RETURN THE
INNOCENT
EARTH

Wilma Dykeman

RETURN THE INNOCENT EARTH

HOLT, RINEHART AND WINSTON

New York Chicago San Francisco

Published simultaneously in Canada by Holt, Rinehart and Winston of Canada,
Limited.

ISBN: 0–03–066640–6
Library of Congress Catalog Card Number: 72–84401

First Edition

Printed in the United States of America

This is a work of fiction. Its characters have lived only in these pages, in the
imagination of the author and the reader.

This book is for

the very old who can remember
and the very young who can believe
and those of the middle kingdom who
have the courage to do both.

". . . and the Lord said in his heart, I
will not again curse the ground any more
for man's sake; for the imagination of
man's heart is evil from his youth;
neither will I again smite any more every
thing living, as I have done.

While the earth remaineth, seedtime
and harvest, and cold and heat, and summer
and winter, and day and night shall not
cease."

GENESIS 8: 21–22

RETURN THE
INNOCENT
EARTH

I

Friday afternoon in Clayburn-Durant's computer department I was ambushed by the smell of ketchup. Tomorrow's mechanized memory and brain was wrapped in the rich cocoon of that earthy aroma, old and warm, familiar and wrenching. Nothing since then has been the same.

The day had started with a phone call from Stull.

"Jon." Not a question, not a greeting, a flat statement and assumption. He did not wait for me to answer. "Wanted you to fly down with Nat and me for the Jackson U. game tomorrow."

I resented that voice—especially at a quarter till seven on Friday morning—arranging my weekend. I did not want to traipse down south to watch the Jackson U. football squad grunt and crunch. I wanted to go to New York and be with Deborah Einemann.

Stull caught my hesitancy. He wasn't stupid. No one had ever accused Stull Clayburn of stupidity, not even when he was a plump, quiet boy standing around awkwardly watching with milky blue eyes which looked and probed and never betrayed the barest hint of emotion or reaction going on in the restless mind behind those eyes.

"First game of the season. And Tech's rated the number two team in the country this year."

"Number one in the Southeast," I said, programmed to a right response.

"Screw the Southeast. It's national that counts. That ought to give the Jackson boys something to fight for."

That's right, Stull: think big. Out loud I said, "It ought to be a good game."

"We'll pick you up at eight-thirty," he said.

"Hold on, Stull." I was sitting on the edge of my twin mahogany bed looking at the empty, neatly made twin bed next to me, and suddenly my feet were chilly and the phone was hard against my shoulder and ear as I tried to light a cigarette and I was chilly all over. "I had other plans for tomorrow."

There was the briefest pause at the other end of the line. From the thickness of Stull's voice I could tell he was having a bad morning, but my sympathy for those bad mornings had run short a long time ago. "There's something else, Jon—"

With Stull there was always something else. Most of us had learned that a long time ago—the hard way. Had I thought for one crazy minute that he only wanted to take me to a ball game to bask forty years later in his glory at Jackson U.? Only?

"What else, Stull?"

"A little problem at the Churchill plant."

"But tomorrow's Saturday. It'll be two-thirds shut down—"

"It's not that kind of a problem." I didn't answer and he went on. "You remember somebody named Burl Smelcer?"

Stull made him sound like an interchangeable part of one of the cabbage cutters. "Of course I remember Burl Smelcer," I said. "Foreman at the Riverbend Farm for twenty or thirty years. I used to pull beets and pick tomatoes on his crew. Two teeth, eleven children, fourteen dogs."

"His wife's sick."

"Perlina." I could see Perlina Smelcer's great freckled arms bulging from the sleeves of her sweat-stained gingham dress whenever she drank from the dipper at the water bucket where a motley crew of pickers would be stripping green bean vines when I was a boy. In her greed for the water, rivulets ran from the sides of her mouth faster than she could swallow and fell on the red, heaving flesh of her neck, then disappeared in the depths of her bosom like a stream soaked up by desert sand dunes. She would see me watching her and she would grin with friendliness and satisfaction, fanning the neck of her dress back and forth to enjoy the full benefit of the cool water trickling down her front.

"Perlina her name?" Stull asked, making it the most inconsequential knowledge since the date of the invention of the yo-yo.

"All right, Stull. Tell me why you've got me sitting here on the side of the bed at this time of the—"

"I thought you might like to see Jackson U. beat Tech—"

"And?"

"And afterward I thought you might run on up to Churchill and check on a few things."

"Such as?"

"The Smelcer woman."

"I'm no damn doctor, Stull. Besides—"

"You haven't waked up yet have you, Jon? The Riverbend is the farm where we've been trying that Morrison fellow's new spray."

"Oh my God!" The chill reached up my back. "How sick is she, Stull?"

"Sick enough. Price Sims called last night, told Nat Lusk about it. She's running a fever, vomiting, on the verge of convulsions."

My mental picture of Perlina Smelcer in a convulsion seemed totally absurd. All her life she had cared for a lazy husband and sickly children who bought third-hand Chevvies and Fords and pulled out for Cleveland or Detroit or New Jersey as soon as they were beyond school truancy age. Perhaps she had earned her own respite from the rigors and duties of health. "And why did Price Sims think all that had anything to do with our spray?"

"Because Perlina had eaten herself a bait of greens the picking machine left behind."

"What about Burl and the children?"

"Price went into that, too. Burl was ailing and didn't eat. As for the others, none of them were home this week—the last two youngsters were in Churchill staying with a cousin to go to the fair."

It all came back to me in a flood of smells and sounds—the September dust and rotten canvas, bawling calves, tattooed sideshow hustlers, glittering prizes, and the music of the ferris wheel as its rickety seats floated up and over and around between the sawdust underfoot and the velvety night sky above. "So it's Perlina."

"We don't know that there's any connection at all between the new spray and her troubles," Stull said. His tongue had lost most of its furred thickness now. "We don't know anything at all. That's why you might do some good down there just looking, listening for a couple of days."

Why me? But I did not ask it. Who else was there? Only Stull and Nat Lusk and I, of all the people who made up the midwestern home office of Clayburn-Durant, knew Churchill, had been born there, lived there, knew the way winter slipped in late or apple blooms broke through early or that a man would shoot his brother's son through the heart because of a rawboned black-and-tan foxhound.

"Jon?"

"Yes, Stull?"

"We can't mess this one up. This spray could mean the biggest break C-D has had in a long time. We can't let some loud-mouthed old mountain woman who doesn't know a snuff stick from a chopstick ruin the whole ball game for us."

I didn't answer.

"You hear, Jon?"

"Sure, Stull. I hear."

"Then I can count on you? I've got Morrison coming in this morning to tell us what the hell may be going on. If he's such a big plant expert and chemist, he ought to know what our risks are."

"I hope so."

"You come by. At ten."

As he hung up I added what he failed to order: "And pack your two-suiter for Churchill." Before I left the phone or even turned on a hot shower to thaw out my chill, I called New York.

Deborah's voice was all that Stull's was not: soft and clear, resonant with her warmth, her inescapable memories, her caring. When I told her I would not be arriving at La Guardia that night, she asked no questions. It was one of her special virtues—this restraint, this lack of prying or probing. "If I listen you'll tell me all I need to know, all I want to know—now or sometime," she said once, soon after we met. Then, with that half-sad smile, "And I shall listen."

(In the beginning was the number, and the number was of Deborah and the number was with Deborah and the number was Deborah.)

When I told her I would be in Churchill and that I might be there all week, she paused a moment and then said, "Don't be homesick, Jon."

How odd—when I would be at home, or where my home once was. "I'm not worried about homesickness," I said. "It's just this damn food business that gets to you after a while."

"I'll be here, Jon, whenever you can come."

I could see the thin scarred wrist and hand laying the phone back in its cradle, her wretched fingers a contrast to the richness of her voice and dark eyes.

When I walked into Stull's office at ten o'clock, Lex Morrison from National Laboratories was already sitting stiffly in one of Stull's Spanish chairs. There was no other way to sit against those hard high backs. The fellow had been to Clayburn-Durant before. The first time, he had done most of the talking, not because he was a talkative fellow but because he had the information we needed. This time Stull was talking. I tried to size up Stull's condition. He was all right, at least for the moment.

"You two met before—" Stull's cryptic introduction left both of us dangling until I crossed the room and shook hands again.

"Jon Clayburn," I said. "You're Morrison—"

The man was pleased. "Lex Morrison, from National Commercial and Botanical Research Lab." He had a good firm grip and his gray-green eyes met a stranger's gaze openly and directly. He was tall and lean and slightly awkward. The sleeves of his coat were a couple of inches too short. His cheekbones were high and stood like small plateaus on his face.

"Your arrested-growth discovery. You've made more tests?"

Lex Morrison looked at Stull. "I guess we're all up against the same shortage: time." He and I sat down on the black leather upholstery of the carved chairs.

Stull pushed himself back from his wide cluttered desk so that the smoggy morning mist rising from the concrete and steel outside created a pale aura behind his large round head. Before him an ornate inkwell and pen, an electric clock with calendar attached, and a tarnished sterling silver cigar and cigarette box were small islands in a sea of letters, envelopes, clippings, reports, and memoranda. To a stranger, Stull's desk must seem incredible, but I know that what he needs to remember is not on file there.

Stull gazed down attentively at his hands. He seemed to be studying the wide flat fingernails, cuticle, pale skin, hair follicles with minute concentration. To Morrison he might have seemed inattentive and indifferent. He wasn't.

"The crunch is on," he had said to me last week when we went down to the company kitchen together to see if the cooking tests had been run on any of the newly sprayed vegetables. "This arrested growth could give us the edge we want in next year's market." I had been surprised but Stull was usually miles ahead of the rest of us in foreseeing what might happen in the canning business.

"Cut the waste at our growers' level," he went on, "ensure peak ripeness in taste and color quality at production level. And if those fellows bitching around down in sales can't sell that, then they ought to be out on their butts."

Stull's vehemence had caught me by surprise. Then I realized there were no positions, not even the president's, secure in this game.

"I was just telling Morrison," Stull said to me now, "that we've tried his chemicals on some of our turnip greens down around Churchill—and a few late tomato vines."

"How did it work?" The scientist was eager as a boy. Perhaps it was asking questions that kept him young.

I grinned at him. "Price Sims, he's our Churchill manager, says the foreman down there claims it's magic. Tomatoes on the vine stayed exactly like they were for ten days. No over-ripening, no spoiling, no rotting."

He was leaning forward in his chair. "And the turnip greens?"

I glanced at Stull. "After a week of sun and rain, less than an inch more growth. Not a tough stalk among the lot. Tender as a baby's bottom."

He nodded. "That's the way it worked on our best farms," he said. "Complete stabilization of the crop. Total interruption of the growth process."

"There are all kinds of possibilities for something like this. That is, if it really works—"

There was a moment's pause.

"You develop this spray on your own time?" Stull hurled the question like a javelin, hard and fast. "University time? Government time?"

Lex Morrison looked straight at us. Obviously he had not expected this interrogation but it did not put him off balance. "It's a sticky question. I teach botany and do research at the state university. Our laboratory has received several grants from the federal government. But none of my college or government time has gone into this. It was my own pet project."

"Why?"

"Plants are what I know. Ever since I was a boy I've studied plants. I care about them. My grandmother taught me that almost before I could walk." He hesitated. "You know she was from your part of the country." He paused but Stull did not pursue the geography. "Down there in the mountains. It's a botanist's paradise."

Haze of smoke, autumn, and exhaust fumes shimmered just beyond the dimness of the room. Then the stranger said, with some embarrassment, "I have a hang-up about time. Since I was a kid, the clock's been my enemy. The changes it brings, the deterioration, the withering—"

"You want to play God?" Stull's voice carried a hint of a dry chuckle.

He flushed. "Don't most of us?" His jaw was hard and set as he answered.

There was a pause before Stull asked if the scientist could give any analysis or reassurance about residual effects.

"No. That's where the time factor enters. It's only been in usable form since last spring. Tested it during my vacation down in Florida and then this summer in my own garden. Arrested plant growth completely—and I ate the fruits and vegetables myself. No harmful effects."

"It arrest your growth?" Stull asked.

"A little late for that, I'm afraid." He half-smiled. "No, it didn't seem to do that, either."

"You find something to keep people from aging," I was trying to relieve the inquisitional air Stull created, "find something to stop this old human machine from what you so nicely call withering—and you can match pennies with J. Paul Getty."

Of course. That was what was in all our minds—from Lex Morrison's and Stull Clayburn's to the Hollywood starlet's and the toothless old farmer's down in Churchill: no change. The great American Dream: Ever Young. Everlasting Eighteen. And if this chemical concoction could achieve that ultimate goal for a plant why not the possibility that it could do as much eventually for a man?

"What do you think about it? Any danger?" Stull laid his hands on the arms of his chair and his eyes narrowed. His hands hardly shook at all when they had something to grasp. "You made the stuff, by God, you ought to have some idea of whether or not we can use it without having our tail shot off."

Morrison answered in the same tone Stull had used. "I know it's all right by itself. I can guarantee that."

"But?"

"But nothing is by itself any more. What I can't guarantee is the effect of any powerful chemical compound in relation to other sprays and fertilizers and additives and even water purifiers."

There was a silence. He went on. "I think it will be okay. But I'm a scientist and I like to be sure."

"And I'm a businessman and I like to be first," Stull Clayburn said.

In the pause I considered why Stull was on the attack, setting up the situation of offense-defense rather than of cooperation in a mutual enterprise. I had personally encountered this arrangement too many times before. When I first joined the company. When Teena and I were married. Stull wanted something. And whatever it was, he wanted it exclusively and totally and at the cheapest price possible. Whoever sat opposite him was automatically an adversary. Winning was all.

Sounds of traffic in the streets below came up in blurred noisy waves—crunching gears and the roaring labor of trucks and screaming brakes. The silence of the room was enclosed in dark paneling and heavy carpet but it was an artificial silence surrounded by the city's clamor.

I broke the pause. "Isn't there a way to be both? Be sure and be first? Take another year for tests but let us have the option until the safety factor is proved and we can begin to use the spray. Then you can be sure and we'll still be first to reap the advantage."

Morrison was nodding. "That might work."

"And it might not." Stull dismissed me in disgust. "You think you're the only fellow working on such a discovery, Morrison? If you've done it, that means there are a dozen bright boys just like you swarming all over the lot, right on the edge of a breakthrough. And a dozen companies right there waiting to grab first. Read your history. That's the story of progress. The names are all there. And they're Fulton and Edison and Bell and Ford and the Wright boys, not the ones who were backing and filling and testing till everything was sure as sunrise. Who the hell remembers the name of the second man to fly an airplane? Or the second man who worked on Salk's vaccine?"

I looked at the photographs on the wall to his left. One family picture of the Clayburn brothers, all the rest glossy photographs of Stull with various groups and individuals, many of the familiar faces around the world. The largest, most prominent, however, was a blown-up news shot of Stull surrounded by the Jackson U. football team. I knew what that picture meant to Stull.

"And what about the Feds?" I intercepted. I knew the question would block Stull for at least one play. I wondered when he was going to bring up the problem of Perlina Smelcer.

He frowned. I saw his old suspicion of me revive. "Agriculture won't have to know anything for a while. We'll go through channels, and channels are slow." He tapped his hands lightly on the desk. "As for Food and Drug, some of these young do-gooders that never had a day's practical experience in their lives are putting the bite on the FDA inspectors, keeping everything unsettled. We'll register our new spray, report in Morrison's own successful tests, ask to be allowed to proceed while we wait for a ruling. Emergency use."

"Sounds all right if it works."

"Sure it'll work—till they can prove something is wrong," Stull said. "Then maybe we can put one of our great senators into the game. Take your choice: an old-guard Republican who understands your problems but won't work on them, or a bright young Democrat who doesn't understand but goes right to work."

Lex Morrison was frowning. "This is something people eat. I wouldn't want—"

The light on Stull's private telephone winked on and off. Without seeming to notice that anyone was talking, Stull pressed a button. We heard his secretary's voice. "I'm sorry to interrupt, Mr. Clayburn, but it's Mr. Lusk here. He says you'll want to see him right now."

"All right." Stull's face held no expression. "Let me see him right now."

The big door swung open immediately. As Nat Lusk entered he nodded to Stull and me but directed his greeting to Lex Morrison. "Just the man I wanted to reach. Met you first time you came here with your snake oil."

"I remember."

"Just had a call from Churchill—"

"Sit down, Nat," Stull said.

Nat Lusk hesitated. His opening run had been thrown off-balance. The deep lines crevassing the leathery skin of his heavy sun-tanned face were even more prominent than usual.

"How's it going?" Stull asked.

And Nat knew that this was a warm-up play. He went along. "Okay," he said, "considering that everything I like nowadays either makes you fat, pollutes the air, or adds to the population explosion."

I managed a smile, but Lex Morrison did not laugh. He was looking at his large bony hands—and thinking.

Nat's Italian tailored suit could not camouflage the rolls of fat which spilled out over his black alligator belt, as the heavy lids could not hide the worry behind his dark eyes. (I recalled the night several years before when Teena had said to me, "There are women, you know, Jon, who like the hint of brutality in a man. Brutality cushioned with luxury. Maybe that's Nat Lusk's appeal." "In that case woman—" I had whacked her lightly on the backside. "It's an appeal I find utterly resistable," she added hastily, laughing. It was one of the last times we laughed together easily, without forcing the gaiety. The next day she went to the doctor and he advised surgery.)

As Nat Lusk sat down he lit a cigarette and took a deep drag on it, then leaned forward, an elbow on each knee, hands dangling loosely between. He looked around like an uneasy old sea lion I had watched once on the water-slick rocks along the California coast, swinging his head from side to side in alert and rhythmic unease.

"Well, Nat?" Stull said.

"I just talked with Price Sims down in Churchill. The Smelcer woman died."

"Damn." As Stull breathed it, it was more a sigh than a word.

I could visualize the scene at the Churchill clinic first and now at the funeral home, although I've been away for many years—can it be more than twenty? Smelcers (the mountains are full of sawbriars and Smelcers, Uncle Whit Ransom used to say) of every size and age, in overalls or housedresses or uniforms, crowding into the poor woman's sick room, certain that this succumbing to a hospital was only a prelude to the final surrender to the grave. And while they watched and waited they would talk and socialize, spying out places to secretly unload streams of tobacco juice. Using up the oxygen in her tight little room, perching on the foot of her bed, they would nevertheless provide Perlina with an indispensable ingredient: the certainty that she belonged, had a place, an identity, relationships.

Nat was explaining the circumstances of Perlina Smelcer's sickness and death to the scientist.

"That was the farm where the spray was used?" Lex Morrison asked.

"It sure as hell was—is," Nat said.

For a moment there was no sound or movement in the office except for the faint wheezing rasp of the electric clock on Stull's desk.

"And there goes the ball game," Nat said.

"Had she eaten the turnip greens more than once?" Morrison asked.

Stull looked at him. "There's the scientist," he nodded, and for the first time there was genuine admiration in his voice. "No hasty conclusions. No pressing the panic button. Questions. Facts."

"How the hell do we know how much the Smelcers have been eating?" Nat Lusk was stung by the implicit reprimand. "Most of those farm tenants just go out and help themselves to the crops whenever they want to. And they glean the fields—get whatever the machines leave behind."

"She probably ingested some of the spray," Morrison said slowly.

"We don't know," Stull repeated. His voice and face were troubled. "But we'll find out—in an orderly fashion." He glanced at me, then looked away. I took the signal, said nothing about my plans for Churchill.

"Those mountain folks are superstitious." Nat lit another cigarette.

Stull spoke on, half to himself. "She might have eaten some other questionable food that same day. Or she may have had some disease for years—all those mountain women are sick half the time. Neither

Morrison nor any of his assistants had any side-effects when they ate fruits and vegetables that had the spray."

"Of course, those were controlled situations—"

"Well, I didn't tell Mama Smelcer to go out in our fields and help herself to our crops. If that's what she did. Hell, I don't want to put anything dangerous out on the market. On the other hand, I don't want to pass up a good thing, work with one hand tied behind me in a competitive situation just because of a scare story."

"Why don't we just by-pass the whole stinking bit, forget about putting ever-fresh fruits and vegetables in our cans?" Nat Lusk stood up and paced across the room, introducing once again his pet idea. "I say switch to some of the cheap and easy, look-alike artificial foods. Most of the half-assed people in the grocery stores and restaurants today don't know what they're getting anyway. Sugar that never came from any plant, cream that was never yanked from any cow's tits, meat that was never on any hoof or wing. If that's what they'll pay for, I say give it to them."

Stull had turned his back on Nat Lusk and sat looking out the window. There was a real splash of gray even in the hair on the back of his head. "No, Nat. We don't want to hurt anybody. We're here to feed people. That's what my father used to say." (*Your* father! I thought. You mean your Uncle Jonathan. Isn't that who you mean, Stull, deep down in your memory?) "We'll set up some more tests in our laboratories. Meanwhile—" he swung back to his desk. His face had tightened, lost much of its flabbiness. In a crisis, his flesh and voice pulled together to become almost firm. "—What's Price Sims doing?"

"Sitting tight," Nat said.

The thought occurred to me that this was no news. By this time of day Price was usually walking tight, too.

"No one down there saying anything about the spray?" Stull went on.

"We didn't exactly advertise," Nat said. "It was all a pretty secret trial run."

"Then they, or we, don't really have any idea what caused Smelcer's wife to be sick, do we?" No one answered Stull. "Maybe it was a new brand of snuff she was dipping."

Nat Lusk was pulling hard on his cigarette. Lex Morrison looked at the three of us Clayburn-Durant men. "I'm not sure I know what you're saying."

"All right. Let's put it right up front where it belongs and look at it. As you yourself asked, what do we know—for sure?" Stull's pale blue gaze, like the level tone of his voice, demanded attention. "Morrison, let's find out why you came to Clayburn in the first place."

The young scientist was surprised. "I told you at our first meeting. There may have been several reasons. I suppose one was the memory of my grandmother talking about the Clayburn cannery, the Clayburn family—"

"Your grandmother?" I asked. I tried to ignore the grim impatience on Stull's face. "Who was your grandmother?"

"Laura Morrison."

I had heard the name before. But this time there seemed to be an echo in my mind. "Before she married, what was her name? Could she have been Laura Rathbone?"

Lex Morrison nodded.

"Well, I'll be damned." I looked up at the picture of five brothers which hung on Stull's wall—five tall, serious young men wearing high, stiff Sunday collars and proper parlor expressions, and I looked at the second one particularly. Jonathan, my father. "Your grandmother and my father—" I began, not really knowing what to say, but Stull interrupted.

"Didn't you actually come to us," he drove the conversation back into line, "because you thought we had the know-how to put your little discovery to good use?"

"The know-how *and* the need," Morrison agreed mildly. "Yes, that was part of it."

"Right now we've got a great big need," Stull spoke softly. "Let's call the game like it is: harvesting crops at their split-second peak of ripeness isn't the biggest hurdle we have to overcome in the canning business. It's just one part of the whole damned obstacle course. But every problem we can lick, or minimize, puts us just that much ahead of the others."

"Of course," Lex Morrison said.

"The way any single plant in a canning company can make us money, Morrison, is to run as near capacity for as many days and nights over as long a season as possible. It costs us almost as much to get everything in motion, cleaned up afterward, for a three-hour day as for a sixteen-hour day. And when we lose time because of lousy harvesting conditions, it costs. And when it costs, we hurt."

Nat Lusk sat down heavily, bored by Stull's elementary education of Morrison. Stull quieted him. "Nat, I want our scientist to understand the basics of the situation."

"Hell yes," Nat agreed. "Let's all understand."

"Well, then," Stull folded his hands together. "We try to regulate our crops by planting at intervals, a week or two apart, and by irrigation. But that fickle lady weather is still hard to manipulate. Too cool, too hot, too rainy—"

"Like most women," Nat muttered.

"But if we could get our pack in the cans, on the shelves, into the kitchens, fresher and quicker and cheaper than the competition"—Stull's milky blue gaze had frozen and fixed on each of us—"we'd show a profit. That spray of yours, Morrison, might make the difference."

It was as long a speech as I had ever heard Stull deliver, except at a board meeting.

"A helluva advertising gimmick, too," Nat broke the silence. "Every bite captured at the tender moment of summer-fresh maturity." His voice assumed the oracular tones of a radio or television announcer.

"I'm not talking about gimmicks, dammit, Nat," Stull said. "This isn't some expensive plan to pour more money into the tube for a return nobody can measure. It isn't some come-on for contests or packaging or promoting. It's good sound production."

"Okay, okay," Nat was waving his hand. His survival instinct told him better than to reopen a basic conflict with Stull now. "But whatever we produce we have to sell—and I kid you not."

Stull was looking at Morrison. "Earlier this summer your spray might have saved us nearly a million dollars."

"That bastard strike," Nat growled.

"Right," Stull said. "This summer, Morrison, three places where our careful planning and growing program brought in bumper tomato crops right on the nose—California, Indiana, and New Jersey—went out on strike. Those tomatoes mildewed, scalded, rotted in the fields. We plowed some under. And we lost a million-two on the whole stinking deal."

All of us winced at the memory.

"Your spray could have saved our damn ass," Stull said to Morrison. "Now we're talking about next season. Not two seasons from now, not a year from now. Next season. Spray in full production ready for our earliest pack, if necessary."

Morrison nodded very slowly. "I understand."

"I doubt that you understand, Mr. Morrison. You've never met a payroll. You've never faced a room full of stockholders who've gone without a dividend twice in a row." Stull leaned back in his chair, but he was tense as a wire stretched for tightrope walkers. "You've never watched a hundred acres of sugar peas rot because they grew too full before the machines could get into the wet fields. But there's no law says you have to understand, as long as you know that we want a reasonably safe spray. We don't ask for the moon. But we want it now or not at all. We'll pay you a fair price. You might even get rich from it."

There was another pause. Morrison shifted in his chair. Nat Lusk took two final draws on his cigarette and smashed the stub in an ash tray on the windowsill.

"And what about Perlina Smelcer?" I asked.

"We hope," said Stull evenly, turning a silver pen around and around in his fingers, not looking at me, "that Mrs. Smelcer wasn't ailing from our spray. And that no one else will be. We wish Mr. Smelcer a long and healthy life."

You could hear the four of us breathing in the room. Morrison was glimpsing the sudden possibility of riches. Stull was grasping at the possibility of stability in an unstable production situation. And Nat and I were groping along in their wake with our own possibilities to push: his for Clayburn-Durant Food Company to go essentially non-food, and mine for us to find a new direction which I couldn't even clearly define.

I looked at Stull's immobile face and the eyes as impenetrable as a pool glazed with ice. Only the hands, locked into a double fist on the pile of papers before him, betrayed any reaction. I was aware of Nat Lusk's disintegrated features and of the eager, troubled openness of Laura Rathbone's grandson. But the other two were only at the periphery. It was Stull Clayburn I saw.

"And do we intend in any way to investigate Perlina Smelcer's illness and death?" I asked.

"We don't intend to throw the goddamned alarm switch," Stull said.

I could feel the hostility fermenting in the room, oppressive as the smog which thickened the air just beyond the windows. But I would not stop. Suddenly I felt quite removed from the executive team of Clayburn-Durant Foods. I was back in Churchill listening to the tales about my great-uncle Whitley Ransom or my uncle Jack Montgomery, who tried to match life's absurdities with their own. Now I was not sure whether I really cared about Perlina Smelcer or whether I wanted to bait Stull.

"Don't we have any responsibility toward her? Not even any curiosity?"

"We have a responsibility to nineteen thousand and twenty-two stockholders." Stull's face was flushing. The change from his normal indoor pallor to this unnatural ruddiness reminded me of watching a summer storm distress the sky with feverish clouds while everything underneath grew motionless.

"And our duty to them begins with Perlina Smelcer," I suggested. Stull and I stared at each other across the desk.

"My duty to them is to keep this company alive."

"And profitable."

"You'd better believe it!" Stull's fist came down on the desk like a thunderclap. The cigarette box rattled. "What's the matter, Jon? No guts to take a risk?"

I smiled. It cost an effort, but I knew that smile would infuriate Stull more than anything else I could say. "I'll tell you what I don't have the guts for. Perlina Smelcer taking my risk for me. Especially when she's not even been told—or asked."

"And now," Stull's voice showered sarcasm, "our executive vice-president massages his bleeding heart. Sweetness and light—and bullshit!" he finished savagely.

I had known for a long time that this moment would arrive. Stull and me. I had not expected it today.

He leaned toward me, his eyes narrow and mean. "We've got a company to run. Whose side are you on, anyway?"

Maybe this was as good a time and outward reason as any. I stood up, shoved away the chair. "I'll have to let you know, Stull," I said.

I turned my back and walked out of the room. Behind me Nat Lusk was making some move and Lex Morrison was saying some thing, but clearer than their actions and louder than their words was Stull's anger which rode on my back as I left his office.

That was late Friday morning.

I didn't eat any lunch. I asked my secretary to call the chairman of the Community Human Relations Council and tell him that Jon Clayburn would not be able to make it to the emergency executive meeting that afternoon. I postponed an appointment with an out-of-town food broker. I tried to act calmly, logically, freezing that moment in Stull's office somewhere in the back of my mind to be examined later. But I could no longer tolerate my own office, next to Stull's.

Then I went down to check the computers—and was subverted by the smell of ketchup.

That stark, uncluttered computer room, with its brighter-than-day illumination and its not-quite-noiseless machines and its flashing eyes of light, seemed like a giant incubator. Sterilized. Throbbing with muted power. Programmed to a single purpose. The new worlds born here would not emerge from geologic upheaval or Genesis miracle but through ceaseless calculation, cool and correct. There would be none of that emotion which I had shown upstairs a short while before when I walked out of the office of Clayburn-Durant Foods.

As I talked with George Hodges in the information systems department, I had a fantasy of these machines secretly breeding each night a new line of managers: sallow, dehydrated young men who would run Clayburn-Durant in silent invisibility. Coupled with this was an image of that overweight, lard-gray human being upstairs in the fifth-floor corner office, in the room whose dark paneling and massive mahogany furniture and decades of accumulated trophies gave it the look and smell and atmosphere of an old and much-used aerie.

In that interval, without design or expectation, between the computer and the aerie, drifted the rich smell of ketchup. It enveloped me and removed me from the the pallid controls of George Hodges or the fierce clutch of Stull Clayburn. It released me into the almost forgotten sensuous well-being I had known as a boy in a roomy, comfortable home in Churchill.

But now the moment belonged to George Hodges, the young expert. He had been with Clayburn-Durant Foods for eight years, ever since I had laid my reputation on the line and said, in direct opposition to Stull Clayburn, that the company should install a central computerized system for handling reports, schedules, orders, records, all vital statistics data, and had insisted that George Hodges was the man to direct such a system.

The fact, which had been pointed out by one of the vice-presidents, that George Hodges was a highly sought-after University of California master's graduate in his field, had as little influence on Stull as the fact, which several of his Southern relatives had mentioned, that George—Nancy Ellen Clayburn Hodges' son—was his nephew. Finally all that had counted was that I had insisted—and acted as though I had the clout. I had presented the case for computers and for George Hodges and backed it with everything I had, which at the moment was largely intangible. From that encounter, I learned something. Next time I go up against Stull I'll have the substance as well as the shadow of power.

But I knew that Stull's capitulation, the decision for Clayburn-Durant to join the age of automation, had come from conviction that this offered the clearest and neatest opportunity to put my judgment to a public test. If I proved right, all was well and the benefit would accrue to Stull's reputation anyway; if I were in error, then everyone would know precisely where the fault lay and the financial loss would be worth the lesson learned concerning potential executive leadership of the company. The days and nights of anxiety that had accompanied the introduction of these computers eight years ago are almost forgotten now, but I can still feel the twinge knifing my duodenum as it did during those long months when success or failure was yet to be proved. (Then Teena's illness came and the triumph of the computers did not even matter.)

And George Hodges, throughout his years with the company, has remained a cool, competent master of his machines, growing in power and reach. A relentlessly serious young man. Two years ago he went to Stull directly and informed him that if he were not immediately incorporated into some of the financial decision-making processes of the company (with a definite possibility of eventually becoming a vice-president) he would accept, on Monday morning at ten-thirty, the offer of a company in Providence, Rhode Island, which had promised him twice the salary he was receiving at Clayburn's. Stull's broad face turned a magenta shade as he laid his trembling hands flat on the arms of his high-backed chair.

"Who in hell do you think you are, quarterbacking in here, a green stripling, telling me what you want? What does the company want? That's the important question."

"But I—"

"Till you know that—feel it down where you live—you're a second-stringer."

And I intervened again, shoving aside the thought that to Stull the Clayburn-Durant Company is merely an extension of Stull Clayburn. I pointed out that while I myself had learned a great deal about foods and canning ever since I was a baby, it was a special knowledge which I could peddle few places. But George Hodges' knowledge is a new language, welcome in hundreds of markets.

"He's the new breed, Stull," I argued, "and we'd better keep him while he's in our reach."

"He's a screwed-up rookie who wants to coach before he's played the game," Stull said.

But George Hodges stayed, and at a new decision-making level. Pale-eyed, sandy-haired, slightly stoop-shouldered—not with age but with concentration—he had no special diffidence or friendship for me. My advocacy was taken for granted by George (the only intelligent course to follow, why any personal considerations?), just as my failure, if the computerized system had not proved practical, would have been accepted by Stull. (Some have it, some don't, and that's where the water strikes the wheel; no personal considerations wanted.) I expected nothing more from either of them. Be right. That's the name of the game.

At that Friday moment, while George Hodges reassured me that the computers were alive and well, and while the anger which had driven me there seethed more quietly, I became aware of the smell of ketchup.

The smell was spicy, thick, tantalizing, at once homely and exotic, astringent and robust, satisfying as the luxury of a vicuna robe swaddled around aching joints. It arrested my conversation in mid-passage. It tugged at memory layered under so many folds of accumulated sediment and upheaval that I could not think of its specific form or dimension but knew only that somewhere, sometime, something had happened (accompanied by this ripe odor) which was as surely part of me as the marrow of my bones. And it related to this day, too.

I brought my attention back to the thin hungry fledgling installed so confidently here on the ground floor. I thought of the fleshy, satiated old hawk entrenched so warily up above. Each of them, though poles apart, had more in common with the other than either had with me. An old familiar sense of isolation laid hold of me.

The ketchup odor intensified. I nodded briefly to a surprised George Hodges who stood aside and watched the executive vice-president of Clayburn-Durant open the heavy door and hurry out into the corridor.

The aroma of ketchup was even stronger than it had been in the tight room. It came from our kitchen-laboratory which occupies a wing at the south end of the block-long building. The odor surrounded me, held me as immobile as any stoutly woven net.

The corridor was momentarily empty. I gazed down its long gray length: freshly polished floors, clean, unadorned walls, all according to written specifications and unwritten image. So! This was to be the time. I would have to decide. Perhaps from the moment I had walked into Stull's office that morning and had exchanged the first few sentences with the young scientist, and then heard Nat Lusk's news, breaking like a scream into our tidy calculations and projections, I had known that this was the showdown. High noon. Only high noon lasts for just one full minute and then it is gone. And it was ketchup, not blood, that bubbled in the kettles and stirred something down in my vitals.

For a moment there it seemed that this building was rising out of a broad field and the field was heavy with scarlet ripe tomatoes bursting their tender skins in juice, and with round, firm, foam-colored cabbage nestled in leaves whose lower layers against the ground gave off a primordial stench of rotting and fertility, and with string beans dangling in slender clusters like long green fingers among their sheltering vines. This mid-town, five-story brick building grew from the wide flat cornfields surrounding this midwestern metropolis where the Durants had built a food empire, and grew from the river-bottom acres in the mountain South where the Clayburns had built their business, and grew from cool acres of clear chartreuse spring peas in Wisconsin, hot fields of orange-meated yams in Puerto Rico, peaches gold as sunlight in California, and flaming pimentos red as the soil of Georgia. The fragrance of the ketchup gathered all up in one bouquet.

Here was the gulf between older Stull Clayburn and younger George Hodges—and me. I could remember. I needed to remember.

"You're still a young man, have your future ahead of you," they said when Teena died.

But all the past is behind me, too, made flesh in Lee and Ellie.

"Don't look back," they had said, even longer ago, when I left Churchill and came to the city. "You're moving on and up now, son."

But what is movement without direction? Stull would dismiss such a question as theoretical, useless. It diverts valuable thought and energy from the main purpose, the indisputable goal: the touch-down.

The smell of the ketchup magnified all that had happened earlier that day, and I left the building.

Even as I backed the Thunderbird out of its parking spot I knew that upstairs in my office my secretary would be making memos of phone calls, assuring everyone that her Mr. Clayburn was somewhere in the building, probably in conference, that he would be back at his desk any minute now, even reassuring puffy-eyed Nat Lusk who undoubtedly had stopped in to ask me about this morning.

I headed north out of the city, toward the stables where Ellie would be riding.

"I *am* Clayburn-Durant," Stull had told me that first day I came to work in the company's midwestern main office. Stull with his round face and wattled jowls and hair loose over his forehead had resembled a wisely innocent, overfed cherub. But neither my cousin's rustic guilelessness nor his detached appraising look had warned me.

"If that's the way you want it," I shrugged. But I knew there was another answer.

I was not prepared, after all the years of postponement, to give that answer yesterday or today. Yet I know this is the time. It is not a good time. Both of my children are having their problems. Lee, in Europe ("I have to see what some other world beyond this screwed-up place is like!"), and Ellie, with her cool adjustments which have impressed me, disturbed me, because she is only thirteen.

Traffic between downtown and the suburbs was clotted. The north end of the city had grown fast, subdivisions popping up like dandelions in spring grass. (Where had I smelled that ketchup in some long past afternoon?) A dozen years ago I had had a chance to buy some acreage out near Green Meadow Stables. I could have tripled my money by now. Today the stables are surrounded by developments with rustic names and urban congestion. Fox Den Hills. Rocky Creek Estates. Wildwood Acres. There hasn't been a fox sighted for ten years, the little creek barely moves along its sluggish run, and the only wildness consists of barbecue campfires on a hundred patios. But three times your investment!

A man could spend his whole life in such speculation. And how did you triple your investment on the time of your life? The old conflict, wrenching me: wanting the money without the cost, wanting to be one of the rich without the impoverishment. Above all, however, knowledge that I want work with meaning. (Perhaps that was, finally, what Lee was saying to me in one of our inconclusive quarrels last summer.)

When I drew up by a lone station wagon in the parking lot at Green Meadow Stables only one solitary little girl and her horse were slowly circling the exercise ring. She was too young and too docile looking to be Ellie. The barns and fields were empty. Everything looked brown and anonymous under the flat midwestern sky.

I climbed out of my car as Bonita Fredericks, the riding instructor, emerged from the nearest stable. It was as though the day had switched to another facet, dialed another part of the forest.

"We didn't expect to see you this afternoon. You surprised us."

"I surprised myself," I said.

She walked toward me with long, firm strides. "Ellie's in the tack room. She'll be out in a minute."

"Fine. No hurry. How's it going?" Our converstion came as easily as dropping a needle in the right groove of a record. My mind was wandering (to my call to Deborah that morning, to the rich aroma of ketchup), but the words flowed out. I looked at Bonita in her trim riding habit with a jaunty scarf at her throat and her long blond hair held back by a silver clasp.

"It's going beautifully. As I've said before, Ellie's a good little horsewoman. She's dedicated. Where are a dozen others today?" She waved a brisk hand toward the empty parking spaces and riding areas. "Oh I don't blame them, at this season, at this time of day. But Ellie's here. Right after school every day, on the dot. She may even ride in the Garden one of these days."

"I hope not." Bonita gave me a look of surprise and then decided to treat my irreverence as some warped kind of humor.

She hesitated. Her face and neck were very brown from riding in the sun all summer. I thought of Lex Morrison's spray. Would an application now, this instant, hold Bonita Fredericks indefinitely at her peak of health and ripeness—gold and tan? Teena was the only person I knew who would remain everlastingly young, forever eluding the subtleties and sweep of change, because that was the way she was captured in my memory. Death alone defied change. Yet it itself was the greatest alteration of all. Who, or what, was Clayburn-Durant that we should defy change and seek to freeze life itself, even for an hour, a week?

As I looked at her, Bonita herself in that interval had changed. I had forgotten how her forehead, when she frowned, puckered in a network of tiny wrinkles. She was frowning now. "Ellie is a little upset today. I think you ought to be prepared."

"I'd like to be." I couldn't quite match her mood of high seriousness at the moment, but I did make an effort to squelch the heretical thought that this was, after all, supposed to be a recreation, a hobby, a pleasure, for an immature little girl, not entrance into a religious order with vows and penance.

Bonita Fredericks planted her feet slightly apart and took her stance in front of me. I felt tall and loose and inefficient before the day's pyramiding demands and her compact self-assertion. The trouble was, I no longer valued efficiency. "I've told Ellie I think we're going to have to get rid of Frolic," she said.

"Oh?" I could only imagine how Ellie had reacted to the thought of giving up her gentle Frolic. "Trouble with that left leg?" The horse had suffered a touch of stiffness back in the spring but I had thought it cleared up.

"It's not his leg." She faced me squarely. "He's lost his nerve."

I didn't say anything. I looked at that strange hopeless little girl out in the ring, riding around and around. Nerve, Bonita Fredericks had said.

After Teena died, several friends who belonged to the Hunt had tried to promote a relationship between Bonita and me. We were paired together at Hunt breakfasts and innumerable dinners and I took her to the opening of the civic symphony season. . . . It all trailed off in a gradual withdrawal on my part. I skipped a number of social functions. I even missed several of the horse shows when Ellie was riding. Bonita was impatient of anything (but there had been nothing between us really) concluding so indecisively. I could imagine that she did not like situations or relationships to dissolve but wanted them amputated—neatly, sharply, promptly.

She was a good-looking woman. That sun-baked flesh and trim, ripe body had nearly trapped me a half-dozen times, and I remembered the pungent sharpness of night-time perfume, sweet and clinging, when I was sick with loneliness. But there was something missing. One holiday we went for lunch to a restaurant out in the country, and I selected an apple from the basket of dessert fruit the waiter brought us. Firm, rosy, flawless, the apple had as much flavor as a bite of cork. I looked at it a long time and then left it on the plate with only one bite missing and the silver fruit knife stabbed to its core.

Then I met Deborah. On one of those weekends when I fled another round of riding and drinking and eating with Bonita Fredericks and our acquaintances, I had volunteered to make a business trip to New York for the company.

On Saturday night, a dripping wet night when streets were shiny and slippery as glistening fish and street lights, floodlights, and neon washed together in blurs of iridescence, a friend from college days invited me to some congested casual celebration (I never did discover its purpose or honoree). There in that old brownstone-front club in the East Sixties on an empty New York Saturday night, I first saw Deborah. Scarred. Flawed. Alive.

"—But the worst thing is that he's been refusing too many jumps lately." Bonita Fredericks was finishing her explanation about Ellie's horse.

I nodded. "I see."

"Of course, Ellie's devoted to old Frolic—"

"Couldn't we send him to some trainer—" I began. I was thinking that he wasn't all that old.

"Not if Ellie's going to be a first-class horsewoman," she answered sharply.

I had forgotten how unpleasant her sharp voice could become when she was disputed, and I was glad to see Ellie come out of the stable.

"Hi Dad!" She gave me a routine smile. She did not even show any surprise at my presence. I knew by the way her mouth was set that she was troubled and probably angry. Her face was pink and moist from exertion and her jeans and sneakers were soiled and smelly. Yet I noticed again, as I had several times recently, that my teen-age daughter was going to be a stunning woman. Small, regular features, teeth that would be straight and even when they lost their braces, curving eyebrows dark and fine as Teena's had been, setting off blue eyes that seemed to be my only gift to her. It pleased me to think that she would be beautiful. It scared me a little, too.

"Why are you standing out here?" Ellie asked. She didn't pause on her way to the car. She climbed in and switched on the radio. I was surprised at the rudeness she had managed to convey to Bonita Fredericks.

I smiled at Bonita. "Thanks a lot for briefing me about the horse. We'll work something out."

"There's nothing to 'work out.' Frolic has lost his nerve. Ellie will have to find another horse." Bonita Fredericks turned to go back to the stables, then hesitated. "I'm sorry, Jon. She's upset now because this is the only horse she's ever had. You get her a real jumper and she'll love you for it. More than ever. He'll make her look good. They'll help each other. And in six months Frolic will be ancient history. I'm just telling you how it is, Jon."

"I know. Sure. Thanks again."

But I didn't know. And I wasn't sure. When Ellie asked, as we drove home, if Miss Fredericks had told me about Frolic and I said yes, I was happy because she cried.

"I hate that Bonita Fredericks," she said. She turned her head toward the window so that I wouldn't see her tears.

"Sometimes we don't like people who bring us bad news," I heard the sententious sound of my words and was annoyed. I decided to keep as quiet as possible.

"I don't want to give up Frolic, Daddy," she said after a while.

"I know you don't, Ellie." I drove slowly, glad that we could have this uninterrupted time together.

"Frolic was the first thing, the first live thing, that I ever had for my very own." She sat not looking at me, arms akimbo, legs stretched out under the dashboard. The tears running down her cheeks seemed unnoticed, someone else's, and I was sorry that she was so ashamed of them. Don't be reluctant to care, Ellie, I wanted to say. Go on and cry. But I didn't.

When she spoke, still looking out of the window, her words trembled like the rust-colored leaves on the oak trees. The lawns surrounding the houses we passed were increasingly spacious. "Miss Fredericks says that unless I have another horse I can't expect to really show—" Her voice trailed off.

"That's what Miss Fredericks says," I agreed.

We were passing Stull's house, that rambling stucco chateau holdover from the 1920s, and I was surprised to see Patrick, Stull's half-black, half-Irish chauffeur, bringing the long empty car down the driveway lined with stunted evergreens. Then it occurred to me that this was about the time Stull left the office every afternoon. Patrick was on his way now to fetch him home. Home? To carry him from one stronghold to another. My day had turned so topsy-turvy and free-wheeling that I had long since dismissed the schedule of Stull and Nat Lusk and Laura Rathbone's young scientist grandson down at Clayburn-Durant.

Then I became aware that Ellie was no longer crying.

"Daddy—"

"Yes Ellie?"

There was a pause.

"Could we find somebody that would take real good care of Frolic?"

I knew there was not any need to answer her question. It had not even been a question, really.

"Because if we could find Frolic a really good home—"

By the time we turned into our driveway all traces of her tears had evaporated as completely as a teacup of water dribbled over the desert sand. I watched her dash from the car as soon as the automatic garage door had lifted its barricade—on her way to a shower, to the hi-fi set on a high decibel, to whatever mysterious rituals crowd a daughter's hours. All at once I was weary. Ellie will survive, I assured myself. Survive? Hell, she'll flourish. And what was wrong with that?

"And something is happening here but you don't know what it is, do you, Mister Jones. . . ."

The words were seeping like smoke through cracks around Ellie's door by the time I was inside the house. This was one of her favorite recordings and I had heard it more times than I would like to admit, but this time it touched a raw place. "No," I muttered, stopping to check the water in the potted plants that adorn our entrance foyer. They dry out quickly indoors and Mrs. Alexander forgets. . . . "No, I don't know what it is—do you?"

"I'm sorry, Mr. Clayburn, were you speaking to me?" It was Mrs. Alexander, my housekeeper, coming from the den, and she surprised me.

"No." I tried to grin boyishly and wound up feeling only foolish. "I was just talking to myself, Mrs. Alexander." I knew she had been in my study watching television although on her birthday I bought her a portable t.v. set and a chaise lounge for her own room. I shrugged. She was neat, dependable, managed the house and Ellie and Lee with a minimum of crises, and was the best I had found since Teena's death.

"You're home early. Should I tell Katie you'll want dinner early or anything?" Her hair was a light blue. I like plain old white better.

"No. Just leave everything the way it is." The carpet muffled my footsteps. "No letter from Lee, is there?" She shook her head.

At the door to my study, I paused. Shelves of books, three English hunting prints on the walnut-paneled walls, black leather reclining chair, wide leather-topped desk, all seemed part of a stage set waiting for the actors to appear. The room was just as Teena and the decorator had planned it. Even the little t.v. behind louvered doors on one of the shelves. "For your news programs," Teena had told me. I had worked here almost every night and many weekends for more than a dozen years. At this moment it seemed a strange, anonymous place. No, not strange at all and that was what was wrong: it seemed so ordinary, identical twin to thousands of other dens.

The only distinguishing mark I could find at that moment was the reproduction, just above the television cabinet, of an old photograph, the same picture I had looked up to in Stull's office that morning. Five young men, self-conscious, self-reliant, facing the camera squarely, braced for any foolishness or disaster that might threaten, fearful of nothing—except the possibility of laughter. They were as serious and ponderous as popes. They were real. Authentic Clayburn.

My father, Jonathan Clayburn, stood second from the right. Not quite as tall as Joshua, not as handsome as Whitley, not quite as young as Cal and Dan, Jonathan was the central figure of that photograph. Often, when I was younger and felt vehemently about such things, I used to test the picture on friends and strangers alike and I would be elated when they chose Jonathan at once as the first to receive their attention and admiration.

What quality was it that shone through a grainy black-and-white photograph with sufficient impact to make people who had never known him look twice at his likeness?

I went on into the den, draped my coat on the back of a chair, and loosened my tie. At the big desk I faced three small gold-framed pictures. Ellie, poised, almost smiling, triumphantly holding the giant blue ribbon she won in last year's regional horse show. Lee, thin and intense, beside our collie when the dog was only a pup and Lee was a little boy. Teena, dimpled, smiling, as she had paused on the circular stairway the day we moved into this house, this dream she had cherished for so long. Teena, Lee, Ellie: the three of them together—apart. Where did Deborah fit into this design? Yet without any photograph or memento she was more real to me just then than any of the others.

Deborah, with the number tattooed on her forearm, who had reawakened me from a sleeping sickness. Across the room at that New York party I had seen her thin arm—in the beginnning was the number, and the number was with Deborah, and the number was Deborah—resting on the plain black silk she wore, and she seemed to me the most tragic and elegant woman I had ever seen.

"Hello. I'm Jon Clayburn."

"And I'm Deborah Einemann." No hesitation. No inquiry. No coyness. Her hand was small and cold, her voice warm and rich.

So it had begun.

I sat in the den until Mrs. Alexander would knock and tell me dinner was ready. Dusk came and I did not bother to switch on a light. There in the twilight I decided that this trip to Churchill the next day must help me discover the truth of Clayburn-Durant Foods. If I looked and listened and remembered, then I might know whether I am part of that world or if I am an imposter. I might know my father —my familiar, forgiving, generous father whom none of us really comprehended, ever—and the strange, forgiving, generous woman I presently love but do not comprehend.

Nerve. The riding teacher said my daughter's horse had lost his nerve.

After a solitary dinner (Mrs. Alexander ate from a tray before her t.v. so that she would not miss the Friday night movie) I called Stull. Patrick answered the phone but he recognized my voice.

"Mr. Stull's not feeling too good right now, Mr. Jon," he said.

"That's too bad, Patrick."

"I'll see can he come to the phone."

"If you would, Patrick, please—" I knew the longtime chauffeur-valet-nurse would be as surprised by my cool as I was.

I could hear Stull's heavy feet shuffling across the handsome parquet floors of his big empty "library."

"Jon. All set for the trip tomorrow morning?" Again, the voice, the statement, the offensive, before I could even speak. A replay of quarter till seven that morning.

"You still want me to go?"

"What else?"

"All right, Stull. To Churchill. Not to the football game."

"If that's the way you want it." His voice had an edge like a razor.

"For this time, under the circumstances. Maybe another time—"

"Wilson will fly Nat and me to the Jackson City airport and I'll see if he thinks he can land on that little strip at Churchill. Then he can take you right to the front door."

"That's fine, Stull."

"Jon. You ready to do a first-class mission for Clayburn-Durant down in Churchill? That was quite an act you pulled in my office this morning."

"It still stands."

"What the hell does that mean?"

"If I have to choose sides, I'll let you know, Stull." I paused before I added, "But let me tell you one thing: I care as much about Clayburn-Durant Company as you do."

"Oh?" There was everything in his tone—irony, sarcasm, incredulity, denial. That tone ("I am Clayburn-Durant") angered me as nothing else had that day.

I was determined to tell him nothing else. He was not one who would listen anyway. It was action, not words, that would reach him down in the gut.

"I smelled ketchup this afternoon, down in the lab-kitchen," I said slowly—not actually contradicting my resolution, for I was not telling him anything, I was confounding him. "And I remembered how much Clayburn-Durant means to me." (What else did I remember? The question nagged at me.)

"What?" For once he was nonplussed.

"Nothing, Stull. Just the good old smell of Clayburn-Durant's quality ketchup. And I'll do my best in Churchill."

"Okay. That's all I wanted to hear—not this crap about ketchup. And Jon—"

I waited.

"There's something else. A hunch of mine—"

I was listening now. Stull didn't speak of hunches often. And when he did they were born more of know-how than of witchcraft.

"Actually it's more than a hunch. And I don't like it."

"What is it, Stull?"

"Someone's buying in heavy on Clayburn stock."

"I noticed the turnover last week. Thought maybe the mutual funds were investing."

"It's not funds. It's not institutional buying, except maybe as a front. It's somebody. Somebody after us."

"He'll have a long pull—"

"He won't find it easy. But we're all vulnerable." Then scornfully, "All these bright boys running around growing new companies like mushrooms, all the Stu Siegels and their conglomerates, they'll wake up with indigestion one of these days. You keep your ears open down in Churchill. Never know when or where you may pick up something."

"Look here, Stull, this isn't a Wall Street junket I'm on for your financiers. And it isn't a data-collecting expedition for George

Hodges' computers. I want to get out and find out for myself what spray we're using on the farms, how good or how dangerous it may be. Dangerous? My God, it could be poison! That's plenty enough, Stull."

"If you think a takeover isn't plenty," Stull's voice cut like a shard of glass even when he wasn't "well," as Patrick put it, and it was also laced with threat, "then you'd better check on your recent history of company mergers and reassess your unemployment benefits."

"That twelve percent of the stock you hold ought to provide some bulwark—"

It was the first time I had ever mentioned to Stull how much Clayburn-Durant stock he owned. It brought the longest silence of all between us.

"I'll see you at nine-thirty," he said abruptly. We hung up.

On the Saturday flight, just this morning, he spoke only half a dozen times. Nat Lusk, casual and dapper in a tawny tweed coat and well-cut flannel trousers for the big football afternoon and party afterward, tried to spark conversation and then gave up as he realized there was something profound, of long-standing, between Stull and me.

As they left the plane in Jackson City Stull only said, "Keep your eyes on the ball, Jon. It's your game, too, you know."

I could have laughed in his face, except for the memory of ketchup choking in my throat.

Price Sims was waiting for me at the little airstrip that used to be Colonel Wakely's cow pasture outside Churchill. Price is one of the new breed, never been lean and hungry. He's plump and balding at thirty-five, satisfied just to hold on to his tiny territory of power. He gets his action from stud poker and the county's illegal cockfights. He came to Clayburn Foods along with the packing sheds and machines of a little cannery the company absorbed in Georgia, and he'll be manager at the Churchill plant as long as he can halfway fill the job because Nat Lusk needs him for those bloody cockfights he wants to see whenever he comes down from the city.

Price is one of the new breed for another reason, too: he is unsure about how he should react to me. The older Clayburns—my father, my uncles Josh and Cal and Dan and Whitley, but especially Jonathan, those five brothers like their father, Elisha Clayburn before them —didn't have any uncertainty in approaching any man. They greeted all alike. They were confident inside the core of themselves, had no need for easy agreement or flattery from untested strangers. But a fellow like Price needs somebody else's definition. That is why I make him uneasy.

A number of the younger men at the central office are like Price. In addition, they are on the way up. And they have figured out just what Stull Clayburn's and Nat Lusk's power is, and that of each of the vice-presidents, but they can't decide what shape or amount or kind of strength I have. They find no slot for me, and not knowing how I may be of use or hindrance to them makes them eye me warily.

We came from the airport to the factory, stopping only at the gleaming new motel on the south edge of town to leave my two-suiter. (There are so many who would have claimed me if they had known I was coming: my brother, Monty, Aunt Nettie Sue, and others. But this time I needed the loneliness of a purchased room. There are some things money can buy and loneliness is one of them.) Price brought me up-to-date on inventory in our Churchill warehouses, told me of plans to cut back to winter production of dry-pack foods. And when he spoke of "Burl Smelcer's wife" he kept his eyes on the road, staring straight ahead. "She never pulled out of the coma after her last convulsion. After all, she was sixty-nine years old."

"Probably looked ninety-nine," I said.

He nodded vigorously. "Old Burl's already given up trying to figure out what killed her off." When I didn't push him he glanced at me briefly. "Her kinfolks will be sitting up with the body tonight and funeralizing tomorrow. Outside of that, everything's quiet as cat fur." Price Sims' effort to talk like a mountain man seemed to me to degrade the poor old woman who had died so agonizingly, who— despite Stull's and Price's efforts to keep her anonymous—had a personality, an entity.

At the factory trucks were unloading the last crop of beans. Late limas, shed of their thick tough pods, and long stringless green beans, as prolific and standard-length as years of cross-breeding could make them, were pouring down the chutes into the washing vats, onto the conveyor belts where rows of women inspected them. Once in the cans, and in the big iron retorts, high-pressure cooking would tenderize them, making them seem young and delicate.

"We sprayed these?" I asked Price.

He nodded. "We're keeping this pack separate, at least for the time being." He picked up a handful of the bright emerald beans. His voice was a low awed whisper. Even I could barely hear it. "They held at this stage of their growth for a whole week. Damnedest thing I ever saw. Right at their prime. And their flavor is the finest we've ever packed, at least since I've been around Clayburn-Durant." In a few minutes we went up to the offices, leaving behind the curious stares of the weather-worn women on the inspection line, and in Price's office we talked with one of the plant superintendents and the sales chief for this region.

Later I borrowed Price's car and in the falling part of the afternoon, as old Cebo used to say, I came out here to the fields. Alone. The gigantic bean pickers were just moving off. I watched them roll out of the fields with the massive tread of dinosaurs, their long mechanical necks (for spitting out vines and stalks and leaves) weaving slightly like the necks of those prehistoric animals, sluggish and cumbersome. A stench of oil and fuel trailed behind them like offal. Where they passed the vines are strewn and crushed, the earth packed hard as asphalt.

I try to stir the dirt with the toe of my shoe. It is as unyielding as the concrete of streets I have just left. When we tended this land we were careful to keep it loose and loamy, never plowing too wet for fear it would bake into clods, making sure it could breathe. I can remember hearing about the day Elisha Clayburn, my grandfather, stood not far from where I am tonight and let the rich black dirt filter through his hands, saying, "The land outlives us all—" and within the month he was dead. Now Clayburn Foods has just about come full term. Now our tractors and cultivators and planters gouge up the earth, turn it to rows, beat the clods to dust, feed it, irrigate it, make it yield whatever those gleaming cans demand. I can trace the ridges of the departed dinosaur's tracks even in the early darkness. Once the Clayburns treated the land as if it were a deep, warm, fertile woman worthy of all the care they could lavish. Now the using is all.

Lightning scrawls across the sky like a match struck against the darkness. It has been a long day. Suddenly it is night and the river below me is drowned in shadows. The distant mountains loom dark and threatening as the humpbacked forms of half-submerged whales. The fields are stripped and deserted.

I should go back into town and phone Ellie. I should go to Burl Smelcer's and talk about Perlina. Above all, I should call Deborah. But I do not leave this narrow strip between the bean field and the river for a few more minutes. Some information fed into my system a long time ago holds me here. It has been years since I have walked these fields.

Thunder rumbles off in the west. Pumpkin wagons rolling, the old farmers used to say. Freshness of approaching rain rides the new wind.

The river down below me murmurs in the darkness. Where it reaches under the banked roots of a gaunt old water oak it gurgles strangely, gradually tearing away the earth supporting those aged roots.

Summer has lingered into autumn this year and only today the giant bean-picking machines finished harvesting this field. It is almost time for killing frost. Trunks of the sycamores along the river shine like bleached skeletons under the fitful moonlight that comes and goes in the stormy sky. Starvation moon, the Cherokees who were once here called it.

I have been a company man for a long time but not so long, quite, that I have lost myself, although I learned yesterday that there is much I have buried and need to remember, for the company, for myself.

The river has made this earth I'm standing on, dragging topsoil and debris down from the uplands to enrich it for generations. And land such as this across America has made Clayburn-Durant Foods, which has been my life. None of the Clayburns has been here in a long while, too damn long.

On the plane this morning coming down the great mid-continent flyway I watched the warrens and hives and colonies of cities and suburbs dwindle and disappear as the mountains thrust up their peaks and labyrinths, and I wondered if there are many others in chrome and steel and styrofoam labyrinths today who know bone-deep, as I, the transition from an old landlocked earth to passage through air.

My boyhood boots pulled against the suck of mud; my present British walkers have been jetted across continents of space and time. Down these muddy rows I used to drag battered crates and baskets; now my Gucci briefcase waits on the seat of the car at the edge of the field. I have two urbane children full of supplementary vitamins and enriched cereals but I remember yanking stubborn beets out of this ground, wringing off the purple-green tops and stems which bled a resplendent juice more royal than blood, bending until my back was an aching stiffness and the smell of roots was bitter in my nostrils.

Canning is part of two worlds and there is no escaping either. Land and computers. Seeds and machinery. Weather and sales charts. The gone-before and the yet-to-come are by-products of every can we fill. Yet in those big, sleek central offices in the midwestern metropolis where I live, we lose touch. Yesterday I learned how incredibly we lose touch.

A nightbird calls from one of the beech trees. Unthinking, I reach for pockets—it is chilly and I am wearing a topcoat—hearkening back to the time when old Cebo, whose face was dark and wrinkled and tough as walnut bark, muttered that a screech owl's forebodings could be canceled only by turning all our pockets inside out. Standing in the deepening darkness, many distances from where I began this day, I wonder if the owl speaks of life or death, the present or future. Or perhaps the past. The past has been thick around me all day, like one of the fogs that sometimes sweeps across these Smoky Mountains, smothering all the familiar landmarks, changing contours, obscuring here and revealing there, until the oldest places are new and the new is made ancient, or seems so.

It is the old past in that scent of ketchup which is here, waiting in the silent furrows, passing like the river in its wrenching, ceaseless course. But only yesterday is still raw within me. I'll have to settle many ghosts while I am here.

In the distance, Burl Smelcer's unpainted house squats on a treeless rise. I must go there. But not tonight, not with the dead woman lying in the narrow room fetid with visitors and heat and food and curiosity—and, yes, mourning. I can see the light from the house, no larger than a firefly in the distance.

I hear the screech owl again. Its quavering cry comes from a nearer tree this time. It makes me apprehensive. I do not seem to

myself the same man who left the city this morning, brisk and businesslike even though in revolt. Here I know that the past is not dead.
Or is it even past? Like all the data programmed into George Hodges'
computers, it waits raw and formless. And no one remembers more
of it happening here than I do.

Blood soaked into the ground. Sweat mixed with mud and crates
of tomatoes and machine grease. Tears and terror and waste, hurt too
deep for scars, pure joy, gall of mistakes, the sweet balm of success,
and the reach out. And out. And out.

I come from a line of remembering people. In generations past
we built churches and ballads and a way of life out of our remembering, handing down words the way others pass along designs woven
into coverlets, carved into wood, or worked into clay. But now that
is going, too—the woven words and the cloth and all.

Another slash of lightning breaks as I leave the field and the
deep-running river and walk along the rutted road toward the car.
Does anyone else care about Elisha Clayburn's violent death in these
dark mountains or the inheritance he left Mary Clayburn and seven
children? Does anyone know of his son Jonathan's improbable journey—so unlike most Clayburn ventures—to unravel the secret of
Elisha's death? Does anyone recollect how another son, Daniel Clayburn, with the strong black arm of Lonas Rankin beside him, dreamed
and pounded into being machines that made a little plant into a
company?

Does anyone recall the face or form of all those anonymous
figures—black and white—who gave strength and substance to the
Clayburns and their dream through patient, wrenching years and
lifetimes? Does anyone at all remember Josh Clayburn's voice, the
wounded look in his eyes as he broke before the ultimatum delivered
by his own son, Stull? Or the ultimatum itself by which the company
became larger than any Clayburn or all the family? And above all,
does anyone remember (or can anyone who knew forget?) Jonathan
Clayburn, carrying them all by his will and muscle?

This is the memory I have come back to claim. My father. Shape
of a world of love-honor-and-obey, of a-man's-word-is-his-bond, of
love-thy-neighbor-as-thyself, of something far and lost, abandoned.

I arrive at my car and climb in, turn the key with stiff fingers,
head toward town. The first drops of rain fall. Their freshness mixes

with the old and acrid smell of mulch and silt left by many floods covering these level plains below the mountains. The dark land stretches around me.

The cold autumn rain is slashing hard against my windshield as I watch the road from the farm into Churchill. A car behind me pulls out to pass in an explosion of impatience. Its tires hiss on the wet pavement and its motor churns. As it cuts back into the right lane ahead of me the rear wheels slip. The driver brings it out of the skid. I wonder if the boy I glimpsed knows how narrowly he escaped plunging down the steep bank to our right. I watch his red tail-light fade into the distance. How did Dan Clayburn feel that long-ago day when his new car stalled in gravel and would not start again?

We are fearfully and wonderfully made, my God-fearing, church-going father and mother told me. Is the foolish boy in that souped-up car? Does he know? Was Perlina Smelcer? Is Stull Clayburn and does he know? Do I know?

No superman of sex or finance or honor. Six-feet-two with hair still dark brown and belly not yet flabby and not-quite twenty-twenty vision. My tennis and love-making are not so unyielding as when I was twenty but they have gained something in form and finesse and enjoyment. I still struggle to keep up with news of neighborhood, city, industry, country, world. The result: frustration, and a dozen riptides pressing in.

A search began for me yesterday: for Jonathan Clayburn, Jr., Jon, in my early fifties, widower, father, business executive, fringe participant in religion and politics and sports and society, secret dreamer at intervals, occasional lover now in love. I ask only to be whole. And I realize the arrogance and impossibility of my asking.

By the time I arrive at the motel the rain has settled to a steady downpour. I stop at the desk to pick up my room key and the clerk makes me welcome. Her formal greeting has been memorized from some innkeeper's manual but as I thank her she adds, "Turning cold yet? I heard thunder a little while ago. My grandpa always said autumn thunder meant a cold spell to come."

I smile at her and nod. All at once I love her. Her hair is set in beatuy-parlor majesty and her dress is a wholesale replica of some high-fashion design shown in a slick magazine, her eyes even bear standard Cleopatra outlines and shadows. But the adaptation has not yet been total. It has not reached all the way inside. "My grandpa always said . . ."

We can still remember.

And I need to remember because I must go on. Without yesterday Clayburn-Durant Foods would not be here. The question is, will any of us—on foot or hoof or wing or fin or root—be here tomorrow?

Deborah brought me to the heart of the question seven or eight months ago when Lee was between his sophomore year and Europe and he and I had quarreled again.

"Can't we talk with each other?" I asked.

"When did we ever do anything with each other?" he shouted, tall, awkward, miserable.

His attack caught me by surprise in what had seemed a casual disagreement. "Baseball." I seized on the first word that came to mind. I was trying to put through a long distance call to our food broker in Chicago, too.

"Baseball?" All at once tears were in his eyes and this increased his anger. "You can't mean that Little League snow job we used to put on because the company needed a better community image?"

"Wait a minute—"

"A minute? I've been waiting all my life. Little League baseball! You've got to be kidding. Tell me the truth, why don't you, just for once?"

I told the operator to cancel my call. "All right, you tell me."

"Old Stull Clayburn was boozing himself every night and scaring the hell out of the directors and word was getting around and you were the good old family type to make Clayburn Foods look good. God!" His voice was almost a shriek. "I didn't even *like* baseball."

Who would have suspected that at ten years old—all those years ago—he knew so much about the company? Or was it only now that he knew? About me? Because I had thought, honestly thought, at that time and during the years when I was treasurer for the Little League team, rounding up money for uniforms and equipment, that I was doing the whole damned bit because I wanted to be with Lee. Yet I knew that I had spent more time raising funds at the country club than coaching or playing ball with Lee. I knew that Stull never objected (as he had with many of my interests) to the hunks of time that Little League consumed. When I had been chairman of the city Symphony Drive, Stull had suggested that it took a lot of time and attention from my work at the company. But with Little League both Lee and Stull had watched me act out an elaborate charade.

"And college. It's a Mickey Mouse world: what can anybody really do to make any difference. Jesus Christ! Wars all over the place."

Before I could answer he rushed on. "But you—you've got some of the pure stuff. Power. You could do something, a little."

"All right. Let's talk about that."

"Run it up the flag-pole and see how it flaps, as your great Nat Lusk would say?" His cynicism confounded me.

"I guess that's about it," I said.

"Well, Nat Lusk and I don't rap to the same language. Talk is nothing. What do you *feel?* What will you do?" He was neither crying nor shouting now. "It's a new ball game, and I'd like to get just as far away from here as possible while you play your innings and I play mine. Because, man, I'm going to feel—and I'm going to do—"

"More power to you." I was trying to recapture a little cool, speak slowly. "If you knew me better you'd know that a long time ago—"

Lee was not listening. He demanded that others hear but he was deaf.

(At that moment I saw my mother's face—wide-eyed, hurt, dismayed—and I heard an echo speaking in my own voice: "This beat-up town is just one cesspool of hypocrisy. Politicians speaking from both sides of their mouth. Preachers gnawing on fried chicken and platitudes with Nigtown on their doorstep. Beethoven and Shelley and Tom Paine roasting in a deacon's hell. God didn't create any such crazy world. It has to be Darwin's."

But Lee could never guess the proportions such words assumed in that remote time and place. To my mother Darwin was not only rebellion but eternal damnation. And matching the fierceness of her love for each of her children, the fear of such an eternity was real, a shattering threat to her life.

I had discovered doubt and the experience of great art and my own humility in one overwhelming dose, and I was afflicting her—because she was so vulnerable, because she did care—with the indigestion of my angry new awareness incompatible with lingering allegiances.)

"Lee—"

He did not answer but he looked up.

"You take a year." I walked across the room and back. "See if you can find out what it is you want—and don't want. It's your life. But I'll stake you to a year."

He was looking directly at me now, suspicious, hopeful. "You mean it?"

"I mean it."

"God!"

"After that, you're on your own."

"Sure." He tossed his head, ran one hand through his hair, dismissing a year as if it would last a lifetime. His resemblance to Teena was remarkable, except that he had more lines in his face already than his mother had had when she died. "I can't make any promises—"

"Did I ask?"

There were a dozen promises I wanted to wring from him and did not, could not. (I remembered the instruction-promise my mother gave each time I left home—camp, college, work, marriage—"Be happy, Jon!" Squeezing my hand, looking with her trusting blue eyes into my heedless face. As if happiness were a commodity and not a by-product. As if happiness were a prize received and not a gift given.)

"That's really fantastic!" Lee looked pleased and forlorn and tender—so open to every low blow and betrayal and fair hit lying in wait for him that I could hardly restrain my need to shield—at least to warn—him.

"Lee?"

"Yes?"

But what else was there to say? I sat back down at the desk. "I'll be going to New York this weekend. Would you see that Ellie gets out to the stables and back?"

"Sure thing."

I carried my wretchedness about the talk with Lee to New York and Deborah that weekend.

We were sitting in her apartment watching Saturday dusk settle over the Tinker Toy buildings of the city below us. It was a yellow, lonely time of day between pale sunlight and artificial brightness and Lee's words seemed an echo of all the desolation.

"Except for his mother's death, Lee's had everything easy—as easy as I could make it."

She brought me a glass of golden sherry, the color of the light melting the city to illusion before us.

"Even I was not born to it. Your Lee and all the others, so young they are, they know."

"Know what, Deborah?"

"How—how fragile it all is. Breath, air, water, a plant, this little plot of earth"—she snapped her long fingers in a small explosion of sound—"like that it can be destroyed."

"I know."

"No. You are thinking of one little part. Your Teena. Your part of the country perhaps. As I think about my little family, and another country. But now it is neither yours nor mine. It is not part—it is all. All can be finished."

Her thin bony hands swept together and fell into her lap with a gesture more eloquent than words. "Let him go, Jon."

When I did not answer she moved down to the footstool in front of me and took both my hands in hers. "Let him go—as he says, far away. It may not be as far apart as you are now."

I nodded. "I told him he could go."

"Jon, don't you see? It is because he is so much like you, still angry after all these years—"

"That many?" I tried to joke. But she had probed to the quick. She knew it. She did not persist. We sat in the semidarkness and watched the city turn on all around us in a bright patchwork.

That night I wanted to make Deborah believe again that life was possible, despite the fragility she had described. I wanted her to know that her flesh was alive and scars did not matter because within her burned something more alive than I had ever found in any other person. We created our own passion and it was as good as a man and woman have ever known together.

But I knew what she had said of Lee was true. And I began to recall my own father.

In my motel room now I open the long sliding glass door which is supposed to remain closed and locked. Smell of the rain drenches my lungs. Sound of its downpour brings the night alive. Up in the high mountains the thick cover of mosses, leaves, mulch, will be soaking up this moisture like a green living sponge. On the farms men will be saying that this puts the tobacco "in case" for grading, puts a good season in the late pastures. Wetness feeds the roots.

I come back in the room and switch on the t.v. to hear the evening news before I go to eat. The picture blurs, then focuses. Men are fighting under trees stark as skeletons from defoliation. While I watch, putting on a fresh shirt, one man seizes his groin and, with a slow tortured spin of pain and surprise, goes down to the ground.

Problems do not come neatly, properly ordered in sequence of time or urgency or our capacity to meet them. I look at the figures on the tiny screen and consider how everything seems to erupt at once, like a smoking, rumbling volcano under which we have lived for many years, until one morning nature blows its top and all the lava, rock, fire hurl down at once, shattering our indifference to the familiar. Work, children, sex, loving—and killing by one means and another, anonymously—they have exploded on my little agenda all at the same time.

I am here tonight, tomorrow, next day, to help determine company policy on the use of certain chemicals, sprays, etceteras, on living plants for living creatures to consume. But policy is not that much a thing apart. Neither is it some predestined set of commandments handed down from a computerized Sinai. Policy is human character. And nature's laws. What is the character of Clayburn-Durant? What is my own? Deborah, Lee, Ellie, Stull, Burl Smelcer's wife, my long-dead father, Jonathan: I am asking.

2

Cebo came up from the fields at dusk, old and sad and slow as centuries.

"Old gray fox down in the cornfield—"

His voice was like grit on sandpaper, scratching from his wrinkled throat and wizened face. Cherokee and Ibo and Scotch-Irish and a half-dozen other bloods and memories had merged in him through the couplings of a hundred cold or steamy nights.

Mary Clayburn, standing on the top step of the back verandah where she had come to the fresh air before bolting the door for the night, shivered and bit her lip.

"Don't begin that spooky talk, Cebo," she said.

Long shadows reached up from the loamy bottomlands below and down the slopes of gaunt mountains in the distance, like an ink stain spreading from a sudden spill, soaking up all distinctions. Only a bend in the river and a single upthrust pinnacle caught final glints of light. The shriveled figure in the yard was blotted out by the swift darkness.

"Old gray still down there in the cornfield," his voice echoed back as if speaking to itself. "Whether we pay him no never mind, he still loping through all free and easy, dragging his brush low behind."

"Hush, Cebo!" Fear wavered through her voice and would not be mocked by what she said. "People who have faith don't need superstitions to live by." The stillness absorbed her words as if she had not spoken. "I guess that old gray is on the prowl for a good fat hen," she tried to turn to lightness. "Bad luck for somebody's flock tonight." Her laugh was a thin melancholy splinter of sound.

"Bad luck," Cebo echoed out in the darkness. His words and tone conjured up all the predators slouching around the margins of life waiting to pounce or nibble wherever there was a collapse or even a wavering of courage, of joy. After the fox, the wolf. And worse than either, the sleek gray rat.

For seventeen years Cebo had been there, part of the life of the brick house foursquare behind Mary Clayburn, part of the spacious barns and tight smokehouses and cribs, so much a part of all the pattern of their days that he had strained the cow's milk for Josh to drink, and mixed it with his own concoction of herbs, when nervousness over her first-born had dried up Mary Clayburn's breasts and left the baby screaming with hunger.

Cebo had washed the corpse and laid out the tiny body of the third baby, born after Joshua and Jonathan. Cebo had rocked the cradle of each of Mary's seven living children. He had sung.

> For I've a home out yonder,
>> Few days, few days,
> For I've a home out yonder,
>> I'm a-going home.
> For I can't stay in the wilderness,
>> Few days, few days,
> For I can't stay in the wilderness,
>> I'm a-going home.

And the little ones listened, quietened by the desolation of the gritty old voice and the dolorous words.

Elisha Clayburn, who was knowledgeable about property and ownership and loyalties, the needs men have beyond salt and meat and drink, had made Cebo a deed for the land on which his weathered two-room dwelling stood. It was a deed of ownership outright so that he owned what few black men and fewer red men and not many white men did in this place and in this year of 1896: his own land and home. Yet no one had ever heard him laugh.

"Cebo," Mary Clayburn called, searching with grave brown eyes where she thought he might be in the darkness, yet not sure. "You do think Mr. Clayburn will be here soon, don't you?"

"Soon enough." But she could tell he was not smiling.

She thought about her husband, trying to bring his face into her vision, trying to hear his voice as he went about chores on this farm and in this house.

To Elisha Clayburn the earth was both a bounty and a barrier. He owned some of the finest acres in the southern mountains—long level stretches of black topsoil—but surrounding him, holding his crops and talents in landlocked isolation, were the mountains.

"The Lord pours out to me on level ground and takes it back in the stony hills," he had said when he watched a master harvest of wheat turn weevily because he could not get it hauled to market.

But Elisha Clayburn came from sturdy generations of men who ate, fought, hunted, plowed, reproduced, and died with energy and profit. The first one in these mountains was a patriot who received his allotted acres for Revolutionary War service to his country. To these he added rich level lands secured by premature, personal (and therefore illegal) agreements with the Cherokees. But no one disputed his possession.

That first Clayburn's wife was scalped by the Cherokees one day when she was gathering herbs for medicine and ran into a stray hunting party of young warriors who were returning from an unsuccessful raid north into Shawnee country. But he found another wife, three more to be exact. He became almost as well known for populating the graveyard as for populating that wild lonesome mountain country. His descendants, seventeen of them, followed his example, at least as far as multiplication and replenishment was concerned. Through experience and expediency, Clayburns accumulated land and did not sell it but handed it down to their children. They believed in the owning of land.

Their finest holding was the plantation on the lower reaches of the river which had been built and owned by Major Hayward Lawes until the Civil War swept all his slaves to freedom and him to madness. Elisha Clayburn's father bought the strong brick house with its rolling acres. When he was only forty-seven, he died of a heart attack. He left behind a farm and home to each of the three married daughters, the home-place to the spinster daughter who lived with him, and Major Hayward Lawes' plantation to his only son Elisha—this last with a debt of taxes accumulated on it. Elisha was twenty, already

married to Mary Ransom. (Nothing was required for the four children buried in the graveyard on the hill behind the home-place, two
taken by fever and one by milk-leg and the other by bloody flux before
it had reached its first birthday.)

Elisha Clayburn's young and secret dream had been to become
a lawyer. His father, however, believed in the independence of the
land, forgetting, no doubt, a farmer's slavery to weather and beasts
and interest on money borrowed. There was deep-seated Clayburn
suspicion of the worth and stability of the word, written or spoken,
except as bond among neighbors.

Throughout his years, Elisha Clayburn was more than a farmer.
He was an unofficial judge and arbiter for people scattered over the
region. In an area where an X was more common than a signature,
he shared his literacy ungrudgingly. Anyone with a dispute could
bring it to him and have it mended justly, without delay. Anyone with
an inheritance to settle could talk with him and have it arranged with
fairness and good will.

Men from far up in the harsh ridges came and told him of their
equal claims on a line-fence strip of land. He listened and pulled on
his short beard and spoke slowly: the swatch of ground should become
a no-man's land, neither of its claimants possessing it but each leaving
it for such birds and varmints and plants as might prove a benefit to
all concerned. They took the decision reluctantly until Elisha Clayburn convinced them. "This is a better way than blood. Use the guns
you left outside my door and your widows and orphans will have to
eat berries and roots scrabbled out of that ground to keep from
starving on charity."

For all who could not write or figure, he answered their needs
willingly, as carefully as if they were his own. "You spend a lot of time
on other folks' work," his oldest boy, Joshua, said one day.

Mr. Clayburn only gave a characteristic little tug at his beard.
He finished the document he was writing for a distraught woman who
denied her church's accusation of bastardy. (Her husband, she explained, in prison for the past two years, had escaped nine months
before and spent a full two hours at home before the law recaptured
him.) Then he pushed aside the ink and said to his son, "I reckon it
as time not spent but invested."

And when his brother-in-law, Whit Ransom, and drunken Edom

Metcalf brewed themselves a fight and tore up the tavern on Churchill's main street, it was Elisha Clayburn who suggested that they share equally the expense of rebuilding it instead of going to court to blame each other for the damage. "Take it to law," he finally told them, "and you can buy a pair of Churchill lawyers a new horse and rig apiece, not counting the tavern repair someone is still going to pay." That quieted Ransom's roaring and Metcalf's cursing. They hated to think of somebody else enjoying their money.

Such counsel, even the writing of legal documents, was seldom repaid and did not put food on Elisha and Mary Clayburn's table or shoes on their children's feet. At last, this year when Jonathan was seventeen and Joshua eighteen, the father made a momentous decision.

It began on an evening more than seven months ago, between late winter and early spring when winds cut sharp as knives at one moment and fanned gently as eiderdown the next. Elisha and Mary were walking up from the barn where they had gone with the children to see a newborn colt. They walked slowly because of Mary's bad left leg. Little Lottie, six, rode on her father's shoulders and surveyed her brothers and sisters below her in queenly superiority. Nettie Sue, eight, held her big brother Josh's hand and this was all the security she needed. The younger boys, Whit and Cal and Dan, had been scuffling on the ground like a den of fox whelps—until they heard their father speak in a grave voice. He was talking to their mother. Neither Elisha nor Mary believed in protecting children from bad weather, only preparing them for it.

"Someone in town," Elisha Clayburn said, "wants to buy this farm. The house, at least."

There was a silence.

Then Josh asked, "Our house?"

His father nodded. "Take it for taxes due."

Mary Clayburn stopped and looked at him. Down in the pasture pond frogs croaked loudly in the fading light. "Can they do that?"

"Yes. They can pay off the taxes and maybe a token sum to us. That's the way half the men around here got hold of their property after the war. And that panic three years ago still has a stranglehold on any fellow trying to farm."

"Who is it wanting to buy?" Mary Clayburn asked.

"Randall Montgomery."

Randall Montgomery was a tall, fleshy, green-eyed man who cut a bold figure in fine broadcloth and boots that shone with the high polish of leather soft and pliable as costly kid. The Montgomerys were town people. Churchill's first family. Randall's father had been circuit judge until a stroke the year before; his older brother, Alexander, was president of the bank; his younger brother ran the store. Only Randall had no settled business—except to be the handsomest of a handsome breed, the most entertaining host of a family renowned for hospitality.

Mary Clayburn may have been thinking of him as she gazed out over the fields and up toward the square house sitting serenely among its oak trees in the sinking light, its white cornices and shutters and Corinthian columns framing the solid substance of brick, tall chimneys, wide steps.

"But this is our home!" thirteen-year-old Whit burst out. "Grandpa gave it to Papa."

Mr. Clayburn shook his head. "Not quite. No one ever finished paying off all the taxes old Major Lawes had accumulated during the war and reconstruction. But there has always been leniency in the county about such taxes—unless someone forced a showdown."

The smaller children looked from one parent's face to the other. They understood that this was solemn business.

"What your grandpa could have done," their father explained, "was pay the taxes first and then beat demented old Major Lawes down to whatever was left over, fair or not." Mr Clayburn tugged at his beard absentmindedly as Lottie clutched his neck. "I'm proud that wasn't part of my inheritance. Your grandpa gave the major all he could muster for the finest plantation in this county. And shouldered the taxes as his own burden."

"Now yours," Mary Clayburn said, but she laid a hand on his arm to show she was not disapproving, only worried. The noise of the frogs was louder in the early dark.

"Why should Randall Montgomery want our place?" Jonathan asked. "He's a city man."

"Maybe he's going to become a country man," Elisha Clayburn said.

"He wants it to make a big splash," Mary interrupted her husband. "The Montgomerys like grand gestures, fine houses, fast horses."

"Except for the one in the bank," Elisha Clayburn agreed slowly, "named Alexander,"

"And Randall is the worst of the lot!" The children rarely heard their mother so vehement. Wisps of her smooth hair had come loose over her forehead, making her look younger and more angry than her words.

"Now, Mary," her husband took her arm and urged her toward the house again. She walked stiffly, the children following close by. "This may be just a notion with Randall. Anyway the judge says I can have until the end of the year to find the money for taxes—"

"Where could you get so much in one year?"

"In Carolina. In the Low Country." He was looking at his oldest sons now, too. "I've been turning it over in my mind. We're going to raise a master crop of corn this year, then we're going to put it on the backs and ribs of big fat porkers and let them carry it down to the South Carolina markets for us."

"A hog drive!" Jonathan said.

His father nodded.

"And we'll make a way to get our crops out of the hills and trade for cash and count a profit." Jonathan's enthusiasm grew like a brush fire.

"Hold on," his father said. "Men been driving hogs through these mountains for years. Can't say I ever heard of a single one getting rich."

"They made a living. But most of them were just traders, like Randall Montgomery when he went last year. It'll be different with us."

"Different?"

"We'll have our own livestock. We'll make our own trades." Jonathan seized his mother by the elbows and would have lifted her from the ground but she braced against him, surprised and unconvinced by his exuberance. His father was looking at Jonathan with an attentive, appraising thoughtfulness.

"I hate those stock drives," Mary said. "They're rough. The men are nothing but licentious rowdies. They can be dangerous."

"Mary, Mary," Elisha spoke gently. "How else am I going to wrench any real money out of this stubborn land? If a railroad ever gets argued and surveyed and funded through these mountains, then we'll have other ways to make a living. But this burden is now."

The mere prospect of all that rowdiness and licentiousness and adventure made the boys' pulses pound. They had watched the hog drives take leave in past autumns. They had observed the gathering of men and animals, the greetings and news and plans, the noise and smells and jostling, the first rush onto the road. For days after the dust of each departure had settled, the boys had longed to go on such a journey. They had talked of the places and had imagined the strangers. They had fancied unfamiliar roads and each of themselves a man among men.

But if they hoped for any such experience this year, their mother had anticipated them and she disposed of the possibility. "One promise, Elisha," she said, as they came to the house.

"Yes, Mary."

"None of the boys will go with you. I won't have them exposed to such carousing and downright wickedness."

"All right, Mary."

Josh and Jonathan, the only ones who had dared to hope, made no protest. They had learned not to debate matters of wickedness.

The season that followed was favorable for growing corn and hogs. Some said that the Clayburn's corn put up two stalks to every seed and every stalk put out three ears. The new litters of pigs grew off plump and healthy and there wasn't a hint of cholera that year. When the young boars were altered, Jonathan held the can of turpentine to pour after his father and Cebo made the cut, and the healing was so quick that only two of the boars died of infection. In the middle of September the boys and the hired hands rounded up every hog roaming the fields and woods and fastened them in smaller pens for fattening. Hauling and husking the corn became a fulltime job.

During an unseasonably hot day in September, Colonel Wakely rode into the yard just at dinnertime and stopped under one of the spreading oaks. Elisha Clayburn and Josh and Jonathan and several other men were coming up from the fields and barn where they had put away the last batch of hay for winter. Sweat mixed with prickly hayseeds clung to their steaming skins.

Colonel Gideon Wakely was like the Clayburns in owning wide stretches of good land. His acres adjoined the Clayburns' along the river. But in addition, he also had money. Or access to ready money, through a bachelor uncle in Chicago who had made a fortune in railroads. This uncle's generosity had built Colonel Wakely a sprawling mansion and filled it with precious bric-a-brac, brought his farm to flourish, and let him marry delicate Drusilla Lusk.

The colonel was a big man and he rode a big horse, white and sleek, and he always rode at a gallop. His mounts never lasted long, but every one he rode was white. His sparse hair and moustache, waxed at the tips, were white, too.

"Lish." He looked down at Elisha Clayburn. "You hard up for help these days?" He did not like to see a man he considered his equal drenched in sweat and hayseed and dirt.

"Not as long as I have boys," Elisha Clayburn said easily. "Come on into dinner, Gideon."

Colonel Wakely shook his head. "Been up to Churchill this morning. Have to get back home and see how many of my hands are playing off." He might not have believed in heavy labor for himself or Elisha Clayburn, but Colonel Wakely was a fanatic in prescribing work for everyone else. Anyone sitting down during a work day—and that stretched from first sunrise to last sunset—drove him into a fury. It was whispered that at wheat harvest once he found Janus Rathbone replacing a quail's nest instead of swinging the cradle and therefore brought a pitchfork down over Rathbone's hand, bracketing it to the ground. Janus Rathbone's left hand became stiff and shriveled.

On this early fall day Colonel Wakely asked, "How are your hogs doing, Lish?"

"Can't complain. Some fat. Some lean. All afoot."

"You've heard that you're going to have company on the road to South Carolina?"

"Probably half a dozen droves along the way," Elisha said, "coming and going."

"Just one other from around here."

Elisha looked up sharply then and Jonathan turned around. "Somebody else driving livestock this year?"

"Randall Montgomery, gathering up all the small herds, going to drive them to market on the shares for the county's one-horse farmers."

"The man's dogging my steps." Elisha Clayburn rubbed his shirt sleeve across his forehead, then seemed to regret his words. "That's his right—to use the big road any time, any way he wants."

"He's already made arrangements with Orvil Gosnell and two or three others who'll go along to drive their own animals, too."

"They know the business. I'd figured on asking Gosnell to help me."

"I hate this, Lish. I had thought to let you take my hogs along with yours, market them the best you can. We big landowners have to stick together. I don't want Montgomery to own a foot of the Major Lawes plantation."

"It's the Elisha Clayburn farm now, Gideon," Clayburn said. His voice was calm.

"Lawes, Clayburn—just so it's not Montgomery," the colonel replied.

But all Elisha Clayburn would repeat was that it's a free world and roads are open to all.

It was difficult to stay angry with Randall Montgomery. When Elisha Clayburn saw him in town a week later, Montgomery spun some of his yarns and no one would have thought he was pressing for the man's home or contending for the Carolina markets in hogs. After a while Montgomery said plainly that he would like to make the drive with Elisha Clayburn. He pointed out that there was no need for folks to be unsociable and keep work from being a pleasure.

When Elisha Clayburn told his family about Randall Montgomery's proposition he added, "I know well enough that Montgomery wants to profit by my experience of hog raising."

After a minute Jonathan said, "It's all right. Maybe you can profit by his experience from past drives. They say he's a horn salesman."

"Good boy!" Elisha Clayburn exclaimed. He beamed on his second son with approval. "You've a level head."

"I've been thinking it over," Jonathan said.

"I've been thinking, too," his father said. "Maybe you ought to come along, help make this drive to the Low Country with us."

"Could I?" Jonathan's face was flushed with surprise and pleasure.

"Would it be all right with you, Mary?"

She looked at them. "You promised me, Elisha."

"I know I did, Mary. But Jonathan's matured this summer. If you're still hard set against it, though, we'll forget I ever spoke."

"No," she shook her head at him, "you and Jonathan decide."

In that case, it was already decided.

The morning of departure came in late October. Elisha Clayburn knew that they would have Randall Montgomery with them every step of the journey, an irresponsible threat prodding them and a high humor entertaining them.

Elisha was determined that they would be on their way as soon as the earliest light broke over Grindstone Mountain. "That first day counts for a lot," he told the children one night as he and Jonathan sat in the kitchen greasing their boots. Josh had gone down to Colonel Wakely's to help him round up his animals, so only the younger ones were there. "The porkers are fresh and spirited then. If a man can break them to the road fast and keep them moving he can cover miles that will never come as easy again."

They worked the grease hard with their fingers, rubbing it into every wrinkle and crevice of the hard cowhide. On such a journey their boots would be their best friends or their worst enemies, whichever they made them be.

"This leather's going to meet a lot of roughness—stone and wet and sharp hooves—it's got to be as tough as tanbark. But it's also going to shoe our feet, so we'd better rub some softness into it, too." Toughness and tenderness. It was Elisha Clayburn's combination. Jonathan marked that fact down in his memory.

To be certain that he didn't lag, Jonathan sat up, already dressed for the journey, the night before they were to leave. When his father came downstairs in the morning, Jonathan was slumped in one of the straight chairs beside a cold fireplace. Elisha Clayburn was startled, then amused.

Mary Clayburn hurried in, jabbing the last pins in the knot of hair piled atop her head, and Delia, the sleepy little cook, followed her. The kitchen became a woman's domain.

"Jonathan," his mother said, as Delia shook down the ashes in the big black range, "take your father's ax and trim me a handful of hurry-wood from the pine sticks in the yard."

"Mama—" he protested, tightening the leather laces of his boots, "the men are making ready to leave."

His words dwindled. His father was already through the door, picking up the double-bitted ax he kept on the rear porch, handy and razor sharp for his own use. By the time Jonathan went to follow him, the older man was coming back with splinters of rich pine and dry cedar. He laid them in the stove.

"A man takes care of his family first." Elisha Clayburn said and went back outside.

"I'm sorry, Mama," Jonathan mumbled, crossing the kitchen. "I was in such a hurry—"

"It's all right, son," she said. She was pouring coffee beans into the coffee grinder on the wall, and the pungent smell filled the room.

"I'll bring more wood," Jonathan volunteered, starting toward the door.

"There's plenty." His mother nodded toward the brimful wood-box. "Kindling was all I needed."

The flame blazed suddenly in the fire-box and the pine began to crackle. The younger boys trooped down from upstairs, rushed through the room, hastened more than usual to finish their morning chores.

"Where's Josh?" Jonathan asked.

"He's not well this morning," his mother said.

Jonathan heard the tone of her voice. He hurried to join the men. Down at the hog lots beside the road, light from a dozen or more lanterns fought the last pale beams of the setting half-moon. The figures of the hog drivers whom Elisha Clayburn had hired threw long shadows across the chilly ground.

"Moon's holding water," one of them observed, "we'll have a clear day."

"Good beginning for a bad end," another muttered. No one paid attention to anyone else's talk.

The morning mounted to a blur of shouts and squeals, strange faces and strong voices, raucous laughter and sly speculation.

"Spartanburg, is it?" a short, red-haired man named Jasper Smelcer said. "I don't much favor Spartanburg for selling hogs—"

"That's the last word I heard from old man Clayburn. Spartanburg's our first aim."

"Aiming and hitting is two different things, as the old man said to his young bride. Now I never had no luck this side the real Low Country—"

"Clayburn said it might be Charleston if worse came to worst."

Jasper Smelcer spat. "That would be one damned long drive." And he wiped tobacco juice from his mouth.

Jonathan had overheard their talk. The thought of Charleston brought images of the ocean and all the dazzle of a city. It robbed him of his appetite for the hot flavorsome sausage and fluffy eggs and buttered biscuits and steaming coffee which his mother set forth for breakfast.

He might as well have eaten.

His father had just taken a last swallow of coffee and carefully wiped his beard when Mary Clayburn came back into the room from upstairs. Her footsteps were heavy. "Elisha, I don't see how we can spare Jonathan for this trip."

The quiet that followed was so complete that even the crackling of the fire in the stove seemed loud. Even Delia made no noise with the pans.

"What is it, Mary?"

"Josh isn't well this morning." She shook her head to forestall alarm. "It's nothing serious. But I don't know how long he'll have to stay in bed and I can't manage without—"

"What about Whitley?" Jonathan said. "He's fourteen—"

"Jonathan," Elisha Clayburn stood up and went around the table and put his hand on his son's shoulder, "you'll have to stay with the family."

Jonathan did not answer. His younger brothers looked away from his face and down at their plates. Mary Clayburn busied herself at the stove. And Elisha turned and went out of the kitchen and down to the waiting men.

When they were ready to leave, Jonathan watched his father bend down from the strong, roan-colored horse and squeeze his mother's hand. "Come back soon, Elisha," she cried.

"Yes, Mary. I'll bring back security for our home and land. Take care of each other—" He looked toward Jonathan, standing alone at one side, and raised his voice. "You must look after each other."

The drovers shouted and the hogs squealed and poured out of their lots and surged up the road in a mighty river of hooves and snouts and bristles and grunts. Elisha Clayburn and Randall Montgomery and another man on horseback rode everywhere—prodding, heading off, driving. The sun was just coming over Grindstone Mountain in a blaze of autumn brightness when the swarm of men and animals disappeared around the last curve in the distance.

They were gone the rest of October and through all of November and now it was Monday in the first week of December.

"I've never heard of a drive taking so long before—" Mary Clayburn said to Cebo, out in the shadows.

"Never had so many hogs before. Never had Randall Montgomery along before." His voice was the same as when he spoke of the fox.

She paused and reached deep into the pocket of her long blue skirt where a letter lay folded, firm against her fingers. "And they never went so far before. After his message—"

But she knew that Cebo was gone now, disappeared to that place where he lived so privately, so much more privately than anyone else on the farm.

The last backwash of light was gone, too, even the lingering reflections. And the savor of the letter's arrival earlier in the day was melted away. The secret pleasure of that piece of paper and small square envelope which Colonel Wakely had brought out from town to her that afternoon was dissolved into sudden raw loneliness and fear.

"Lish all right?" Colonel Wakely had demanded even as she stood reading the crowded page of Elisha's writing.

"Yes, oh yes, he's very well," she choked, unable to relieve the tightness which had gripped her throat when she saw that firm, legible, familiar script delivered there into her hand.

In addition, the colonel had always frightened her in a vague, illogical way. Astride his big white horse there in the yard he had seemed to dominate the world—powerful, ruddy-faced, sharp of tongue and eye.

"Word in town this morning warns that the market in hogs is breaking." The horse jerked nervously and Colonel Wakely tightened the hold of the bit. Mary Clayburn stepped back, uneasy before the animal's power and its harshly controlled fright. There had been a period of time when she could not come close to any horse. The drag of her foot whenever she moved was testimony now to that bad past time. "Where is Lish?" the colonel was asking.

"He writes from Charleston," she said, suffocating under the thin warmth of the midday sun and the colonel's scrutiny and the excitement of Elisha's letter. "He has only one more batch of animals to sell."

"Charleston? Uh oh! Those Charleston belles are hard to pass by." He made a grimace with his large full mouth. "Well, Lish may still make some money on this project. God knows how he'll manage if he can't pay those taxes." His short strong legs increased their pressure on his mount. "Well, I won't put on mourning if Lish brings me home a roll of cash for those hogs of mine he took along."

Mary thought of Elisha's anxiety over the extra burden the Wakely drove had put on him. But she knew there had never been any thought of refusing the favor. The Wakelys and Clayburns were neighbors.

"Take care, Mary." Colonel Wakely left as he had come, in dust and hurry, the horse suddenly released from taut confinement to a spurred rush and gallop. Mary turned to read and reread her letter in peace.

And Elisha had reassured her. Across the long hard distance his words had drawn the sting and threat from Colonel Wakely's words as a poultice draws poison from deep wounds and infections.

A little wind had risen as Mary Clayburn stood in the darkness leaning against one of the columns supporting the tall roof of the long back porch. The smell of leaf smoke spiced the wind. The younger boys, Cal and Whit and Dan, had raked the yard that afternoon after she had read them the letter saying that their father would be home soon. Not all the leaves had gone into the barn for winter bedding in the stalls. A few piles must have been disposed of easier and faster by bonfire. She herself had been so busy making poundcake, Elisha's favorite of all desserts, that she had not noticed the fire. She wondered if the boys had been careful to rake around the fire and make certain that it was down to ashes for the night. The smell of the smoke came again, rich and bitter, the essence of autumn. It soothed her, quieted Cebo's omens of predators, whetted her longing for Elisha.

He had gone down the winding road under the brilliant maple and poplar and hickory and sweet gum leaves in the late October morning. Through choking dust and clinging mud, across rivers where a half-dozen hogs drowned off the crowded rafts, over rocky beds where some grew lame and fell behind, he finally reached the cotton lands where meat was in short supply and could find ready buyers. From one market on to another, if the need had already been glutted by an earlier drove; from one city to the next until, at last, Charleston. There, beside the ocean, must come the final trade and the turn toward home.

That was what the letter today had said. Elisha was settling his last transactions. Prices at some of the earlier towns where he had often found favor before were sunk to starvation level, and he had determined to push on until, finally, at the coast he had found good fortune. He had been the first drover to arrive in Charleston this season with good mountain pork, sweet from the fattening of mast on the hillsides, rich chestnuts and chinquapins, and corn in the pens. He would be returning to her and to the children any day now. And the long money-pouch he would be bringing home was fat, fat as the roundest fattening-hog they had ever owned.

Leaf smoke, darkness, the river moving down there between fruitful fields that belonged to her good husband and her five growing sons: these mingled in Mary Clayburn's mind until she felt the world flowing out from her in circles and ripples of light.

Where was the gray fox now? Long gone from the cornfield. Prowling some woods or hen-roost, curling up in his own secret den. Mary was shamed by even the moment's shudder she had allowed to stir in her. What hope for the world when those who were blessed and gifted, as she, did not live daily, hourly, by their faith? She tried to summon all the devotion with which she had been instructed in her religion since infancy.

"Mama?"

She jumped. Jonathan appeared below her in the yard. His voice had changed so recently that she was not yet accustomed to its depth and timbre. "You startled me. I thought you were in the kitchen playing checkers with Edom."

"Josh took my place." He sat down on one of the steps below her, leaning forward to rest an elbow on each knee. "I came out to look once more where the boys had burned their leaves this afternoon, make sure no one left any fire."

"With this wind that's rising—" she began.

He nodded. "That's what I thought. But everything is all right."

His authority reassured her. There inside the cozy room he had heard the threat of wind and had come to meet it. His calmness reminded her of Elisha.

The dry leaves clinging on the oak trees rustled. "How many of Colonel Wakely's hogs did Papa take to South Carolina?" Jonathan asked at last.

The question surprised her. "Maybe four hundred."

"Without that extra drove to sell, he'd have started home already when he wrote to us." There was more of a boy's longing than a man's resentment in his words, and Mary Clayburn smiled to herself. Since toddling days Jonathan had been his father's shadow.

She sat down on the step beside him, favoring her left leg, letting it follow the sudden bend more slowly. "Your father didn't begrudge the extra work and wait, so we mustn't either." She would not remember that initial irritation he had later regretted. "Anyway, Jonathan, slow as the mails are, he ought to be hard on the heels of that letter."

After a moment he asked, "Do you think he'll bring any new books back?"

"Knowing him, and you," she answered, "I shouldn't be a-tall surprised."

"And he can tell us about the ocean, and Charleston, and the cotton and rice crops, and what the people there are like. . . ."

They sat on the steps quietly. "Jonathan," she said at last, "I'm sorry you didn't get to go with him. . . ."

"Don't brood about it, Mama. It's all past."

"Charleston is a wicked city. . . ."

Dan, eleven, burst out of the kitchen door and crossed the porch and found his mother and brother sitting there. "Cal's telling ghost stories. He's telling the ones that scare Nettie Sue and Lottie."

"But not a big chap like you?" Jonathan teased. They went into the house. Inside, the yellow lamplight made them blink as they came in from the December darkness.

Later that night, after the children were asleep for several hours, and Edom Metcalf was in his room off the kitchen and Cebo in his dwelling down the hill, the wind blew up the storm it had been threatening. Mary Clayburn heard a loose shutter rattle at a downstairs window. She waited, lacking the will to leave the warm nest of her bed, hoping the noise would go away of its own accord. But it persisted. She sighed, threw back the cover, looked at little Lottie asleep in the trundle bed beside her, and went out into the hall. She negotiated the stairs slowly because of her leg.

She found the neglected shutter at a pantry window above her reach. She dragged a chair from the kitchen and climbed up to grasp the hinge. The wind outside was strong. Just as she gave an extra tug and made the shutter secure, she felt the chair slip from beneath her feet. A grasp at the windowsill broke her fall so that she did not plunge instantly to the floor but slid down as the chair slid away from her. She lay in a heap, the long white flannel nightgown billowing like a tent around her, the two braids of rich brown hair falling over her shoulders like a decoration added to the fine lace insertions in the yoke of her gown.

When she pulled herself up and finally stood again, disgust and fear and relief left her trembling. No bones had been broken. "Thank God, thank you, God. . . ." The words were a murmur, over and over, as she climbed back upstairs to her bedroom.

Beads of sweat glistened on her upper lip and rolled down between her full round breasts. She caught sight of herself in the walnut-framed mirror above the marble-topped washstand and she heard Colonel Wakely say again, "Uh, oh! Those Charleston belles are hard to pass by."

The mirror reflected plain brown hair and brown eyes, a square serious face with firm chin and pale, almost sallow, complexion. Bearing eight children had taken its toll on her figure. But there was no qualm about Elisha and the Charleston ladies. Freely, and without any artifice or even hope on her part, he had chosen Mary Ransom for his wife, and after she had recovered from her initial astonishment at his choice she had accepted it as a total and permanent commitment.

Sometimes, however, she wished that she might have cameo features, grace, and liveliness, as the Montgomery women in town had.

Mary Clayburn had not always been awkward and plump. Once, as her handsome father's only daughter and her rollicking brother's only sister (her mother had died when she was born), she had been a lithe strong tomboy of a girl. Then, when she was seventeen, the fragile promise of her life poised at a critical moment, her brother's horse had thrown her. Whitley Ransom, a relentless prankster, had thrust a stalk of cockleburs under the saddle of his horse one day "to see what would happen."

He had not seen, because he was in the house eating a dish of apple cobbler when his sister decided to take the unsuspecting horse, which had been standing at the hitching-post under a broiling sun, down to the barn. After that, she remembered nothing except the pungent reek of leather and horse sweat. She had settled her weight into the saddle. Suddenly there was a whirlwind, and darkness.

Afterwards, Whitley and their father and everyone else who knew them had watched Mary's long recovery while the bone broken in two places mended poorly, was set and reset. Since she had been seventeen she had never walked without the little dragging limp that was sometimes inconspicuous to others but always conspicuous to herself.

Her father and brother had labored to prove their sympathy, which was real, and their love, which was token. No one could help its inadequacy and none of them could admit its cruelty even in his innermost thoughts. It was then that Mary Clayburn had turned to the love of God.

Unwanted sympathy and the facade of her family's devotion had come perilously close to exposure when Mary reached the age of proper marriage—and beyond the age. There had been only one who came to call seriously: Elisha Clayburn. Even later she could scarcely bear to recall the unconcealed amazement of her father and brother when they realized she was being courted. Their disbelief had turned to jubilation and then to caution as they watched one of the most eligible and able young men in the county, or in that part of their state, come to see their Mary. They advised her. For the first time in her life she did not listen. She was herself and Elisha had sought her out.

The night of their wedding, when she had flushed and stammered at her ignorance and innocence, Elisha had told her outright what that gift was he had sought and found in her. "Of all the women I knew, you were the one I would rather have to be mother of my children." He had tried to be gentle with his strong calloused hands and muscular body. "It's the best kind of love, Mary, to want a woman to bear your seed and birth your sons and daughters."

"Yes, Elisha, yes," she had responded, wanting to understand, longing to believe.

"It's love that lasts for more than a night and a spasm. It endures." His voice was quiet and straightforward, as if he were discussing matters of land and seasons.

"I want to have your children, Elisha," she whispered, still shy and shamed by her own honesty.

"I knew you would," he said.

To neither of them had this seemed an arrogant or one-sided exchange.

As each child had been born she recalled Elisha's words and touched the infant's groping fists and wrinkled eyelids and hungry mouth.

The Clayburns, for generations before Elisha Clayburn, had garnered a reputation for being men of judgment and foresight and planning. It was appropriate that the Ransom farm, where her bachelor brother, Whitley Ransom, now lived, adjoined the Clayburn farm along its southern boundary.

Mary Clayburn settled back into the deep featherbed she had left to seek out the banging shutter. Waiting in the kitchen on the cut-glass cake stand was a luscious poundcake, made of yellow butter she herself had churned fresh that day and yellow-yolked eggs she herself had gathered fresh from the nests to fold into the batter. When he saw the cake Elisha would nod, look at her, and smile and nod again, after he broke off a tiny corner of the first slice, tasting it carefully, delicately, in tribute to all her care and effort. She smiled to herself.

When the full force of the storm broke, raging against the brick walls and through the great tough limbs of the oak trees, Mary Clayburn was already asleep.

By morning the storm had passed. The sky was still heavy and the clouds were like clusters of soggy gray feathers settling over the horizon and nearby fields. Along the avenue of oaks that lined the driveway leading from the state road in the distance, and between the oaks and maples that canopied the lawn about the house, lay scattered debris from the wind's fury. A dozen limbs the size of a man's thigh had been twisted from the trees and hurled asunder. Smaller branches and twigs were strewn everywhere.

Edom Metcalf was already out surveying the destruction when Mary Clayburn came onto the porch. His strange hazel-colored eyes did not focus in the same direction and he had the appearance of gazing in two directions at once. Mary looked at the distorted trees and broken branches and littered yard and driveway. She could see the cows huddled by the pasture gate down near the barn. She even saw the old Dominecker rooster lead a flock of bedraggled hens from one of the woodlots. Next time they would use the good tight hen-house.

Edom pulled the sweat-stained work hat lower over his forehead and spat an amber arc of tobacco juice into the nearest pile of limbs. "Looks like the wind was playing hopscotch with the devil last night," he said.

She nodded slowly. "It's the worst devastation we've had since the year of the big flood. And that was all down in the fields."

"Mr. Clayburn came home now," Edom said, and his eyes looked both at her and toward the road, "he'd think we'd all deserted. This about the way Shiloh looked after all the shooting was finished."

"Then we'd better eat a stout breakfast and begin to put everything to rights again, hadn't we?" she said.

When her summons to cheer met no response except another stream of amber, she tried again. "I'll turn all the boys into the yard and we'll see what we can get done in a day."

"More like a week," Edom Metcalf muttered.

She had turned back toward the door when she heard the horses approaching. She swung around, forgetting to favor her left leg, and winced. There were three men coming down the long drive. Slowly they picked their way through the debris, careful so that none of the horses should stumble. She crossed the porch and stood on the top step, trying to make out who they were.

When they were close enough so that she could recognize one of them as Randall Montgomery, she searched the other faces again, thinking that one of them should be Elisha. But they were two men from town.

The three visitors rode up to the steps where she stood, reined in their horses and dismounted in unison, as if none of them wanted to be the first. They spoke her name so quietly that Mary Clayburn barely heard their voices. Edom Metcalf went over to them and took the lines and held their horses. The horses began cropping the last tufts of green grass at the edge of the lawn. The sound of their big yellow teeth pulling and chomping the wilted grass was loud in the stillness.

The men walked toward Mary Clayburn. Their motions were slow and reluctant. The low gray clouds curtained off the mountains in the distance and wrapped this scene into itself, a world drifting apart and alone. Trunks of the oak trees, glistening from the night's rain, and the four tall chimneys like sentinels at each side of the house, stood clear and bold in the leaden light. Everything else appeared shrouded, water-logged, sluggish. Even the three men seemed massive and sodden.

"Morning, Mrs. Clayburn," Randall Montgomery said again. His polished leather boots shone like the tree trunks but his dark eyes did not sparkle with their usual mischief.

"Mrs. Clayburn—"

"Mrs. Clayburn—Mary—"

The other two men echoed their earlier murmurs. She recognized them now: Janus Rathbone, an honest rawboned farmer from the nearby Dark Hollow district of the county—"as dependable as morning," Elisha had said of him once not long ago; and Alexander Montgomery, Randall's older, heavier, steadier brother, president of the bank in town, and also of the mill and the lumber company and the railroad promotion association.

Mary spoke to them, calling their names in turn, inviting them into the house. But they remained standing just below the steps.

"Where's Elisha, Randall?" she asked then. "You're home already. Why isn't he with you?" Still no one answered. "I'm looking for him any day."

"That's why we're here, Mary—" Alex Montgomery began, then paused. Janus Rathbone twisted his hat awkwardly in his hands.

"Elisha and I were together," Randall Montgomery said. "We were on our way back from Charleston. Mary, Elisha was hurt."

For the first time she noticed the bandage around Randall's neck, a heavy white cloth which gave the incongruous look of a clerical collar. She heard a door slam deep inside the house. Footsteps came out on the porch behind her.

Janus Rathbone walked up the steps slowly and stood before her.

His long bony face was set in lines of suffering. His deep-set eyes looked at her steadily and kindly. "Elisha wasn't hurt only," he said. Mary Clayburn's breath left, squeezed from her by the sudden blow of knowing what his words told more slowly. "He's dead, Mrs. Clayburn."

In the distant woods a crow called, harsh, lonely. She stood as if frozen.

"How?" The word was a whisper.

"We were coming through the mountains," Randall Montgomery began hurriedly, then paused. She waited and he went on. "It was early in the morning. Yesterday morning. Just at daybreak. We got a soon start from the Dorseys' stand. Lish was anxious to get home. He hadn't even taken time to buy you the pretty or Jonathan the travel book he intended." Montgomery struggled to get a hold on the events, to re-create that moment. "We left the Dorseys while it was still dark, and first light was just breaking when we started through Wolf Pen Gap."

There was no movement on the porch. In the hallway just behind her, the great Clayburn grandfather clock struck the hour. Randall Montgomery did not continue until the clock was silent. "Right in the gap, where there's thick laurel and ivy and all manner of undergrowth, two outlaws jumped us."

Her eyes were fixed on him.

"Their hats were pulled low over their foreheads and they wore long cloaks and kerchiefs tied over their faces. One of them never spoke a word. The other told us to hand over our money. They sighted their guns dead on us."

Mary Clayburn's gaze never left his face. "Oh, let them have the money," she murmured.

"We threw down our wallets. The one who did all the talking picked them up. We were turning our horses." Randall Montgomery looked at the other two men, beseeching them for relief they could not provide. He moved closer to the steps. "All at once a queer thing happened. The oddest surprise dawned in Lish's face. He swung back around and looked again at those two scoundrels and before he knew what he was doing, I think, he exclaimed, 'I know you!' It was only a breath, a gasp more to himself than to me or to them. But that gun ripped a blast so quick you couldn't think."

"Elisha!" she cried.

"That robber's first shot killed him, Mary. He went off the horse slow and easy, just eased off so gentle that I didn't know what I was seeing till it was all over. I jumped to help Lish and that's when they took a crack at me. Just a flesh wound." He touched his bandage. "Elisha was already dead."

She made no sound. For a moment she made no motion. Then slowly she raised one hand and arm in front of her, to her cheek, palm turned outward as if fending off a blow.

"I fell when their shot hit me. They must have thought I was dead. I wasn't sure myself for a minute. But by the time I'd found the wound between my neck and shoulder and stanched the gush of blood, they'd fled. Off through the underbrush, down into Wolf Pen Creek ravine, I reckon. Slick as vulture's beaks, they disappeared."

One of the men listening whispered an oath. But Mary Clayburn was not thinking of the killers. "Where is he now, Randall?"

"They're bringing him home. We took him to Moseley's." He would be coming in the long black carriage of Moseley the undertaker. "We rode on ahead, to break it to you—"

The raw, damp wind blew strands of hair free from the knot into which she had bound it earlier in the morning and now those wisps clung across her stricken white face and clammy forehead like welts from a lash.

The men could not know it then but Mary Clayburn afterward vowed, in family enclaves, that she saw her husband's face at that moment. It was Elisha with his plump cheeks, firm jaw, neat brown beard accentuating the oval shape of his face, and heavy eyebrows shading round blue eyes which flashed a brilliant alertness. The expression she saw on his face as it appeared to her was the same expression—compounded of pride and surprise, strength and vulnerability—that she had seen twice before in their lifetime together: once when he folded back the knit blanket and he saw their first child, Joshua; and again when he told her that his father was letting them have the Riverbend Farm, as everyone in the county called this home where she lived now and had raised their children and crops.

But gradually the blue eyes and familiar features faded. Someone's arm was at her back, steadying her. She thought it must belong to the Rathbone man until she heard Jonathan say, "Mama—" Those were his footsteps she had heard behind her a while ago.

All of the men were up on the porch now, awkward, anxious, urging her to go inside the house, to sit down.

"Cal," she heard Jonathan tell the younger boy who appeared at the door, "run get Delia. Tell her to come. Quick!" The boy's footsteps pounded down the long hall toward the kitchen.

Then she shook off Jonathan's arm and clasped her hands in front of her until the knuckles showed white, and she nodded for the men to come into the house with her. She had no tears but her throat was as parched as her eyes, burning with a dry, dull pain, and she could not trust herself to speak until she sat down on the black horsehair sofa in the gloomy, damp-smelling parlor. She saw them seated one by one on the stiff, straight-backed chairs in front of her. Then she spoke.

"I'm all right, Delia," she looked at the small alarmed face of the black woman who appeared in the doorway, "if you've a pot of strong coffee brewed, why don't you bring us each a cup?"

The men, uneasy, started to protest. "I wouldn't care for any, thank you ma'am," Janus Rathbone began.

"Don't bother about us," Randall Montgomery was saying.

"No, it's no bother at all," she spoke urgently, but as if from a distance. "You've ridden all this way—"

They sat, erect and tense on the edge of the small hard chairs, and waited for her to go on. When she did not go on but sat looking at the hands in her lap, watching her blunt fingers lock and unlock, Alex Montgomery spoke. "If there's anything we can do, Mary—" He hesitated. "The loss of all of Elisha's money—"

There was a shuffling of footsteps in the hall and into the room but she did not even look to see who might have come in. "I don't know, Alex. I hadn't thought about the money." They were all watching her, and then in embarrassment they all looked away. "I don't know." She lifted her eyes and looked at Jonathan who had come inside with her and stood beside her now, his hand at her shoulder. His eyes were wide with a comprehension that seemed to be growing slowly, awesomely, within him. His face was parchment pale.

"What do you think Papa meant," Jonathan said, looking at the three men carefully, "when he said that he knew who the robbers were?"

"That's the big riddle." Randall Montgomery leaned forward eagerly, relieved to be discussing facts and circumstances. "That's the mystery, Mrs. Clayburn. I've turned it over and over in my memory. There wasn't one thing familiar to me about either of those scoundrels. I don't know what Lish saw that I didn't."

"One thing you haven't told her," Janus Rathbone said.

Randall Montgomery looked at her and then at Jonathan. "They weren't white men," he said.

There was a barely perceptible stir around the room.

"But Papa always said there weren't but a handful of black folks back in those mountains," Jonathan said.

"That's right," Janus Rathbone nodded.

"Well, two of them were there yesterday morning," Randall Montgomery said. He crossed his long legs encased in the polished boots. "Swooped down like turkey buzzards after carrion. They knew right where we'd be. Knew we had a roll of money."

"But how could Papa have guessed who they were?" Jonathan persisted.

The men could only shake their heads. "Like I told you, son, that's the riddle."

By now the other children, except for Nettie Sue and Lottie who were still asleep, had come into the parlor. Their faces were grave and frightened. Mary Clayburn patted the sofa beside her and the three younger ones crossed the room carefully, as though negotiating unfamiliar territory, and sat down with her. Then Daniel, the youngest boy, looked up at her. And it was Elisha's grave expression and firm mouth she saw. She looked at his five sons there in that frozen moment in that shadowy room—Joshua, Jonathan, Calvin, Whitley, Daniel.

"Dear God!" The words strangled in her throat, a bitter accusation and a cry of irredeemable loss.

She wept.

The men were uneasy before her tears but not so uneasy as they had been before her initial calm. They nodded to each other that it was well she should cry, and they looked courteously away, out of the tall windows draped with heavy burgundy-colored velvet hangings, and down at the richly patterned carpet, toward the pictures of Clayburn and Ransom ancestors on the walls. The room, unused except for special occasions and Sunday afternoons, was chilly but no one had thought to light the fire under the logs waiting in the deep brick fireplace.

Delia came in. China coffee cups rattled against their saucers as her hands shook, passing the tray before the men. She saw Mary Clayburn crying and tears washed down her own small sunken cheeks and fell on the silver tray, mingling with the brown drops of coffee which had sloshed from the overfull cups. When she tried to urge acceptance of the steaming hot coffee on Mary Clayburn, there was total refusal. "No, no. Let me alone. I can't swallow."

The children's eyes stayed fixed on their mother. At first they had looked at the three men, surveying carefully their boots and high-laced shoes and the hats lying beside their chairs because Mary Clayburn had forgotten the habit of a lifetime and had failed to deposit her visitors' hats on the brass stand in the hallway. But when they saw their mother crying as they had never seen her before, they did not look away. Daniel and Whitley began to cry, too. Cal's mouth trembled. He looked at Jonathan and then at Josh. Josh was a little apart, still by the door, the last one to come in and know what had happened.

"Why?" she asked, the sobs shaking her body. "When he had already let them have the money freely, why did they have to kill him?"

"They were blackguards, ma'am," Alexander Montgomery answered, vehement before her sorrow and loss, yet holding in leash the fury of his anger.

"Varmints," Randall agreed. "Varmints to be hunted down."

The men were relieved to express some of their emotion. They drank the scalding coffee in quick gulps.

"Why would he be killed when we need him, when all of us need him—"

But they did not want to veer into this uncharted area of questioning. "We'll find who the killers were, Mary," Alex Montgomery said quickly, mustering confidence into the words.

"We'll find them," Janus Rathbone nodded. "A man like Lish Clayburn, a good man, he can't be just cut down in his prime with no one punished, nobody knowing. . . ." He floundered, looking to the other two men for help, for confirmation.

"That's right."

"Folks in Churchill are torn up pretty bad about this, Mary," Alex said. "Last night after Randall came in with his neck all hurt and bloody, bringing Lish and the horse, a crowd of men went back up to Wolf Pen Gap and on to Dorsey's tavern to see if there had been any sign of the renegades."

"They'll hunt down any traces of Lish's killers."

"But it's Elisha I want," she cried.

During the long night that followed, a night broken by days during which decisions were made and patterns were followed, people Mary Clayburn had known and many she had not known came to help her. But Elisha was not there. Because he was not there none of the others became real to her. She was most unreal of all to herself.

Her brother Whit arrived and swollen Irish tears coursed down his purple-veined cheeks as he hugged his sister to him. "A dastardly thing! This whole countryside is cut up over Lish's death. Don't you fret. We'll avenge this outrage." Before the end of that afternoon she heard him in a back room sharing belly-laughter tales with some of the men who had ridden from adjoining counties to pay respects to Elisha Clayburn.

Colonel Wakely and his wife came. "The scoundrels made away with all the money Lish was carrying? Uh oh!" the colonel shook his head. "Lish should have divided it up, should never have carried it all in one place." Those who were gathered in the big room, as well as those elsewhere on the first floor of the house, could hear his booming reassurances which followed. "Don't worry, Mary, you'll be looked after. You and the children won't go begging. And I'll never dun you for a penny of the money Elisha was carrying from the sale of my hogs."

As he talked, tiny Drusilla Wakely squeezed Mary Clayburn's hand, reminding them both of times long ago when they had been lonely girls and close friends, as close as long distances and infrequent visits would permit. "Dear Mary," she whispered at last, her spidery fingers tightening their grip. "Poor Mary. But you have had so much, so very much."

Clayburn kin moved in and out. There were Elisha's two sisters, Malvina and Kate: Malvina, unmarried, who had unpacked her trunk in the upstairs sewing room and now made herself useful in running the house; Kate, who had married a Nashville lawyer and seen four daughters find adequate husbands, who came for the funeral and started her long journey back to the mid-region of the state the next morning.

There were cousins, friends, neighbors, curious strangers. "Have they caught the killers yet?"

"What will Mary do now?"

"All those children! And their year's crop tied up in that hog drove, the money stolen."

"This is a master farm, all right. Never was a Clayburn didn't have an eye for good land."

They were all there, wondering, whispering.

But Elisha was not there. His body lay in the parlor, surrounded by flowers and people. But when his wife and children looked at the marble face and folded hands, he was not there. The person they had known was somewhere else.

Time stood arrested. Days merged into one endless, drowsy Sabbath with no work in the fields, a surfeit of platters and bowls and trays of food heaped up in the kitchen, too much to eat at the long laden tables; and voices droning in yard and hallway and parlor, as men, uneasy in their best black suits on a weekday, and women in their best silk at midday, clustered in little coveys and talked through the days before and the hours following the funeral.

The church was a white frame building with a simple steeple. It stood in a grove of cedar trees on a hill above the river. The Clayburns and Wakelys and Ransoms and a scattering of other neighbor families had built it and kept it painted and in good repair through the years. Once each summer there was a weekday "working" at the church, when all the members came and the men outside cleared underbrush from the little woods and trimmed the trees, the women inside scrubbed the hard wooden seats and floor and washed down the walls and polished the wood-burning stove; then all met together to mow and trim and weed and plant new shrubs or flowers in the fenced-in cemetery. Elisha and Mary had spent many hours helping keep the old tombstones in repair, planting the boxwoods that would now be at the head of Elisha's grave.

The little building was not large enough to seat all those who came to the funeral. The minister, Luther Pryor, old and wise in his knowledge that such an audience would not be his again for many another year, took the occasion to speak for an hour and a half: eulogy, parable, warning, threat, plea, and finally eulogy again.

Relatives and friends looked at each other and shook their heads when they saw Mary Clayburn's pale face and distant gaze. She tried more diligently than ever to hide the limp of that twisted left leg, for she could bear only so much of their well-meant sympathy.

"She's always had strong faith," they agreed.

"It will stand her in good stead now."

Those who lived on the farm knew Mary Clayburn best. "She's walking a lonesome path," old Cebo said. He did not speak to her once of grief, but each night just at dusk he went through the barn lots and woodlot and made sure that all the chickens were safe in the new tight henhouse, as she wanted them to be.

And her children never forgot this ordeal they saw her endure. It sealed her hold on them. Unwittingly, Mary Clayburn and her God molded Clayburn character for several generations to come—both in the practice and the breach—at this vulnerable moment in seven young lives.

The night after the funeral she roamed the house, her black silk dress still buttoned high around her neck and tight around her wrists. The silk rustled at every step like dead leaves on the oaks outside.

At the door which led into the narrow room that had been Elisha's office, she paused. She had not been inside since the October day he went away. Slowly she turned the heavy knob and opened the door, then paused in fright and shock. There was a lamp on the desk, its wick turned up for full light. Someone was sitting at the high-backed chair pulled up before the desk. She saw a head of chestnut-brown hair, dark and thick as Elisha's had been when he first courted her.

"Come in, Mama," Jonathan said.

Her son's voice and face startled her. She looked at him as she had not looked at anyone or anything since the morning Edom Metcalf showed her the damage from the storm and Randall Montgomery and Alex Montgomery and Janus Rathbone had come riding toward her through the debris. She saw him. She saw that his young face, usually ruddy from weather and farm work, was pale. There were traces of new lines around his eyes. His shirt was rumpled. As he leaned back in the chair and then stood up, he stretched his arms above his head and she realized that he must have been sitting there for a long time.

"What are you doing, Jonathan?"

He looked around at the rows of shelves and the dim dusty

bindings of the books that filled them, at a yellowed, frayed map of the world tacked against the back of the door, at the stacks of ledgers and papers and boxes in and on the massive roll-top desk which was the room's only furnishing. "There was so much I ought to have asked him."

A fly, late survivor of summer, mistaking the lamplight for day, suddenly spun across the room and struck against the lamp chimney. It fell, then buzzed frantically once more, and whizzed like a bullet to some hidden corner. The sound was loud—garish and accidental —in the surrounding silence.

Jonathan turned the chair toward his mother. But when she sat where he had been, the leather still warm where he had sat, she turned back to see what he was reading. One of the thick black ledgers lay open on the desk. In bold ink and a careful familiar script were written dates and names and entries after each name. She glanced at some of the entries and saw that they referred to a dispute settled, a line fence established, and—at least twice—small loans extended.

She remembered the morning he had made one of those loans. A sallow-faced, stoop-shouldered man in patched coat and pants had come to ask for help in buying a cow. "His heifer died. There are nine young ones, the baby two weeks old," Elisha had told her afterward. "We're short on money, but not that short." And he had not bought a new buggy that spring.

The handwriting which recorded all of these personal crises was firm and clear. On some of the capital letters there were even fancy curlicues. A film covered her eyes and the words blurred.

"He must have known everybody in this county and the next," Jonathan said.

Her smile was wan and slightly crooked, but it was the first one that had come in days. "Not quite. But many. And many people he didn't know, they knew him."

Jonathan nodded. He looked at the shelves. "I'll have to plow deeper into all these books—"

Her gaze followed his around the room. When he pulled a little stool out from one corner and hunched down to sit on it, she looked at him again. Her son Jonathan, stamped with his father's features of round face and blue eyes, muscular shoulders and height and ample foot size. As inheritance from her she recognized only that serious countenance which she had always regretted in herself. When, in younger days, her brother Whit was entertaining hordes of friends who flocked to his bright, easy laughter, she had often been neglected because of her sober, reserved expression. And among all her children, Jonathan most resembled her in the seriousness that reflected some inner responsibility. She felt a surge of mingled pride and sympathy for him.

"Can we realize anything from these?" Jonathan was asking, looking at the ledgers filled with names and obligations from many years. During these recent days while she had been locked away through grief, her son had been moving outside himself, considering what must be done for her and for the family. Without the money from their drove of hogs they were in a serious situation. Jonathan was the first to face it.

"I don't know," she said. "Maybe when some of these people learn that your father's family—" Her voice shook and she did not finish.

"He's owed a lot."

"He never did it for the money."

Jonathan nodded. "I know."

"He always said he didn't have any official degrees, all he had was common bay-horse sense. But he was a mathematician. He had judgment. People would listen to what he said. That's why they came to him." She was happy to be talking about Elisha, reminding Jonathan of the many times his father was called from the dinner table, or kept from the farm, or otherwise engaged by someone who could not afford or would not trust one of the costly town lawyers to settle his affairs.

"Surely those who borrowed money outright—not time or judgment or patience, but cash money they've signed for—surely they'll feel obligated," Jonathan said.

"I don't know," she answered. "He never mentioned it to me."

And Jonathan noticed: she did not suggest that if Elisha Clayburn had kept his money, had not loaned it to every hard-pressed farmer needing help for taxes, for medicine, for seed or a mule or fertilizer, he might have had enough to leave his family without worries at this moment.

"We'll get along all right, Mama," he said. "Josh and the others, none of us wants you to be worried."

"Then I won't be," she said. "But you and Joshua must go to

college next year. Your father always planned that. We'll have to find a way."

The flame in the lamp had gradually smoked the clear glass chimney until the light in the room was dimmed to a glow, dull and glistening as old gold. Shadows cast monstrous designs around the walls and reached from the lamplight out to where Jonathan sat, almost hiding him from her. The old house was quiet around them. Not even a board creaked in the pine floor polished to a smooth soft surface by generations of footsteps.

"There's something I have to do first," Jonathan said. "I have to help."

"Help what?"

"Find Papa's killers."

She did not know how to answer this.

"Why did Papa say he recognized who the robbers were? There's some answer. I'll never be satisfied till I know."

She nodded.

"I can't tolerate it," Jonathan was speaking faster and more clearly, "that out there somewhere are two murderers, and my father's dead while they're free—"

"Don't, Jonathan," she cried as sharply as if he had struck her. "Don't say it ever again. Go with the men if you have to. But Jonathan —take care. Take special care."

"I will."

"We need you, Jonathan."

After a few minutes he took the lamp and lighted their way upstairs. She walked slowly, because of her limp and because of the burdens the past days had heaped upon her. "Thank you, Jonathan," she said. The square room and the big walnut bed, smelling faintly of furniture polish, looked cold and dark and empty before her.

"Good night, Mama. Don't worry about anything."

She watched his boy's shoulders, broadening into a man's, disappear downstairs.

After she had undressed and pulled on the white flannel nightgown and plaited her hair in two long braids, she knelt by the bed— going down cumbersomely because of her leg—and prayed as simply and earnestly and fervently as if her Lord must now take the place of her husband at the center of her life.

Before Jonathan could join the search, it came to him. Late the following afternoon men on horseback rode down the Clayburn road again, but instead of stopping at the front this time they rode on around the house. There were six serious, unsmiling men with tightly buttoned coats and guns handy in their saddle holsters. Their horses were well fed and had been ridden hard. In the back yard they paused.

Josh and Edom Metcalf were on their way up from the barn when the men rode in. Josh had always been a special help with livestock. Men on the farm already respected his judgment of cattle.

There were no preliminaries or niceties. "You got a nigger helper here?" one of the men, who wore a red beard, said to Josh.

"No," Josh answered matter-of-factly.

The man was surprised. "You sure about that, son?"

"Of course I'm sure." Josh's face was open as daylight.

"What about that feller called Cebo?" another rider spat.

"Cebo?" The red-bearded man swung around.

"Oh, Cebo's just himself," Josh explained carefully, "Indian and black and a whole mixture of things."

"He must be the one we got in mind," the man said. "He around here now?"

"At his place, I reckon, just down the slope there," Edom Metcalf volunteered.

"His place?" The reddish eyebrows lifted.

"Mr. Clayburn gave it to him, legal, free and clear, a good while back."

No one responded to this.

A fat fellow at the rear spoke. "Fetch Cebo." A couple of the horsemen pulled away from the group and galloped in the direction Edom had indicated.

By now others were gathering from inside the house and outside as well. Jonathan came from the woodyard. Mary Clayburn clutched a thick gray shawl around her as she hurried out onto the porch and down the steps. To stay on the porch would revive too clearly in her mind the scene on that other porch, at the front, on that other morning—was it a few centuries ago?

When they saw her coming they removed their hats and spoke solemnly, respectfully, then put the hats back on. They explained that they were friends of Elisha Clayburn's, having known him as fellow squires on county court, or at the stockyards where he had often traded cattle, or on the road commission where plans for county thoroughfares were made and days of labor together on the roads themselves forged common bonds of sweat and callouses. Wherever they had known him, they held him in respect. They did not intend for him to be gunned down without protest, without discovery of the killers, without retribution. If a man such as Elisha Clayburn could be murdered without revenge, who among them would be safe?

She returned their greetings and looked at them, trying to understand their message, and a long, hard shudder gripped her. She had seen all of these men before. Several she knew by name. Orvil Gosnell, the dark-bearded one, was from this corner of the county, a squire and farmer. Jasper Smelcer, who had given the order to find Cebo, was a part-time preacher and an occasional salesman of books, photographs, medicines for men and livestock. There were other familiar faces whose names she didn't know, especially the sallow, stoop-shouldered one riding a scrawny nag.

These men were not a mob, howling, lusting. They were something more implacable: serious, sincere men moving relentlessly to carry out what they considered their duty. They were strong men appeasing their fear by action, lawful men seeking vengeance outside the law, sad men who would satisfy their grief through inflicting greater pain. They claimed to seek a criminal but their need was for a culprit. They had whispered to themselves that they were doing this for Elisha Clayburn, his wife, his children, but it was their own need that drove them. They were acquaintances and neighbors who might have remained, except for Elisha Clayburn's death, unacquainted with their own capacity for fear and ferocity.

"They've gone to get Cebo," Josh said.

"What do you want with Cebo?" Mary Clayburn asked.

"We want to talk with him, Mrs. Clayburn," Orvil Gosnell said.

"But we can tell you anything you need to know from him," she said.

"Even if he's got a strange nigger hiding here?"

She was startled.

"That would add up to two niggers," one of the men stated. His words, slow, deliberate, fell heavily into the silence.

"Mrs. Clayburn," Orvil Gosnell said, slouching in his saddle, but sharp-eyed, "some of us feel pretty strong about the fact we got paid off and we come on home from Charleston ahead of your man and Randall Montgomery. If we hadn't been in such a push, if we'd rode through the mountains together—"

" 'If' never made the river run uphill," Jasper Smelcer said shortly.

"But I'm a-wanting this lady to know—"

As Mary Clayburn started to speak, the men who had gone to Cebo's came into view. They rode slowly, for Cebo was walking in front of them, stooped and shriveled.

But it was not at Cebo that Mary Clayburn looked. Striding along beside him was a short, heavy-set black man she had never seen before. Suddenly she was confused and dizzy. Josh and Jonathan stood on either side and steadied her. There was a ripple of movement among the men who were waiting. As the little group came up to them, one of the younger riders called, "You, boy!"

They all stopped, but Cebo and the black man with him turned.

"We found them all right. The young buck here was up in the loft, old one tried to keep us from looking. We went up anyway. Had him treed."

A grunt of satisfaction from several of the men.

"Miss Mary—"

She heard the quavery old voice and responded. "Cebo, what's happening? Who is this stranger?"

"Everything all right, Miss Mary," Cebo said to her. "All right, don't fret. His name Lonas from Carolina. Lonas Rankin."

"But what is he doing here?"

"He come, Miss Mary, to help Mr. Hartwick in town."

"Old Sledge?" Jasper Smelcer demanded. When Cebo nodded, Smelcer said, "Old Sledge Hartwick needs extra help the way a rattlesnake needs extra teeth. What does this boy know about blacksmithing anyway?"

"He make the hammer ring," Cebo answered. "Show them your muscle, Lonas. Make a frog."

Reluctantly the younger man lifted his left arm, clenched his fist, bent his arm at the elbow. Muscle humped to a hard bulge beneath the shining dark skin of his upper arm. Only then did Mary Clayburn realize that he did not have on coat or shoes against the December chill.

"But what's he doing here, with you?" she asked, and two of the men on horseback nodded. "What?"

"He come because he scared. Long time ago, over in Carolina, he learn my name and this place. Hear the name Clayburn and Old Cebo and after he on his way here all the trouble about Mr. Lish break like a dam busting. Everything washing away, everything getting dangerous and ugly. Little twigs got to find shelter. He knew folks looking for a black man—so Lonas remember my name and he come to me like a limb washed ashore till the looking passes."

"You see?" Mary Clayburn turned in relief to the men. "Cebo has explained it."

But they did not nod or answer. Finally one said, "What about this 'Cebo,' too?" He set the name apart in scorn. "These the only two black folks I know of anywhere right around close."

"That's so."

"And Lish Clayburn would have recognized at least one of them, even in disguise."

Mary Clayburn interrupted the swift exchange. "You can't mean —are you trying to say that you think Cebo—?" She did not finish and they did not answer. They did not yield an inch.

"Cebo was here that night and the morning Papa was killed, too," Jonathan said slowly.

Everyone turned to look at him.

"You saw Cebo? Right here?"

"Right here. And I'd swear the truth of anything Cebo says, this world or the next."

Mary Clayburn wanted to speak but the silence seemed eloquent enough. The winter afternoon was fading fast. She was frightened and tense, every muscle in her body drawn tight. Just as she felt the pressure slackening a bit, the second man who had gone down to Cebo's rode to the front.

"Where'd this come from?" he asked. He held aloft a roll of bills, curled into a small green cylinder and bound by an old shoelace, for all to see. "This was up in the loft in the toe of the nigger's shoe—"

Mary gasped.

The man threw the roll toward Cebo but the old man made no move to receive it. It fell on the winter grass and lay like a round cartridge between white men and black, ugly, threatening.

Two of the horses tossed their heads and moved uneasily, breaking the stillness.

The younger man with powerful black arms and round, shining face stepped slightly away from Cebo, planted his feet firmly apart on the half-frozen ground, and folded his arms in front of him. He seemed to have made a decision. No matter the turn of events, he would not cringe. He would meet these accusers foursquare. His stance, to Elisha Clayburn's widow and sons, did not seem that of a skulking robber.

"Yessir, that's my money," the man named Lonas Rankin said distinctly.

Cebo looked up at him with aging bloodshot eyes and forestalled the question on the tongue of every other person there. "Where you come by it, then?" he asked.

"At Mr. Dorsey's tavern," the black stranger answered. "Going through the mountains my horse turns lame from all the sharp rocks underfoot. I stop off at this stand to buy corn for my horse, some food for myself, to carry us on through to Churchill, the county seat down here, and to Mr. Sledge Hartwick's blacksmith forge."

He paused. The men sat unblinking on their horses. Mary Clayburn and her oldest sons and Edom Metcalf stood attentively in the yard. Out in the pasture a cow bawled, the sound low-pitched, drawn-out, lonely. The silence of his listeners urged the stranger on to fuller explanation.

"That Dorsey woman, she spotted the lameness, set in to try trading me out of my horse. It was a big, good-blooded horse. I put all the cash I ever laid hold of and a full year's work at toting cotton bales into that horse. I hadn't no mind to sell it. But first that woman set in and then her man." He slowed, picking his way through a thorny path in explaining to one set of white people the ways of another pair of whites. "They never let up. All the time I ate out there in the yard, under a shade tree, from the plate she fixed, and all the time I watered and rubbed down my horse, every minute they after me to trade. Then they done went and brought me this roll of money."

His listeners' eyes flickered for an instant to the cartridge of bills lying there on the grass.

"I want my horse," he continued, his voice mournful with enormous loss. "But something behind their talk makes me say all right. And I leave my horse and take the pay and glad to get away. I come on through the mountains by foot."

Jasper Smelcer's horse grew impatient. Its sidesteps were the only movements that broke the sullen listening of the tight-faced men. The black man waited a moment. Then he concluded in a rush.

"By this time, talk of Mr. Elisha Clayburn's killing has spread everywhere. From Mr. Dorsey's tavern on, the few folks I meet up with are full of suspicion. They afraid. I afraid. I come on to Cebo's at Mr. Clayburn's. I can't find that blacksmith. I never killed any man in my whole life. Never kill nothing."

Mary Clayburn was the first to speak. "Cebo," she said, "is he telling the truth?"

The old man nodded. The web of wrinkles on his face and neck crumpled and held like seasoned leather. "Too true to be a tale," he said.

She looked at the man.

They wavered for a moment. Then Jasper Smelcer rode up beside the red-bearded man. "All due respects to you, Mrs. Clayburn, that boy ain't giving us nothing but hogwash." He turned to the others. "Anybody here know them Dorseys that run the stand beyond Wolf Pen Gap?"

Two men nodded.

"Be the Dorseys folks that would likely pay big cash for a lame horse bought off a strange nigger?" Jasper Smelcer asked.

The two men shook their heads.

"All due respects, like I say, Mrs. Clayburn," Smelcer repeated, then turned full-face toward the cluster of a half-dozen men, "I ain't swallowing any such swill as I just heard."

They hesitated. Orvil Gosnell said, "Don't seem very likely. I always heard the Dorseys named as a mighty grasping set of folks."

"And how'd this fellow here know right where old Cebo lived at?"

All of the men were muttering now, moving restlessly, like cattle before a storm.

"Joshua? Jonathan?" Mary Clayburn began and faltered. She did not look at either of her sons as she spoke but gazed straight ahead at these men in her yard.

"I don't know what we can do, Mama," Josh said. He frowned, troubled and puzzled.

"Your father trusted Cebo. Your father wouldn't want us to let anything happen to Cebo."

"No, Mama," Josh said.

Jonathan had turned and without a word was hurrying across the yard, up the steps, into the house. They could hear the back door as it slammed heavily behind him.

Mary Clayburn pulled the wool shawl close around her and took a step forward. "Friends," her voice was higher than usual and it trembled, "I appreciate your intention to respect Elisha and to help me and my children. But can't you see that Cebo here, who was completely trusted by Mr. Clayburn, isn't anyone you're looking for?"

"And his visitor?" Jasper Smelcer asked.

"Cebo could never shield anyone who harmed Mr. Clayburn," she said.

The dark face of the stranger, Lonas Rankin, was smooth and immobile. Although the air was frosty his skin gleamed with oily sweat. That was the only sign he gave of fear. He looked from one group of whites to another. He did not go back to stand with Cebo but remained where he had landed when he first stepped forward to give account of his presence and his money.

"Well, that's not good enough for me," Jasper Smelcer said. "No disrespect to you, Mrs. Clayburn, but you're a woman under heavy grief. Nobody could expect you to be right *at* yourself."

"It stands to reason you can't think anybody you know would harm your man," Orvil Gosnell said.

"This is man's business. We ought not to fret her anymore," a gray-haired rider beside Gosnell said. "Bring them two along, and we'll finish elsewhere."

Mary Clayburn looked around at Joshua. He took her arm. She looked at Edom Metcalf. He was squatted on his haunches, a blade of grass between his teeth, gazing intently into the distance. The shawl tight around her shoulders—askew so that the fringe of one end almost dragged the ground whenever she moved—she walked the few steps over to Cebo. "You're forgetting," she said to the men on their horses, "vengeance is mine, saith the Lord."

"We're remembering Lish Clayburn," Jasper Smelcer said.

Her face grew even paler; her hands trembled.

"Not vengeance, but justice," another man spoke up.

"Then be certain," she said, "be certain that you do justly—"

She was aware of Jonathan coming down the steps, striding toward her. At first she could not make out what he was carrying. Then she saw. In his arms he cradled several of the bulky ledgers from his father's desk. His face was set in determination. The riders who had already begun to move toward Cebo and Lonas Rankin paused as Jonathan walked in front of them. They watched as Jonathan handed to his brother Josh all but one of the heavy account books.

Jonathan held the other one up high enough above his head for all to see. "Anybody know what these are?" he asked. His voice was not loud but everyone heard.

The men stared, puzzled and irritated by the diversion.

"See here, Jonathan," Jasper Smelcer began.

"What you up to, son?" the gray-haired man asked.

"You've seen these books before?" Jonathan insisted.

The men glanced at the well-worn ledgers and looked away. "Reckon those be your father's account books," Orvil Gosnell said.

"This ain't proper time to go into all that," Jasper Smelcer said quickly.

"We got a bigger account to settle," Gosnell agreed.

"Stand back, son."

But Jonathan remained beside his mother, between the two black men and the group of riders pressing in. "It's a proper time," he said. He laid one hand on the big ledger he held. "If any settlement of accounts is to be made, then these debts ought to be reckoned first— they being oldest, maybe largest."

The men looked at each other and at Jonathan Clayburn and there was no ready answer. Someone said, "Maybe so, Jonathan. But this business we're on this morning, it's life and death. Them accounts of your pappy's, they can wait for a more fitting time and place."

"Some of them have waited a long time already."

"You have anything special in mind, son?"

Jonathan looked at the gray-haired man and nodded. "I have something in mind." He turned slightly. "Orvil Gosnell, you remember buying a stout young work-horse from my father when your woman was ailing and you needed to haul tanbark to pay for her doctor's bills—was it five, six years ago?"

Gosnell straightened himself in his saddle. "Something like that."

"And there was your dispute with a neighbor over a line fence, Jasper Smelcer," Jonathan looked at the fat, self-satisfied man in the forefront of the group. "Papa spent the better part of a week finding a fair settlement out of court, without bloodshed."

"I was much obliged to him," Smelcer said, flushing, glancing around at the others. "And no one can say I don't finally meet all my obligations."

"Of course." Jonathan stepped to one side and touched the ledgers stacked in his brother's outstretched arms. "For most of you, maybe every one of you, there's some debt set down in these pages. That debt is owed my mother now."

In the pause that followed the gray-haired man at the rear spat loudly and then said, "Nobody's disputing it."

There was a longer silence. "Then we're offering all of you a chance to set the record even now," Jonathan said. His mother laid her hand on his arm and he knew that she understood what he wanted.

The men were still uncertain. "We'll make a trade," Jonathan said.

This was something they understood. "What you mean, son?" one of them leaned forward slightly.

"My mother and her children want you to leave Cebo and Lonas Rankin here. In exchange we'll close the accounts left behind by my father. You—none of you—will owe anything."

The men, old and young, Cebo and Lonas Rankin as well as the whites, were trapped by surprise.

"You'd trade for your father's slayers?" Jasper Smelcer asked in his preacher's voice.

"Cebo's guilt isn't proved," Mary Clayburn protested. "Can you doubt, Jasper Smelcer, that I want my husband's killing brought to justice? That I shall have it brought to justice? But not till I've witnessed the blood on these men's hands more plainly than I've yet seen it."

Their will was shaken.

"There are entries in these ledgers for loans of money, and many a winter's provision of food. There's other indebtedness, too, that might come as a surprise if it was made public," Jonathan said. The mildness of his tone did not deceive them of the determination behind his words.

"You dunning us for your pappy's favors?" one asked.

"Papa would never have dunned anybody. But he was a master trader. You can't deny that."

They nodded slightly and stole glances at each other, glances of respect for this surprising boy.

"Papa would have relished a trade to settle your debts," Jonathan said.

"Would he have relished this trade?"

"I can't know for sure, Mr. Smelcer," Jonathan answered. Then, after a pause, "All I can do now is use my own judgment."

"Don't seem like the nigger would come right to the dead man's farm." Their unity and drive were collapsing.

"I don't want to go against a dead man," one said, "if Lish set such store by this Cebo."

But the thought that was fastening in each of their minds, slowly but firmly, was the advantage this trade brought to them. Quickly, cleverly, they calculated. In one action they would free themselves from obligations that were costly and troublesome, debts some of them would never be able to repay in full even if they wished to. Why should they hold out to avenge Lish Clayburn's death if his own family were willing to forego bread and butter for these two hides? Their appetite for justice was replaced by their hunger for easy gain.

"This boy's offer agreeable to you, Mrs. Clayburn?" the gray-haired man asked suddenly.

She nodded. "I'm praying you'll take it."

"Well, if that's how *you* want it—"

"We've each other as witnesses that these debts set down against us are canceled," Jasper Smelcer said.

"I gave my word," young Jonathan told him.

"The boy's got grit in his craw," the gray-haired man said.

There was a moment's wait, uneasy and tense.

"Then if it's settled," Orvil Gosnell jerked at his horse nervously, "if we're leaving these two here—" he looked at Cebo and Lonas Rankin, spat, and finished hastily—"I'm of a mind to be on my way." He turned his horse's head and disappeared around a corner of the house.

The others followed close behind, swiftly, murmuring to each other, to Jonathan, and—the last one—to the black stranger. "You watch your step, boy." One man rode his horse close to the unflinching Rankin. "You hear?"

"I'm hearing, Mister," Lonas Rankin said softly.

The men left quickly, apart from one another. As they galloped down the long driveway toward the public road their faces were shrewd from a bargain well made, but they were not satisfied. They had come in the sweat and smell of hate. They had wanted to purge the community and themselves in a violent catharsis, and they had been thwarted. They slouched in their saddles and headed for their homes in surly silence, skirting town, curiously relieved and frustrated at the same time.

When they had gone, the last horses gouging up turf as they galloped away under heavy spur, the familiar sounds and sights asserted themselves once more. Winter limbs rattled in the brisk wind that was rising. The cow bawled again and again. The tableau in the yard broke apart. Joshua carried his load of books inside the house. Cebo and his younger friend still stood near Mary Clayburn and Jonathan.

"You believe old Cebo," his voice rasped. His bent shoulders were jerking under the homespun shirt he wore. "You know I ain't taking any life on this earth. Lord knows I saw that old raven bird winging close there for a little while."

"It's all right, Cebo." She was shaken and weak with relief herself. "The Lord looks after his own."

"I'm obliged to you, Missus," the young black man said. "And to you, Mister. Not likely I'll forget what you done for me this day."

All of them left in the yard—his mother, Edom Metcalf, these two victims—looked at Jonathan.

"You your daddy's son today," Cebo said. He might have been

an Egyptian priest pronouncing ancient rites. "You your own man today."

"I just hit on something that worked," Jonathan said. He held the big ledger under one arm and with his other guided his mother back toward the steps. "If I were you now," they all knew he was speaking to Rankin although he did not look at the stranger, "I'd move on pretty quick—"

"I aim to find Mr. Hartwick—"

"No. I mean to another state." Jonathan helped his mother up the steps. "We just bought you some time today, we didn't win any verdict."

"That's right," Cebo nodded. "You go to work at that black-smith's, even saying he'd take you on now, which ain't likely, them men would pick fights, make trouble with you ever' way they know."

Shoeless, coatless, he spoke bitterly. "Nothing left. My horse taken away from me—"

And they all thought of the money at the same time. During this brush with violence the little roll of bills had been forgotten, but now it was crucial again. Someone, however, had not forgotten. It had disappeared from the spot where it had fallen. Cebo and Rankin were on their knees searching the ground.

At the top of the steps Jonathan turned and looked at Edom Metcalf. The older man shifted and spat a long stream of tobacco juice into the brown grass. Gradually the gaze of the others turned to him, too. He did not respond. A dull flush flooded his face under its growth of beard. Jonathan, still looking at him, nodded slowly toward Lonas Rankin. "Give it back to him, Edom."

While no one else had noticed, when the men on horseback were taking their leave, Jonathan had seen the deft hired man flick the tight wad of money into his hand and pocket.

Metcalf made a move to protest, then thought better and was quiet. He thrust one hand deep into his baggy trousers and reluctantly drew forth the small cylinder of bills. With a gesture half of contempt and half of wrath, he flung it toward the black man. In one spontane-ous reach and leap, Lonas Rankin caught the pitch. His hand closed around the money. The curious little pantomime was over before Mary Clayburn seemed to realize what had happened. "What is it, Jonathan?"

"Everything's all right now, Mother," he said.

Cal and Whitley, who had just emerged from the woods and fields which lay to the east of the house where they had been since noon hunting rabbits, saw that some excitement had happened and they hurried to discover what it was. When they came into the yard they stared at Lonas Rankin. "Get busy, you two, and carry stovewood for supper," Jonathan said.

"I told you," Cal whispered fiercely, "we ought to stay out there till black-dark. Now they'll nag at us till suppertime. And we don't even know what's been going on—"

Inside the kitchen Mary Clayburn sat down in a chair beside the round pine table. Delia had gone home, as she did every afternoon to her cabin down the road, after she had prepared the main part of supper and left it on the back of the stove and in the oven with the fire banked low. The rich odor of baked spareribs and tart spicy apples filled the kitchen, making it a warm familiar firelit haven from the barbarity they had glimpsed outside only a few minutes ago. Hardworking, secure, prudent, the Clayburns followed a pattern established by others before them, confident in the rewards of their faithfulness. Then all of the order had been swept away, all the virtue nullified, on a wild foggy mountain one morning, and here on this late gray afternoon. They were shaken by the destruction that swirled around them, but they persisted, returning to this refuge of home and family and established ways.

Wearily Mary Clayburn pulled the shawl from her head, let it fall to the floor and lie there. "Jonathan, did we do what was right?"

"We did the best we knew, Mama."

She leaned over on the table. "Those men were ready to kill, Jonathan. They wanted to kill." He nodded.

"Was their thought for Elisha?"

He did not answer.

"I was scared," she said in a moment. "I couldn't even pray. I just called the name of the Lord over and over in my mind."

"We were all scared, Mama."

Josh came down the hall from the room that had been his father's office and into the kitchen. "I put Papa's ledgers away. I don't expect we'll be needing them again." He paused. His broad face was distressed by a network of lines, like a puzzle. "That was a lot of money, Jonathan. Couldn't we have got Cebo off for less?"

"It was a tight race, Josh. Those men weren't in a mood for dickering."

Josh's face remained uncertain. "I guess not."

"We may never get a nickel from the other accounts on your father's books," their mother said. "We've little enough to live on." And she believed it. In the Ransom-Clayburn-Wakely-Churchill world she knew, people were brought up to believe that they lived by meat and bread earned in sweat and foresight, by cloth and brick and fuel won through clever trades, by plows and harnesses used on uplands and bottomlands alike, by walnut sideboards and gold watch fobs and brass bedsteads. Her actions had just denied all this, had revealed that she knew with instinctive certainty that the intangible nourishment she and everyone else needed for survival had little to do with the obvious assets in which she believed she believed. She saw no contradiction in holding a complete trust in her Lord and at the same time needing the reassurance of material security.

"We do have the farm," Josh said.

She looked up. "Right now we do."

And they thought of Randall Montgomery. Since Montgomery's return from Charleston, neither he nor anyone else had mentioned his effort to buy the Riverbend Farm. Perhaps it had seemed inconceivable to the Clayburns that two disasters could strike them at once. But with Elisha's death his livestock money had disappeared, too, and the threat of loss of the land hovered even closer.

"If we could find who killed Papa," Jonathan said, "maybe we could find the money, too."

Cal and Whitley were on the back porch with their loads of stovewood. Josh held the door open for them. "You know," he said slowly, "I can't help but wonder if that Lonas Rankin might not have known more than he let on. Where there's so much smoke there's likelihood of some fire."

Jonathan, leaning against the window with his back to them, looking out into the empty yard, answered. "Tomorrow I'm going up to Wolf Pen Gap, to Dorsey's Stand, all the way to Charleston if necessary. Before I come back we'll know something about Papa's killers."

Thus began the strange time.

The family never knew whether Jonathan hesitated to talk about the rain-chilled sojourn in the high mountains—short days and long nights when the narrow road was either a mush of gumlike mud or a hazardous passage between jagged boulders that had tumbled from overhanging cliffs—because he wanted to forget as soon as possible or because he wanted to remember as long as possible.

Whatever his reason, Jonathan left a small stark island of uncluttered fact, classic in its simplicity, in the full, debris-cluttered river of Clayburn memory. Only Janus Rathbone offered supplementary details so that those who came in later generations would have full knowledge of what happened.

Jonathan had asked Janus Rathbone to go with him. Rathbone lived on a small farm in the Dark Hollow corner of the county—a poor area of upland woods, wild birds, small animals—whose outer edge began at the northernmost boundary of the Clayburn farm. He was a quiet, unflinching man who had ridden with Randall and Alexander Montgomery the morning they came to tell the Clayburn family of Elisha's death. The day Jonathan went to ask Janus about the trip, Jonathan met Laura Rathbone for the first time. She was fifteen.

While Jonathan spoke bitterly of the sheriff's indifference and idleness, even as he and two deputies tried to placate Elisha's many grieving, enraged friends, Janus chewed his tobacco slowly, pleasurably as a cud, listened to the boy's argument. "You're right enough, we've got nigh no law here. Your pappy's death deserves a lawful ending." He agreed to go with Jonathan. First, he said, he would like to "ask around" about one or two matters he'd been "thinking on" in relation to Elisha's death. So they did not leave immediately but waited a week, and the mid-December rains caught them in the mountains.

Instead of one day, it took the better part of two for them to reach Wolf Pen Gap. Jonathan never afterward related to anyone how he felt when he first reached that opening at the summit of the Unakas, shrouded on a late winter afternoon in bonechilling clouds settling down over the mountains. At that season of year and time of day there would have been only quiet everywhere, except for the splattering drips of moisture gathered from the thick fog on twisted limbs and twigs of an occasional giant chestnut, and from the leathery green leaves of laurel bushes which grew in an impenetrable tangle in the gap and down a wide swath of the slope. In other weather there would have been a far view opening on either side of this notch in the hills, luring a traveler to pause, then linger, and gaze at a blue-green, swelling sea of Tennessee mountains on one hand and North Carolina mountains on the other. But with clouds curtaining off the view the gap was closed in wet and cold and silence.

The riders paused for a moment of grief and curiosity beside the great boulder where Randall Montgomery said he and Elisha Clayburn had been waylaid. Then, as Jonathan later told it, Janus Rathbone wondered if the two of them might rest their horses briefly after the hard climb. They loosed their grip on the reins, sat relaxed in the saddles for a weary interval, suspended in this upper world of cloud and silence where all human traces seemed erased. Any sign of passage, struggle, death had vanished.

Then simultaneously Rathbone and Jonathan swung around until they faced the farthest edge of the boulder. It was as if that mass of granite had somehow shifted to permit passage to the pair on horseback who suddenly appeared there. They seemed to have materialized out of fog and chill.

Jonathan's horse gave a startled step sideways and whinnied. The strangers were swaddled in black from the crown of their wide-brimmed, homemade woollen hats to the muddy hems of their long enveloping cloaks. And in the space above the rags covering the lower half of their faces, and on the hands that were barely exposed under the cloaks' sleeves, the skin that was visible was also black. Jonathan sucked in his breath.

"Your money," the one slightly in the forefront said. His voice was harsh as a raven's. The gun he leveled at Janus did not waver. His mount was well trained. It did not move or break the aim.

"Your money," he repeated, a shade louder. "Pitch it on the ground—over here—wallet, pouch, whatever you're a-carrying. All of it. Both of you." The words slurred in an effort to disguise the voice. The metal finger of the pointing gun was unyielding.

"Whatever you've got on you, son," Janus Rathbone said, "let them have it." His voice was firm, careful as a barefoot boy treading among chestnut burrs.

Jonathan reached into his pocket, drew out the faded wallet

nestling there and threw it on the ground with a thin tinkling sound. Rathbone was making almost the same moves. He and Jonathan might have been performing an overly familiar ritual or ballet. Jonathan could hear his mother's cry echoing in his ears, "Let them have the money, Elisha!" Rathbone's worn leather pouch, long and stuffed like a sock, hit the ground with a solid thud. Jonathan was surprised that his companion should be carrying so much money.

The man made a small motion with his gun. "Get it," he growled, as to a reluctant bird-dog.

The second rider dismounted quickly, crossed the rough ground swiftly, and, back to Jonathan and Janus Rathbone, scooped up the muddy purses, handed them up to the man with the gun, and remounted. It was all done as quickly, as effortlessly, as drawing a deep breath.

"Try to follow after us and you'll never know the shot that dropped you." The man's voice was unemotional and convincing, stating a noteworthy fact. He nodded and his companion wheeled; horse and rider disappeared around the boulder and into the single narrow strip of woods not choked by laurel and dog-hobble thickets. When his threat had had time to gather from separate words into one bulletlike impact and settle in Jonathan's and Rathbone's minds, the rider followed his partner, crashing loudly through dead underbrush. Then he, too, disappeared into silence.

Janus Rathbone spoke first. "We'll wait here a minute—"

Something in his voice alerted Jonathan. The suddenness, the success, the repetitive and nightmarish quality of the robbery had benumbed Jonathan momentarily but now he threw off the horror. (This was how it happened before, only at this stage my father lay strangling, dying, feeling the warm ebb of his own blood when it was all over and the black-cloaked figures had disappeared.) What did this old countryman with him mean by such casual direction? His words and tone hinted that he had been braced for the day's events to fall out as they had.

"Now," Rathbone was speaking again. "Let's follow after the hellhounds. Go quiet. Quiet as your pappy's ghost." Before Jonathan could question or probe or agree, the older man had spurred his horse around the boulder and onto a narrow trail that led into the dark woods.

Jonathan followed. The trail was scarcely visible, but Janus Rathbone followed it easily. His sharp eyes neglected no detail. A crumpled cluster of waxy galax leaves, a torn bed of velvet green moss and trailing arbutus, a scatter of limbs and fallen twigs: each served as a marker to point the way.

"Set your mind to it, son," Rathbone said.

They urged the horses on.

Fog made the dark round tree trunks, moist and shining as a lizard's skin, appear like heavy columns reaching up into some gauzy canopy of gray and evergreen. The path led a winding route between them, deeper into the balsam woods. Jonathan's muscles were stiff with cold and tension, but he was unaware of the hurt and ache. Straining to see what lay ahead, he leaned forward in the saddle and kept his horse close behind Rathbone's.

There was a sound. It was not a wood's noise of scampering feet or falling branch or alarmed wings. The older man halted, held up his hand, cocked his head. It came again, a small explosion of sound. He listened and nodded, and to Jonathan's astonishment a slow satisfied hint of a smile crossed his face. He moved on at once, Jonathan following, the sound of their horses' hooves muffled by the thick woods' mulch.

Only a few yards ahead the woods opened suddenly and fell away in an abrupt cliff. Just at the brink of the mountain, overhung by a wide ledge which thrust out from the earth like a promontory above the abyss, was a sheltered spot. Two horses stood tethered nearby and two figures hunched on the ground beneath the gray, lichen-covered ledge. One of them was still making the sounds, only now they had become loud, unmistakable sneezes interrupted by choking coughs. Janus Rathbone's long pouchy wallet, clutched in the man's hand, shook with the violence of his sneezes.

"That older feller," the man was growling, rubbing watery eyes with his free hand, "he's tried to fox us. Might trail us, too. We best keep watch—"

But Janus Rathbone was already around the edge of the over- hanging rock; he reined up between the two thieves and their horses. Jonathan, close behind, was surprised to see a pistol in his hand. "Freeze right where you be," he said.

Before Rathbone had finished, the sneezing man lunged for his gun on the ground nearby. Rathbone's pistol shot split the silence. Its sound echoed in the cavelike space underneath the rock and out over the chasm which plunged away beneath them. The black-clad man fell.

"My God!" There was a high shrill scream. The second figure looked up at Rathbone and Jonathan on their horses. "You've shot him. You've killed my husband."

Hampered by the bulky clothes she wore, she knelt beside her fallen companion. His hat had toppled to one side and now she flung aside her own and laid her head against his chest.

Jonathan, probably for the first and only time in his sober Clayburn life, wondered if he had taken leave of his senses. What he saw before him in this improbable cave and confrontation was not only one revelation but two.

"It's a woman!" he gasped. And then to Janus Rathbone: "And they're white people."

Rathbone nodded. "Looks so. Pick up their gun, son." Jonathan did so, still looking at this strange couple.

Around the edges of neck and forehead which had been concealed by their hats, and along the upper arms now exposed by the pushed-up sleeves of their cloaks, the skin was hardly white, but at least a sallow yellowish gray. Elsewhere it shone with a greasy concoction of black which had been rubbed on in hasty disguise.

"You've killed him," the woman was screaming. A stain of blood oozed onto the fallen man's cloak.

"Just winged him, I reckon," Janus Rathbone said. "Nicked him in the shoulder. He won't be doing any more shooting for a spell."

There was a muffled sneeze from the ground. Janus Rathbone winked at Jonathan. "Guess my old black pepper did its job."

"Your pepper?" Jonathan asked.

He nodded. "A batch I had left over from curing my hams and meat a little while back. Ground that pepper fresh night before last, so it would come out strong with that paper stuffed in my wallet."

"You expected they'd waylay us?"

Rathbone shrugged. "Figured somebody might try. I had word bruited about that two fellers fitting our description would be on the Carolina road today with a lavish of money. Then it come to my mind that if we had any chance to follow, some plain old pepper might give just the edge of advantage we'd need. Leastways, there'd be no doubt who prowled through that old pouch of mine."

Jonathan shook his head. "I wondered about that fortune you seemed to be carrying." He grinned at this mountain man who had become so resourceful a friend. "Paper!" he said. "And you'd spread word ahead—"

"He's dying!" the woman shrieked again.

Rathbone gazed down on the man. "Get up!" he barked suddenly, sharply.

The man, who had not moved, scrambled to his feet. He clutched his left hand to his right shoulder. Angrily he jerked his head signaling his wife to stand beside him.

Jonathan leveled the gun at them. The man was short and heavyset. His hair, half-gray, was thin and matted, his eyes narrow and filled with fear, watery from his attack of sneezing. His wife was sturdy as a man. Her hair was drawn into a tight knot atop her head and her skin beneath its camouflage was coarse and wrinkled as old canvas.

"You were the ones—" Jonathan began, "my father—" Now that he saw them he could not believe creatures so tawdry had been the cause of a good man's death. Surely there was something larger, more majestic than this ignobility. His father killed by these greedy prowlers: it was as if a lofty eagle had been brought down by weasels.

"These were the varmints all right," Janus Rathbone was saying. "Killed your pappy, robbed no telling how many other victims."

"But how?"

Rathbone looked at the couple cornered under the ledge. The silence of the woods above and chasm below was broken only by the faint, distant roaring of a waterfall somewhere deep in the valley. "You the Dorseys?"

The man nodded spitefully.

"I figured so." Rathbone looked at Jonathan. "They keep the tavern down under Wolf Pen Gap. Travelers spend the night there, like your pappy and Randall Montgomery. These two can discover which ones carry money. Then black themselves up, waylay the travelers when they get to the gap."

"But don't people see them in these cloaks and hats and—"

"Reckon they hide their paraphernalia here in this cave."

Involuntarily the woman's eyes shifted toward the deepest recess under the ledge. Rathbone swung from his saddle and handed his reins to Jonathan. Keeping his gun on the couple, he stooped and made his way to the back part of this low room sheltered under rock. With the toe of his heavy boot he shoved a square, metal-covered box into the light. "Open it."

The man did not move, but the woman shuffled across the dirt and pried up the heavy lid. Inside were only stained, threadbare black gloves and empty wallets of several styles. One by one Rathbone held these up, mute trophies of a half-dozen robberies, until Jonathan finally nodded. "That was Papa's. I'd know it anywhere."

"I warned we ought to burn that trash," the man snarled to his wife.

"We'll be wanting the money was in these, too," Janus Rathbone interrupted calmly.

"You'll not have it!" The woman was cruel as a shrew, her snuff-stained teeth showing between her narrow lips. She seemed ready to slash at them with fangs or spring upon them with talons.

In the sickening futility and illogic of her fierceness, Jonathan encountered what seemed to him the very essence of money-greed. This was blind, insatiable ravenousness capable of the ultimate sin, taking of life.

Jonathan's own course was influenced by this early vision of rapacity. It was an evil old as Eden. (Jonathan in later years would argue with preachers and neighbors alike that it was not curiosity that had driven man out of the Garden, but his greed to devour everything within reach.) It was also as prevalent as man himself. In his time, Jonathan would see many varieties of wreckage resulting from the infinite variations of hunger, but his initiation into the primitive, meaningless violence which had cost the life of the person he most loved and respected never lifted its imprint.

Janus Rathbone and Jonathan Clayburn brought the Dorseys— shamed and defiant in the mixture of grease and soot and bootblack- ing which streaked down their faces and hands—back to the county seat. "Great Excitement in Town and County," the weekly *Herald- Citizen* announced in its next issue. "White Bandits Masquerading as Negroes Captured in Robbery Attempt."

In breathless gasps and leisurely repetitiveness the editor-reporter- printer-owner told of the Dorsey's tavern, of their career of robbery which had begun, by their confession, some two years before and had reached its climax in Elisha Clayburn's death.

"We hadn't planned on killing him," the man Dorsey was reported to have said.

And a friend of Elisha's had answered: "Killing is the work guns are made to do. You had a gun."

There was no report of what Orvil Gosnell, or Jasper Smelcer, or others who had been ready to kill Cebo and Lonas Rankin for Mr. Clayburn's death, thought and said.

Later, when Jonathan realized that the horse Dorsey rode was the one he had traded from the reluctant black man, Jonathan bought the horse and brought it to Cebo. "If you know where Rankin is, take it to him."

"He long gone now. Days and nights. And far."

"He may come back this way—"

But Cebo did not answer.

Clippings of the *Herald-Citizen* account of the Dorseys' capture, of his hanging and her imprisonment, and of the subsequent return of Elisha Clayburn's money to his family (money found in a milk can in the loft of the rambling old tavern) lay in family Bibles and cedar chests and linen presses for decades to come, growing yellow and brittle. Orvil Gosnell made a ballad called "When Death Wore a Mask in the Wolf Pen Gap," and he sang it to the music of his own guitar. Others adapted it and changed it as they wished, and eventually it became a well-known tale of grief and loss, set down in D-minor key. This mournful song and the fading bits of paper preserved the public experience that Clayburn order and purpose had had with mystery. It was the mystery of darkness folded in the innermost leaf of man and nature. Sudden death, forestalling inevitable age or final achievement or expected disease, had come as random as a bolt of lightning. Tempering all their practicality, awareness of mystery lay within that generation of Clayburns as hidden and real as the decaying newspapers that lay in their chests and Bibles.

Elisha Clayburn was dead.

The family he had begot and the routine he had established lived on. There were mornings and evenings when Mary Clayburn or one of the older sons paused and looked at the broad waiting bottomlands, the surging river, the books and pen on his desk—and everything was the same and yet forever changed. This, too, was mystery, for it lay not in the outer world but in the interior vision of that exposed reality.

Money from Elisha's trip to Charleston paid the bank and the tax collector for old debts. Now the land and house of the Major Lawes plantation was theirs, was the Clayburn Riverbend Farm, beyond dispute. Even a few of the obligations on Elisha's books were paid and the family had money in Alexander's Montgomery's bank.

At Jackson University, Josh became captain of the first football team. They were a squad of muscular farm lads with sunburned necks and innocent faces framed between wide ears spread out from their heads by years of wearing winter caps and summer hats pulled low behind their ears. They were more expert at tossing horseshoes than at passing pigskin, but they were learning fast.

Also at the university, Jonathan was elected president of his class. At graduation with Josh, after three years, he was valedictorian. Neither of their lives ever actually left the farm, however. During long winter evenings of study in the drafty library, on drowsy autumn Sunday afternoons of preparing speeches for the debating society to which they belonged, in the midst of their prank-filled friends at the battered old boardinghouse, Josh and Jonathan remembered the spacious woods beyond their pastures, and the waiting fields and barns now tended by hired help and younger brothers. Experience reduced to numbers and Latin grammar and high-flown English seemed anemic when compared to the steamy challenge of new ground in spring, the acrid fertility of manure pile and pigsty, the rough demands and satisfactions of land and animals and a pragmatic natural world.

A total alien in the world of books, Josh endured (by the grace of football) and graduated and went home with the hope that he might never leave again. Jonathan took all that the professors and books could give him and returned home and found that neither he nor the family was the same as before he had gone away. He was looking larger, farther, wider now.

In addition, there were five others, younger—Cal and Whitley and Dan, Nettie Sue and Lottie—to educate.

The two older boys came home from college in late spring. They put away their celluloid collars and Sunday suits. They laid their books beside their father's on the shelves in his little study. They told Cebo, bent with rheumatism, that he would no longer need to take the plow or hoe into the fields, but he could feed and water the livestock —mules, horses, cows, hogs, chickens, turkeys, geese, guineas—and keep the woodbox filled for their mother and Delia in the kitchen.

Before daybreak the morning after their return, Jonathan stood alone at the back steps looking down toward barns and pasture and the river in the distance, listening to the first clear calls and warbles of birds busy in the newly leafed maple and elm and tall spreading oak trees. Cebo, passing through the yard from the corncrib to the barn, paused when he saw Jonathan, then sat down on the lower step, placed the wide brass bucket between his knees, and began to shell the ears of husked corn. His hands, rubbing one bare cob against a full ear to pull the hard grains loose, looked like weaving spiders. The corn rattled into the bucket.

"You seeing night out or day in?" his raspy voice asked presently.

"Waiting for daylight," Jonathan said.

The grizzled head nodded.

"Had a dream," Jonathan said softly. "Guess it waked me up and I couldn't go back to sleep."

The chatter of the corn against metal stopped. Cebo did not look around. He waited.

Jonathan watched the birds winging back and forth. "I dreamed—" He paused. Cebo waited. "I was back in the mountains, farther in the mountains than I've ever been, and the valley around me was totally hemmed in. Narrow, dark, no entrance, no exit. Then, just as I began to feel pressed down and a cold sweat was breaking out on my face and hands and body, I heard an unbelievable sound. It was running water. When I looked, I found the boldest, clearest river ever seen on this round globe. And I lay right down in its swift, deep current and it carried me through a passage in the mountains and out near home."

The birds rustled in the treetops.

"Clear water, you say?" Cebo asked.

"All the way. So clear that in the deepest places sand and pebbles shone like a buck's eye in firelight."

A grimace twisted Cebo's face. He nodded with satisfaction, and the corn began to fall with quick new patter into the bucket. "That about the best luck can come," he said. "A dream of clear water."

Jonathan had never seen the old man so close to laughter and cheer. "Well now, I'm glad—"

"Old clear river rolling out of that dark penned-up valley. Something good on the way, boy."

Jonathan could feel the tug of Cebo's words. He shrugged it off. Luck was for the wishbone, not the backbone. "We need something," he muttered, "something to let us break out and make a better living, use this farm to its best—"

"Clear water a-rolling—"

The sound of Cebo's voice was happy as singing. Jonathan watched daylight wash across the sky and down the distant hills.

"Clear water—"

An English teacher at the university the previous winter had read aloud passages from that thornbush of an old Yankee writer, Thoreau. One sentence had lodged in Jonathan's memory. "Only that day dawns to which we are awake."

Well, he was awake.

3

That was the way it came to me: larger than life, less than life. Legend and anecdote, fact and imagination, pieced together like a stained-glass window that is not a window at all—opening neither out nor in—but an illumination of legend, of belief, myth, or transcendent passion carefully created, frozen in rich and brilliant permanence.

Stained glass, of course, is obsolete today. As our memory is considered obsolete by many. It has been replaced by ingenuity. Information systems they are called. They store facts, statistics, formulas, names, data. And when someone in Clayburn-Durant needs an answer he can go to George Hodges' computer and feed in the question —and after a momentary rumble of digestion the Word will come forth.

But that elaborate tool cannot supply the answers for me. It cannot even direct the search, the search more important than answers. These come from my own information systems: labyrinths of brain, organs, senses, spasms of fear, loneliness, intuition, and hungers. There is more here than any computer can contain. There is layer beneath layer of myself and others.

The past is dead! Long live the past! If I think Stull Clayburn or Nat Lusk or Deborah Einemann are more real than my father, Jonathan Clayburn, or my grandmother Mary Ransom Clayburn or even Laura Rathbone, I am a fool.

For how is it that we come to knowledge of ourselves and those strangers around us masquerading as lovers, parents, children, friends, adversaries? A dozen names and roles which are assigned in pompous singleness but which in fact are always fluid, overlapping, and several.

By so-called facts: dates and places, figures, events, a neat record of births and deaths and marriages and mergers, reports in newspapers and journals, which the mothers, aunts, cousins accumulate in fat, neat scrapbooks where the paste crumbles and yellows, the paper clippings turn brittle and brown as dead leaves, and gray mildew finally whiskers the untouched crevices and spine of the bindings.

By unwitting fragments: a word, a glance, a breath, telling nothing but revealing all, buried only in some convolution of the brain until it surfaces at an unexpected moment to slice through accepted myth like a laser beam of reality.

By legend: gradual, constant, unconscious flow of family stories, anecdotes, reverences, judgments, communicating more by the single turn of a phrase, the lift of an eyebrow, the tone of a voice, than pages of words can suggest. All these sucked into us with milk and water, fed to us as surely as bread. Finally we "know"—not what happened so much as what someone, or several, believe happened. And at last not so much what someone believes happened but what it meant to those who were there. That is the legend we receive and transmit: of something that happened somewhere and sometime and how someone was there—one person at the beginning, a different person at the conclusion.

What happened on that remote, fog-wrapped mountain during the incredible morning when my young father (is it ever possible to see one's father young, smooth-cheeked, naive, frightened?) found that paltry pair who had blasted the orderly Clayburn life? Were they real, those horses stamping on the green turf before the old brick home, the trapped black man sweating the oil and juice of flesh because he smelled the unjust presence of death, those bearded neighbors hot for blood until traded out of it by my father?

Violence was a part of the air and place and time our fathers knew. Public hangings with the stretched neck and the gorged eyes of a man like a pulled gander, impromptu burnings with kerosene sloshed on at the excruciating moment or pine splinters stuck in the flesh ablaze, chain gang labor: these were justice.

Heavyweight, lightweight fights until a mortal brain was sufficiently damaged to permit only blackout, knockout: these were entertainment. The lash, the cudgel, the bullet: these were strength. Oddest, most difficult for me to realize, is the fact that this recognizable
one-to-one physical violence, which my father Jonathan knew, was
infinitely easier to encounter than the subtly masked total violence
surrounding my son Lee.

When I was young I sometimes fell asleep at night longing to
have been with him, with my father and Janus Rathbone, during that
dreadful moment of discovery when they knew beyond dispute that
Elisha Clayburn had been killed for money, money only, money all.
I would lie under the eiderdown comforter listening to my mother
pace the carpeted hallway beyond the door and I would think of the
protection and strength I should have given my father. But I cannot
seem to give them to my son who is here, now.

Whenever I return to Churchill for more than an afternoon's
inspection, they seem to return, too: those who first shaped this company which now shapes me. There are men in the Clayburn-Durant
Company, able, hard-hitting managers and salesmen and directors,
who can barely remember the maiden names their aging wives once
bore; they would consider me a madman if I should lay aside our gin
rummy cards on the plane one day and mention the name of my
grandmother.

What would I say of Mary Clayburn? What do I even know of
her? Only my suspicion that the dogma which was her faith and
strength became the doom and weakness of some who came afterward?

Her seven children revered her. I heard their voices, even in
elderly years, grow meek and respectful when they mentioned her
name. Yet I never "knew" her. What was behind the plain solemn face
with its high forehead, slightly flaring nostrils, brown wavy hair?
What unspent force within her called forth that religion which totally
controlled her and reached into all our lives? What was her strength
which left its legacy of weakness?

Not only the blood-kin, the obviously influential, are part of my
information systems, however. There are those who were taken for
granted as the scenery, and as essential. The forgotten ones. Old Cebo.
Lonas Rankin. Delia. Serena, later on. How else except through them

and through a childhood of white innuendoes, nods, grins, frowns, approvals, rejections, could I have gained the love/fear, need/hate, identity/indifference sunk deep beneath my tanned and tended flesh? Lonas and Delia I never saw, but a dozen not unlike them moved through my boyhood—the proud strangers destined to stir unease and guilt and destruction, and the unassuming hands and feet, carrying and fetching, lifting and building, doing for—always for.

Cebo was no faceless name to me, however. Cebo was a pair of enormous eyes whose dark pupils were surrounded by purple-veined orbs the yellowish color of aged mutton suet. With those eyes which seemed as ancient as the pyramids and his rasping voice as raw and harsh as rock, that small, inescapable man held me motionless, intent, for hours of childhood.

There is no need now for me to be ashamed or unashamed of the small square room of our big brick garage where my father brought him from old Major Lawes' Riverbend Farm, where he hunched before a round, coal-choked stove in winter and steeped himself in the sunlight which slanted through the open door in summer. There I would find him.

"Hello, Uncle Cebo."

No spoken greeting from him. The lid of one round old yellow eye would descend in the long slow ritual of a wink. That one small gesture enclosed us in a private world. I hunkered down on my haunches until he, on his low-slung, tattered cane-bottom chair, and I were face to face.

"How's your spirits today, Uncle Cebo?"

"Spirits low today, dragging low, boy." His head, small and shriveled as a sun-baked prune, shook slowly from side to side. In my mind I could see clouds of demons, magicians, and protectors hovering in this dusky little room, armed with knowledge given only to Cherokee shaman, African priest, Highland chieftain. For he would tell me then, or later perhaps, some bizarre tale of his encounters with a world that seemed to lie all about us but that I could never enter.

A fierce dog met on the road one midnight was not a dog at all but a man disguised for evil reasons.

The distorted leaf of a certain shrub was a token for making medicine.

The deep-throated gurgle of a mourning dove before rain bespoke warning.

And anyone who would shoot such a dove would call down on himself the curse of heaven, for his name was written in the Bible.

I reveled in the tingle and chill his words aroused in me but I was ashamed to share it with anyone else, even my brother Monty. Now I feel differently. I know there is mystery. Even in the coils of company finances and crises, clubs and committees, and cars and planes, I have been reminded. Teena's death and Deborah's presence and numerous stifled intimations are my link back to that smoky cubbyhole and a touch with old Cebo.

Yet he has come forward with me, too, into my city, my now, my business. The Community Human Relations Council on which I sit is there because of Cebo. Memory of his gnarled hands with their bleached pale palms affects me more than all the volumes of statistics our council has compiled. Wasn't it delayed recall of Cebo's repeated nightmare of a strange fettered wolf—crippled, stifled, dying—that finally made me undertake a new labor-hiring program for our company? But if it was Cebo's memory, then why didn't I move sooner? How our actions and beliefs are barnacled with self-deceptions and comfortable justifications that help us survive, only to drown more deeply!

Only once did I ever visit with Cebo outside his little room. My mother planned a day's journey "down into the country," as she called it, which meant that we would go from our house in Churchill down to the Old Home-Place, the Riverbend Farm, our father's home and not hers, as she always reminded my brother and me. And since our father could not leave business that day but had duties to attend, Cebo came along. There was no danger that Cebo could overcome by his frail knotted hands or legs, there was no mechanical repair that he knew how to make on our cumbersome new automobile, but my mother insisted on taking him as symbol of protection and assistance. Symbolism was reality to her.

Aunt Nora and Uncle Joshua Clayburn lived at the Riverbend Farm then. Of their children only Stull aroused my curiosity. I did not see him often but he seemed aloof and perplexing, different and therefore interesting, and on this day he was to teach me the gulf between our years, between ourselves.

When we arrived my mother and aunt met in a flurry of all those niceties that are the distillation of a perpetual hostility. Before they could turn their attention and kisses to me I fled around the house.

Uncle Cebo was standing in the back yard. His eyes were fixed on a stump beyond us, near the barn. It was a new stump, clean and wide as a table-top, only at its heart there was dark decay.

"Next to last," Cebo was muttering. "I remember you, hardhearted old man. But now you cut down, gone, and your heart rotted. Nowhere no more. Next to last."

I looked again at the new stump and saw beside it a great, wide-branched tree still standing. "What kind is that, Uncle Cebo?"

He looked at me scornfully. "Oak, boy."

"Was it there when you were a boy?"

His scorn doubled. "That old oak sprouting there long ago as your great-great-great-grandpa, or maybe long ago as old Nebuchadnezzar himself. Just growing quiet and steady." Then he turned his gaze on me, weighing, making judgment on the ripeness of a moment. "Come along, boy."

We walked across the brown grass of late summer and into the deep shade of the tiers of oak leaves layered above us. We walked up to the tough round trunk of the tree so large I could not embrace even half of it between my outspread arms. Cebo reached out to touch the shaggy bark and so did I. Then I saw that where he touched, higher than his shoulder, there was a difference in the bark and the wood underneath. The scar was old, very old.

"Major Lawes was his name, boy. Major Lawes. He owned this land and all on it, above and underneath. He put the ring in this oak, the iron ring." Cebo's hoarse old voice paused a moment as he stroked the scab of bark beneath his bony fingers.

"They making the brick for this big fine house, toting the brick for the mansion, all the black slaves working for Pharaoh in the latter days. And when the firing didn't go right, when the fetching and laying wasn't fast enough, somebody got fastened to the iron ring."

Suddenly I was listening more attentively than I had ever listened to Cebo before. I knew that this was something I had not even heard whispered before, something as vicious and compelling as a lurking copperhead. I did not move. I scarcely breathed.

"My mammy, she one of the fast toters. Lots of days she set the pace and I toddled behind her, a nubbin of a boy with two bricks in my hands, proud to hear her named the fastest, looked up to. A high-built brainy Ibo tribeswoman, they always said she was, although born this side the ocean. But one day toward the end of the building, they was topping off that last chimney on the northeast corner there—"

We turned and looked at it in the full hot sun, as strong and steady as if it had always stood and would remain so in centuries to come.

"Things was going hard and whatever anybody tried to do just seemed like they were trading the witch for the devil. Old Major Lawes had lost time—and his temper to boot. And just after noontime thunderheads began to roll up out of the west, I guess my mammy was nervous and all. . . ."

When he paused there wasn't any sound but the rustle of a bluejay high up in the oak leaves.

"What did she do, Cebo?" I asked at last.

He leaned against his hand flattened against the tree. "She dropped two of them satchels of bricks, one first, then right on the next trip up the hill another. And the bricks, striking against one another and the ground, chipped and broke. I was running along close behind and when they fell I saw all those scattered pieces and the look in my mammy's eyes and I fell on my bare knees and started trying to put them bricks back together again. But they wasn't no going back. . . ."

I waited.

"They tied her up to the iron ring. Laid her back open with a special little whip Major Lawes had traded once from an Indian packman."

I tried to visualize a back "laid open" and the "little whip" but even with my vivid child's mind I could not see it plainly. Its blur of blood and pulpy flesh made my stomach churn. "What happened then?" I had to know.

"She passed." He looked at me patiently, then acknowledged my ignorance again. "My mammy died."

I looked back at the scar on the tree in horror.

"Not right there. Not then. Soon after. While Major Lawes' foreman was whipping her, that storm broke loose. Everybody run to shelter, didn't have time to unloose her. During that hard lightning and thunder and then the downpour of rain that come after, she was out here chained to this old tree. I remember one of the workmen held onto me, finally fastened me up in the corncrib when he got tired holding, so I wouldn't run out to my mammy and get in trouble, too."

"But Cebo," I cried, "why didn't your daddy look after you?" My throat was tight. I didn't want his story to end this way. To me it was still a story he could make up as he chose. "Why didn't your daddy come and protect your mother and you?"

"Lord God, boy," Cebo shook his head, "it was Major Lawes doing the punishing."

I still didn't understand. Even when he added, "Major Lawes would have to protect us from hisself," and I knew enough to hush. I didn't actually understand what Cebo said until years later when I became familiar with the arrangements by which a man divides himself.

"I'm sorry, Cebo," I said. But even then I knew my easy regrets were useless. They cost me nothing, made no restitution.

We waited. I could feel the tree all around me. "Then what happened?"

"That evening, after the storm moved on, they moved her back to the cabin, her teeth chattering, her eyes wild as a doe's caught in the light on a fire-hunt. Lung fever carried her off."

There was a pause. The bluejay had long since abandoned his perch in the oak tree, and all was quiet.

"Major Lawes mighty regretful of his loss. Even after the war and jubilee had been laid on him, he still sickest at losing mammy. That and freedom drove him to the old black pit." And for one of the few times in my life, I heard Cebo chuckle. It was not a good sound. And the lines of his face did not seem to fit into a smile. "When your grandpappy buy this place, old Major Lawes a lunatic roaming its rooms calling on the devil to snatch all niggers into hell and brimstone."

I had no knowledge to fit his words or the glee of his high mirthless cackle. Lung fever. Death. Madness. But I mourned his proud, industrious mother. God, I mourned her.

Even then, however, a cool, self-centered corner of my mind was thankful that the cruelty and sadness had not actually driven my stomach to rebellion and betrayed me into sickness. I was glad I had not vomited in childish upset, because I had seen my cousin Stull, fifteen years older than I, during the final minutes of my conversation with Cebo, watching from the porch in the distance. Now he came toward us.

He was medium-tall and plump. His hair lay flat against his head. It was never possible to guess what he was thinking. Or feeling.

"What are you two doing down here?" he asked. No greeting, no pleasantry, no acknowledgment of us as visitors.

"Hello, Stull," I tried to be older. But he did not respond. He waited. "Oh, Cebo and I were talking about this old tree."

I looked to Cebo to find some signal about whether or not I should tell any more. But he was gazing off toward the mountains. "This old tree has a lot of stories," I went on desperately. Somehow my words seemed to be separating me from Cebo, pushing me toward my indifferent cousin.

"Stories?" Stull said. His tone, his face, discounted the word and all it described.

"But Cebo's are true," I rushed on. "They really happened. Didn't they, Cebo?"

He did not answer.

Then Stull demolished me. "Well, it must be fun to be a child, able to spend the day telling tales." He turned, in ballooning knickers and self-esteem, and walked back toward the house. "As for me, I have to go in to Churchill," he was saying as he left, "and help Uncle Jonathan with the sauerkraut pack."

There was no sound after Stull's words. Presently the screen at the back door slammed behind him.

Cebo only looked at me. I was brimming with disappointment and chagrin and jealousy. Then Cebo shuffled away, moving toward the barn. I looked at the scar on the oak again. Actually it wasn't a very large wound. Considering the size of the whole tree it was almost nothing.

At dinner I asked Aunt Nora if Stull had really gone in to work with my father at the plant.

"Goodness yes." She smiled, pleased, and gave me an extra helping of banana fritters. Then she said to my mother, "Jonathan is one person who seems to appreciate Stull's abilities. You know—"

My mother nodded. "Jonathan has put himself out to train and teach the boy—"

It seemed to me that when my mother and aunt talked, none of their sentences was ever quite completed. They trailed off into laby-rinths of meaning I could not follow.

But I did know that being part of the emotion-rich back-yard world of an old black man was nothing compared to being Stull and part of the practical upper world of making and selling, of trade and profit. The food I ate, even Aunt Nora's banana fritters, had lost all flavor.

On the way home I had nothing to say. I thought about Cebo's story. My attention, my caring, seemed weak and insignificant before Stull's detachment. I thought about Stull working with my father. And I was miserable with jealousy.

After all the years, the jealousy is weaker, easier understood and dismissed. But Cebo's iron ring and mother are fastened in my mind. Not consciously—I haven't thought of them in ten, maybe twenty years. But now I have discovered they are still with me.

Cebo was only one of the first and now forgotten. Time carries them away and they all—even the central ones—diminish in the family and public vision just as a figure standing at the wrong end of a telescope recedes to a speck of dust with a few twists of the lens adjustor. Yet they all made Clayburn-Durant, wrought it from noth-ingness, sweated it into stability until now it grows larger each day and magnifies at the other end of the telescope.

In our information systems somewhere we must have filed at least a memo of the awkwardness and intuition, the vision and error, the lonely decision and grinding labor which accrued, accumulated, became this company and us. Yet we do not reach for it. Deborah says we are terrified to look back and so we keep running. But that is because she has seen the wolf pit, the snake den, the bare fang—not over her shoulder or far away but gaping at her feet, tearing at her flesh. I am determined to cancel out her memories with mine—or discover the point within us where they merge.

4

The idea gathered slowly, steadily, like a soaking summer rain. While Josh and Jonathan were away at college the railroad stretched through the mountains.

"If only your father could have been here the day the cars came to Churchill," Mary Clayburn wrote her oldest sons.

After they came home, whenever they went into town Jonathan paid close attention to the freight unloaded from the mammoth boxcars along the short spur track beside the station.

At Montgomery's brick store which dominated the street opposite the railroad station, Jonathan took note of the products arriving from the big wholesale houses to the north. A large part of each shipment was foodstuff. He was surprised at the quantity. "These mountains are a land of make-do or do-without," he had heard old-timers say, especially those who had come through the winters of 1860–65, when coffee was parched corn and salt was scrapings from smokehouse floors and meat was whatever could be found in fields or woods.

He remembered that his father had given a talk to the farmers' convention in the state capital only a year before he died—a yellowing copy of it lay in one of the ledgers above his desk—and his topic was: the South must feed the South. Jonathan often thought about that talk.

One afternoon in mid-summer he came up from the river bottoms earlier than usual, leaving Cal and Whit to load the last wagon of tomatoes. In the kitchen Delia and his mother were canning. Through an open window he could see a half-dozen plump hens wallowing in troughs of dust at the edge of the back yard. Their wings raised little golden clouds which settled lazily in the drowsy heat. His mother sat near the window, an ample blue-checkered apron covering her lap and bosom. Painstakingly she selected one of the scalded tomatoes heaped in a granite pan on her lap, then began to skin it with quick, careful strokes. Her broad face shone with perspiration. The skin on her hands was bleached and puckered by hours in water and juice. Nearby Delia was bent over the wide black kettles bubbling on the stove; a white towel tied around her head gave her the appearance of a devotee tending a sacred ritual.

Steam turned the room into a humid furnace permeated by the rich and satisfying odor of the tomatoes cooking. On the long wooden table in the middle of the room stood a row of glass jars, gleaming and newly sealed. In a wide dishpan on the side of the stove, empty jars, sterilizing in boiling water, bounced lightly and struck each other with tinkles. Baskets, buckets, boxes of tomatoes spilled over from the kitchen to the porch outside. Nettie Sue and Lottie, impatient in juice-stained pinafores, were picking out the specked or rotting tomatoes. Dan stoked up the fire in the stove.

"I don't begrudge the devil his job." Dan wiped sweat from his reddened face with his right sleeve. There was a dark smear on his cheek. "If his climate is anything like this, I'm going to stick with the church."

"Daniel!" Mary Clayburn said.

"Eternity no joking thing," Delia pronounced solemnly.

"Now Delia, how do you know for sure?" Dan leaned against the wood-box, his eyes brightening with the prospect of a tease. "Like Cebo told me the other day when I asked him about Bryan and McKinley: 'You can't any more talk about what you don't know than you can come back from where you ain't been.' "

"Pshaw!" Delia slammed the lid on a kettle. "That Cebo got nothing but constipation of thought and diarrhea of words."

"Delia! Mind your talk!" Mary Clayburn was shocked and amused. Living on a farm, she had not been able to insulate her family from nature's functions. But she had learned thoroughly all the subjects which brought shame and embarrassment to polite people.

Jonathan was not listening to their talk. He stood in the door, feeling a rivulet of sweat run down his chest, aware of the lazy chickens outside and busy women and the robust voice of his younger brother; and he looked at the tomatoes still waiting on the porch to be handled and examined and graded by his sisters, and at the tomatoes already canned on the table—crimson ripe, tender in their sweet juice. He thought about the tomatoes already in the cellar: two long shelves of jars left from last year and the year before that. He thought about the tomatoes rotting in the fields.

He went to the table and picked up one of the quarts and nursed its warm smoothness in his hands. "Why couldn't we put some of these tomatoes in cans and sell them?" he asked.

His mother paused in her peeling and rested the knife in her right hand against the edge of the pan in her lap. With her left wrist she brushed a loose lock of hair back from her moist face.

Dan, at the hallway door, halted and looked at Jonathan.

"The South should feed the South," Jonathan said, half to himself, turning the jar and looking at the tomatoes.

"Your father believed that," Mary Clayburn nodded.

"I read it in some of his papers," Jonathan grinned. "But it's not just a theory, it's common sense."

"How?" Dan asked.

"Well, we have good land, we have plenty of rain, the right climate—why, our growing season gives us weeks longer than they have up north." Jonathan's thoughts tumbled forth as rapidly as the raw tomatoes Delia was dumping from Mary Clayburn's pan into one of the pots on the stove. He set down the glass jar, thumped on the table, then strode across the room to where Dan stood. "We'd have a head start every year. We'd be close to big markets. Don't you see—"

"Of course I see," his younger brother said. A ready smile lit up his plump face and bright brown eyes. Dan was quick, responsive.

"Well, you can count me out," Nettie Sue wiped her sticky hands across her apron, "I'd rather play the piano than fool around with this old mess."

"And we have the people," Dan said to Jonathan, "people to help us grow the food and put it up and eat it, too." They looked at one another and nodded. . . .

The idea took root.

Throughout the rest of that day and night Jonathan and Dan talked of nothing else. Doing the evening chores, at mealtime, sitting in the yard after dusk hoping for a random breeze, those two could not be diverted from their germinating ideas and swelling plans. During the following week and month the thought of turning their hand to a cannery dominated the family's talk. It shaped their work and channeled their play and brought them to decisions.

Mary Clayburn was the first key. Her approval came slowly but in the end completely, because she was convinced that this business could cement the unity of her family.

"Joshua is already away from us this year, running that sawmill and timber operation for Gideon Wakely," she said regretfully. "We can't stretch this farm enough to make it provide a living for five grown men. But our family must hold together as long as we can. Putting up a cannery might give us a way to work and thrive together."

The next morning Jonathan wrote to the state's agriculture department and to the state university for information about small canneries in the southeastern region and for advice about growing crops for commercial canning. That afternoon he and Cal rode over to Colonel Wakely's to talk with Josh.

"We'll want Josh in on this, too," Jonathan said.

"If he's so minded," Cal agreed.

They found Josh helping oversee a timber crew on a remote tract of the colonel's woodland. Amidst the uproar of crosscut saws and axes and drivers shouting and lashing at mules and oxen, Josh was harried, tired, and more than able to contain his enthusiasm for his brothers' idea.

"Look here," he said, propping one foot on a giant chestnut log freshly cut from the raw stump, "we've just begun furnishing tanbark to that new tannery in Churchill. They'll gobble up all we can provide. My pay here is sure as day. I'm of the opinion it's our lumber and minerals that will be the future of this region."

"For a while," Jonathan said. "But they won't last forever."

Josh looked at the heavy forest stretching on either side. "I'll take my risks on them lasting as long as I need them."

"There's risk in starting something like a cannery," Cal admitted.

Their mother was disappointed that Joshua did not come home at once. "Likely he feels under obligation to Colonel Wakely to stay the year out," she said.

The following week Jonathan announced, "I'm going to make a little trip up to Virginia and talk with a canner there. Alexander Montgomery at the bank told me this man's the only one he knows who's made a success of such a business in this part of the country."

"We'll run the farm while you're away," Cal said.

"Like we did when you were away at school," Whit reminded him.

Their mother nodded. "Joshua and Jonathan and Calvin in their turn, and you and Dan in your turn, Whitley." She looked at Jonathan, "Find out all you can in Virginia. And remember to make that fellow show you all the debit side of the business as well as the bright credit side."

"Don't worry, Mama. We don't want to go into anything without our eyes open."

"And our sleeves rolled up!" Dan clapped his brother Whitley on the shoulder. "If we make a go of this, it'll take sweat and gristle." He looked as though he welcomed the possibility. Whitley frowned. He did not like people pounding on him.

When Jonathan returned from Virginia, Robert Lee Buchanan came with him. He was a courtly man, quiet, set on achieving the purpose of his visit. He himself was leaving the canning business—a larger firm had purchased his small plant, which had only been a side-interest to his tobacco manufacturing—but he yearned to see industries home-born in the South.

"We'll never be free of Appomattox, sir," he told Jonathan during their long train ride, while flakes of soot from the laboring engine streaked their faces and stiff collars with soft coal smudges, "never free until we can run machinery as well as plows, until we can count money in our own banks as well as medals and memories."

"Mountain folks set considerable store by their independence," Jonathan said.

"Then, sir, remind them that independence has to be won in the marketplace no less than on the battlefield. We're a subject people down here, not so much because of Gettysburg and Vicksburg and the Wilderness, but because we've given our all to cotton."

Jonathan nodded, listening to the click of the wheels on the rails punctuating this man's emphatic words.

"Tobacco, timber," Mr. Buchanan continued, "a few other of the money crops we need most desperately—but mostly cotton, the raw product: all sent up north for someone else to make the manufacturing profit. Yes indeed, sir, I will do all in my power to help you and your family start your little cannery."

He walked over the fields with the boys—tall Jonathan, serious, quiet-spoken; and medium-sized Cal with his affable, shining round face; and Whitley, whose dark hair and heavy eyebrows framed the wide-set sockets of his intense keen eyes; and buoyant, tousled Dan. When Robert Lee Buchanan left, the Clayburn boys had a new kind of knowledge of crops, of where a packing shed might best be built, of machinery and cans, of details that would be trivial if forestalled but could compound into disaster if they went unanticipated.

Before Mr. Buchanan left, Jonathan took him to visit Colonel Wakely. The colonel was impressed by this man of substance and manners. "A gentlemen, Jonathan, a gentleman," he concluded as the visitor took leave of fragile, embarrassed Drusilla Wakely in the parlor. "You pay heed to what a gentleman like that says."

"He says for us to try our cannery," Jonathan spoke carefully. "Seems we've got the land, the labor, the seasons, the crops—everything but capital, right now."

"That so?" The colonel glanced back to the genuine Virginia gentleman releasing Drusilla's bony bit of hand. "Money's scarce right now, but I might help you out on capital, boy. For Elisha's sake I might give you a chance to prove yourself."

Jonathan flushed. "That's a big offer, Colonel Wakely. We couldn't make any guarantees—except to do our best." He wondered about the truth of the colonel's reputation for being a hard, grasping man.

"That might be enough." Wakely turned expansively to Mr. Buchanan. "Jonathan and I have just concluded a little business alliance. I'm going to help out these Clayburn boys, help them put some of your knowledge and advice into practice. I'll lend them financial support."

"I congratulate you, sir. You are a patriot and a businessman.

You've made a wise decision." Robert Lee Buchanan extended his hand.

Jonathan later told his brothers: "The colonel worked himself into a promise, then had no way to get out of the corner but jump. He mentioned several thousand dollars for us. He can't back out now, even if he wants to."

Jonathan's suspicions that the colonel might want to were justified. Colonel Wakely was attacked by second thoughts. In mid-August Joshua came home for two rainy days while work on cutting and stripping the chestnut bark was delayed, and he told Jonathan that Colonel Wakely had said launching off on such a big venture as a cannery might be foolhardy. The boys should weigh their position carefully. The colonel had pressed Joshua hard: where would the boys get the rest of the capital for machinery and labor and raw materials? How could they be sure of enough crops to fill their cans? Once packed, where and how would they sell their product? For his part, the colonel felt it a mighty heavy gamble.

"Tell him," Jonathan said to Josh, "that if he backs out of his pledge to put up some capital for us, a pledge made to us in his home, we'll have no out but to write Mr. Buchanan up in Virginia and cancel our order for his soldering irons and cooking vats. Buchanan offered to let us have them at a big discount."

"Colonel Wakely wouldn't like to go back on his word to Mr. Buchanan," Josh said.

"I know," Jonathan said.

Joshua looked at him quickly, then nodded.

Their conversation took place as the two brothers rode into Churchill in the family's best buggy. The rain had slackened and the freshly roached team of grays was stepping briskly. After a silence, Jonathan spoke.

"I just wore my middling-best clothes today." Jonathan surveyed his older brother's high collar and dark suit. "You're all turned out in your Sunday finest."

Josh blushed and looked straight ahead.

"Reckon I'll have to load up our supplies at Montgomery's while you meet that little teacher."

"Pshaw, Jonathan, she may have the worst case of the uglies this side the Atlantic Ocean."

"Miss Nora Stull Buchanan of Richmond: that doesn't sound like the uglies to me."

Jonathan himself had looked forward to meeting the niece of the man who had been so helpful about their new enterprise. When Mary Clayburn had told Robert Lee Buchanan of her search for a schoolteacher to live at their home and teach her little girls, as her sons had been taught before they went away to college by a scholarly old uncle of hers who had since died of lung-fever, Mr. Buchanan had mentioned his niece, a cultured girl recently graduated in fine arts from a small women's institute. Nora Stull, as he called her, hoped to teach, he said, but in cultivated, pleasant surroundings, not in a common public situation. After correspondence it was agreed that she would spend a season tutoring in the Clayburn home, and if all went agreeably further arrangements could be made. Now Jonathan wondered if it were really the weather that had brought Josh home for this interval.

When the train came into Churchill, Jonathan was helping Randall Montgomery gather and load a long list of household and farm supplies: a new plow point, coffee beans, a bolt of bed-ticking for fresh featherbeds, turpentine, lamp chimneys, salt, and six cans of salmon. It was Josh, his big hands (calloused and stained from working in the tanbark) hanging a bit too far below the sleeves of his coat, his eyes and smile tentative and shy, who met the pert, well-dressed girl as she stepped confidently off the train.

Nora Stull Buchanan waited until the porter wiped his cloth along the brass rail of the exit and adjusted his square yellow stepping-stool for her; then she put her hand in his, reached a tiny foot down until the hand-crocheted trim of her petticoat showed, and finally made a small, graceful leap to the ground. She bestowed a smile on the porter, disengaged her hand, and rearranged the froth of a hat perched atop her brown hair.

"Miss Buchanan?" Josh said.

She bobbed her head. The little hat tilted. "Nora Stull Buchanan," she said. "You would be—" She studied him a moment, one gloved finger on her chin. "Joshua."

He reddened.

"And that's Jonathan." She looked at his brother crossing the street, coming up to them.

"How do you know so much about us?" Joshua asked.

"Goodness, I don't know 'so much,' " Nora Stull Buchanan said, "only your names. My uncle told me how each one of you looked."

"Well, we're all going to look wet if we don't hustle you and your baggage into the buggy before that black cloud yonder opens up," Jonathan said as he hurried within earshot.

On the drive home, Nora Buchanan securely protected between them, Joshua found more and more to say. Jonathan had not suspected his older brother even knew so many words. When Nora remarked on the blueness and tallness of the distant mountains, Joshua launched into a list of names and altitudes: "We've got plenty above six thousand feet. Big Balsam, Clingman's Dome, Old Grindstone."

When Nora noticed the imposing Montgomery house at the edge of town and, farther on, the old Ransom farm, Joshua acquainted her with their histories. Jonathan had never heard his older brother talk so readily. They were almost home before Jonathan had a proper opportunity to ask Nora Buchanan about her uncle.

"Uncle Robert Lee's just fine," she said. "And he sent you a message."

"Anything he says is gospel to Jonathan," Josh said.

"But I should charge you postage fee!" she tipped her head to one side.

"We'll repay you," Josh said eagerly, then stumbled, "with something—something really fine."

"No," she clasped her white-clad hands together. "I'll bring your message in exchange for this nice buggy ride."

"What did Mr. Buchanan say?" Jonathan asked.

"He sent word: 'If possible, begin your business with enough capital to last through two seasons. One year isn't sufficient test for a cannery.' Those were his very words."

"That's right," Jonathan said, "but I don't know where we'd find more capital."

"You're not in the canning adventure." Nora turned full-face to Joshua.

"Not right now," he said. "Right now I'm in lumber. It's a thriving business—"

Jonathan considered Mr. Buchanan's message. What could he do about it? When he had gone to the bank, Alexander Montgomery had remarked on his youth and inexperience. His uncle Whit Ransom had not even let him introduce the subject. "All the Ransom cash is tied up in livestock and land. A curse on it all, I say. Millstones worrying me to my grave." Jonathan had no other sources of support at the moment.

His friend's advice gnawed at him—that evening, the next day, all the while that the rest of the family spent welcoming Nora Buchanan, arranging her room (upstairs beside the two little girls'), and planning her schedule (classes all morning to just after noon, the rest of the day and evening free to be part of the family, crochet, read, walk, do as she wished).

Before he went back to Colonel Wakely's and the timber, Joshua took his three oldest brothers to one side. "I'd count it a favor, while I'm away," his face and voice were embarrassed, but he pushed on, "if none of you would pay attention to—her."

"To who?" Cal asked innocently. "Her? Who's he talking about, Jonathan?"

"You know who," Josh said. "Miss Buchanan."

"Oh!" A great light dawned in Cal's face. "Miss Nora Stull etcetera, etcetera."

"Well now, Josh," Whit spoke earnestly, "I don't see how we can just pay no attention at all to her. Say we're at the table and she asks for the salt, should we ignore her—"

"You know what I mean," Josh said desperately.

Jonathan agreed. "Why yes, Josh. We know what you mean." And the way he said it was devastating to Josh's tranquility.

Thereafter, however, they followed Josh's request studiously. And they noticed that he came home from Colonel Wakely's more often than he had before.

Later in the fall, when the maples were flushing red and gold in the woods, after Whitley and Daniel had gone off to the university (reluctant to leave the excitement of plans for the cannery that multiplied each day—plans for setting up a sawmill to saw the Clayburns' own lumber for a canning shed, plans for securing seeds and crops and machines and cans), Jonathan, Calvin, their mother, and Colonel

Wakely met in the Churchill office of lawyer Littlepage distant cousin of Mary Clayburn's. There they signed a of partnership to become effective January 1, 1901, in an months.

The capital was meager: all of the savings in Mary bank account, twelve hundred dollars; a matching twelve from Colonel Wakely; and from Jonathan and Calvin, six hundred dollars apiece: earnings of recent crops, of all their labors, scraped together bit by bit. The final fifty dollars to make their six hundred each had come from the sale of a fine little cow Jonathan had raised from a calf. Thoroughbreds were rare on mountain or lowland farms in the region, and this dainty-hoofed Jersey had been their pride. "We can't have everything," Jonathan told Cal, "successful cannery and rich man's herd too. Something gained, something lost." So they scratched the money together like grabbling small new potatoes in the spring.

In their agreement, Jonathan and Calvin pledged to manage the company during this first year. Their salary would be whatever portion of the new profits (if there were any profits) they all should agree on at the end of the year. With thirty-six hundred dollars in cash, their land, and themselves, Clayburn Brothers Company was born.

That night, after they had returned home and checked to make certain Edom Metcalf and Cebo had finished the chores, after supper, Jonathan walked out by himself. It had been a momentous day.

The moon was risen full and dazzling over the dark bulk of Grindstone Mountain in the distance. Its light washed old familiar landmarks of rail fence, gnarled trees, worn paths, with mysterious new dimensions of highlight and shadow. The strangeness reflected Jonathan's mood of exultation laced with apprehension.

At last they were under way, he and his family. From this farm they could build something for all of them, and for the community, too, something that might reach out over the state, something that could, if Mr. Robert Lee Buchanan were right, move across the whole region. What better work, or more permanent, than to preserve good food, provide for people's hunger, and earn a living at the same time? This combination of practicality and idealism was deeply satisfying.

Where the leaves hung thick on the trees, patches of darkness covered the ground. It was as though Jonathan, walking under the alternating lightness and blackness, moved under some live jungle cover—the sinuous skin of splattered leopard or tiger or those other exotic beasts seen only in geographies and circuses. The night was like other full-moon nights, and yet unlike. This time there was a stillness, a brilliance. . . .

He came to the lower pasture, open and unshaded, and there was only the light, moonlight everywhere, and the immense disk of the moon in a limitless sky.

Loneliness squeezed his chest to tightness, his mouth dry, but it was no more unbearable than the loneliness that had driven him out here away from a familiar shelter, the loneliness of loving and leading his family. Here was both isolation and largeness, inevitable companions under a moon drenching the earth in light as remote and irreversible as time.

The quiet excitement that he had felt that afternoon, as he was driving his mother and Cal and himself home in the surrey, lingered. ("Think about it, Jonathan," his brother had said, "we're businessmen now, Clayburn Brothers Company, legal, with a name and debts and everything!" And his mother had said, "I hope we're doing the right thing.") There was the responsibility of the documents in his breast pocket and the recollection of Colonel Wakely's hard gaze fixed upon him as he thought of what Mr. Buchanan had said about the likelihood of an enterprise's first-year failure. But this one year was all they had. There would be no second chances. If there were success, it would be for his whole family; if failure, it would be his alone.

He glimpsed a motion beside the rail fence along the south side of the pasture. He paused, waited. But there seemed to be nothing. He walked on again. This time the movement was unmistakable. On the other side of that weatherbeaten zigzagging fence, something was either following him or watching him. He turned and walked directly toward the spot. There was no way to conceal or protect himself.

The girl on the other side of the fence did not try either. As Jonathan approached, she stood up, so clear and startling that he sucked in his breath sharply. Only a few feet apart, they paused, hesitated, looked at one another.

Then the girl broke the silence. Her laughter was free and full and easy as wind. "Anybody watching would think we're two varmints—fox or some such—run upon each other out here in the pasture."

"Oh?" His voice was stiff and cold compared to hers. He did not accept being called a varmint.

"Foxes are best. I've spied on them at feeding and hunting and play—and outsmarting old Whit Ransom's hounds. They're dainty as dancers. When they come upon a stranger they look just like we did, heads thrown up, sniffing, asking, taking, or leaving." Quickly, before he knew what she was about, the girl had swung herself over the fence and stood beside him.

Jonathan was surprised that anyone could seem at once so tall and so small. Standing there in the moonlight she reminded him of a silver birch he had seen in the woods not long ago—full-grown yet slim and lithe and tender—surrounded by massive oaks and sprawling beech and an old fat pine, but holding its own space of ground and sky easily, surely.

"You surprised me" he said, not knowing how else to respond to her talk of foxes and dancers.

"That's because you thought you were alone," she said. "Daddy says I'm always surprising people."

"You are?" The girl left him tongue-tied. It was not only her odd intimate way of talking but the way she looked—that long wheat-colored hair falling around her shoulders in the moonlight, framing the intense radiance of her thin face.

Her conversation doubled back like a fox's trail. "It seems like you're alone out here." She made a motion which involved arms, shoulders, total body, indicating the surrounding silent landscape. "But I found out a long time ago you're not alone. There's all sorts of little creatures, and big too, hiding, nesting, peeking, running, searching—everywhere."

"Why yes, I guess so," Jonathan said.

Suddenly she whirled and leaned over the fence behind her. Carefully shifting the loose top rail, she picked up something clinging there. When she held out her hand to Jonathan, a sprightly katydid perched in the palm, its beady eyes, gauzy wings, busy legs all still. "See?"

She was a strange girl, all right. She seemed in some ways younger than Nettie Sue or Lottie, yet she must be at least eighteen, six or eight years older than his little sisters. "I guess I hadn't thought about the bugs," Jonathan said.

She looked up at him. The expression on her face was hurt, closed. He realized that he had seen her before. Somewhere, not too many years ago, he had seen that same puzzled watchfulness, but he could not remember where. She was putting the insect back on its bit of wood.

"It's unusual," he began lamely.

"No," she turned around quickly—he tried to recall when and where he had encountered this unpredictable girl before—"it's not one bit unusual. That's why I showed it to you. Creatures like that —smaller, bigger, prettier, uglier—all over this place, everywhere."

She left him nothing to answer. He paused. "I'm Jonathan Clayburn." It seemed as sensible as anything else he might say.

Now she was laughing again. "Did you think I disremembered who you were? Oh, I see," she leaned back against the fence, "it's you who forgot. I'm Laura Rathbone."

"Janus Rathbone's girl." He could have given himself a thrashing. "The day he went up on the mountain with me, when Papa was killed—"

"No, a week before. You came to our house to ask him about going."

"But you were a little girl."

"Well, you weren't near as old then as you are now."

They had nothing more to say for a moment.

"Daddy might begin to fret if I stay away the plumb night—" She smiled.

"Which way do you go?"

"Down beyond this pasture, through your lower woods, the way leads right to our place. Lots prettier than the big road."

"I'll walk back a piece with you—"

But she was already across the fence, moving away. "I'm proud I saw you, Jonathan Clayburn."

"Wait! Laura—"

"Be careful the way you go walking out in that lonesome moonlight—"

She was running. He had not even noticed what she wore but now in the distance it looked soft and light, blending with her long hair which lifted softly and fell, following the rhythm of her running, up and down over her shoulders. It had not occurred to him to ask her why she was out alone in the night, wandering. As he walked back home he wondered why he had not asked, except that at the time it had seemed perfectly natural that she should be there.

Laura Rathbone. He spoke the name aloud. An idea came to him. Clayburn Brothers needed a man who could help build the canning shed, set up machinery, put the little factory to running; a man of judgment and common sense. Jonathan and Calvin's first job would be to find growers, in addition to their own family, for the tomatoes they would need. Then they would have to find equipment and supplies. Meanwhile someone would be needed to stay on the job at the building of the plant. Why hadn't he thought of Janus Rathbone before? Janus had already demonstrated his loyalty to their family. He was held in respect in Churchill and throughout the county far out of proportion to his land and holdings. He was a man of general knowledge, practicality, ready wit. Jonathan grinned, remembering the pepper in the bag of paper play-money the Dorseys stole from Janus that day at Wolf Pen Gap. Somewhere, a long while ago, someone had said that Rathbone had no wife, only a girl-child, and that to see the two of them together was to know that the twig didn't fall far from the tree. Janus Rathbone, if he would come to work for them, would be a balance of strength and useful knowledge.

Jonathan walked home briskly. After all, there had been purpose in his evening's wandering that had started so aimlessly. Nothing satisfied his Clayburn instinct more than discovering a profit where none had been foreseen. His mother must have known something that he could not yet say he knew for certain when she spoke about the ways of the Lord, mysterious yet rounded with pattern, aiming toward good. Right now, it was all too remote for him. He would meditate on it in the future, when he had more time, more understanding.

Janus Rathbone became part of Clayburn Brothers Company and Laura Rathbone became part of the family's life.

"Why not set up that sawmill right here close by where your factory will be?" Janus Rathbone said to Jonathan and Calvin the first week they discussed their plans. The three of them, along with Cebo, were standing beside Old Mill Creek, which wound through the level upland, second-growth woods that Mr. Buchanan had suggested as a location for their plant. The autumn sun shone benignly warm on the clumps of heavy-podded sumac in the open spaces, on the swift stream, on the fading bronze and russet foliage of the woods, and on the four varied men who stood giving careful attention to the site.

"We had thought about using the timber just above the river bottoms," Cal replied. "It's bigger, would saw out the boards quicker."

Janus nodded. "That's right. But you'll be having to clear this place anyway. Why not use these trees and save these fine ones down nearer the river for something better than a packing shed?"

"That's good sense," Cal agreed.

"Whatever you lose in time taken to saw the smaller trees up here," Janus went on, "you'll win back by not having to haul the lumber all that distance."

Jonathan's instinct about Janus Rathbone's worth to them was proved throughout the autumn and winter and spring of cutting, sawing, building, and finally equipping the crude shed which would be their factory that summer.

While they worked, using Edom Metcalf when the farm could spare him, sometimes hiring Orvil Gosnell who came by one morning in the winter and asked if he could work for day-wages whenever the weather was open, the life at their home stretched and flourished, too.

The teacher, Nora Stull Buchanan, had won Nettie Sue's and Lottie's allegiance that first day when she unpacked her horsehair trunk and showed them some of the newest dresses and muffs and hats from Richmond; she was turning the girls into regular scholars—or so their brother Daniel teased. In addition, thin-lipped, red-haired Rilla Bryant—who had become, somewhere back along the endless line of generations, "Cousin Rilla"—arrived to spend a weekend and spent the next few years. The dress she was to help Mary Clayburn make (Cousin Rilla was a seamstress who paid her way through a hard world by using a sharp needle) turned out to be more difficult than anticipated. And when its tucks and pleats and buttonholes were finished, Cousin Rilla offered to make the little girls new pinafores. Then there was a uniform for Delia; its model had appeared in an English household journal. Then the nimble-fingered, nimble-witted woman turned to shirts and work clothes for the boys. She was a person who knew how to be useful and undemanding, female company for Mary Clayburn, and acceptable to preoccupied menfolk.

In addition, there was Brother Luther Pryor who came once a month to preach at the simple white church and spend a long weekend at the Clayburns'. His visits were as regular and unquestioned as the seasons.

In their work, school, farm, church, home, the Clayburns' public and private life merged, rich and inseparable. In their parlor Brother Pryor held the Saturday night prayer meeting which both unkempt Edom Metcalf and strutting Colonel Wakely attended. In the little storeroom off the kitchen, which had been converted to a classroom over the years, Nora Buchanan taught spelling and grammar and arithmetic and penmanship and polite literature. At first there were only Nettie Sue and Lottie. Then Mary Clayburn talked with Janus Rathbone one day and discovered that his daughter had been to school for only the few three-month periods that Mrs. Clayburn's uncle had taught long ago in the church's Sunday School room.

"But that isn't enough," Mary Clayburn said. "She must come and have schooling with my girls."

"Now that's thoughty of you, Mrs. Clayburn."

"She could ride over with you each morning when you come to work with the boys—"

Janus Rathbone gave a little smile. "Walking is nothing to Laura."

But Mary Clayburn was caught up in her own plans. "And she can stay each day with us. That Nora Buchanan is a quick teacher—"

"And my Laura is a quick learner."

"I'm sure she is. Let's be thankful we've found a way for her to put that mind to use. She won't be—well, embarrassed—or self-conscious, will she, being older than Nettie Sue and Lottie?"

Janus smiled again and shook his head.

She was magnificently unselfconscious. When Laura Rathbone arrived at the Clayburns' the following Monday morning and saw Nora Stull Buchanan she exclaimed, "Now aren't you the prettiest little thing since a March pink?" And she flung her arms around Mrs. Clayburn's shoulders. "It's tonic to see you again," she said. "I'll never forget the days you used to come over to your uncle's school, Mrs. Clayburn, and bring Whit and Dan and the rest of us there some special treat." Then she placed herself squarely in front of Delia and looked into the deep brown eyes of the older woman's wrinkled face.

"Here you are, no bigger than a piece of soap after a hard day's wash. One day when I was seven or eight years old, you helped me put some young doves back in their nest." She caught Delia's hand and squeezed it.

And to the little girls, flinging off her thin cloak, "Hello, schoolmates. London bridge is falling down—" She had to stoop to catch their hands and make an arch while she danced with them. Her hair spilled long and shining over her face, down the waist of the oatmeal-colored homespun dress she wore.

And Nora Buchanan laughed with surprise; Mary Clayburn smiled in pleasure; Delia clucked her tongue and chuckled softly; the children clapped with excitement.

The work of setting up the sawmill, cutting the trees, piling logs and then the lumber, went forward steadily. There were no well-defined working hours, only sunrise to sunset with little time at home except during bad weather. In addition to the usual autumn chores of gathering fodder and apples, turning the river bottoms, and butchering hogs for winter meat, there were the numerous unfamiliar arrangements to make for setting up the cannery itself.

At his father's desk, Jonathan wrote careful orders to wholesale offices in Jackson City, fifty miles downriver, for solder and soldering irons (Mr. Buchanan had not sent enough), peeling knives, kettles. The American Can Company of Baltimore seemed to him as remote and impressive as the United States Treasury, but he pressed them for consideration. "Inform us as to the best possible price you can make a small country concern in the South, a business that will be trying its legs for the first time this summer but might become a going concern, with considerable trade to give eventually to some can manufacturer—that is, if we can stand up to this year's pressure," he wrote in one breathless sentence. The company shaved another ten cents on the hundred from the "rock-bottom wholesale price" they had quoted earlier, and Jonathan ordered eight thousand cans.

After Janus Rathbone, working at the mill, sawed out building boards for the packing shed, Jonathan pressed Cebo into use in making tomato crates from the narrow lengths of lumber that were left over. Proud to become a part of the new project, Cebo sat on a rough plank stretched between two saw-horses, sawing the thin boards, nailing them together, until suddenly there was a square new crate, then a growing stack of them.

Shad Kendrick helped Janus and Cebo. Shad was a neighbor farmer's son with a flat ruddy face, wide blue eyes, slow and deliberate movements, and quiet integrity. The possibility that he would work anywhere but on his father's farm had never occurred to the Clayburns and they were astonished and pleased when he came and offered, not to work for them but to "help them out."

Before the buildings or crates or cans, however, came the tomatoes. "There's no way we can grow all we need on this farm," Cal said.

"Not if we're to have any land left over for corn and wheat and hay," Jonathan agreed, "and we don't want to go plumb out of livestock."

Cal smiled. "Not unless we want to live on tomatoes next winter."

"Besides," Jonathan said slowly, "it might be a good thing to get farmers around here into the way of growing something besides corn and tobacco. Maybe they'll tie into our company."

But the farmers of Churchill and the surrounding county were wedded to the idea of grain and livestock and not eager to abandon old ways. During late winter, Jonathan and Calvin rode over the country roads—through cold and freeze and thaw—searching for men who would agree to put a field out to tomatoes in the coming summer.

"They listen close enough," Jonathan said one day to Janus Rathbone when he had come back by the sawmill, "but then they shake their heads. Or if they do agree to think it over, inside two or three days they've changed their minds."

"Too risky for them maybe," Orvil Gosnell muttered, lifting a fresh plank to the stack in the clearing.

Jonathan was surprised. "No riskier than corn—and not as hard on the land," he answered. But he rode home more discouraged than he had ever been since the partnership was formed.

He met Laura on the porch. She was going down the back steps with one arm full of books as he came up from the barn where he had fed and rubbed down his horse. It had been a long while since he had come home before dark.

Ever since that night in the pasture Jonathan had eagerly anticipated chance encounters with Laura, but he had avoided talking with her alone. Conversation with Laura was like going through a

March day. From one hour to the next you never knew what the weather would be—fair or stormy, up or down. Yet he'd admit he liked to hear her, liked to be part of the excitement of her voice, the enthusiasm of her awkward-graceful gestures.

"Your daddy will be coming along directly," Jonathan said.

"No need for me to wait. I'll go on home and kindle up the fire. Besides, I like to walk through the woods and over and under and around all the fences." It was a chilly gray day but she wore only a light coat, and even that unbuttoned and loose over her white shirt-waist and dark skirt. "I'll run lots of the way," she added.

Her smile unsettled him. "Are you liking the school work?" he asked.

Her eyes shone. "Liking? That's a whittled-down word! All the things I'm learning—" She held the books for him to see, then shrugged and smiled at him as if abundance left her speechless.

"Stay till your daddy comes," he said. "Maybe you could help me think up a label for our cans. You know, until Christmastime we'd not even given a thought about the need for labels. When the boys were home, Dan asked me what we were going to call our canned goods."

"Yes," she nodded eagerly, "you ought to have a—a remembering name on those cans you mean to sell." He smiled at her choice of words but sobered hastily at her next question. "Have you found folks to grow the tomatoes for you?"

"Nobody except ourselves, yet." Janus must have told her of their difficulties. It was odd to think of a man talking over business affairs with his daughter. But then Laura was different. Jonathan admitted that. "No," he said, "we may not have enough tomatoes to get us through this first year. Not unless we can get more farmers to agree to grow an acre or two apiece for us."

She had come down the steps and they walked out across the yard under the brown-leafed oaks. "You're wanting them to give their word they'll grow tomatoes and let you have them, come canning time?"

"We have to know what we can expect. We'll furnish plants free and pay a fair price per crate delivered at our factory."

"I don't know about such things," she said, scattering a cluster of leaves with the toe of her shoe, "but I was wondering,." She did not look at him but at the leaves through which they walked. "Could you give them something to expect—for certain—too?"

Jonathan stopped and looked at her. "What do you mean?"

"I don't know exactly." She gazed out under the trees and to the pasture and fields beyond. "But before they put out all those tomatoes on some of their old cropland, or before they set in to bull-tongue out patches of new ground," she paused and shrugged, "well, could it be likely they'd want to know what they'd be getting, too?" She spoke so slowly she might have been one of the farmers wrenching roots and rocks out of newly cleared land.

"Maybe."

"Anything happen those tomatoes weren't used," she rushed on, speaking more naturally now, "lots of folks would have a considerable waste on their hands. Couldn't even feed them to the hogs."

Jonathan felt that her talk of these matters, crops and hogs and such, was somehow not appropriate, yet inwardly he acknowledged the sense of what she was saying. "Sign a contract, you mean?" he asked her.

She began to walk again, still not looking at him. "Oh, I don't know about contracts. I just know folks have to think about what-all might go wrong in such a chancy thing—"

"But sometimes there's need to risk—"

"Oh, I'm not scared by chancy things myself," she looked directly at him now. "I was talking about most folks."

As she left him, hurrying down the slope, she turned and called, "I almost forgot. Tell Miss Buchanan I might be late tomorrow morning, if my little Jersey brings her calf tonight."

Nora Stull Buchanan blushed when Jonathan gave her the message at supper. Nothing could have spoken more clearly of the difference between Laura and Nora. Obviously Josh, who had come home for this evening, buoyed up by prospects he had for making a good nest-egg of money from Colonel Wakely's timber, liked Nora's blush.

A little later, when Jonathan raised the question of drawing up agreements with the farmers, he did not mention Laura Rathbone. Her suggestion had been so casual he had accepted it as his own, a gift.

After the family finished eating and the dishes were cleared away, with Cousin Rilla Bryant helping the girls in their quick disposal, they remained around the long table covered by its white linen cloth. They hulled chestnuts and peeled apples brought from the cellar in a big wooden bowl. The hickory-log fire burning to red-hot coals in the wide fireplace made the room cozy and cheerful. Now the family could relax, sort out happenings of the day just past, and plan the day ahead. Mary Clayburn manipulated five steel needles to round the heel on a pair of heavy gray work socks she was knitting. Cousin Rilla was basting the hem of a dress. Josh sat near Nora and gave her the choicest tidbits of the nuts he cracked.

Cal spoke uncertainly about Jonathan's proposal to give contracts to the farmers. Mary Clayburn said nothing. The little tattoo of her needles clicked steadily.

"I know I'm not a legal part of your deciding—" Josh began.

"You're a part of the family," Jonathan said. "That's enough." He peeled a Winterjohn apple, slowly, carefully.

"Well, for what it's worth, my idea would be to keep things like they are. Contracts and such only serve to stir up trouble."

"Now Josh," Cal looked at his brother with a wide-open gaze, "I'd think you were a man in favor of contracts. Especially right now. All kinds of contracts." His gaze shifted artlessly to Nora Buchanan.

The blood rose in Josh's face. "See here, Cal—" he stammered. "Look here—"

The peel from Jonathan's apple was a thin curl. His sisters sitting beside him watched with fascination as it grew longer and longer. "Can I have it, Jonathan?" Nettie Sue whispered.

He nodded, then said to the others, "I can't see where it would hurt to give a fellow extra assurance if he wanted it toward growing his tomatoes."

"Maybe so," Cal said, without conviction.

"It'll mean extra work, drawing up all those agreements," Josh was not convinced. "I don't know, seems like there's no trust when everything has to be set down in writing."

"Depends on how you look at it, I guess," Jonathan said. The sharp blade of his pocketknife was reaching the bottom of the Winterjohn. The peeling separated from the apple was so thin that the steel was visible beneath the transparency.

"What do you think, Mama?" Josh asked.

Mary Clayburn rested the unfinished sock and its framework of

needles on the ball of yarn in her lap. "We'll be obligated either way
—by our word, whether it's spoken or written."

"And since we're making about as little headway now as it would
be possible to make and just stand still," Jonathan said, "maybe we'd
better give up on the spoken and try the written word."

Josh watched the slow turn of the knife. After a pause he said,
"Well, maybe."

The peeling fell from Jonathan's apple. Nettie Sue picked it up
and cradled it in her hand carefully as an eggshell. "Give it to Nora,
Nettie Sue," Cal suggested. "Let's see if she's got a sweetheart."

"Yes—please!" Lottie clapped her hands, and even Cousin Rilla
laid her sewing aside.

Nora accepted the apple peeling. She stood up from the table and
twirled around before the fireplace. She was petite and lacy and glow-
ing as a rosy valentine in the firelight. The peeling arched over her left
shoulder and broke in two as it plopped to the floor. They crowded
around to look. "What letter does it say?"

"I can't make out anything—"

"Why, there's a J plain as a wart on your nose."

"Where?"

Cal showed them, tracing the more-or-less straight line with the
more-or-less curve at the bottom.

"It is! It is!" Nettie Sue said.

"Well," Nora tilted her head and examined the apple peeling, "it
might be."

"Course, we don't know what that means," Cal went on. "Lots
of folks' names begin with J. Two right here in this room."

The others obviously had thought of only one.

"A whole bunch of foolishness," Josh said. "Besides, it should
have gone over Nora's right shoulder, to be true prophecy—"

"My, you were watching sharp, weren't you, Josh?" Cal said.

"Well, we'll notice tomorrow morning," Jonathan said, "if we
spend all night here on foolishness—"

Cal assumed hurt surprise. "You think true love is foolishness,
Jonathan?" He clucked his tongue in reprimand.

"Calvin Clayburn," his mother warned, "you curb that teasing."

Jonathan stretched and walked toward the door to the hallway.

"When I come across true love," he said, "don't reckon I'll need any apple hull to tell me who it is."

Mary Clayburn smiled. She knitted a final round on Joshua's new socks.

During the following month Jonathan and Cal found their luck improved in signing up farmer-growers. Shad Kendrick's father was the first. He agreed to cultivate three acres in tomatoes. Eventually, by early spring, they had sixty-three acres contracted in addition to their own. They had promised to pay sixteen and a half cents for each satisfactory bushel brought to the cannery. That last half-cent was hard won. Cal had been impatient and said, when Shad Kendrick's father held out for seventeen cents and Jonathan insisted sixteen cents was all the company could pay, "Let's give them seventeen cents and go broke."

"No," Jonathan said. "Mr. Kendrick here can come out with some profit at sixteen cents. With our capital for this year eaten up by the sawmill and building everything from the ground up, along with the canning itself and our uncertainty about a market once we do have a product—" He shook his head. "We can't go in deeper than sixteen cents, Mr. Kendrick."

After a while the old man said, "Sixteen and a half cents." And they shook hands and signed on that.

By the time Whitley and Dan came home from college in mid-May, the little plant in the Old Mill Field was almost finished: raw rough lumber formed a shake-roof shed with three open sides, sitting beside the winding stream. Orvil Gosnell and Cebo were at work now building boxes in which to ship the cans once they were filled with food. Janus Rathbone and Shad Kendrick were making ready to set up the boiler.

"Give Dan time to shed those college clothes and all those big new words," Cal said to Janus and Shad, "and he'll be out here to help you on that machinery."

Dan was already looking at the boiler and the places being readied for the big kettles. "You know, Shad," he was saying to his friend who had greeted him with a hearty handshake, "don't you think we should set these at the opposite side, considering that most of our hard winds come from the west and at that end the smoke and steam would be carried off?"

Kendrick studied the lay of the land. "You're plumb right, Dan."

"I'll be here tomorrow morning," Dan strode across the opening, "itching to get my hands greasy." His good humor was contagious. Even Jonathan seemed to relax a bit.

When they stood above the broad upland field and looked at the long rows of spindly tomato plants taking root there, Cal said to the younger brothers, "You two sure timed it right. Got home just the day after that back-breaking job of setting plants was finished!"

"Use your head and save your back." Whitley said.

"Those plants look thrifty," Dan encouraged.

"They'd better," Cal's voice was unnaturally serious. "What they manage to produce, along with those sixty-three acres under contract, decides whether we're canners or wild goose chasers."

And the four of them stood quietly, bound by the enormity of their undertaking.

"Canners up in New Jersey, Indiana, all around, they're mighty close-mouthed about the kinds of tomatoes they plant, their formula for cooking, that kind of information," Jonathan told his brothers.

"Damn Yankees," Cal added.

"However, Mr. Buchanan did some investigating for us." Jonathan went on. "We think we've got the best seed on the market to make bright, tough-skinned, flavorsome tomatoes."

Dan kicked a clod of dirt. "Can't have the best without the strongest roots."

"That's right."

"Jonathan," Dan said abruptly, as though Cal and Whit were not there, "I'm not going back to Jackson U. next fall."

Jonathan was taken by surprise. "Look here, Dan—"

"No. I've made up my mind."

"But you're just in your second year. You have to finish."

"I'm going up to Boston. I've already written the Massachusetts Institute of Technology," Dan grinned. "I'd kind of like to see what one of those Yankee schools has to offer."

"So that's it!" Jonathan nodded.

"Little brother's reaching mighty high," Cal said. " 'Simmons on the lower limb just as sweet as those that shine at the top."

"It's not persimmons I'm after," Dan retorted.

Cal grew sober. "No. You'll be a real help to us if you can

graduate from a place like MIT—if we keep this business running that long."

"I haven't mentioned anything about it to Mama."

"If it's best for you, she'll want you to do it." Jonathan said.

"It'll cost more money."

"Come autumn, we'll all be a lot better—or worse off than we are now. Either way, you go to MIT." Jonathan smiled. There were new lines, dark circles under his eyes.

That night Dan spoke about Jonathan to his mother. "Jonathan's working too hard," she agreed. "I worry about him but I don't know what to do."

"I'll try to lighten his load all I can," Dan said.

Unexpected problems brought delays. Jonathan improvised and labored and planned each day the night before. There was one day he could not have planned, however.

It was a Wednesday and Colonel Wakely brought Joshua home in the middle of the day. Joshua lay pale and motionless in the big rubber-tired buggy and as she saw him Mary Clayburn cried out with fear and ran to him. "Joshua!"

"Now don't get excited, Mary," Colonel Wakely said as he climbed down from the seat. "The boy's going to be all right."

"What's wrong? What happened?"

"Let's get him carried into the house, Mary."

"The men are all down at the factory."

"Factory!" Colonel Wakely snorted.

"Delia! Cousin Rilla! Come quick!"

They made an odd assortment—the small cook whose thin arms concealed surprising strength, the startled seamstress, limping Mary Clayburn, and the colonel—awkwardly carrying Josh indoors to his bedroom, pulling off his heavy shoes, laying him on the wide walnut bed. Delia brushed up the bits of sawdust which had fallen from his shoes and socks.

"It was on his hand, Mary," Colonel Wakely explained, puffing from exertion. "Best place it could have struck—"

"What, Gideon Wakely? What?" she demanded.

"The snake. Coiled under a pile of tanbark Josh was helping load this morning. A mean-looking copperhead."

"Copperhead?" Cousin Rilla gave a small shriek.

"Lord save us," Delia murmured, and hid her head in her apron.

Mary Clayburn's hands covered her pale face as Cousin Rilla put a comforting arm around her shoulder.

"We've treated him already," Colonel Wakely hurried on. "One of the men cut the bite immediately, criss-cross so it could bleed, carry off the poison—"

Mary Clayburn picked up her son's swelling hand and arm swathed in white muslin, held it gently, laid it back on the sheet. Josh stirred slightly, opened his eyes. "Mama, Colonel Wakely—what are you all doing?"

"You're home, boy," Colonel Wakely said heartily. "You just had a pretty jolty ride home in my buggy, fainted away for a spell—"

"It's all right, Joshua," his mother was stroking his forehead, brushing back the tousled hair, "it's all right now—"

"Oh Joshua!" There was a choked cry from the doorway.

Nora Buchanan and her two young pupils stood there. Just behind them there was the sound of running steps and then Laura Rathbone joined the trio.

"It's all right, Nora, children," Mary Clayburn continued in her soothing tone, "Joshua's had an accident—snakebite—and he's lost some blood."

"Snake?" Nora's eyes widened in horror. She hurried to the bed, then looked around in self-conscious embarrassment until Josh spoke. "It doesn't hurt too bad," he said, looking at Nora with a pathetic pleading.

"Colonel Wakely," Mary Clayburn said, "there's no one here for me to send so I must ask you. Will you go in to Churchill at once and bring Dr. Maclin?"

"Why yes, Mary, if you think it's necessary."

"Necessary? The boy has been bitten by a copperhead!"

"Don't worry, Mama," Joshua tried to reassure her, but weakness and pain contradicted his words.

The colonel was readjusting his broad-brimmed hat as he made for the door. "I'll bring Maclin back, yes indeed—"

After he had gone, there was quiet in the room until Laura Rathbone touched Mrs. Clayburn's arm and said softly, "There's a poultice will draw the poison. I'm going out in the woods to find the leaves and roots."

Mary Clayburn nodded, distracted by a chill which seemed to be seizing Josh. "Yes, Laura, anything—" She drew a heavy quilt close around his back and shoulders. "Put a brick on the stove to heat, Delia. We'll put it to his feet."

It was a strange, bitter-smelling concoction that Laura Rathbone applied to the swollen angry wound late that afternoon. But she moved with such authority that Mary Clayburn could not refuse her help. Laura had interested and disturbed the older woman ever since she had been coming to share Nettie Sue's and Lottie's classes. Her responsiveness and generosity were magnetic. But Mary Clayburn held back from full acceptance. Even the girl's hair ("Long and loose as tassels," Cousin Rilla had described it one day) seemed an affront to the buns and knots and hairpins and combs that the other girls and ladies arranged so elaborately. Still, no one could deny Laura was a girl alive, as spontaneous as the gestures that punctuated the rapid stream of her talk. Shortly after Laura laid the poultice on his hand, Josh seemed to grow easier. He slept.

His brothers had hurried home from their work in the tomato field and at the packing shed when one of Colonel Wakely's timber cutters brought them word of the accident. In work clothes and dusty high-laced shoes, they sat and stood awkwardly in the hall and the adjoining room and heard their mother's whispered account of what had happened. Whitley said Nora Buchanan was worried about the herbs Laura Rathbone was using on Josh. Jonathan reassured him. "She knows the woods."

"If I remember right," their mother said anxiously, "Laura's grandmother was part Cherokee. She may have special talent—"

"Besides," Cal interrupted, "old Dr. Maclin ought to get here pretty soon, unless Colonel Wakely took a side trip by Memphis Gibson's."

"Cal!" Their mother was shocked and troubled.

"I'm sorry. I didn't mean any—"

"Poor time for jokes, Cal," Jonathan said.

The doctor arrived just at dusk. Colonel Wakely, he said, had had to go on home to his wife who became nervous when she was left alone with only their servants after nightfall. The tiny gray-haired man with slow gentle hands and quick angry-looking eyes examined Josh and talked with Laura about her remedy, gave Josh a dose of white medicine from the pharmacy in his worn leather saddlebags, pronounced a hopeful diagnosis, and said he would spend the night.

His presence gave the women something to do, making up a fresh bed, cooking, bustling. While Cousin Rilla sat by Josh's bed, Mary Clayburn spent a long interval in her room. They all knew she was praying.

Laura, on Dr. Maclin's advice, made fresh poultices twice during the night.

"I wish there was something I could do," Nora Buchanan said the next morning when she came downstairs, fresh and pretty in a pink-sprigged dress. "It's not proper I should sit up with him if I don't know how to make your medicines, Laura. And in a few days I'll be going back to Richmond!" Tears filled her eyes.

"Don't cry," Laura commanded. "Just don't cry. You do think a lot of Josh, don't you?"

Nora nodded, reluctant to make the admission.

"Suppose I make up the medicine and you put it on today?"

"Thank you, Laura."

"You will be coming back in August or September to teach again, won't you?"

"I hope so," Nora nodded quickly. "Unless something should happen to—him," she glanced toward the closed bedroom door.

"He'll be all right."

Dr. Maclin confirmed Laura's optimism when he left at mid-morning. At Mary Clayburn's request he had made a brief examination of the rest of the household, testing eyes, tonsils, lungs, and assorted bumps, callouses, and aches. Then he looked at his patient. "Joshua may have to take it easy for a while."

"We'll see to that all right, doctor," Mary Clayburn promised.

"Don't go making an invalid of him," the doctor added quickly. "His system has had a shock. Let it recover. Then go on normally. And Delia," he turned to the wiry black woman handing him his saddlebags, "you take that tonic I gave you. Take it regular, you hear?"

"Yes sir, I sure will, Dr. Mac," she agreed.

Nora Buchanan stayed an extra week during Joshua's recuperation until her parents wrote insisting that it was past time for her to come home and enjoy a rest from her teaching. Josh, pale and weak, had little to say for days after she left.

June arrived. The mornings were fresh, increasingly warm, the afternoons long and filled with the buzz and drone of bees and other insects in weeds and fence-rows. Rains came, welcome at first on the delicate green plants and crops putting down their heavy root systems for summer growth. But the showers persisted, keeping each successive day damp and gray with heavy cloud cover.

"If this keeps up," Cal said to Jonathan one day, as they chopped weeds in the tomato field and then gave up because the ground was too wet and would clod if they worked it so, "we'll have a master harvest of moldy vines and slim pickings in tomatoes."

"Maybe it'll let up tomorrow," Jonathan said.

The rain did not let up. It came heavier than before. A few of the tomato plants in the lowest parts of the field turned yellow and died.

Jonathan rode over to Shad Kendrick's farm and to Janus Rathbone's to see how their crops were doing. Both lived on upland farms and their tomatoes, planted in fields only recently cleared, had not yet suffered from the rain.

"New ground almost always does best for tomatoes," Janus Rathbone said.

Jonathan agreed. "We didn't have time to clear any this year."

"Your crop will be all right," Janus said. "Just a little wet spell."

"I hope so, with Mama's faith and your hope. But there's a lot at stake this year," Jonathan said. He looked around inside the house where this friend and his daughter lived. It was a log house, well made of large sound chestnuts tightly fitted and chinked together, enclosed between two tall stone chimneys at each end of the house. Downstairs there were two long rooms connected by a wide breezeway or dog-trot from which steep stairs led up to a second story.

The furnishings were spare, the floors bare except for a braided rug, but these were scrubbed to a dull luster by years of sand and lye. The cold hearth and fireplace of the sitting-bedroom were clean and shining. On the walnut slab of mantel lay collected a hornet's nest (gray and fragile as if spun from layers of silk paper), a thick, hard twist of lichen shaped like an ear and attached to a piece of bark, laurel burls in forms resembling animals and faces, dried stalks of weeds and wildflowers in muted shades, and Indian flints of various colors, sizes, shapes.

"Those are Laura's fancies," Janus Rathbone told Jonathan. "She's always bringing in oddities from the woods. Used to be crippled birds and varmints and such, then a little owl she was raising caught its neck in wire and choked to death. She never brought in any other creature to house-tame."

"This is a nice room," Jonathan said. He said it because he liked the uncluttered freshness of the wall logs, hearth stones, hand-hewn cherry beds and chest and table and oak-splint chairs. It was a room of essentials, ample, well-made, well-tended essentials.

Janus did not answer him directly but pointed to the old long rifle cradled on pegs above one of the doors. "That's a curiosity," he said. "My great-grandpappy carried it into these hills after the Revolutionary War."

"Does it still shoot?"

Janus nodded. "But Laura won't let me take it out. She's an odd sort of girl, stubborn-minded against any killing. Even crows, they rob my corn patch every year—" He smiled, puzzlement, indulgence, affection mingling in his face.

"Janus, were some of your folks Indian?" Jonathan asked directly. He was not given to overtures or embellishments.

The older man looked at him sharply. "Not my own people. But my wife, her mother was half-Cherokee."

"I see. I'd never know—"

"That's Laura's grandmother," he said plainly. He turned his head away from Jonathan. "When my woman died a-birthing Laura, her mother come here and lived with us. She was eighty-odd years old then. That's where the girl got her woods ways. Galloping consumption took the old woman when Laura was just eight, maybe nine years old."

"I'm sorry," Jonathan said. He was recalling a conversation he had overheard once when he was a child. Years ago. Forgotten until this moment. His mother and Brother Pryor, a new minister to the community then, were sitting in the parlor. Jonathan was on the floor. The claw feet of the table in the center of the room held his attention: big immovable paws of worn, scratched mahogany. Overhead the drone of older voices was a comforting umbrella of sound. Down below, there was the ugliness of the carved claws.

"—And it's nigh impossible to rid them of that superstition for spirits, ghosts, unseemly things we can't acknowledge," the preacher above him was saying.

"She seems such a lonely old soul," his mother answered slowly. "And kindly natured."

"If she wants to renounce her heathenness," Preacher Pryor went on, "we stand ready to accept her repentance—"

"Heathen—" The word had a strange ring. Jonathan the child stared at the big mahogany paws and nails and feet. Were they marching toward him? He repeated the word until it became a little sing-song: heathen, heathen, heathen. Was it reaching toward him?

A long time afterward, some boy told Jonathan that Janus Rathbone's hand was stiff because an Indian witch had laid a spell on it. Jonathan hadn't paid that any attention because he knew Janus's hand was stiff where Colonel Wakely had put a pitchfork in it. Now he understood that both the boy and Preacher Pryor must have been talking about Laura Rathbone's grandmother.

He wished Laura were home now and not out in the mountains somewhere. "Maybe once we get into canning proper, Laura can help us with the tomatoes," Jonathan said.

"I know she'd admire to," Janus told him.

"That is, if we have any crops."

Janus smiled. "Don't get downhearted. There'll be tomatoes. All we can manage."

But it began raining again when Jonathan was on his way home. That night he and Cal and Dan talked about what they might do if the tomato crop failed completely. Could they close down the packing shed before it had ever been put to use, leave what money remained in the Churchill bank, and raise another crop next year? They doubted if Colonel Wakely would be patient that long. And now that Josh was unable to continue working in the tanbark for him (and Mary Clayburn had forbidden it even if Josh had been able), they noted that the colonel's cordiality toward the Clayburns had fallen away.

The following Monday, however, the rains stopped. The rest of June and the first weeks of July brought ideal weather. Corn grew tall along the river; wheat thickened into tides of grain rippling under the wind; gardens flourished and Churchill people sat down to steaming dishes of new peas and tiny potatoes, lettuce wilted by hot crisp bits of bacon and vinegar, fresh green beans boiled in iron kettles, strong slices of raw onion, ears of milky, nut-flavored corn, brittle cucumbers. And tomatoes reddened on the vines.

Days were not long enough for all the work that needed to be done, and so Jonathan and his brothers—except Josh, whose attack of grippe and high fever following the snakebite had left him thin and weak—worked before and after daylight. The first shipment of tin cans arrived from Baltimore and Cal and Dan drove into Churchill to fetch them.

"They're number three cans," Jonathan instructed before they left early on a dewy morning. "Check for size on the bill of lading."

"Could we spare Cebo, too?" Dan asked.

"What do we want him along for?" Cal asked. "We won't need anybody extra loading empty cans."

"I thought it would be a treat for Cebo to ride in to Churchill, see the big sights, help bring our first cans."

Jonathan nodded at Dan, smiling. "Cebo goes, too," he said.

The tinkle and rattle and bang of the empty tins preceded the wagon and mules and men down the road late that night. Jonathan and Shad Kendrick were waiting at the deserted shed to help unload the cans. They watched as the sure-footed mules came in sight, pulling the high-piled wagon along the rutted, rocky road. Dan, holding the lines, snapped the long whip over their backs with a shout so that they pulled up to the shed at a tired trot. With a lurch they halted, metal banging, wagon wheels squeaking, Dan bracing himself. "Whoa-a, Kate. Whoa-a, Frank."

The yellow flames of the lanterns spilled pools of light around men, wagon, mules. "Well, boys," Jonathan said, stepping back from the side of the wagon, lowering his right arm and hand which held the largest lantern, "looks like we're ready to set up a cannery."

"Folks in Churchill seemed to think so," Cal said, climbing down from the wagon seat. "You'd doubt they ever saw a can before in their everlasting lives, way they loafed around watching us load up."

"Those courthouse, cracker-barrel farmers," Dan grinned. "They're strong on wishbone, weak on backbone."

"Some of them watched mighty close, too, while we hired our new helper," Cal went on.

Jonathan looked around quickly. "How's that?"

"You can ask Dan about it. It's his big trade."

Even as Cal was talking, a figure Jonathan recognized as Cebo came from the back of the wagon—followed by a larger, sturdier man. For a moment the past seemed to be repeating itself.

"It was like this," Dan said, handing the reins to Shad Kendrick and jumping to the ground, "Kate here went lame on the way in to Churchill and we had to stop by Old Sledge's and have him do some shoeing. That's why we're so late getting back. Well sir, at that blacksmith's we met an old friend."

"Lonas Rankin," Jonathan said.

The black man, self-contained, unsmiling, nodded and stopped beside him. "Evening, Mr. Clayburn," he said.

"Lonas only been back in this country less than a week," Cebo said, "already Old Sledge calling him the best smithy he ever seen work at the anvil."

"That's right, Jonathan," Dan said. "I never knew a man to work as fast and sure as Lonas. But—" a frown puckered lines of worry in his smooth face, "Old Sledge was doubting if he could keep Lonas there. Said there was still feeling in the county running contrary to Lonas."

Jonathan nodded. Once, not long ago, he would have protested that Lonas Rankin had been shown innocent of anything except being a victim of the same evil that had overtaken the Clayburns, and that therefore he deserved amends, not suspicion or punishment. But Jonathan had learned, first with dismay and finally with acceptance, that there were limitations to logic. "The blacksmith's is too public a place," he said.

Dan nodded, pleased by his older brother's perception. "And so I brought him here to help us. Handy as he is with tools, Jonathan, he'll save us time and money, too. And if I can learn what I'm hoping for up at that MIT, between us—Lonas and me—we can keep Clayburn Brothers Company machinery humming." He gave the black man a slap on the shoulder.

"Hold on," Jonathan said. "We're barely keeping our heads above water wading upstream for this first season and already you've got us swimming in the deep water three or four years from now."

"Well, it's like this," Dan concluded triumphantly, "you've got to look ahead."

"Lonas he can share with me," Cebo was saying. "I've lived in lonesome walls too long, be joyful to share with somebody."

Jonathan said, "That's fine Cebo." He thought of their dwindling capital and expenses yet to be met. "Tomorrow, Rankin, you come by the office up at the house and we'll decide pay, all the rest. Now, are we going to stand around talking all night or are we going to unload cans?" Jonathan was moving to the back of the wagon. The mules jerked restlessly.

"Can't the cans wait till morning?" Cal asked.

"They can wait, all right," Jonathan said, trying to cheer the others on, "but we can't. Too much to do tomorrow."

They set up a relay line—the three brothers and Cebo, Lonas Rankin, Shad Kendrick—and in the warm summer night they emptied the farm wagon of its merchandise from Baltimore city.

The second week in July, Jonathan and Cal went to each of the farms where they had contracted to buy tomatoes. They decided on how fast the tomatoes were ripening and set a tentative date when each farmer might start hauling to the canning shed. They found it necessary to repeat their warnings over and over: "Remember, bring only when we say to. And ripe, firm tomatoes. We want to put up a pack that makes folks think of sun and summer—and tastes that way."

On the last sweltering Monday in July, Daniel and Calvin fired the boiler before daybreak. Edom Metcalf and Cebo brought the first wagonload of tomatoes up from the field where the pickers were filling the crates scattered along each row. Lonas Rankin tended a hot fire under the molten solder and Shad Kendrick waited between the cooking kettles and the soldering irons and the mountain of cans.

At two long rough tables women in fresh aprons, hair tightly combed and pinned (neighbors, Shad Kendrick's mother and Orvil Gosnell's wife, and Laura Rathbone, among others), took up gleaming new knives and sorted and peeled buckets of morning-fresh tomatoes. Jonathan was everywhere: at the wagon unloading, with the women peeling, beside Shad tipping the lids with solder, over the cooking vats.

Excitement mingled with the heat. When the first batch of cans was lifted from boiling water and set aside, bright and steaming, everyone paused a moment—and looked—and nodded. "Well," Jonathan Clayburn murmured, "we've come this far."

Another wagon rolled down the rough road to the shed. He could tell by its lurching that many of the tomatoes would be bruised and he hurried out to check the driver and his load. But first he had to pick up two of the women's buckets of peelings and empty them in the stream that ran beside the shed. "Tonight," Dan called to him, "I'll rig up a sluiceway to carry that waste off into the creek."

Their canning season lasted four weeks. The weather held hot and dry, tomatoes ripened overnight on the loaded vines, and pickers and wagons moved through the dry, packed fields easily and quickly. But there were emergencies.

Orvil Gosnell's wife, scalded by steam down her left arm and side and leg, had to be rushed to Dr. Maclin and did not return to work again. During the next week Mary Clayburn came for at least half of each day and filled the vacancy, working beside the other women at the rough plank tables. Her presence brought a sense of family and steadfastness into the urgent trial and error of the packing shed.

In early August Shad Kendrick and Orvil Gosnell each had to take time off to catch up with his own farming at home. A short while later, one total run of cans was not properly sealed and after standing a couple of days began to spew bubbles of tomato around the edges. Pressed for time and help, Jonathan had Lonas Rankin haul the spoiled cans out into the woods and dump them under a thicket of white oaks.

Most aggravating of all, several of the farmers who hauled in the tomatoes that they had contracted to grow persisted in acting is if they were handling rocks instead of tender, perishable vegetables. When Jonathan pointed out that many of the tomatoes were coming in bruised and smashed, the men spat and looked at the crates and pointed out that these tomatoes were just going to be cooked and smashed up anyway.

Then Jonathan told them, "I don't know how many cans we'll fill this year, or if we'll go on to another year. But as long as we last at it, we'll put the very best we've got into every can. And that's what somebody, opening them, will find. You understand?"

They nodded. The next day a few of the tomatoes were still bruised, but not so many as before.

Jonathan was exhausted at the close of each day. His brothers were tired, too, but not from the same burden of responsibility in addition to the work. As Josh grew stronger he took over other farming chores at home. He and Edom Metcalf looked after the livestock, cultivated the river-bottom cornfields, and tended the garden as they could.

Late one afternoon as work in the Old Mill Field shed was finishing for the day, knives and kettles washed, fires banked, and crates stacked, Laura Rathbone stopped to see Jonathan and gave him a small packet.

"To help you sleep," she whispered. When he started to protest she would not listen. "Those circles under your eyes, they're not from work but from losing rest. You seem calm to us but you fret inside. This medicine my grandma used to make for her own self. I can remember the spicy smell of the dried leaves when she poured hot water and brewed them. 'Balm to my after-dark worries,' she used to say to me."

Jonathan liked the smell and taste, too, after he sheepishly asked his mother to fix Laura's remedy that night. He slept seven straight hours, not waking once to plan tomorrow's order of work, or to decide whether they should send for an additional five thousand labels bearing the "Clayburn Quality" insignia, or to consider the sales trip he was arranging to some of the important grocers and food dealers in nearby cities.

When Jonathan thanked Laura the next day, she smiled and went on working. Her face was flushed with heat from the steam under the shed, her arms were stained, and tendrils of her long light hair clung to her cheek and throat.

"You better get us some more buckets here," she said, "or we'll all be twiddling our thumbs."

"Yes ma'am," he obliged her.

He was glad she had been here during these long, hot, good days. He would not acknowledge even to himself that he looked every morning to reassure himself that Laura Rathbone was at the tables —talking animatedly with the other women, laughing often, peeling bucket after bucket of tomatoes quickly and easily. She teased and talked freely with the men, too. Jonathan decided that in growing up with only her father, Janus, Laura had not learned the niceties of women's ways. Her buoyancy alternately refreshed and embarrassed him. But the embarrassment only occurred around other people, as on the last morning that Colonel Wakely stopped by to scrutinize operations.

The colonel had come often during the past three and a half weeks, in his white suit, using his stocky riding crop as a pointer and plaything. "Just seeing how you boys are getting along," he announced upon each arrival, dismounting from the tall white horse, shaking the dust from his wide white hat. His jovial words were canceled by the narrow, hostile gaze he turned on them.

"How are the growers measuring up?" he inquired. And Jonathan pointed out the plentiful supply of tomatoes.

"Now you boys got all these tomatoes inside the tin, how you going to dispose of them?" he demanded. And Jonathan explained their plan to ship down the river, which would be closer at hand and cheaper than the rail to Jackson City, fifty miles away. Then they could shift to rail freight.

"Creek keeps shriveling under this dry spell, you boys going to have to find you some other place to dump your tomato stink," he pronounced. And Jonathan wearily agreed.

The colonel's last remark had been prompted by sight of Lonas Rankin carrying two brimful buckets of waste. Under his torn shirt and trousers, arm and leg muscles bulged with the effort and he seemed impervious to everyone around him. At a narrow point between the peelers' table where Laura Rathbone worked and the passage where Colonel Wakely stood, one of the sloshing buckets tilted from Lonas Rankin's grip. A blob of tomatoes splattered to the floor —and onto the colonel's snowy trousers.

The thick skin of the colonel's cheeks mottled to the hue of the stain on his clothes. As promptly as he would right a runaway horse or correct a headstrong hound, the colonel raised his riding crop. And in the moment's interval between its lifting and its falling, while Lonas Rankin stood frozen and all movement in the shed ceased and a tense silence fell, Laura Rathbone took a single step from her table, thrust up the unexpected barrier of her arm and seized the riding crop from the colonel's hand.

While others in the shed stood motionless as actors in a tableau, the girl turned in one total graceful gesture, strode to the cooking area, and stoked the whip into a hot leaping flame. Then, without a glance behind, she walked out of the shed, across the open space, and down the dirt road. Her quick steps sent a half-dozen insects buzzing, flying on paper-thin wings into the dry roadside weeds.

"What—" Colonel Wakely groped. "That girl! That brazen girl destroyed my property. I could have the law on her."

"It's done, Colonel Wakely," Jonathan shook off his astonishment, made an effort to sound respectful. "I guess she's high-strung."

"Who is that girl? Who are her folks?" The colonel's anger mounted, especially as he became aware of the others in the shed staring at him.

Jonathan made a brief nod to the black man. Lonas Rankin moved away, toward the stream. The women turned slowly and began drawing their knives under the silk-thin peelings of the scarlet tomatoes.

"She's just one of the girls helping out for a little while," Jonathan said quietly to Colonel Wakely. "I can't imagine what got into her. I'm sorry about your riding crop—"

"And that nigger." The colonel looked down at his spotted trousers. "Are you going to let him get away with his impudence?"

"It was an accident, Colonel," Dan said.

"Not just these stains, boy. The way he looked, and stood—his whole manner—" The older man could not express his anger adequately. "A fine gang of helpers you boys got together here. A nest of white and black." He left the shed. Before mounting his horse he beckoned to Calvin, who had followed him outside. "You get rid of that nigger bastard and that white trash and you do it today!"

Each person in the shed picked a careful way through the rest of the day.

At dinnertime Cal spoke to Jonathan. "You heard what the colonel said, as he was leaving."

"I heard," Jonathan answered.

At the end of the afternoon, when the women had gone home and the packing shed was empty except for Lonas Rankin and Jonathan, the black man lifted the last gleaming cans from their cooking vats and mopped the sweat from his face. He spoke to Jonathan. "You want me to go?"

Jonathan did not pause in his work of stacking empty crates

outside the shed. "If I did, you wouldn't have to ask. I'd tell you."

There was a silence. "If he had whipped me with that riding crop," Rankin said, "I'd have hit him."

"Lonas," Jonathan said, "it never does anybody good for a man to act the fool. You stay out of Colonel Wakely's way."

Laura Rathbone did not return to work for the rest of that week. Without her quick efficient hands the schedule of the canning suffered. And no one mentioned the loss of her easy laughter and friendly voice, but there was a different mood under the flat shed roof. On Monday, without apology or explanation, she appeared again. Her long hair was done up in a bun at the nape of her neck, so that it would not be in her way as she worked, and the blue and white gingham dress she wore was covered by a crisp fresh apron. There was a great deal of laughter in the shed that morning.

By the end of the afternoon, Jonathan reported to his brothers, "We've put up a record pack today. Things are looking good."

5

The Clayburns believed.

They believed in the brick house. Home, foursquare against the storms that swept down from the mountains in summer, high and cool under the slow lingering burn of summer sun. Secured by deeds and taxes, paint and repairs and sweat. Durable, permanent brick.

They believed in the white clapboard church. It sat on a hill flanked by a cemetery on one side and a grove of poplars on the other. In the cemetery time vanished. Tall, imposing shafts of chiseled granite coexisted with crumbling homemade headstones. Shallow letters gradually eroded under rain and freeze and thaw and a green beard of moss. The stones recorded death and spoke of life: "She Is Gone But Not Forgotten." "We Shall Meet On That Beautiful Shore." For all their certainty of heaven and simplicity of statement they revealed anxious fears and sorrows. In the tangled weeds and vines around the stones small chipmunks hid and insects ticked noisily on autumn afternoons.

They believed in the concrete courthouse. At Churchill's core, it filled a ragged square of trampled grass. Its windows were blinded by years' accumulation of dust and grime and smoke. Inside, the rooms were saturated with stale smells of human bodies and old paper. On the once-varnished shelves rested documents of boundaries, ownership, wedlock, inheritance, as well as murder, theft, and countless variations of petty and monumental evil brought to judgment. The records, written in long hard-backed ledgers, accumulated in piles as thick as layers of sediment built up during the slow geologic passage of time. Their glossy red spines, faded to match the number of years they had lodged there, indicated the era of each legal stratum. On the second floor stood the judge's bench and jury's box and public seats and spittoons of the county courtroom. On the top floor rested the county jail. The bars across its windows gave the building a top-heavy appearance of grandeur masked, of majesty hoodwinked.

They believed in the rock-veneered bank. Solidly it fronted on Churchill's fickle main street which alternated between such extremes as a suck of mud or a wallow of dust. The bank's doors opened and shut more regularly than clockwork. The men in high collars who sat behind its desks and stood behind its counter-windows appeared as imperturbable as the fixed countenances of G. Washington and A. Hamilton on the paper they handled each day.

These were the boundaries of Clayburn belief, translated into wood and solidified into mortar. Family. God. Law. Money. And these translated into the big slippery words: love, purpose, order, security.

I try to understand how the rightness of their faith was also error, why it did not create for my children Lee and Ellie a world less destructive and corrupt. Was their vision as limited as mine is? Family as refuge. God as scorekeeper. Law as vengeance. Money as life.

They believed in the words and in the institutions. And from that belief they drew strength. I grew up surrounded by this strength. It was as familiar as the drone of my family's voice in the yard on a summer evening, as unselfconscious as my Aunt Nettie Sue's anthems at Easter and Christmas, as unquestioned as the slightly tarnished badges of the county sheriff, as tangible as safety deposit vaults. I could receive the strength, but it was not my father's strength because I could not also receive his belief. That is an anchor each one puts down for himself.

Is there anyone who grew up in the mountains, the South, America, as I knew them, who did not experience a crisis of belief? Perhaps so. It is not easy to question in the midst of total acceptance. It is not easy to strike through the thorn bushes when the highway has been cleared and smoothed by so many ahead.

By the time I was growing up, the Clayburns no longer lived on the farm, no longer attended the little white church. They had moved into Churchill and its First Baptist Church. (Many of the factory workers attended the Second Baptist, a frame structure on the opposite side of town. At the Open Door Baptist Church, in what was called Jaybird, Delia and most of the black population of Churchill worshiped. As for the farm hands, they erected a Clayburn Primitive Baptist Chapel on Grindstone Creek, six miles from town, where they shouted and washed each other's feet and "came to glory." Farther away, near the head of the creek, nestled the one-room Grindstone Hard Shell Baptist Tabernacle, where during long summer services certain mountain men and women handled copperheads and rattlesnakes to prove their trust in all-watchful Heavenly Father.) The Clayburns had joined with the Montgomerys in enlarging the First Baptist building and giving it the permanence of brick. (The Clayburns set great store by brick—neat and orderly, without the unexpected shapes and jagged edges of stone or the weathering and decay of wood.) It was there I heard my first Bach, disguised as a hymn, and my first poetry, disguised as Solomon's description of the church as a bride. Church defined the boundaries of our lives: culture and entertainment and therapy as well as religion.

Above all, reality of the world's evil and possibility of heaven's existence were etched deep in my consciousness there. Week after week the stylus moved, biting deeper, whether or not I listened, whether or not I accepted, simply repeating until it buried the message within me.

How could I ever have told Teena, with her cool Episcopalianism, her midwestern practicality, what it was like to be a small boy on Sunday morning in Churchill? How can I ever convey it to Deborah, with her experience of the disciplined intellect and the raw horror? Yet if they do not understand this, they know nothing.

(Teena said to me, just after Lee was born, when I was ready to leave Clayburn-Durant—then talked with Aunt Lottie and considered the responsibility of having a son and being a son—and stayed: "You Southern boys really are tied up in knots, aren't you?" Teena smiled so that her words did not bite but merely stung. "Carrying that burden of family and salvation and God knows what else around with you, like a tortoise with its precious shell—")

Sunday morning was Puritan in its outer sternness and pagan in the abundance of its inner physical sensations: the smell of starch and toilet water and oiled benches and fraying hymnals, the throb of an organ swelling off-key on the bass notes, the radiant mystery of stained glass, the whisper and tinkle of the collection plates' passage through the congregation.

Above all, Sunday morning was the music—sad, sentimental, militant, tightening your throat and chest for all the loss or glory of the world—and it was the minister's voice, angry or pleading, moving or awesome, cultivated or half-wild, but onto something no one present could dismiss or disprove. We might dislike, but we could not escape. Sunday was a day to ponder on our immortal souls and feast on fried chicken.

"Blessed assurance, Jesus is mine, oh what a foretaste of glory divine. . . ."

Afterward the melting delicacy of golden corn pudding.

"Onward Christian soldiers, marching as to war. . . ."

The sweet rise and fall of the rhythm, the pulse-pounding beat of the march, the primitive blood and beauty, the sincere, solemn faces upturned briefly with all the hint of rapture they would ever know: such memory—even in the boiler-room pressure of today, even in this world which seems as far removed as the Pre-Cambrian age or the time of the great fern forests—mellows my attitudes, touches me to unaccustomed pity for those who could believe so faithfully, as well as for those who cannot believe at all.

There was another dimension to the belief. Revivals came in mid-summer during seasons of parching drought or drenching flood, when the land, like the people, lay ready for either renewal or rescue. Again, in my present world of young George Hodges and instant answers from the machine, of knowledgeable Bonita Fredericks and stylish conformities, of inter-office memos and board meetings and daily decisions for sixty-four plants and people ranging from Madison Avenue admen selling Clayburn-Durant's image on t.v. screens to Mexican wetbacks in the Rio Grande valley harvesting fruit for our cans—in this world the residue of long-ago revivals seems thoroughly submerged.

And yet—

One of those summer meetings brought my first personal knowledge of my cousin Stull.

In mid-August that year the brown canvas tent spread wide like a shallow, muddy pool in one of Alexander Montgomery's empty fields at the edge of Churchill. Pungent odor of the canvas mingled with the smell of fresh pine lumber from one of Colonel Wakely's sawmills that was used to build row after row of benches. Around the outer edges of the tent, dry stalks of weeds and Queen Anne's lace and fading purple thistles persisted like a stubble of beard. On the bare plank platform in front of the banked seats stood a small home organ and a lectern. This established the domain of Kincaid and Truesdale, musician and evangelist of "world-wide fame."

For two weeks in the August heat they sang and shouted and exhorted and pleaded and it seemed to me that the town and everyone I knew was forever changed. Great-uncle Whit Ransom, tears streaming down his florid face, took an oath to give up strong drink for the rest of his natural life. Old Sledge Hartwick, overcome by the spirit, vowed to the singing, watchful congregation that no matter how hot his blacksmith's shop became or how heavy the hammer he would never use curse words again, be damned if he would.

Memphis Gibson and two of her girls cried at the mourner's bench and promised repentance of their carnal ways. (I overheard Uncle Cal tell some men the following day that he bet there were a raft of good male citizens hated to hear that promise made, even for a little while. I wondered what he meant.) And cautious Alexander Montgomery wrote a check for one thousand dollars to launch the final love-offering for Brother Truesdale.

Of all the moments or events which startled and stirred us during those emotion-laden days, however, none equaled for me the sight of my cousin Stull Clayburn walking to the front, grasping the outstretched hand of Mooney C. Truesdale, committing his life to God and accepting the Holy Spirit.

That night at home in bed I tried to remember what the Reverend Truesdale had said. Random sentences lodged in my mind like driftwood scattered from the waves of warning, threat, and strange angry love that had washed over the congregation before him.

Oh, let the wind blow, brother. Let the wind howl and the rivers rise and a flood of lamb-purified blood descend into our withered church-baked hearts. . . .

Some say: Brother Truesdale, I've got my own religion. Yes, my brother, but do you have God's religion? Folks don't like to hear the truth about their corruption and their devilment. But I'm not preaching folks' way. I'm preaching the Lord's way. God be praised! That's the rocky trail I've follered since that day I was ploughing in the hillside fields and the Lord called on me to lay down the plough handles and take up the sword for Him. "Lord," I said, "I may be a poor old worthless varmint, but if you're a-wanting me I'm all yours, bone and shank and head and hand," and that's the way it's been and the Lord has blessed me beyond all deserving.

Oh, you say, Brother Truesdale, I don't have time to work for the Lord God Almighty. I've got to run my store and see after my mill. I've got to tend my tobacco fields and feed my white-face heifers. Oh dear brother, the mercy of the Lord God be upon you. God hates a proud look. God hates an owner's grasp. You're just a steward and tender of His earth. And if you can't humble yourself you're headed for brimstone where the fire is never quenched and the worm is never fed.

Your time here is short as a borrower's memory, no matter how young you be. The days of the little babe at its mother's teat are brief as candles. Too soon the hour of wrath will come upon us like a rending storm. That's why I'm a-pleading with you now, this breath; accept the Lord; be baptized in the flow.

I want to see an old-time sin-killing Holy-Ghost revival. I came here on fire with the Lord and I'm not a cinder yet. We'll burn out the proud flesh in our secret hearts.

Let the agnostics and the atheists, the haughty doubters, have their little day on earth. The gathering of the believers and the faithful, the saved and the chosen, will be in heaven. It will come for eternity. It's the gift of God; you have only to reach out with your own pitiful little mortal hand and accept—tonight, now, this minute.

You may never live to return back to this old tent tomorrow night. You're making your eternal choice—for heaven or hell. Don't, O brother or sister, don't disinherit yourself forever from the love of God.

I did not want hell.

Was I a haughty doubter? I did not mean to be.

I wanted love. I wanted to be the faithful and the chosen. I wanted eternity. And heaven.

Yet I sat on the plank bench with my feet anchored in sawdust and I could not move.

Then I saw Stull. Stull walking down the aisle, a serious young man (and I still a child), wearing a watch fob like my father. He was sweating lightly so that his face and forehead shone in the flickering light. His shoes squeaked slightly with every other step but no one heard or paid attention in the midst of the rapturous singing.

> There is a fountain filled with blood
> Drawn from Emmanuel's veins,
> And sinners plunged beneath that flood
> Lose all their guilty stains. . . .
> Lose all their guilty stains. . . .

The vision of a fountain flowing with the warm sticky scarlet of fresh blood made me shudder.

Stull looked straight ahead. The congregation stirred as everyone craned to see him. All of the adult Clayburns and most of the children above infancy, including my brother Monty, had professed faith and joined the church long since. At that moment, only Stull and I did not belong, only we had not washed away our guilty stains, and it appeared that very soon I would be the only one left in that wretched condition.

Stull's father and mother sat on the seats just in front of ours, and when my mother leaned forward and patted them on the shoulder they turned to smile radiantly. I saw tears glistening in Aunt Nora's eyes. If my mother had been crying I would not have been surprised, for she laughed and cried easily. Aunt Nora, however, was another matter. She did not yield often to any display of her inner feelings. Her tears, brimming like iridescent bubbles ready to break, confirmed for me the solemnity and importance of the moment.

I looked back at Stull. Preacher Truesdale had stepped down from the platform onto the grass and sawdust, laid a long shirt-sleeved arm around Stull's shoulders. He held up his other hand for a pause in the music. His shirt was wet, sticking to his skin, outlining the undershirt he wore.

His voice was hoarse and triumphant. "Our fine young brother

Stull Clayburn comes to God tonight. Let us all rejoice. Oh, there will be gladness among the angels in heaven this night."

I could feel the surrounding waves of emotion rolling over me. I tried to see Stull again but he was kneeling now. Suddenly I felt my mother's hand in mine and a strong squeeze. I looked up into her face. She was gazing at me with a question. A hope. And a longing. My chest tightened with love for her.

But I could not go down the aisle. I could not join.

On the way home my mother spoke to my father but I knew she was addressing me. "Little old Stull! I know how Nora and Josh must feel tonight to know that he's accepted the Lord."

There was a short silence. My father spoke quietly, almost to himself. "Stull has a good head on his shoulders. He's a smart boy."

"That shows you," Mama nodded, "no one is smart enough not to need the Lord's saving grace."

"Why don't you get saved, Jon?" Monty piped up from the seat beside me. He had been a loyal Baptist for two years already.

"Don't push Jon, Monty," Mama said. "He'll know when he's ready. The Lord works in mysterious ways—" She reached back and patted me on the knee. But I knew she was glad that Monty had asked, had reminded me, had prodded.

Alone in bed with my guilt that night I wondered about the awesome experience all of those around me had had, which I had not yet known.

"There is a fountain filled with blood. . . ."

The sound of old Number Seven, the midnight train from Chicago to Charleston, came up to me from the tracks through Churchill at the bottom of our hill. The engineer played a long tattoo with his whistle. Mike O'Leary! He was famous from the Great Lakes to the Atlantic seaboard for his spit-and-polish engine, gleaming black with bright brass bell and hand-holds, and the voice he gave to that resonant whistle.

"Whoo—oo—oo, whoo—oo—oo—oo, who. . . ."

The clear lingering call, with each note falling pure and separate as drops of rain, seemed a cry of such distilled loneliness, echoing from the valley into the hills, that it brought me a sad, self-conscious comfort.

The next day I could hardly wait to see Stull.

My father had put Monty and me to work for the last two summers in the Riverbend Farm fields picking tomatoes. I was eight years old and Monty was ten and all the men told us that since we didn't have so far to stoop our backs didn't ache the same way theirs did from the picking. Maybe not. But during the first days each season I didn't see how anyone's back could ache more than mine. But then I learned how to give to the bends, how to rest on one knee at an especially heavy vine. The ground yielded hot and soft under our bare feet.

At noon Stull brought a fresh supply of water for the pickers.

As he drew up at the end of the field under the shallow shade of a row of sycamore trees that grew along the riverbank, I left my row without waiting for anyone to tell me to help with the water-kegs and ran toward Stull. In his work clothes, squinting against the midday glare, he didn't appear much different from the way he had every other morning that summer.

"I hope you get these kegs unloaded as quick as you can," he was saying to old Orvil Gosnell, the field foreman, as I came up panting and breathless. "I've got to get home to dinner so I can take Uncle Jonathan to Jackson City this afternoon."

I could tell by the way Orvil Gosnell spat a wad of tobacco juice into the bushes that he didn't like the way Stull spoke. He banged the kegs onto the ground.

"Stull, I want to ride back with you," I blurted. The idea had just come to me. "I've got to go home. I'm feeling sick to my stomach."

My cousin looked at me. The expression on his face did not change a fraction.

I turned to Orvil Gosnell. "My mother would want me to come home. She always worries the worst way if our stomachs are upset."

"That's true," the old man spat again, remembering I suppose all the paraphernalia of separate water jugs and dippers and straw sun-hats that my brother and I had brought to the fields. "You go on home."

As Stull and I bounced away, I looked over at him. He did not speak. For all I could tell, the miracle of the night before at the Kincaid-Truesdale meeting might never have occurred.

"I was at the revival last night," I said.

He did not look around. "That man can really talk."

I clutched at the door handle. It was hot from sitting in the sun and I let loose quickly. "But you were saved," I said.

"That's right."

When he did not go on I tried to. "You professed your sins and your faith and you accepted the Lord Jesus Christ."

He was looking at me now—back at the road and then at me.

Was I breaking some unwritten code, committing some unforgivable breach? Was Stull's testimony, his act of faith, beyond all explanation or statement or discussion? But the guilt throbbing through those hymns, the loneliness wailing through Number Seven's whistle, remained inside me from the night before, and I had to try to know; I had to know.

"Stull," I swallowed dry spit and began again. "Stull, how does it feel?"

His gray-blue eyes—the no-color of the hazy summer sky—stared at me. "How does what feel?"

"The change. The change inside you. Knowing that you've accepted God's love, and eternity and heaven—"

"You trying to make fun of me?" He was scowling.

I could feel the blood flushing my neck and face.

"Oh no, Stull. I just want to know how it is to believe—"

He stopped scowling. I saw that he was convinced of my sincerity and, simultaneously, of my stupidity. I grew even redder. I wanted to stay silent but I went on talking. "You and I were the only ones in the family who hadn't made professions. I would—if I could," I went ahead lamely.

The car hit a ragged chughole and we bounced on the hard narrow seats. Stull put in the clutch and shifted to second gear.

"That's what I wanted to ask you about this morning," I made a last weak effort, "how it is—"

"How what is?"

I did not know what else to say.

We turned from the farm road onto the county highway. I had begun to suspect that there were no chariots of glory to envelop our spirits, only cars that rattled on errands for our business.

"Mama and Daddy, they'd like it if I went down to Preacher Truesdale, too—"

This time he answered me. "Why don't you go then?"

"I don't know." And that was a completely honest statement.

"It's the smartest thing," Stull said.

I looked out of the window at the dusty road straight ahead.

"You know you believe in God," he went on more easily. "After all, even if He isn't there it hasn't done any harm."

I nodded. But I was not satisfied.

"So I say, might as well join on up. The church can do good for you, too." He winked at me in a camaraderie we had never shared before. We did not share it now.

I sat huddled on the seat with my hands beneath my legs, legs weak as if from a long sickness. We were nearly home. At our driveway Stull paused and I crawled out of the car. Before he continued on to the adjoining driveway, his own, he leaned out the window and said, "Don't think so much, kid. Go on and join. It'll make you feel better. I'm glad I did." He didn't often say "kid," a holdover from his college past. Any other time but this I would have been flattered to have him address me so.

When I told my mother I had come home from the tomato fields because of an upset stomach, it was no longer a total untruth. Everything seemed upset at that moment. My mother's reaction to any suggestion of sickness satisfied the sufferer totally. Her concern sufficed for the situation and made it easy for everyone else to take a calm and reassuring outlook. My mother's personal catalogue of illnesses permitted no minor ailments. A runny nose heralded pneumonia; a single pain in the region of the abdomen became a symptom of appendicitis.

Of my stomach disorder she gasped, "It's the season for—for typhoid!" And her blue eyes widened in alarm as she telephoned my father at his office. After talking with him she grew calmer. She brought me baking soda in a glass of water and put me to bed.

It felt strange to be in bed at midday. My mother had drawn the shades against the noonday light and the room took on a golden cavelike glow. From a sewing nook down the hall came the clean smell of fresh smooth cloth. I knew that Serena's daughter was ironing there. The familiar thought and smell comforted me.

But I knew the code I had broken with Stull. Even then I knew, although I could not have put it into words. We (especially we boys, we men) were not supposed to discuss the innerness of life. We were supposed to observe true division of Sunday from Monday. We were splintered into a half-dozen fragments and our maturity was measured not by trying to make the parts into a whole but by juggling the pieces cleverly, separately, so that no one saw the empty spaces.

That night, the last night of the great revival, I stayed at home. My mother brought me salted chicken broth in one of her white Haviland consommé cups. The gold band around its edge gave the broth a slightly metallic flavor as I sipped. I swallowed its delicacy slowly. It reminded me of times when my stomach really had been churning and this salty golden juice had soothed and nourished me back to normal. Remembering made me sad, made me feel older in a way that I did not want to feel.

From that August day forward I never discussed any but matters temporal with Stull. And I remained acutely aware of the embarrassment most Clayburns felt in confronting or discussing the creative, spiritual, moral, sexual, intangible forces of their lives.

Yet those older ones—my grandmother, my father, my uncles— believed. And who am I to judge their belief? Shall I judge them against their descendants, against my friends, against all those lukewarm bodies who do not believe or disbelieve—who have only arrangements, conveniences, patchworks for their lives?

When Teena died there were letters, condolences, murmured conversations. Those who knew us assumed that this would be my trough of the wave, my time for asking why and who and seeking some reconciliation between the master plan and the daily drone. Lee and Ellie had their questions, too. But I was arrogant, maybe even apathetic, not to say that they were really my questions, also.

It was not Teena's death but Deborah's life that led me to think less about Clayburn-Durant problems and more about belief.

> There is power, power, wonder-working power
> In the precious blood of the Lamb.

Was the blood that drenched Deborah's life precious? My memories and questions weave into nets. At this moment I find less need to understand my cousin Stull's power than to appreciate my father Jonathan's strength.

6

Summer reached its zenith, and waned. The number of wagons rolling down the dusty road dwindled to a trickle. Fewer cases of tomatoes were processed each day, and the season steadily drew to a close.

During these final days Jonathan and Cal, instead of being at the factory, were in Jackson City, Chattanooga, and Atlanta, making the initial effort to tell grocers and food distributors about a new brand of tomatoes: Clayburn Quality.

Preparations for their departure had turned it into a major event. Their mother and Delia and Cousin Rilla had put Jonathan's and Cal's suits, shirts, and collars in first-rate order and had packed them carefully in valises. Dan and Whit had shined their brothers' shoes until the worn leather shone. With fresh haircuts and firm handshakes and bright new cases of number three size cans of tomatoes, they went to the cities, self-conscious in their immediate lack of sophistication, confident in knowledge of their own worth. Jonathan's equanimity soothed Calvin's alternate chagrin and anger before the various responses they received.

"Churchill? Where's Churchill? Must have slipped off the map I studied in school."

"Clayburn Brothers Company? Never heard of it."

"Tomatoes? That your only product? Need a little more variety don't you, fellers?"

A few, in Jackson City and elsewhere, listened and nodded, then agreed to look at samples. Jonathan and Cal cut the cans carefully, not looking at one another, knowing that although they checked the cases each morning to be sure of no apparent leaking or swelling, there remained always the possibility—indeed, likelihood—of some spoilage.

After a dozen trials, as they laid back the lids and exposed tender red tomatoes and juice to the sight and smell and taste of the grocers, Jonathan and Calvin were encouraged. The can tops had been well soldered. But still the buyers were reluctant.

"If we had some assurance your other cans would be as good as these. . . ."

"Tell you what, Clayburns. You come back next year. We'll talk business then."

"Much obliged to you for thinking of us. But right now we're swamped with tomatoes."

In each city there were men who took time and interest enough to look at Clayburn Quality canned tomatoes and taste them. They were complimentary and encouraging. But only a half-dozen of them placed small orders.

Each night when Jonathan and Cal returned to the succession of hotel rooms, they added up their orders, discussed reactions, and gradually came to an admission: if four thousand cases of cans, hand-picked, hand-packed, and hand-soldered, were going to be hand-moved, business would have to improve considerably. Yet, before they had realized or intended it, they were already talking about next year to their customers and prospects.

"We're counting on being able to get our product to you at least two weeks earlier than any of the northern canners next season."

"Using water as well as the rails, we ought to shave prices by the case for next year's customers."

But back in their hotel room, Jonathan remarked with a faint smile, "Mr. Alexander Montgomery and his bank board will be glad to hear our plans for another season."

"Not to mention Colonel Wakely," Cal said.

"Before we sell our first crop we're already talking up our second." Jonathan sat on the edge of the sagging bed and rubbed one weary red foot. "Looks like we may have a company without any customers."

That night Cal was wakened by his brother's voice. Jonathan, talking in his sleep, was quoting figures and prices. It was unusual for Jonathan to show any signs of discouragement and Cal tumbled from his own high spirits and jokes to glum despair.

During the next several days they sold a few hundred more cases. Then Jonathan said, "We might as well tackle Waverly Company and see how we fare." Cal advised waiting until their luck was running better. "We need to know now," Jonathan said.

Late Saturday afternoon they came to the cavernous emporium of Hugh Waverly and Son, which filled half a city block near downtown Jackson City. They had stopped here once before but Mr. Waverly had not been able to see them. Now they stood nervously waiting, trying to appear calm and judicious.

On one side of the long store were crowded groceries of all descriptions. The opposite walls and counters displayed dry goods and household wares. The dusky rear of the building offered tools and implements of many kinds from iron wash kettles and sewing machines to shiny new hoes and rolls of barbed wire.

The heavy Saturday trade began to thin while Cal and Jonathan waited patiently to see the tall, deliberate man in black broadcloth and celluloid collar who sat behind the glass windows of a cubbyhole in the center of the store. His office, with its dusty roll-top desk and high-backed chair and wooden crates of papers, was a hub from which his long glances radiated into various parts of the store like spokes that kept the bulky vehicle moving.

The two heavy cash registers which served both front and rear of the large store indicated the prosperity of Waverly and Son. Each time the high clear bell of one of the cash registers clanged, the man in the cubbyhole lifted his head and peered briefly in that direction as if registering in his mind, too, the name of the clerk and the dollars rung up there.

The Clayburns' attention centered on the shelves of canned goods along the left wall—a carefully arranged selection. Little wonder that men in Atlanta and Chattanooga and right here in Jackson City had advised association with Hugh Waverly, if possible. There was an atmosphere, a promise, of bustle and progress which permeated this establishment. Its source was obviously the character of the man who controlled it, as Jonathan and Cal realized after their first minutes of conversation with him.

When Hugh Waverly discovered their business he pushed his glasses closer over his eyes and laid down a barrage of questions: the location and size and productiveness of their farms, the beginning of their cannery, their plans for the future. His curiosity was more than an aptitude for cordiality and anecdote, which the Clayburns had already encountered among several other gentlemen businessmen. This was a questioning based on a drive and purpose larger than congeniality. Waverly peered at them over narrow gold-rimmed glasses and held his hands clasped behind his back. His unchanging expression and stance, his rapid, penetrating questions—not about the product they were trying to sell him but about every other phase of their business—disconcerted Cal. He was relieved when the older man finally agreed to look at the tomatoes.

"All right. Let's see what you're offering."

Cal snatched one of the half-dozen cans from the small valise they carried. Without a glance he set it on a nearby counter and hurriedly cut the lid. Red juice spewed a small geyser over Cal's cuff and sleeve and the worn wooden top of the store counter. Mr. Waverly's eyebrows raised.

"That's a bad one," Cal choked back embarrassment. He looked at Jonathan but found no help, only a reflection of his own dismay. Then, straightening his wide shoulders, he faced the storeowner directly. "Mr. Waverly, that's one of only two cans we've found spoiled on this whole sales trip."

There was no reply.

"You know and we know that we'd rather it happened anywhere than here, with you."

The older man continued to look at the juice on his counter and on Cal's sleeve. He motioned for a clerk from another part of the store to come and mop up the mess.

Cal went on desperately. "Look here, Mr. Waverly, you're a man of common bay-horse sense. If you've never found any flaw in those bolts of cloth up there on your shelves," he waved one arm in the direction of the dry goods department, "or if you've never got hold of one of those machines that had something bent or misfit or lost, we'll take our cans and leave right now and not bother you again. But if you've put up with mistakes before, Mr. Waverly, grant us this one."

The older man returned Cal's straight look. He removed his glasses, blew a spot of dust from the lens and returned them to the bridge of his nose. "Cut another can," he said.

He looked at the fresh can of tomatoes, then tasted the contents carefully. He stood, hands tight behind his back, and peered at his displays of canned foods along the shelves.

"It's our policy," Jonathan said in the long silence, "to make good any can that doesn't hold up."

Mr. Waverly turned abruptly. "A guarantee?"

"Our word is bond on it."

"Step back to my office."

They sat in the crowded fishbowl office and Mr. Hugh Waverly wrote out a formal order. "How many cases have you left?" he asked.

Jonathan and Cal looked at each other. "A little better than three thousand," Jonathan said.

"I'll take them."

The scratch of Waverly's pen-point on paper made the only sound in his office and Cal and Jonathan tried to subdue their incredulity. When Waverly had finished writing he handed the order to Jonathan and said, "If your tomatoes run as good as that second can I saw, this firm will be proud to handle Clayburn Quality. One request: I want to be the only outlet you have in this city."

Taken unaware, they did not answer immediately.

"It will work to both our advantages." Mr. Waverly removed the gold-framed glasses again and rubbed the upper bridge of his nose slowly. "You see, I've learned something running this store and other smaller ones before. First, I buy people. Then their goods. I can get tomatoes lots of places. Right now I'm buying Clayburn Brothers."

"You won't be sorry, Mr. Waverly," Cal gripped his hand impulsively. "No sir, you'll never regret having early confidence in Clayburn's."

Jonathan said, "We'd be proud to have Hugh Waverly and Son as the sole outlet for Clayburn foods in Jackson City. In return, would Waverly's offer only Clayburn brand tomatoes to their customers?"

The older man was nonplussed. He tilted back in his chair, studying Jonathan.

"Our prices will match any others in the market," Jonathan went on. "We're two hundred miles closer and two weeks earlier than our nearest competition. We'll be working to make the costs cheaper."

There was a long delay. Outside the glassed-in cubbyhole, clerks and customers went about their business. Inside, the three men sat tense and alert.

"All right. On those conditions—high quality and low prices—we'll handle Clayburn's exclusively as far as their tomatoes are concerned. I won't promise how long we'll continue such a policy, but we'll give it a trial."

Jonathan leaned forward and extended his hand. Cal followed suit, more soberly this time. "We'll do right by you, Mr. Waverly," Cal said.

"We'll do good for each other," Jonathan added.

Mr. Waverly nodded briskly. "I believe we will. People here are using more canned goods. I've remarked the change. You've come on the scene at a good time, Clayburns."

"We'll try to make the most of it."

"I can believe that." The older man chuckled for the first time. "By God, I believe it."

Jonathan and Cal caught the train to Churchill late that afternoon. They felt no need to pay for an extra night's lodging at a hotel when their business was finished. Tired from the tension of their trip and grimy with feathery coal soot from the train's engine, but elated by the final success of their first sales venture, they came home.

After the heat of the deeper South, the cool shadows of the sprawling oaks and the breezes sluicing down from the mountains in the evenings were refreshing. The family gathered on the front porch to hear a report of the trip.

Cal gave a dramatic account of the early rejections and discouragements. Mary Clayburn murmured, "Perhaps we should never have gotten away from farming—" And then Cal described their encounter with Mr. Hugh Waverly.

"Well, that was nice," their mother concluded.

"I knew you'd do it!" Dan beamed.

"Wish I'd been along," Whit sighed.

Disappointment clouded Cal's face. He looked around at Josh

and his trusting sisters and attentive Cousin Rilla and saw that none of them could realize any more fully than his mother the desperation of their call at the Hugh Waverly Company, and the triumph that had followed.

"You should have heard Cal when that first can turned out to be bad," Jonathan spoke urgently. "You'd have been proud of your son, Mama. He took the bull right by the horns and admitted our failure, and then he challenged Mr. Waverly's sense of fair play."

"I had to say something." Cal's dejection at the family's casual acceptance of their victory was melting before his older brother's unexpected tribute.

"You said just the right thing. I was watching Mr. Waverly's face. I could tell. Guess we'll have to make you our manager of sales, whenever we get high-toned enough to need such titles."

"The Clayburns are noted for being good traders," their mother said.

In the security and familiarity of this comfortable vine-shaded porch, surrounded by love and care, Jonathan saw that it was impossible for some of the family to understand just how impersonal and indifferent that other world out there had been, the world of trade, of competition, of success, which brooked no mistakes.

"Then we're a company!" Dan stood up. "We'll go on canning next year, too."

"And we've made a profit," Cal said.

"I was afraid it might all end before I could be part of it," Dan grinned at all of them. "Now I've been thinking about blackberries, and maybe green beans. They'd stretch the canning season and they're easy to grow."

"Don't forget apples," Whit added.

Their mother interrupted. "Before plans swell too big I should tell Jonathan and Cal that our partner in the company isn't well satisfied."

"Colonel Wakely?" Jonathan asked.

She nodded. "He and Drusilla came to see me a few days ago. Drusilla wanted to ask if I would speak to you boys about taking her brother Nate to work in the company."

"Then she must have some hopes for the company," Jonathan said.

"Oh, she didn't speak to me before the colonel," Mary Clayburn said. "He was very discouraging about the prospects for canning."

Jonathan frowned. He was grateful to their mother for not going into a long list of all the colonel's dissatisfactions. They all sat silently while dusk descended over the porch. At last Jonathan turned to his mother. "I guess we could find a job for Nate Lusk," he said.

"I hoped you might," she answered, rocking in the big white chair. "The Lusks were once one of the leading families in this part of the state. But now only Drusilla and her younger brother are left. And Nate has just never found his place in life."

"Did he ever look for that place behind a plow?" Josh asked, reminding them all of the untended acres in the old Lusk farm, of the sagging rafters in the old Lusk barns.

"The Lusks were always gentlemen farmers," Mary Clayburn said.

"And gentlemen tipplers," Josh added.

Their mother frowned, and nodded. "That's where the money, then the land, then the name finally go. . . ."

"We'll offer Nate a job next year, Mama," Jonathan said. "Now, are we beholden to Colonel Wakely in any way? Because of Papa or debts or anything I don't know about?"

"Why no, Jonathan," Mary Clayburn shook her head. "We're beholden to no one. Only to the Lord—and to everyone."

"Would it fret you if the colonel wasn't one of our partners?"

"Pray about it. Do what is right."

The next morning Jonathan Clayburn went into Churchill. As he rode along in the late summer–early autumn morning, he was equally indifferent to the hot sun and chilly shadows. "Right," his mother had said. "Do what is right." The choice was risk, the action chance. Right for whom, and when, and how? Situations developed, changed, dispersed, came together again in new forms. A man acted and discovery of whether rightness was in it or not came later.

At the bank he had a long talk with Alexander Montgomery. When their business was finished, the older man invited Jonathan to dinner at the great brick mansion on the hill above town. Alexander's wife and two of their four children were also present around the long, damask-covered table heavy with food for the midday dinner.

"Livvie Lee!" Alexander Montgomery's wife spoke softly to the nimble, pretty child who did not touch a bite of food on her plate and looked only at their tall, grave visitor. "Olivia Lee, we never stare!"

Jonathan tried to smile at the little girl, but he was uneasy at being the center of attention. He had been to the Montgomery home on many other occasions, but never before as a guest of Mr. Alexander Montgomery.

The oldest son of the family, Pettigrew, called Pett by the people of Churchill but known at Washington and Lee where he attended college and in the bank where he now worked by the full South Carolina name of his mother's family, was Joshua Clayburn's age. Jack Montgomery, who had spent a year traveling around the world in preference to college before he began clerking at the Montgomery store for his father and uncle Randall, was the age of Dan Clayburn. Their sister Josie, for Josephine, was sixteen months younger than Jonathan. And the little girl, Olivia Lee, the baby, was only ten years old.

Jonathan had been at political rallies and revival meetings and various sociables with Pett and Jack Montgomery and he had been paired with Josie often at parties. She was a lively girl who liked people and gaiety. She had her mother's natural charm (which counteracted a hint of natural arrogance), and Jonathan enjoyed being with her. But Josie Montgomery made it quite clear that she did not intend to waste any significant part of her popularity on a young man who lived on a farm and would probably always live on a farm and would undoubtedly want his wife to live on a farm, too. Her brothers shared this attitude, especially thin, purse-lipped Pett, who enjoyed wearing black serge with a gold watch-chain across his vest on weekdays as well as Sundays.

Jack was the most popular member of the family, and if he and Jonathan had little in common it was because Jonathan had never learned to play the games Montgomery knew as second nature: lawn tennis and billiards and poker and ballroom dancing. Jonathan liked Jack Montgomery, even envied him perhaps, and a visit to the Montgomery store, with Jack as its relaxed and affable mentor, was decidedly more pleasant than a visit to the Montgomery bank and an encounter with Pett's sharp eyes and haughty greeting.

Today Pett, astonished when his father invited Jonathan to their home for dinner, had stated that he would remain at the bank.

"Farmer from down in the Dark Hollow promised to come by today and settle the interest on a note. I wouldn't want to miss him."

"Well, I wouldn't want to discourage such dedication to duty, Pettigrew," his father said. "Hope that farmer stops by right away. Come along, Jonathan."

Josie and Jack had greeted Jonathan warmly. "You and Cal didn't come to our last ice cream supper," Josie pretended to pout.

"We were away," Jonathan said, then added, "on a sales trip."

Her attention was arrested. "Oh? Where did you go?"

"Just Chattanooga and Atlanta—and Jackson City, of course."

"Just? Why, I'd sell half my interest in heaven right now for a visit to any of those cities."

"Josie," her mother said. But her voice was so soft it was hardly a reprimand and Jonathan wondered if Mrs. Montgomery had ever really disciplined one of her children as his mother had had to do. He vaguely remembered some comments he had once heard his mother make to Cousin Rilla about "the wilfullness of all the Montgomery children."

"Well, I do want to go to the cities," Josie said.

"Sales trip for your cannery, Jonathan," Jack said, half-question, half-statement. "I hear you're becoming a big industrialist."

"Not very big, I guess," Jonathan said.

"Not yet," Mr. Montgomery said, "but it wouldn't surprise me—" As he hesitated, there was the announcement for lunch.

Jonathan did not become conscious of the younger girl's presence until Mrs. Montgomery whispered her name. "Livvie Lee!"

Through the rest of the meal he could not escape her gaze. Her eyes were as oval and as pure a blue as a robin's egg. After a while Jonathan decided that he liked the wonder and the adoration that seemed to be in Olivia Lee Montgomery's eyes when she looked at him.

The crystal chandeliers, the closely textured carpets, the over-abundance of furniture, the heavy baroque gilt mirrors, gave the Montgomery house a more sumptuous atmosphere than Jonathan remembered. Even the midday food, served by two solicitous maids in proper uniform, was highly seasoned, rich. Jonathan felt enner-vated in such surroundings.

Under the warm cordiality of the Montgomerys, however, Jonathan found himself expressing thoughts he had not spoken before. When nuts and fruits followed the dessert of Lady Baltimore cake, Jonathan said to Mrs. Montgomery, "This may seem odd, but sometime I would like to try packing peanuts."

The announcement was greeted with a little silence.

"You know, peanuts are really hard to parch just right."

"I'd never given it much thought, Jonathan," Mrs. Montgomery admitted.

"I can tell you a good deal about a man's character by his ability to parch peanuts. Over-cooked is easy. Under-done is just as trifling. To strike a medium calls for patience and a steady hand and judgment."

"Are you a good peanut parcher?" Mrs. Montgomery asked, and their was a hint of teasing laughter behind her voice.

"Oh, the best," Jonathan replied promptly. He knew teasing when he met it, and how to respond to it. The others laughed, too. But the little girl still looked at him with unswerving clarity.

As he went home that afternoon, drowsy from the heavy dinner, he felt a new sense of confidence. In the world of the Alexander Montgomerys and the Hugh Waverlys, the Clayburns were making their own place.

That confidence reinforced him when he received word the following week that Colonel Wakely wanted to talk to him as soon as possible. They had not seen each other since that awkward day in the canning shed.

At the colonel's home they sat in the shade overlooking the river and the fields beyond. Wisteria vines, now almost bare of their leaves, clustered in a tangled mass over the end of the verandah.

"How'd you boys make out on your sales trip?" the colonel asked, without preliminaries. When Jonathan told him of their success, he did not respond immediately. Then he said, "It'll be a chore, getting your cans shipped in first-rate condition."

Jonathan agreed that transportation would be a problem.

"How do you boys feel about another year?" the colonel asked.

"We ought to make a little money this season," Jonathan said. "No figures yet?"

Jonathan shook his head. "Not till our sales are all billed and paid. But I've roughly figured up the situation. Barring some catastrophe, we'll turn a profit."

"You and Calvin decided what salary you expect to be paid out of that?"

"That's for all the partners to decide," Jonathan answered. "Whatever's fair."

He rocked back in his chair and it creaked under his weight. "You made those changes I asked you to, Jonathan?"

The question was a surprise. When there was no response he went on. "You know: that sassy nigger and feisty girl."

Jonathan nodded. "I remember. I don't see how we could manage without them."

The colonel slapped one hand down on the arm of his rocker. "Then I don't see how I could manage to stay on as one of your partners."

Jonathan felt the sweat gathering around the collar of his shirt and running down his back between his shoulder blades. "We'd hate that, Colonel Wakely," he said quietly.

The mildness of his answer shocked the colonel. "Maybe you don't understand, Jonathan."

"I guess I do, Colonel." He focused his gaze on a field in the distance, a small, fenced-in field holding seventy-five or a hundred hogs. "We were thinking we might put any profit back into the company—this first year," Jonathan said.

"I might have gone along with that, but now I'll admit straight out that you've shaken my confidence in your judgment. Especially your judgment of people."

But Jonathan hardly heard this pronouncement. He was remembering his father and the long drive Elisha Clayburn had made to Charleston. "Look after the family," he had said to Jonathan before he left that brilliant blue October morning.

"Besides," the colonel unfolded a finely initialed linen handkerchief and wiped his forehead, "I'm not sure but that the canned food field is already over-crowded. Why, you take your fine friend Buchanan from up in Virginia. Even he was crowded out."

Jonathan did not seem inclined to dispute. He sat and looked at the distant hogs and thought of his father's acceptance of Colonel Wakely's drove which had delayed Elisha Clayburn on that hard, final journey home.

"Making a big business success isn't always as easy as it seems," the colonel said.

"No," Jonathan agreed, remembering the several inheritances the colonel had received, "it isn't easy." His face was open and attentive and slightly naive. "I guess the thing for us to do now, Colonel Wakely, is settle on some give-or-take figure so that one of us will be able to take over the cannery—"

The older man's eyebrows lifted. " 'One of us' take over?" The thought seemed to amuse him. "Surely you don't expect to—"

Jonathan seemed unperturbed. "Of course we wouldn't be able to offer a very high price. But would you be willing to agree on a give or take, Colonel Wakely?"

"Of course. Of course."

"What figure would you have in mind?"

"Today?" Movement of the colonel's rocker stopped. "Now?" He had been caught by the oldest offensive maneuver: surprise.

"I was under the impression you'd been giving it some thought," Jonathan said mildly. "I'd like to know what you had in mind."

Colonel Wakely hesitated, spoke slowly. "Of course I've given it thought. To my mind, the offer will have to include the twelve hundred or six hundred, as the case may be, that each of the partners invested in the beginning, plus six percent interest—"

He paused but the expression on Jonathan's face did not change as he gazed out toward the remote mountains.

"—Plus a fair share of the profits."

"Would four hundred dollars on your investment seem fair?"

"Well, of course we don't know the profit yet. I don't believe I could pay you boys and your mother a sum that large."

"Then that's what we'll pay you," Jonathan said. He looked straight at the startled colonel. "You agreed to give or take."

The colonel's face froze. "You and your mother and Calvin will meet those terms I named?"

"Yes." Jonathan knew that the colonel assumed that he himself would be the buyer, not the Clayburns, and that he would have set a higher profit and more than six percent interest if he had suspected that the Clayburns might be the purchasers.

"By damn!" the colonel said. "You must have turned a profit if you can buy me out all at once, lock, stock, and barrel."

Jonathan did not answer.

The colonel's chair creaked again with sudden motion.

"Well, where's the money coming from?" he fired point-blank. "I'll expect all cash."

"We'll have it," Jonathan said. "We'd like to be the takers in this proposition."

Reluctantly, the colonel agreed to withdraw. He had not intended to continue in the cannery, but he was uneasy over the thought that the Clayburns might persist without him. "I don't know—"

"But you said—" Jonathan began.

"Damn what I said!" The colonel stood up. Shadows of the wisteria vine cast coiling patterns of sunlight and shade over his mottled face and white shirt. "All right. You can have my share."

Jonathan stood up, too, and held out his hand. "We could meet in Churchill next week," he said.

"Monday morning at ten," Colonel Wakely snapped. "In Littlepage Ransom's office."

By the time they met on Monday the colonel had figured out that the money the Clayburns were using came from Alexander Montgomery and the bank. The discovery that the Montgomerys had a confidence he lacked unsettled him. Did they have information that he lacked? The colonel was suspicious. There was the matter, too, of Jonathan's foresight, the unexpected way he had handled that give-or-take proposition and had made the cannery solely a Clayburn affair.

The colonel was proud of his reputation as the wealthiest man in the county; he believed that he was also considered the most sagacious, and he wanted nothing to blemish that reputation.

"See here," he said in Littlepage Ransom's office, after the papers were signed, "we'll just keep our transactions here this morning a private affair. No need for all the riff-raff to know our business." He tried to smile and shrug lightly but the result was a stingy grimace.

As for Jonathan, all he wanted was the dissolving of that old partnership.

On Monday night when the family gathered at home after the

signing of the papers in Ransom's office, Josh said to his brother, "I believe you could have traded with the colonel for half as much cash profit, Jonathan."

Jonathan did not deny it. "Maybe. I don't know. I just wanted him out of our business. And our offer was fair. I'd rather tip the scales a little in his favor, if there's any question." He looked around at his mother and the others. "And now there's no one but our own family in the company. We won't have to worry about making money or losing money for the other fellow."

"That's right," Cal said. "Look ahead, not back."

"We should look to God," their mother said, "and be thankful." After a moment she asked, "Now that we're reorganizing, shouldn't Joshua have a share in the company?"

Jonathan and Cal and Whit and Dan looked at their older brother. "You're not going back in the lumber business?" Cal asked.

"No." Josh shook his head.

"You know he isn't, Calvin," their mother said with a sharpness that surprised them. "There will be no more talk of it."

"All right, Mama," Cal said. But he could not resist an opportunity to tease. "Now, Mr. Clayburn, you do know that you're coming into a flourishing business on its way up—"

Josh was all at once sensitive and aggrieved. "If you don't want me in with you, it's all right."

"Now, now, sir. I didn't say that. We just want you to realize what a progressive, what a prosperous, what an amazing organization—"

"I know as much about it as you do," Josh said.

"Beware exaggeration! With my own wide and varied experience in the field of growing, preserving, and peddling foodstuffs—"

"Just because I'm looking after the livestock while you and Jonathan are riding the rails and visiting big cities doesn't mean that my work counts for nothing."

"Your brother is teasing, Joshua," their mother said hastily. "Everyone does his part of the work and it's all important to our family's well-being. You had a test and trial with that snakebite and the rest of us are just thankful that we didn't lose you." Her solemn look fixed on her four younger sons. "From the profit with which the

Lord blessed us this year we'll advance your share to make you a full partner in the company."

Jonathan was first to respond. "That's right, Josh. We ought to be in this all together. Whit and Dan will have their turn as soon as they get educated."

"That sounds fine, Jonathan," Josh said. "If you're all sure." He looked around at each one. "I want to do my part."

"We're sure," Jonathan said. The others agreed.

Whit stood up. Even in work clothes he managed to appear more fastidious and well dressed than his brothers. His thick dark eyebrows and strong chin gave his face authority. "You're sure for Josh. But I'm not at all sure that I want to stay in Churchill the rest of my life and trade in beans and tomatoes."

"Just what did you have in mind?" Cal inquired.

"I had in mind," Whit's tone squelched his brother's waiting laughter, "to become a professional man and live in a city in style. Maybe go to law school."

"Uh—oh," Cal exclaimed, "you've got a dude on your hands, Mama."

"It's a poor family can't afford one dandy." She smiled. They all relaxed, happy that the unusual moment of tension between them was dissolved. "I want my children to do as they think best—and right— for their own lives. But whatever it is you do, you must always help each other."

"That's why we'll each have to work twice as hard this year." Jonathan pulled their thoughts back to the company. "Now we have a name and reputation to live up to. Did you tell them about the letter from Mr. Waverly, Cal?"

"It only came this morning." Cal assumed an air of grandiose announcement. "Mr. Hugh Waverly writes us to the effect that the prosperous public of the metropolis of Jackson City has responded well to Clayburn Quality tomatoes. In fact, he estimates that he will be ready to receive another shipment on his contract sometime before Christmas. By late spring we should have our whole pack sold, delivered, money received."

The others murmured approval, satisfaction.

"Mr. Hugh Waverly also mentioned that he would like to come to the mountains sometime this fall to see just what the Clayburn Company is, and perhaps do a little hunting on the side."

"Mr. Waverly is coming here?" Mary Clayburn asked. "Why didn't you boys tell me at once?"

"We haven't invited him yet, Mama. And besides, it would be at least two months before he would come," Cal replied.

"We'll invite and he'll accept," she said. "There will be lots of preparation."

Mary Clayburn was right. Mr. Waverly wrote that he would welcome an opportunity to visit in early November, and from that moment on his visit became the focal point for all plans.

Meanwhile, Whit returned to the university and Dan left for faraway Boston, the Massachusetts Institute of Technology, strange food, a cold hard climate, reticent people, strenuous studies. Dan's letters home made Jonathan and his mother smile and the others laugh outright. "I had quite a time finding MIT," he wrote. "After I had ridden all over Boston on that street-car I found myself back where I had started, which turned out to be right across the street from MIT." With a suggestion of homesickness he asked what they were doing in the company now. The first early snow in Boston led him to admit that he had been thinking of the late autumn woods of home, with russet oak leaves underfoot and the warm sun at midday on old gray ledges and familiar paths. "Of course, the Boston Commons provides an interesting site," he added in a lame attempt at his usual optimism.

A short while later Dan wrote to his mother, in a private letter: "They are having a banquet and dance here at the school. Most of the fellows are wearing their fancy clothes. If you won't tell anybody around there I thought I might rent one of the dress suits and go to the party. Of course, I wouldn't be dancing but I would like to watch. Mama, don't think I'm not well-dressed usually. Both of my suits are in good shape."

When the others in the family learned about Dan's letter they roared with laughter. Cal sent a post card to Boston, asking his brother if the Ward McAllister of Churchill should wear rented clothes in the big city.

Mary Clayburn pointed out to her children that Dan understood if dancing were sinful in Churchill it would be sinful in Boston as well. His rejection of it was a source of deep satisfaction to her.

After Whit and Dan left, Jonathan and Joshua and Cal developed plans for the coming year. They agreed that Joshua would remain in charge of the farm as the backbone of their enterprises; Jonathan would arrange the finances and run the cannery and be the chief manager of all activities; Cal would represent Clayburn Brothers to the farmers on the one hand and to the buyers on the other, and he would help enlarge their production and their market.

They also decided to build two other packing sheds. These would be several miles from their first little plant—one in the lowlands near the Ransom farm and another on the uplands where new ground was being cleared for more tomatoes. Beans, blackberries, cabbage, and apples would be added to their products.

While these plans went forward, Nora Stull Buchanan, plumper and pinker than ever, returned to the Clayburns, and school was resumed for Nettie Sue and Lottie. Josh grew animated and confident again.

On the way from the railroad station when Nora Buchanan asked him her first question—was he a part of the company yet?—he was proud that he could answer yes. "I'm a full partner now, Nora," he said. The trace of a pout left her mouth and she nodded happily at the news. Her eyes twinkled as she nestled closer to him on the buggy seat.

And Laura Rathbone came up through the fields again, ready for whatever the woods had to offer or the books to yield. She borrowed volumes from Elisha Clayburn's study and her father proudly complained that his daughter was bankrupting him with the "Lamp oil she burns over those books of a night."

When the beeches and hickories were turning the color of old gold in the valleys and the oak leaves were burning red on the hillsides, Mr. Hugh Waverly arrived for his weekend visit. He brought the young man of twenty who was the "and Son" of Hugh Waverly Company, a pale, quiet person who spent most of his time nodding agreement with his father's words.

"Well now," Mr. Waverly told the Clayburns, "this is the quiet little interval before Thanksgiving and Christmas, and it's good to get up to the hills. Are there birds hereabouts?"

Mr. Waverly prided himself on being something of a hunter. He had brought his field clothes with him.

"And I'd wager he can't count a dove's pinfeathers at fifty yards through those little gold-rimmed glasses," Cal said.

Jonathan nodded. "You and Edom will have to take over this hunt for Saturday. I'm due to go into Churchill and see Mr. Montgomery that morning, stir up a little additional capital for our Ransom farm plant."

"Cebo knows where the doves are, too," Josh said.

"He won't go with you," Jonathan told them. "You know Cebo says killing doves is contrary to Scripture."

"Don't let him tell Mama," Cal said. "If old man Waverly wants to hunt birds here, I say let's find him birds."

Josh winked.

Early on Saturday morning, after a breakfast of fresh sausage and eggs, crisp waffles and coffee, molasses and blackberry jelly and hot apple turnovers, Josh and Cal, Mr. Waverly and son, led by Edom Metcalf and Orvil Gosnell and two good bird dogs, set out for the fields. Jonathan had already left for the day in Churchill and Alex Montgomery's office.

As Jonathan rode back late that afternoon, he took a shortcut across country. He met Laura Rathbone running toward him across the rough stubbled ground. She stumbled, almost fell, kept on running. He turned the horse and galloped to meet her.

When he reined up beside her, she leaned against the horse's side, half-crying, panting. "You have to come with me, Jonathan. Come and see what they've done."

"What is it, Laura? Who?"

She shook her head. "I don't know who. But you have to see." Her hair was tangled and wild from her running. The plain brown dress she wore, with white collar and cuffs, was torn at the hem around her ankles. Looking down at her long, tense, delicate body against the hard sleek side of his horse, Jonathan felt the surge that had come before when he was near Laura. He reached down his hand.

She rode in front of him and he could smell the wetness of her hair where it clung to her neck and cheeks. The warmth of her body heated him. The rhythm of the horse's motion bonded them into a single unit. She seemed as light as a thistledown that might have blown onto his saddle, yet he knew she was as tough, too, as the leather of that saddle. He could see the bone and muscle of her strong hands. And there was the curiosity, the novelty, of never knowing what she might say or do.

The field where she brought him—between her home and the Clayburn farm—was a trampled, bloody sight. Jonathan looked at it in dismay. The wide brown meadow was splotched with dead quail. Loose feathers floated here and there in the light breeze, and caught on a stalk of weed or fallen twigs near the surrounding woods.

Many of the neat little birds lay in torn, bloody clusters. The blood—on feathers, grass, bare ground—was not bright and scarlet but a brownish crust spread in muddy ugliness. Around Jonathan's feet and stretching on across the field were fluffy, stiffening carcasses: tiny beaks agape or clamped close as scissors, eyes bright and sightless and fixed as shoe-buttons, feet as delicate and useless now as cobwebs.

Laura cried, walking among the trim, speckled quail. She circled wide, searching the torn, beaten-down grass to know the dull destruction, and finally met Jonathan again at the edge of the field opposite his tethered horse. "What could pleasure folks about just pure killing?" she asked him.

"I don't know," he said. He thought of the excitement of hunting —the trigger carefully squeezing under his finger while his eye held the game steady in its sights. But not this way, not wholesale, not wasted. "Lots of folks just like to see something fall," he suggested lamely. He wondered that a man as small and correct as Mr. Waverly could find satisfaction in a ritual of havoc. "Surely they'll be back for these birds."

She looked up at him. "I hate them." It was very late in the afternoon. In the half-light her pale face was streaked with tears. "My grandmother used to tell me about the pigeons that used these mountains and skies when she was a girl. Flocks so great they blotted out the sun when they flew over and broke giant trees when they roosted. And not a wild passenger pigeon left today outside a zoo somewhere —none left after the traps and nets and clubs and guns men brought." She sank down to the ground and huddled there sadly, angrily. "I hate them."

Jonathan went to her and knelt beside her and laid one hand on her head. He began to stroke her tense shoulders. Suddenly she lifted her face. They looked at each other. And their mouths were together. Their bodies were together. The grass was November brown underneath them and they could smell the chill of earth and hear the early-evening cry of a screech owl in the nearby woods, but they were aware of nothing beyond their own tumult and hunger. Beneath their burdensome clothes he could feel her softness and she his hardness, and they could not deny the yielding or the thrust. They had waited a long time. They had followed rules and commandments and expectations. But all those outer regulations lay abandoned with their clothes as they discovered the reality of themselves, of their manhood and womanhood no longer separate but whole.

In the midst of the plundered field of birds Jonathan made love to Laura. And she made love to him.

Full dark came and with it a deepening chill. Laura shivered. Jonathan shivered, too. It was the first time he had ever held anyone else's body close to his, feeling the warmth of legs and belly and arms pulsing with his own, lying together, and it was an experience of such delicious sensuousness that he wanted it to go on and on. His arms around her provided a fullness of possession he had never known before. They clung together. The night owl cried again.

"Jonathan," Laura said, "I love you." Her voice was small and strange in the darkness. When he started to speak she drew her finger over his lips. "I wanted to tell you first." She laid her head full on his chest so that her long hair tickled his arms and shoulders and nose and chin. "You must wait and tell me—if you want to—some other time."

There was no explaining Laura.

As they rode home Jonathan held her so close she could scarcely breathe. Before this evening he had always been a solitary, lonely person, not so much because he wished to be but because he did not know how to break through the seriousness and reserve which surrounded him. The burden of his father's death, the responsibility to his family, the expectations of his mother, had made him both larger and lesser than himself. But they had made him prisoner. Only this night, with Laura, out on the wild dead grass had he felt released into a largeness and fulfillment he did not know existed. He had given and received sex, but more—he had given love, received love, made love. And, by God—as his uncle Whit Ransom would have said—it was good.

$\diamond$

7

Part of the programming was the words. There were blasphemous words and words that were whispered behind barn doors or during drunken rages, but there was one word that was never spoken outright. Sex.

Not that sex claimed such a minor part in our lives. On the contrary, it dominated. With brute urgency or gentle insistence it dominated. I suppose the reality was so powerful that we thought to contain it by avoiding any recognition, definition, rational discussion.

But it was there all right. Since that first patriarch had buried four wives in rocky mountain land and sired twenty-three children. Since every one of the big-boned, meat-eating, westward-pushing men had come from the crowded British Isles and claimed land, women, a world along the way.

It was there in trampled barn lot and dusty nest and wallowed pen and open pasture, in cabin and woods and mansion: hot, craving, not to be denied. Sex.

Yet in their world as in mine a generation later, there was no simple admission of the word. Powerful, invisible, its reality disturbed and fed our lives like the flow of a mighty subterranean river. But we came to its tides and currents vulnerable, without warning and naked, without preparation. My father, my uncles, my brother, I—each of us in turn feeling that we were unique and lonely and shamed in the intensity of the surge and undertow gripping us.

("Jon," Deborah said to me one night, covering the scars on her small white breast with my hand, "do not be so afraid of yourself. There's nothing anyone has done or thought that you might not think and also do. For better, for worse, we acknowledge our humanity."

"Is that how you survived, Deborah?"

Her face became even more pale and still, until her brown eyes seemed to swallow up the other features—and me. And she did not answer.)

Did part of the reason for our Puritanism in sex lie in the fact that so many Clayburn families were reared by women, those Clayburn women left widows by blood clots and accidents and violence? My grandmother. My mother. And their world had assigned them a role. If they were prisoner to that role, so were we all.

One of the stories which was bequeathed to each child among the Clayburns, each one receiving it at some special preordained moment from maiden aunt or watchful uncle or waiting cousin, was of Dan. My uncle Dan.

It was the season after his father's death. The rest of that winter had been long and confining, with record-breaking snows and a new-born calf frozen in the barn stall and the two girls choked with chest colds. The smell of onion poultices and hot flannel and steam from boiling teakettles filled the drafty halls and chilly bedrooms. When spring finally came there was a release of energy and jubilation.

"The back of winter finally broken," Cebo said, the first day that birds winged busily among the tree-tops.

The boys attacked the farm chores, trying to recall what their father had done in previous years, making their own decisions carefully. Their mother and Delia and the girls dragged pillows and featherbeds, quilts and rugs and curtains out into the wind and sun. They beat and shook and draped clotheslines and shrubbery and porches with bright patches of fabric and color.

At the close of one demanding day when rocks beneath the plot had summoned all of Josh's and Jonathan's determination, when clearing stumps in the pasture had drained the energy of hired men and even young Dan, when brooms and mops had tolled the women's strength, they all rested after supper. Their talk was desultory. And somehow, drifting, the conversation took a turn toward teasing, that trademark of the Clayburn clan.

They teased about Whitley's eyebrows. "Mama ever runs short on mattress stuffing, she can shear Whit's brows, gather all the padding she needs."

And about Joshua's feet: "Give the feller some oars, he could navigate the Great Lakes in those boats."

So on—with Jonathan's ears, Colonel Wakely's pomposity, the Montgomerys' social aspirations in Churchill.

"And there's a Montgomery girl just right to make Dan a sweetheart," Josh turned to his younger brother.

"Now that would be mighty convenient," Cal said, "with all those Montgomery mills and banks and houses."

"I'll bet Olivia Lee Montgomery would like our Dan, too; a boy with plenty of freckles and ears and—"

"Hush up, Josh," Dan said.

"He's blushing! Little brother is blushing—"

"I am not."

"No. Brother's not blushing like a girl. He always turns pink as a turkey's wattles this time of day."

"Olivia Lee Montgomery Clayburn," Whitley chimed in. "You'd have to admit it has a certain class, Dan."

"I don't know," Dan muttered, trying not to look at them, not to hear, "and I don't care."

"When he gets out of bibs and grows a little, him can think about sweethearts."

"Hush up, Josh. Just hush!" Dan leaped out of his chair. His temper flared like a fuse exploding in the fire. "You—you're nothing but a—a horny prick!"

Silence froze the room.

No one moved. No one spoke. The sound of the clock ticking on the mantel was as loud as a drumbeat. Even the younger children who had no idea what Dan had said realized that some awful taboo had been violated. Dan had broken the bonds which held the world in place as metal circles bound barrel staves in orderly, useful shape. And they all looked at their mother.

Mary Clayburn's face had turned ashen. The skin bleached not white but gray, the ugly mottled color of cold ashes. Her eyes widened with an alarm unlike any of her children had witnessed. The knuckles on her hands which grasped the arms of the master dining-room chair (the chair her husband Elisha had always filled until a few months before) were shiny white.

Dan was the first to move. Overwhelmed by the reaction to his outburst, he turned to his mother. "Mama—" The word stuck in his throat, was swallowed up in their silence.

"You little whelp," Josh said at last. "You ought to have your mouth cleaned out with carbolic acid."

"Hush, Joshua. I can't bear it for my children to quarrel." Their mother spoke stolidly, as if from a far distance.

Jonathan crossed to where Dan was still standing and righted the chair which was tumbled on the floor behind him. "Don't you want to sit down, Dan?" he said.

And Dan sank onto the chair.

"Where did you hear such words?" Mary Clayburn asked.

Dan was relieved at the chance for explanation. "Down in the field, this afternoon, one of the men called Edom Metcalf—that."

"You tell Edom in the morning, Jonathan, that that man isn't to work on this place another day." Mary Clayburn looked at her youngest son. "You knew it meant something not nice, something nasty, didn't you?"

Dan choked. He nodded.

"What shall I do?" His mother spoke the words to herself only, heavy with the burden of her lonely responsibility. "How can I make five boys into five upright men without Elisha here—" she broke off. After a moment she went on, "Lord, you'll have to give me strength."

The children, awed by what seemed an eavesdropping on their mother's weakness and despair, did not look at one another. They gazed at their hands, at the clock ticking so loudly, at the flame in the lamps.

Abruptly she stood up. "Daniel, go outside and bring the stoutest switch your pocketknife will cut from the birch at the edge of the yard."

Nodding, almost eagerly, he dashed for the door. "And Daniel," his mother added, "bring the birch to the back room. I'll be waiting." She picked up one of the smaller glass lamps and went out into the hall.

In the silence the ones left behind could not help but overhear what followed in the schoolroom to the rear. They heard Dan return and their mother send him out again for a larger switch. They heard his slow steps down the hall once more and their mother's instructions on his second return.

"Are you ready, son?"

"Yes, Mama."

"All right. I'm holding out my hand. I want you to switch it with that birch limb as hard as you can."

"Mama!" The cry of startled protest echoed through the house. Its meaning was reflected in the shocked looks exchanged by Jonathan and Joshua and Nettie Sue and Lottie in the room where they sat, waiting. "Mama, Mama," Nettie Sue whimpered. "He's going to hurt my mama."

"Be quiet," Cal said, and put his arms around the two distraught girls.

"I've told you what to do," their mother's distant voice was firmer. They knew she would not swerve.

"Mama, I can't."

"You will!"

There was a pause. Then Mary Clayburn said, "If I have failed to make my children pure of thought and word and deed I should be punished."

"But it wasn't you," Dan cried. "You're the best, the finest mother—"

"Better that I should be punished now for a minute than that you should be punished for my failure through an eternity."

"But Mama—"

"Use the switch, Dan! Lay it across my hand. Hard."

The tension in the big room was as palpable as the spring night wind that blew unnoticed down the hall and through the door. They all knew that Dan was crying. The one who remained constantly indifferent to his own sprains and scratches and hurts (in contrast to Josh and Cal who nursed and discussed and magnified each pang to its ultimate affliction), the one who always laughed and made a joke when his brothers had succumbed to pessimism, the one who never cried was sobbing now.

The sigh of the supple birch bough echoed down the hall.

"Again, Daniel. Harder."

The sound of the striking and the crying mingled.

"Much harder."

Eventually the ordeal was finished. They heard the switch strike against the wall and fall to the floor as Dan flung it away from him. They heard him run upstairs.

Then their mother came down the hall, dragging her left foot ever so slightly, and into the room. The girls rushed into her arms. She reassured them. Her face was composed now and it had lost that ashen color. She held her left hand behind her back.

"It's time for bed," she said, "and our prayers." She looked at each one in turn. "Each of us must remember the prayers."

"We will, Mama."

"And Whit, you sleep with Cal tonight. Let Dan be alone."

"All right, Mama."

"I know my boys are good, but snares lurk everywhere, and as you become men's bodies—" She broke off, stumbling on the word "bodies." Then she concluded, "We'll have to trust the Lord."

Fact, memory, legend: that evening was imprinted in family annals. What its confused mixture of anatomy and colloquialism and atonement, its overtones of sexual intercourse and shame, seared on the Clayburn conscience, I would not attempt to say. What guilt (was she his first belated groping for sex?) did it infuse between Jonathan and his free, natural, loving Laura?

At any rate, the inheritance of family virility and satisfaction was not diverted. The Clayburns took sober second thought for their spirit and salvation of their soul. But the body was also part of that steward-ship and it was here and now, imperative in its yearnings and appetites.

After all, they did become (and I did become) canners and preservers of beans, beets, corn, kraut, and half a hundred other foods for appeasement of the belly, not philosophical explorers of the baffling mind, or painters, composers, poets, raw to the quick with the search for the vision, the melody, the word that would reveal a clue to the secret.

8

"We need that piece of land the worst way," Joshua said. He watched Nora as she disappeared into the downstairs bedroom, then he followed his brothers down the long hall and onto the verandah where they stood, straightening and stretching for a moment in the midday June heat. "It would round out our farm just right."

"It does snuggle up to those lower acres we planted last year," Calvin agreed. He pulled off his broadcloth coat and hung it on the back of a porch chair. Then he began loosening the buttons on his vest.

"With the Ransom farm cannery on one side and this Rathbone place on the other, we'd be sitting pretty," Josh went on. "After all, with three years of canning behind us we've got to be sure we have plenty of farmland."

"Our big brother has big ideas," Cal said, "now that he's an old married man."

"With an heir on the way," Whit nodded.

Dan, already in his shirt sleeves, looked at Jonathan, who stood at one end of the verandah with his back to them. Dan started to speak, reconsidered, and sat down quietly in one of the rocking chairs.

"Janus Rathbone has enough timber there to provide all the picking and shipping crates we would need for at least the next half-dozen years," Josh persisted. "It would be easy to get to, too. Set up a sawmill in those white oak flats—"

Cal glanced at Jonathan's back and interrupted. "It's not the lumber we need so much. It's the new ground for tomatoes." His voice was casual, affable. "The way our tomatoes have been selling the last three years, we may need to clear old Grindstone Mountain before the decade's out."

Whit, still buttoned into vest and coat, fingering the gold watch fob his uncle Whitley Ransom had given him when he turned twenty-one the year before, nodded in agreement. "Jonathan, I remember you forecasting that if Clayburn Brothers succeeded in this year of our Lord, 1904, it would be largely because our own farms could guarantee a supply of raw material."

When there was no response, he added, "That was what Mr. Buchanan lacked at his cannery up in Virginia. You said that's what hurt several of the fly-by-night factories our supply salesmen had told us about."

"And there's no land like new ground, the first season after timber's all cleared, for bringing in fine quality tomatoes just right for canning," Josh said urgently.

"She wouldn't want the trees cut," Jonathan said quietly, so quietly that the others hardly heard his words.

In the house behind them there rose a distant clatter of dishes. Their mother, growing heavier and more pronounced in her limp, came outside. Each of the sons moved to help her: Jonathan pulled up her favorite chair and Dan settled her in it.

"You're looking mighty nice in that blue dress, Mama," Josh said.

"Thank you, Joshua. It's the first dress I've had that wasn't black since your papa died."

Her broad cheeks were pink from heat. When she discovered that she had misplaced her fan, Cal went to fetch it. As soon as he handed her the stiff round palm leaf she began to stir an almost invisible breeze before her face.

"What are you five hatching up?" She looked from one to the other of them. "Must be a serious business."

No one answered for an interval, then Josh said, "We're trying to decide whether or not we ought to buy the Rathbone land that joins ours down in the Dark Hollow section."

"We need it for tomatoes," Cal added.

Their mother fanned a moment. A board in the floor under her rocker creaked rhythmically. "What does Jonathan say?"

There was a pause.

"I wonder how you know so certainly that Janus Rathbone will sell his land," Jonathan turned to his older brother.

Josh was surprised. "Why, anybody will sell anything—if they're offered enough."

"I doubt that Laura would sell those woods," Jonathan said. "For anything."

"And I doubt that the deed is in her name," Josh answered, then flushed as he watched the still, remote expression close over Jonathan's face.

"Of course," Cal's eyes widened in the innocent expression he assumed when he found a new source of teasing, "there *are* ways to get land in a family other than by buying it—" His voice trailed off. But no one laughed.

Jonathan spoke quietly. "I would be willing."

The creaking in the floor and the whisper of the fan ceased abruptly.

"Well, Cal, that is a little far-fetched," Josh said.

"Are you trying to tell us, Jonathan," Mary Clayburn asked, "that you—you could like Laura Rathbone? I mean like her that way?"

"I would marry her, Mama."

"Marry?"

"That is, if she would have me."

Their mother's surprise was shared by her other sons. They stared at their brother who always appeared to be under such control, exercising so much wisdom. They had vaguely suspected Jonathan's attraction to the girl (and they would admit she was arresting in a strange, intense way), but no one had imagined marriage. And, if she would have him? What did that mean?

They sat in a momentary tableau, each trying to understand a situation that might abruptly alter their lives. This was more than they had bargained for on a leisurely Sunday.

Well-fed, unhurried in the beckoning afternoon, comfortable in an enclave surrounded by allies and competitors, the Clayburn brothers used this Sunday interlude in the shade of the long verandah or the warmth of the big square parlor, depending on the season, to digest events of the week past, lay plans for the week to come. Sometimes one of them took their mother to visit Drusilla Wakely and the colonel. Another might visit a friend or go "courting" across the county. But their nucleus remained there each week for a business and a personal reconnoitering.

Jonathan was the one most often at home. After Nora Stull Buchanan and Joshua married and continued living with the family, they often went off for the day on Sunday. Mary Clayburn explained, "Nora's cooped up here with her in-laws all week long. And Joshua is on the farm working with just Edom and Cebo and the field-hands. He and Nora need to be away on their own on the Sabbath."

Cal was popular with the young people of the county, and few picnics or gatherings were planned where he was not one of the organizers and centers of activity. There was no special girl in Churchill he liked, but following his elder brother's marriage he wrote regular letters to Isabel Buchanan, a cousin of Nora's he had met at the wedding in Virginia.

Dan and Whit had only recently returned from up north. Whit would go back to Yale Law School in September, but Dan had finished MIT and was, as Cal said, like a race horse at the starting gate. In fact, it was the need to determine Dan's position with the company that had kept all of the family at home this fine Sunday in June. Discussion of buying Janus Rathbone's property had been brought up and dropped previously, due to Jonathan's resistance. It had been introduced today only by a casual question of Nora's at dinner: "Where are all those crops coming from to keep five plants running?"

Which had brought the remark from Cal, "You're a mighty bright girl, sister-in-law, to look like such a helpless little thing." Nora had blushed prettily and smiled at him.

And Josh had pursued the question as they came out to the verandah.

Now Jonathan stood at a corner of the porch, leaning against a column, in his high Sunday collar and tie and shirt sleeves, his face controlled and expressionless as it often was at the cannery when problems seemed insurmountable. He was telling his family that a mountain girl without proper background or acceptable resources could refuse to marry him.

"It's not very flattering, is it?" he smiled at them in tolerant gentleness.

"Jonathan, you haven't actually asked her?" his mother said.

"I've asked." There was something in his voice that barred other questions.

During the years since Elisha Clayburn's death, the family had come to take for granted Jonathan's leadership. His labor and attention seemed rightfully to belong to them as much as to himself. Laura Rathbone was the first claim he had made solely for himself. Suddenly they were dismayed and chagrined, not at themselves that they had failed to notice Jonathan's caring for the girl during these months and years, but at him for the possibility of embarrassment and change which threatened their equilibrium.

Mary Clayburn was trying to fan again, but the stiff palm shook in her hand. "Laura is generous-hearted and pretty enough, I suppose, in her own way—" The effort at diplomacy collapsed. "The girl has always made me uneasy."

No one spoke. The tinkle of glass and china echoed faintly from inside the house, followed by an occasional female voice from the depths of the kitchen. In the distance, those on the porch—if they were looking—could see two figures plodding along a path between the upland fields: Delia and her niece, in silk hand-me-downs and dimity made-overs from the Clayburn closets, on their way to their church. The two women moved slowly but steadily, weary from the day's work already accomplished since daylight but anticipating this brief afternoon of exemption from being servants. Except for their receding figures, the landscape was motionless, suspended in afternoon drowsiness.

Josh felt the need to respond to their mother's comment about Laura Rathbone. "She's always so notionly."

"She's not one to be easily predicted," Jonathan agreed.

"Well," Dan ran his hand through his hair, "Josh makes that sound like a crime and Jonathan makes it seem like a pleasure. Guess we'll have to leave everybody to his own mind."

But even Cal was finding it strenuous to be light about Jonathan and Laura Rathbone. "I just can't understand how I never noticed— between you—" he murmured.

"Maybe you weren't looking," his youngest brother said.

"None of us was looking, I reckon, Dan," Cal admitted.

"Well now, there's not been that big an event—or secret," Jonathan said. He straightened and stood away from the column where he had been leaning. "All that's happened—I found a girl I liked and she likes me I know, but so far she won't hear any talk of marriage."

"That's unnatural in itself," his mother said, "especially in a girl already twenty."

Jonathan almost smiled. "Laura says that she won't ever go into marriage for a name or a house or safety or anything but the two people involved."

"There! That shows in itself that the idea of a name and a house has crossed her mind," Mary Clayburn said.

"They've crossed other people's minds—and tongues—too," Jonathan said. "That's what she knows."

Since the morning, years ago, after his father's funeral, when he had struck a bargain between his father's ledgers and the men bent on vengeance and had eased his mother's dread of a fearful injustice, this was the first occasion on which Jonathan had seriously differed with his mother. This made him uncomfortable. At other times, when Josh had wanted to borrow an advance on his company salary and take Nora to Niagara Falls on their honeymoon, when Dan had wanted to go up north to MIT, when Whit had wanted to be separate from the family company and become a lawyer with his graduate training at Yale, at all these and other critical times Jonathan had interceded, thoughtfully weighing every pro and con of the situation. He had persuaded their mother in each instance by the balance and unselfishness of his judgment. Now he needed someone else's consideration in his behalf.

"I still don't understand," his mother said, "if she likes you—"

Jonathan could not explain to them what he did not understand himself. And then there was the guilt. How could he tell them of winter afternoons in the scrubbed cozy simplicity of that house he liked so well, before a roaring hickory fire? And of one afternoon in particular when Laura looked up at him with tears in her eyes?

"You're going to be somebody. Not just in Churchill or this little mountain county but in big places as well. I couldn't bear the time when you'd be ashamed of me, Jonathan, or I'd long to be away from you, back in the woods and fields among things I understand."

How could he describe for them the summer evenings when she had shaken her long soft hair until it touched his cheek like a caress: "My mother was Cherokee. Half or whole or one single drop, you know the amount doesn't make any difference, she's called Indian. And I'll never be shamed by it. What would you say, Jonathan, when they asked you about that at one of your company meetings?"

How could he re-create for them one pulsing moment of the desperate, loving effort he had made to reassure her that nowhere he could go, no one he could know, would diminish his caring, his loyalty? And the fierceness with which she had cried, "That's what I couldn't bear: your loyalty. I'd want your loving, Jonathan, all of it, always. Or nothing." And he had to admit, briefly as a shadow across the sun, that deep within himself he was dismayed, almost frightened, by her passion.

"If she likes you—" his mother said now.

"I don't know." He spoke on edge. "Maybe she doesn't like me. Maybe she only loves me."

The Clayburns were clearly unaccustomed to such outbursts from Jonathan. Embarrassed by any discussion of emotions, they did not look at him now, or at each other. Only half-intentionally Jonathan had maneuvered them into position to welcome a change of subject from his personal affairs. He felt, all at once, lonelier than he had ever felt before. Even on the mountain long ago when searching for his father's killers, he had had Janus Rathbone with him. Even in that first packing shed when the first lid had been soldered on a can and the can had been handed to him to hold and examine, he had had Cal and Dan with him. This time there was no one. Dan was trying to understand—at least he was being quiet—but that was not enough.

"Well now," he said, pulling up a chair so that he could sit facing Dan and his mother, "no more talk about hearts and flowers. I thought we were going to make some business arrangements today, take a new member into our company."

Dan responded immediately. He nodded and slapped one knee loudly. "That's right. When are you fellows going to let a good man get into the canning business and straighten you out?"

They all welcomed the respite from dabbling in the quicksand of Jonathan's strange behavior. "Guess we'll greet a good man—when we find one," Cal rejoined. "Till then, we'll have to make do with whatever we can pick up."

"Now that Whitley and Dan are Yankee swells," Josh said, "and know important things—all the right places to pay three dollars for a fifty-cent dinner—I reckon we'll have to mind their good advice."

"Now, what do you partners think we ought to offer this new expert?" Jonathan asked, looking in turn from his mother to Cal and then to Josh.

"What about the same starting pay that we had?" Josh mentioned tentatively.

"I hadn't given it much thought," Cal said. "What do you think, Jonathan?"

"Well now," Jonathan looked at Dan and then at the high ceiling above them, "I wondered about this proposition: Daniel Clayburn, upon payment of a thousand dollars, to become a full partner in Clayburn Brothers Company. Also to be production manager of the main plant we're opening in Churchill this year and technical overseer for the other plants as he can get around to check their machinery and methods. Payment for this work to be the same salary received by Joshua and Jonathan and Calvin Clayburn: eight hundred dollars a year and one-fifth of the net profits of the company for this year."

Their mother listened carefully to each word and gave quick nods of approval.

Dan interrupted. "Objection. I like everything about that proposition—but one thing. I'll accept your letting me come in now with almost the same investment you risked years ago. And I'll accept your offer of a salary that's the same as the other partners'."

"Well, then, what's your big hold-up?" Cal asked.

"I won't accept a fifth of all the company's profits. My work ought to help earn bigger profits than came in last year. Otherwise, I'm not much account to the company."

The other brothers looked at each other, then back to their youngest member.

"So," Dan said, leaning forward, his voice eager and excited in spite of himself, "whatever we earn over and above the amount of profit last year—of that I'll take a fifth."

Their mother watched each of them.

"That sounds plumb fair, baby brother," Cal said.

"It sure does," Josh nodded earnestly.

Jonathan stood up and walked to the end of the porch. He paused a moment, gazing toward the rear of the farm and the river's wide sweeping bend between the greening fields, then he came back to the others. He stopped beside Dan. "I guess our father would be mighty proud to know he has a son like you—"

"He knows," their mother nodded confidently.

"Lots of men can graduate from MIT," Jonathan went on, "although we're pleased enough about your record there, too. But I guess there are very few men could make as fair a proposition as you just made us."

Dan smiled at his older brother. "I guess I've had a pretty good model to follow after in how to be more than fair." In that slippery moment their eyes met. Then they turned away.

Their mother had resumed her energetic rocking and her usually impassive face was a regular catalogue of contentments. "Your father, where he is, knows as well as I know here that our sons care for one another, help one another. That's as good a part of heaven as we could want."

"We'll always do our best by each other, Mama," Josh said. His voice was strained with virtue.

"Better come on in and join the company circle, brother Whit," Cal said, "then we'll all rise on our wings or fall on our backsides together."

"Cal!" their mother said gently.

"Thanks, Cal, but I'll not be coming into the canning business. I might help out, though." Whit fingered the gold watch chain. "Clayburn Brothers may need good legal advice all along—"

"It's going to grow," Dan promised.

"And it's going to need a lawyer." Jonathan sat down again slowly. "A good one to help us keep the law, not get around it."

"Companies don't get fat that way, Jonathan," Cal said, then added quickly, "no, I agree with you. We'll try to be upright as a company as we are as individuals."

"And we'll try to see that others are upright with us," Jonathan said. "Whit, maybe after you finish your big Yale education and after you're admitted to the bar, you can begin by doing something about the freight rates down here."

"Maybe so," Whit agreed.

"It's squeezing us," Jonathan held his arms behind his head and leaned back in his chair. "The cans and fertilizer we had shipped in last week—it cost half as much as we'd pay for a like amount of our canned goods being shipped out. I told the stationmaster last week, 'These freight rates will suck the South dry just as long as goods can be brought in to us for less than we can send them out.' "

Dan grinned. "You ought to hear some of those Boston folks stammer and stutter when you ask them to explain such facts of life. They can't see that we're still an economic colony down here."

"It's like Nora's father up in Richmond says," Josh told them, "the war didn't change anything, didn't settle anything, except for the worse."

"But the new railroad siding you're building—" Dan began.

"*We're* building," Jonathan corrected him. "You're in this now as deep as any of us, young fellow."

"With that railroad siding we're building at the new plant and warehouse in town, we'll be ready to take advantage of any favorable circumstance that offers itself."

"That's so, Dan," their mother said, "and I'm glad to see my boys' work prosper. But I'll have to admit I'm sorry to see Jonathan leave home and move his office into that plant."

They all laughed outright. "Mama," Cal said, "Jonathan isn't going to the Sandwich Islands. And he's not leaving home. He's just going up the road a piece to have an office in our warehouse where all our business can have a central control. And he and Dan may think they'll board in town part of the time, but knowing yours and Delia's cooking I don't judge they will be away too often."

"That's so, Mama," Josh assured her.

"What's so?" Nettie Sue asked from the door. She and Lottie were still rubbing their hands, puckered from hot dishwater, as they came out onto the porch.

"That your brothers will still spend lots of time here with us in spite of the new warehouse and office in town," their mother said patiently.

"Oh, I hope so, Jonathan," Nettie Sue said. She was sixteen and wore her hair piled on top of her head.

"You will, won't you Dan?" Lottie echoed.

They were agreeable girls with clear scrubbed faces. The features which made their brothers attractive men—broad faces, firm chins, strong noses and mouths—made them innocently plain. They seemed totally without guile or mystery. When her brothers teased Nettie Sue about Mr. Hugh Waverly's son, who had come on a bird hunt last fall, she giggled and protested and hoped that her brothers knew something she did not, for the young man had never as much as written a word to her.

"We'll still be here so much you'll have to shoo us off like a visitation of locusts," Dan assured his sisters. "That is, unless Shad Kendrick failed his business course down at Jackson City and can't be of help to your big brother, the president. Or unless Lonas Rankin lost his way with machinery and helping this old brother of yours, the new plant manager."

"Dan? Oh, good, Dan!" Lottie cried.

"That reminds me, I saw Shad at church this morning," Jonathan told his brothers. "He's coming to work tomorrow. He seems to feel that he's made lots of progress, learned a great deal at business school."

His mother nodded. "I'm glad. Shad Kendrick comes from a good generation of people."

There was silence. Her remark had turned each of their thoughts full circle back to the subject that was lying just beneath the surface: Laura Rathbone and the importance of blood. Jonathan pretended not to notice the sudden lull. "Shad is a good old boy," he said. "Now, would anybody besides me like a good cold drink of water?"

Everyone would. "I'll get it for you, Jonathan," Nettie Sue volunteered. She beamed under her brother's thank you and added, "Better still, I'll make some lemonade."

"What about trying some of that ice we packed away last winter?" Cal asked.

Jonathan considered. "Wouldn't it be best to wait until our really hot weather sets in? We put such a good layer of sawdust around the icehouse door this year, it seems a shame to break into it till we're ready to make full use of the ice."

"Maybe so," Cal agreed reluctantly. "Come July we're going to be glad to remember that February day we spent chopping blocks out of the pond."

"Meantime," Josh hesitated, then plunged on, "would there be any harm in us walking down to the corner where our line joins Janus Rathbone's? Could we just take a look at the soil and the trees and the general lay of the land?"

Whit cleared his throat. No one spoke. Nettie Sue's footsteps receded down the hall.

"With five plants running full blast every year, we're going to have to haul in a real crop of tomatoes—" Josh's sentence died in mid-passage.

"It's too late for Rathbone's land to do us any good this season," Cal said. "We can think about it."

"Josh is like all the old Clayburns and Ransoms," his mother said, "all he wants is the land that joins him."

"I'll have to think about it, Josh," Jonathan said.

Summer came in at a trot, went at a gallop, and ended in a sprint. Days melted away as quickly as the ice carried up from its sawdust storage in the icehouse in the ravine. Beans, cabbage, beets, blackberries ripe and juicy, and plump red tomatoes rolled into the sheds. The Clayburns continued to woo, cajole, educate the small farmers who contracted crops and gradually listened, learned about seed, about fertilizer, about careful timing and handling during harvest.

Jonathan gathered samples from the various canning plants, marked them, and took them home at the end of each week. As meticulously as if they were potential customers, the family cut each can, tasted the contents, savored and pondered and rendered verdicts.

"Those tomatoes seem like the firmest we've ever packed for their color and size."

"Bet old Hugh Waverly will be proud to get a shipment of these."

"He should be. But I'm not so sure about this run of berries. Some of them are mushy."

"Rain last week held up the pickers. They just pulled every blackberry came to hand, didn't cull out over-ripe ones."

"Tell Shad Kendrick to send out a notice about that: any more over-ripe berries brought into the receiving shed will be docked from the pay-check."

And Jonathan said, "One thing we have to do: our cans must be uniform. In color, size, seasoning, our product just has to come out the same from each packing shed. Otherwise we'll never build up trust among our customers in every can they buy."

At the new cannery and warehouse in town, Jonathan and Dan pushed each day far into the night, stretching their energy to the outermost edges. With the help of Lonas Rankin, Dan set up a box-making machine, and its success led him to push forward work on an automatic capper.

"Better look out for those machines," Lonas said one night, "pretty soon we won't need no folks around here a-tall."

"Don't need spoiled food any time," Dan answered. He was filing the end off of a bolt and he frowned in concentration.

"You're sure right. I hauled a run of swollen cans from the Ransom shed, dumped them in the river last week," Lonas said. "Now all that muscle work lying down on the river bottom, money wasted."

"Tighten the vise there, Lonas," Dan said. Then, as the sound of his file grated in the quiet, he asked, "The river? Is that still where we get rid of the bad goods?"

The black man nodded. "River's the only thing around here big enough, deep enough to swallow up a load like that."

Dan bore down on the file.

" 'Course, when this old feller's finished," Lonas said, looking at the capping machine, "don't reckon we'll need to dump any cans under the river. They'll all be floating off to market on top the river."

"That's right, Lonas," Dan said vigorously.

The capping machine, under Dan's adjustments, and the box-maker, tended by Lonas, speeded up the crucial weeks of canning. But for a brief interval it appeared that there would be no canning at all. The Friday night after the automatic capper had gone into operation a group of men and women from the Churchill plant came after work to speak to Dan.

"We're quitting," one of the younger ones, Orvil Gosnell's son, said bluntly. He held his thumbs in his suspenders in a gesture of defiant unconcern.

An older man joined him. "You see, we never worked nowhere with colored before. We don't aim to start now—"

Dan glanced at each of their faces, then broke into a broad grin and pretended ignorance of their meaning. "Now I reckon you're mistaking me," he said, "and if I'll just wipe this grease off my face you won't have any complaint."

"It's not you," one of the women spoke up, but Dan did not let her go on.

"Black's only skin-deep," he said, and drew his handkerchief from his pocket and swiped a broad, clean streak across one cheek.

Finally the Gosnell boy said, "It's Lonas Rankin we're naming."

A great light seemed to dawn on Dan. "Why, he's not working with you, son," he explained. "Didn't you folks understand? He's with me. I need him to forge the iron and steel for our machines. Lonas is with me and the machines."

The perturbed group did not know what to make of these assurances but they liked Dan and trusted him. They wanted to believe what he said, and so they accepted it.

The following week Dan discovered two processes with the green beans which could be combined into a single handling, and one line of women was freed to work with the sauerkraut. By this saving, two products could be canned on the same day in the same plant. Jonathan was jubilant over the improvement. "You'll turn us into a real going concern yet," he said to his brother.

Dan laughed, scratching one grease-smudged ear. "Me and Lonas here," he said. "And I've been wondering if the assistant to the manager shouldn't have a raise in salary, too?"

"Maybe so," Jonathan agreed, "Probably so." But he was frowning and did not look at Lonas. Later, in the office, he told Dan that such decisions should never be mentioned impulsively or decided before the employees.

"It just seemed like the right thing to do," Dan said.

"It was, but not till all the management had talked it over and agreed."

Dan granted that he would try to follow procedures more closely.

When the season reached its height, Nettie Sue and Lottie came to work at the canning sheds, and when some of the women had to be absent from the plants because small children kept them at home, Lottie offered to look after their children while they worked. She asked her brothers if she could use an old storeroom, which she converted into a room where a dozen children came each day to play and eat lunch under her supervision.

Lottie was a serious girl who took with literal piety each precept in the copybooks, every adage of her mother's counsels, all the Bible's admonitions—and their weight lay heavy on her heart.

Although Nettie Sue was two years older, Lottie seemed, at least to her family, much the more mature, perhaps because she seemed less happy, less infected with romantic dreams. For Nettie Sue Clayburn harbored a desire: she wished to become a singer. It was a hope that had little support from her family, chiefly because they never, even for a moment, took it seriously. Such careers—acting, singing, painting —were for strangers, foreign sorts of people with long names and languid seductive bodies and incomprehensible upside-down habits of work and sleep and play. The Clayburns refused to think that Nettie Sue might actually consider joining such bizarre ranks. Therefore, her "voice" remained a whim, a pastime, and no one gave her trembling soprano more than casual, infrequent compliments. Lottie's talents and inclinations seemed much more practical and praiseworthy.

As Lottie's number of hours in the "nursery" grew from six to twelve, while the mothers of the children put in ever-lengthening days at the sorting benches and peeling tables, Lottie's brothers considered giving her individual wages. None of the Clayburn women had ever received any direct pay for work, and this innovation needed serious consideration. At last it was agreed that although Lottie's name would not appear on the formal payroll, she would advance beyond "missionary" status and receive regular cash each week that she performed her special service to the company.

On the Riverbend Farm, Josh increased the herd of cattle. Vines from some of the vegetables that were canned, along with the pasture corn and hay, made good feed for the livestock. And Josh was gradually becoming an acknowledged expert on both dairy cows and beef cattle. The department of agriculture at the state university at Jackson City occasionally called him in for practical advice and consultation.

When Nora gave birth, in late August, to a son, Josh was awkward with the pride and humility that had warred within him on so many occasions. He was swathed in security. He had managed to win a pretty, aristocratic wife and yet continue to live near his mother, and now the addition of Stull Buchanan Clayburn, bone and flesh and blood of his own, completed the idyll of success and prosperity slowly accumulating through his brothers. Of all the Clayburns, Josh had become most nearly satisfied with the direction and events of his life.

During the first week of September, Jonathan grew quieter than usual. Fatigue, even in the fresh hours of early morning, dragged at him like a heavy yoke. Two nights he went to bed as soon as he had eaten a few meager bites of supper, but each morning his legs and arms moved as if they were relentless weights. Then, a week after Josh's and Nora's baby was born, and while Jonathan was still at the breakfast table listening to Dan's plan for an automatic cabbage-chopper which he and Lonas would build during the winter for canning kraut next season, Cousin Rilla collapsed on the kitchen porch. Jonathan began to carry her upstairs, but thin and light as she was under all the staves and petticoats she wore, he stumbled on the second step and pitched forward and lay there because he knew he could not get up.

His mother cried out and Dan came running, followed by Cal. Together they brought Cousin Rilla and then Jonathan up to their bedrooms.

That afternoon Dr. Maclin was pacing across the floor and speaking. "The ice is our villain. I'm positive of it."

"But we've all had some of that ice," Mary Clayburn replied.

"Then you may all come down with typhoid," Dr. Maclin snapped.

Typhoid. A raging fever. Delirium. The lining of the stomach inflamed and delicate as tissue paper. Life hanging by a balance that was more often than not tipped on the side of death. Typhoid, the scourge.

Four days after her collapse, late in the afternoon, Cousin Rilla hemorrhaged, and died. Lonely, dressed in silk she herself had stitched, she was buried in a corner of the Clayburn plot where she would rest as she had lived, without intruding over-much on any family group. Brother Pryor, standing on the freshly cut grass and ragweed near the raw hole of red clay, spoke a brief benediction for the "faithful departed sister."

Only Cal and his sisters and a handful of neighbors showed up to hear him, however, for the rest of the family seemed immobilized by anxiety. Jonathan was still delirious. The doctor shaved his head and Delia sponged him with cool water and his mother took her vigil by his bed, saying that she herself would give him all medicine and would not leave until his fever had broken.

Others came and went like ghosts around the house. Cal and Dan finished out the canning season, put up the last apples and decided to wait on pumpkin till next year. There were so many decisions only Jonathan could make, yet each day they experienced the benefit of some judgment or foresight he had shown in the past. Women left the canning sheds and came to offer their help at the brick house where time appeared to be standing still.

"Any word of Jonathan Clayburn today?" people in Churchill asked each morning.

Mary Clayburn rested at brief intervals on a cot set up beside the carved walnut bed where Jonathan peered forth gaunt and wild from ciderdown pillows and disheveled sheets. Time after time he seemed to try to call, but no name came from between his parched lips.

"Tell me, Jonathan," his mother leaned over him. "Tell me, son. Anything you want—"

But from the abyss behind his eyes no message formed.

Throughout long nights and days old Cebo brought ice for bathing and carried waste and comforted Mary Clayburn merely by the constancy of his presence.

Laura Rathbone came. But not into Jonathan's room, not into his vision.

As chance arranged it, Nora Stull, as her uncle back in Richmond had always called her, was in the downstairs bedroom with her baby when she heard Laura at the front door and then in the hall, calling softly in the mid-afternoon drowse and Indian-summer heat.

"Here, Laura, come in here," Nora answered.

She appeared in the door like a genie, her thick, burnished hair caught back and confined by a ribbon into one long fall down her back, her face sad and tense.

"How is he, Nora?" she asked, without prelude or formality.

The family had not seen Laura for a long time. They had not understood why until the startling Sunday afternoon conversation with Jonathan three months before. When Josh had told Nora about it later, she had been angry, angrier than he had ever seen his wife before. "Jonathan can't marry somebody like that." She stamped her foot. "He positively cannot make Laura Rathbone my sister-in-law."

And when Josh had tried to reassure her and quiet her she said, "He can't bring a woodsgirl, a nobody, into the family."

Now Nora looked at Laura's face, surprised to observe how she had changed. For all her air of freedom and natural grace, a sense of pain lodged there, too.

"How is he?" Laura repeated softly, urgently.

"Who, Laura?"

"Jonathan. How's Jonathan? Will you tell me or not?"

"He's just the same," Nora Clayburn said.

"Oh, God!" Laura leaned against the door. Afternoon sunlight slanted between the lace curtains and across the cradle swathed in blue beside Nora's bed. In the moment's silence Laura did not seem to notice the cradle. "Has he asked for me?"

Nora Stull's eyebrows lifted. "You?"

"Yes, me, Nora. Has Jonathan called for me?"

"As far as I know he hasn't spoken anyone's name, least of all yours. They say he just lies there and stares and grows weaker while the sweat pours off him as he groans and his mother gives him medicine."

"Would they let me see him, Nora?"

Slowly, deliberately, Nora shook her head.

Laura turned her face away, toward the door.

"You're not so welcome around here any more," Nora said. "If I were you, Laura, I'd go on home and spare making myself an embarrassment."

"But you're not me." Laura faced around, her green-gray eyes hard upon the snug, round-faced girl in the bed. "You're a little pink and white fluffy kitten aren't you? All softness and purrs—and claws."

Nora Stull stared, almost frightened.

"Oh, you've all got claws. Taking my woods, taking the trees and hidden green places and mosses and Christmas ferns and bold little stream. Taking it because my papa thinks we need money—" From her voice she might have been crying but there were no tears in her eyes.

"I don't know anything about their trades," Nora said, stroking the smooth hem of her sheet.

"Oh, you know all right. I'll wager you knew when they only had it in mind."

Nora showed a flicker of triumph. "I knew Josh thought they needed more land for crops for the cannery—"

" 'Josh thought?' " Laura gave a short laugh. " 'The cannery?' Why poor Josh doesn't know the first ABC about that company, or care—unless his little schoolteacher makes him. If it weren't for Jonathan—" her voice caught. In a moment she went on. "But Josh is doing this on his own. He's buying our woods from my papa. I doubt that Jonathan knows."

"He doesn't," Nora answered impulsively. "There are some things the company can do without Jonathan's direction."

Laura looked at her and away and she spoke more quietly. "I won't live on there without my woods. Josh might as well buy it all. Because I'll be moving somewhere else, somewhere farther in the mountains."

"That will be nice, Laura." The relief on Nora's face was bold as print.

"Nice?" Laura shook her head. "Nice?" she repeated scornfully. "You don't know anything about it, Miss Buchanan."

"Mrs. Clayburn now," Nora said, patting the bed softly.

"Mrs. Clayburn, indeed." And Laura laughed again. "Oh, they don't know what they've gotten themselves into with you, do they?"

They looked at each other a moment. "I don't know what you're talking about," Nora said. "I only intend that Joshua won't play second-best all his life."

Laura left the door, took a short step back into the hall. "Well, I won't be around for your little games, Nora Clayburn. You tell your Joshua he ought to speak to my father about buying our cabin and house-plot, too. He can likely make himself a real sharp trade." She looked toward the stairs at the end of the hall and upward toward the faint sounds in the distance. "If you swear to me that he hasn't called my name—"

"No, he hasn't. I swear," Nora cried.

Laura glanced at her once more. "Scared, pretty kitten?" And she went the way she had come, suddenly, lightly, freely as a forest creature.

That night Nora told Joshua only that Laura Rathbone had come to see her and the baby, and that the Rathbones wanted to sell their cabin along with the woodland. Josh, weary and distraught (he had just helped hold Jonathan in the bed during a surge of wild delirium), was cheered a little. "As I've said time and again, it'll round out our holdings just right. I believe Jonathan will be proud we went ahead—once he's well."

No others in the family were brought down by the typhoid, but the rest worried about their mother's strain.

"She's tired to the bone," Josh said.

"She won't rest," Cal protested.

"Leave her alone," Dan advised.

Nettie Sue and Lottie cried when they carried meals upstairs and saw their mother's haggard face. She would not let them cry in her presence so they kept control until they returned downstairs and could sob in Delia's sympathetic arms. Nora, fragile and unsteady after fourteen days in bed following Stull's birth, found the kitchen and dining room such doleful places that she wondered if her milk and the baby's nursing might be affected. The whole household assumed the dimensions of a loose wheel careening along without center or direction.

And then Jonathan's fever broke. From raging heat his body plunged to wracking chills. Under Dr. Maclin's guidance, Mary Clayburn and each of the others in turn labored to keep Jonathan breathing. At last, quiet and gasping, he turned to them and in a weak but rational voice that they had not heard for an eternity asked, "What time is it?"

"It's six o'clock," his mother whispered because all at once she could not trust herself to speak louder.

"Morning or evening?"

"Why, morning."

"That's good," he said, and went to sleep.

A long struggle followed, a struggle between Jonathan's impatience and his weakness, a struggle between his ravenous hunger and his weak digestive membranes which could bear only the softest, simplest food in small quantities. But Jonathan slowly recovered.

His brothers developed a new optimism. They came to feel an unspoken certainty that their mother's Lord, in sparing Jonathan, had granted them a special dispensation. Brother Pryor reinforced that belief, reminded them of Cousin Rilla's death, which might just as easily have been Jonathan's, passed the collection plate, and received pledges of tithing from the company profits for that year and the next. This assured a new organ for the church and raise in salary for himself.

Gradually Josh and Cal and Dan gave Jonathan an accounting of the business's progress during his illness. Josh told of the farms' good harvest and the cattle they would keep during the winter. Dan said that closing the canning season earlier than planned had cut down on the pack they expected but its quality was the most uniform they had yet achieved. And Cal reported that he and the new salesman, Nate Lusk, with only one trip, had sold almost half the cases that were not already taken under contract. Nate would go out soon on a sales trip on his own. And Shad Kendrick had done a thorough, conscientious job in the office. Jonathan was pleased.

Last, they told him about the transaction which had been concluded only last week in Littlepage Ransom's law office: the Rathbones' sale of their woods and cabin to the Clayburns.

"Laura's woods?" Jonathan said.

Dan and Cal glanced at each other uneasily. "The woods down there between our place and theirs. I guess they were Laura's and her father's," Cal said.

"What did she say?" Jonathan asked, his voice so low that they had to lean toward the big couch where he sat propped against a nest of pillows.

"Why, she didn't say anything," Josh answered after a pause. "We didn't even see her. Her father was alone at Littlepage's office. He took the deed home for her to sign."

"But he said she wanted to sell?" Jonathan persisted.

"He said so. And she said so, too, the day she came here to see Nora and the baby," Josh said.

"Laura was here while I was sick?"

Josh nodded.

There was a long wait. "I know the very day it was. Did she come up to see me?"

"No," Josh said. "She and Nora talked a little while and then she just up and left. You know how she is."

Jonathan looked out of the window at the tops of the leafy oak trees. "I know how she is," he said. It was a windy day and a sudden gust brought down a thick scampering of leaves. "I know. That's why I can't believe she would leave that place—" The sentence died.

"Well, all I know is, everything went smooth as silk in Little-page's office. And although Laura never said outright, I think Nora got the idea she wants to move farther up in the mountains. Or maybe she did say so, come to think of it."

Jonathan continued to gaze out of the window. After a few minutes Dan jumped up from his chair. "Look here, Jonathan, if you don't like this trade we can call it all off. Janus would go along." When he received no response he rushed on, "We thought you'd like that land. But we'll do whatever you say."

Another tearing of wind stripped more leaves from their limbs. "No, Dan," Jonathan said. "You can't paste wings back on the dead birds."

His brothers looked at each other and shrugged, mystified. They didn't know whether Jonathan was recovering as well as they had thought.

"Keep the land."

"All right, Jonathan, if that's the way you want it. Now we'd better let you get some rest." And Josh led the retreat downstairs with Cal and Dan.

It was not the way he wanted it. It was the way it was. During his delirium he had seen Laura Rathbone, reached out to her, called to her, and he had ridden through endless foggy mountain passages with her father Janus. Always he had returned to Laura's name. Yet he knew that the cry had never mounted into his throat, had remained choked and imprisoned inside the churning, seething fantasy of his mind.

Now the longing was burned out. She had told him the reasons why she would not marry him. "The Clayburns want to con-quer the land—plow it, plant it, turn it to their use; all I want is to know it, live with it. We're too different, Jonathan, and your way will win."

Now he would accept her judgment. She and her father had sold their woods and the neat, sturdy cabin. He would buy them. He was too tired, there was too much work to do, for him to try any longer to understand Laura Rathbone.

Later that night when sleep would not come, he lay in the dark-ness listening to the wind—clean, willful, free, irresistible. Perhaps Laura was right and there had to be a definite choice between the wild and the useful, the free and the profitable. Well, the Clayburn Company partners had made their choice and he would bend his best effort to making it successful.

He wondered if Nate Lusk had included freight costs in prices he quoted customers or if he had made the shipments f.o.b. Churchill. Tomorrow morning he would check on that—first thing.

9

Faces and events roll backward. Time transposes. The data in my memory flickers like home movies run in reverse when divers leap out of the swimming pool feet first and soar onto the diving board or when people walk backward down streets and through doors which close mysteriously behind them.

"Will Stull be quarterback on the ball team this year, Nora?" Aunt Josie Montgomery asked.

They were playing rook in Aunt Josie's long dusky living room —Mama and Aunt Josie, Aunt Nora and Aunt Nettie Sue, four of them wearing summer dresses as colorful and fragrant as a bouquet of flowers gathered from Cebo's garden, while I turned the pages of the musty Montgomery family Bible opened across my knees. It seemed an unbearable penalty for my being a child that I should have to sit here with my mother and aunts through a long afternoon in late August looking at Doré's illustrations of righteous saints and writhing sinners while my cousin Stull was part of my father's real world outside.

Aunt Nora's voice was tight and defensive as she answered. She knew, even as I did, that Aunt Josie Montgomery didn't care a snap for any "ball team" in the country; that's why she didn't even bother to designate whether it was football or baseball or whatever. "Of course, he won't be playing quarterback, Josie," Aunt Nora said.

Then she added, "As a matter of fact, I wouldn't be surprised if Stull didn't play at all this year."

By the time my aunts had unraveled all those negatives, Mama exclaimed, "Oh Nora, he's not hurt himself or anything?" She was always alert to the possibility of injury or pain.

"No, Livvie Lee, he's all right." Aunt Nora was brisker than ever. "It's just that he will have a lot of studying to do this third year at the university and he wants to come home a weekend during apple season to help his Uncle Jonathan—and then I guess that new coach didn't put him on the team this year—"

They all looked up from their cards, even Aunt Nettie Sue from her rook card (you could always tell when she had drawn the plum because her face turned whiter than ever under the chalk powder that caked her face and the folds in her neck, and she worked to look innocent and indifferent), and Aunt Nora looked back at them.

"Oh Nora, I'm sorry," Mama said. She sounded very sincere. But I really knew how much there was to be sorry about.

Aunt Nora confirmed my knowledge. "He's disappointed, of course. For two years he's been hoping—" Aunt Nora's small fingers searched out a handkerchief. "You know how Josh was captain of the very first team Jackson U. ever put on the field, and Josh just never had any thought other than that Stull would be right there, too." She dabbed at her eyes.

"Well, I wouldn't let something like a little old ball team whip me down," Mama vowed. She didn't realize that to the Clayburns such comfort was heresy. "I think Josh ought to go down there and see those people." She threw a card sharply on the table.

"That's just what we're going to do, Livvie Lee!" Aunt Nora said. "I'm so glad you feel that way. You see, when Josh mentioned it, Jonathan didn't want us to go."

Mama flushed. "Oh, Jonathan is always so—so fair!" she waved airily. "He's so shy of special favors that sometimes he won't even do justice by his own family."

"I say when you have an advantage you better make use of it," Aunt Nora said. "Everyone else does." I looked at her pretty pink and white face and was surprised by the implacable thrust of her chin. I had never noticed it before.

Aunt Josie nodded. "As brother Jack says, it's chickens today, feathers tomorrow. Why wouldn't Jonathan want Josh and Nora to get Stull on the team, Livvie Lee?"

It worried me that they seemed to be criticizing my father. I felt that Mama sensed it, too. I didn't realize what a good infighter she was. "Of course," she said, "that's why Jonathan works himself to death as president and treasurer and had about a dozen other jobs during that old war and its aftermath and won't take a penny more salary or vacation or anything than any other official of the old company."

"What does that have to do with football, Livvie Lee?" Aunt Nettie Sue asked.

"Jonathan doesn't believe in any special treatment," Mama said. "That's what it means, Nettie Sue."

Aunt Nora and Aunt Nettie Sue looked back at their cards. I wondered why the conversation had suddenly died. I wanted to hear more about Stull.

I thought of the times he had stationed Monty and me out in the yard so that he could throw the big slippery football to us over and over again. Although I could barely hold the ball I suspected that Stull was not a very good player. I could see that he had no natural sense of rhythm or timing or ease with the ball. Even then he was overweight, and something about his appearance, his awkwardness, indicated reluctance for direct physical encounter. There was nothing about Stull that suggested the athlete—except his hunger to win.

"Well, Josh is going down to Jackson City and we're going to talk to them," Aunt Nora said. "Did you name green to be trumps, Nettie Sue?"

I took one last look at the full-page picture of terrified sinners under a lowering, agitated sky, clutching a rock as the waters of Noah's flood lapped around them. Then I closed the Bible and laid it carefully beside me as I slid off the sofa. "Aunt Josie," I said, and she turned—still looking at the cards in her hand but listening. "Can I go upstairs in your attic?"

"Why yes, of course you may, Jon."

"Is there anything up there he can hurt himself on, Josie?" Mama asked, a little frown making crow's feet between her pretty eyes.

"No, Livvie Lee. Let him explore. Just be careful, Jon, wherever you see boxes stacked up, don't pull anything down on top of you."

She laughed lightly. Aunt Josie was not noted for meticulous housekeeping. She had a great flair for decoration and everyone in Churchill wanted to come to her parties, but no one ever believed that her unseen attic and unused basement were in immaculate order. Aunt Josie had had "servant trouble" for years; she managed to keep only the non-essentials accomplished. All the fundamental housekeeping "just slid," as she would merrily explain. Certainly Josephine Montgomery was not going to wear herself out on the drudgery of scrubbing and lifting and polishing.

"I'll not spend my days chasing dust when I'm going to be dust myself soon enough," I heard her tell Mama one morning just before a party. And Aunt Josie bought new sash curtains so that no one realized the windows hadn't been washed since the winter before. (Of course, actually, everyone did know. They kept track of such things in Churchill because most of the ladies had very little to keep track of besides such trivia.)

"Go easy, Jon," Mama called as I walked down the hall. "Remember about the boxes."

I loved the attic no-man's land for it was timeless and lonely. The light that came from two small windows at each end of the tall narrow room was filtered through layers of a golden dust which lay over all the massive odd shapes tumbled back under eaves and crevices. The smell was always the same—of old leather trunks and dry paper and of raw lumber cured through generations of heat, for none of the attic had been finished except for rough sub-flooring underfoot. Overhead, rafters slanted like rough exposed ribs from the long spine of the central beam. And the sound was of a fat green fly droning at the window, careening from one window to another and landing like a shot put, all the while continuing its buzz and drone.

I have wondered if Aunt Josie's attic was not a map or diagram or mirror of her mind. Stored in the attic as in her mind were deep, forgotten layers of useless trivia and unsuspected treasure. No logical inventory of the contents existed, because it was impossible to determine or define all that was there.

There were labyrinths of narrow passages between the attic's accumulations of years. Broken dolls and chairs, cups, drawers without handles, wire skeletons of abandoned lampshades took up large spaces between square packing boxes carefully roped and stacked.

Random cartons overflowed with long-forgotten mementos. This seemed to be chaos without any effort at order. (Perhaps that was why it appealed so strongly to a boy—I could participate in anarchy and chaos for an interval without any nagging, nasal voices calling me to civilization and to order.) Anything known to the annals and fancies of man might be tucked away here and dredged up at the most unexpected moment.

There were three aunts who played a role in our lives. (Aunt Cornelia in Atlanta and Aunt Isabel in Richmond were glamorous because of distance and interesting because we hardly knew them, but they had little impact on us.) But Aunt Nettie Sue and Aunt Lottie were my father's sisters and Aunt Josie was Mama's sister, and among them they defined the Clayburns and the Montgomerys and the paradoxes and contradictions that were/are our character.

"Poor old Nettie Sue," my mother would say, "she's what I guess you'd call a real old maid. Of course, all that Clayburn teasing may have hindered her. And I don't know, she may have had lots of beaus, she may have turned down ever so many chances to go to the altar, I couldn't say—but if she did I never heard about it."

Everyone in the family spoke of Aunt Nettie Sue in that fashion, agreeing to some fixed, unspoken law that the worst fate possible to a woman—remaining unmarried—had befallen her. She was becalmed in the backwaters of life.

"Poor Nettie Sue," my father would say as he watched his sister negotiate her Dodge down the winding driveway.

"Poor old Nettie Sue," Mama would say before she telephoned her sister-in-law to come and share our Sunday dinner with the preacher and his wife and the choir leader.

"Poor Aunt Nettie Sue," Monty or I would whisper to Stull or Nancy Ellen or another of our cousins whenever we went for summer ice cream on their porch.

Aunt Nettie Sue was considered quite stingy, in contrast to her sister, our Aunt Charlotte, whom we called "Lottie" and honored for her selflessness and generosity. Not that Aunt Nettie Sue gave us gifts that were cheap. It was not their price but their utility that alienated us.

Aunt Nettie Sue lacked all sense of timing. A fine black umbrella with a carved ivory handle would have been my Uncle Whitley's pride and joy at fifty. To my cousin Stull at fifteen it was an insult and a burden. The golden oak desk I would have welcomed at twenty-one was an incomprehensible present at half that age. (What boy needed such anchors when his world was furnished with living green oak trees and a live river, weekend woods and knee-deep meadows, and on Saturday afternoon, the release into a silver-screen world of riders of the purple sage under the light of Western stars where the good guys and the bad guys were always, without fail, clearly separated, defined, rewarded, or punished justly?) As for my brother Monty, the time would never have been ripe for the *Book of Knowledge* in twenty volumes which Aunt Nettie Sue presented him. Monty wanted to know everything that was happening in Churchill and he wanted to know all that was necessary about eternity, but toward the whole vast continent of knowledge that lay between the infinitesimal and the infinite, he was totally indifferent. Hostile, in fact. Aunt Nettie Sue's books gathered dust on his shelves.

Aunt Lottie, on the other hand, gave us sweets and promises. Genuine Atlantic City taffy ("Half the price of each box will go toward support of an orphan's home in the Congo—" so that we could feel virtuously benevolent while we chewed and pulled on the talcum-powder flavors). Sometimes each family received a fruitcake at Christmas (baked by the inmates of a needy religious institution), and once there were fifty shares of Clayburn-Durant stock to divide among the children. The cake, which ran heavily to raisins, was dutifully eaten, while everyone silently acknowledged that Lottie would leave, one of these days, a great deal of Clayburn-Durant stock to be divided among immediate kin—fifty shares being only the appetizer signifying the feast to come.

"Lottie's always had faith in the family, I'll say that." Aunt Nora would say that and a great deal more. "Now poor Nettie Sue has sold so much of her Clayburn stock and bought heaven knows what else! She worries Josh so with her speculations and talk about the market. For a woman to be so involved in money—it's just downright unattractive."

It was not Uncle Josh she really worried, however, but Uncle Whitley. And, I suspect now, vice versa. For Aunt Nettie Sue lived alone and was therefore always vulnerable to advice and other people's arrangements of her affairs. Two areas she kept under her own control, however: her singing in the church choir (no matter how often nieces and nephews snickered) and investment of her money (no matter how her brothers discouraged her). One provided her with her only pleasure, the other with her only power.

Aunt Lottie, on the other hand, was married. Yet somehow she and Uncle Penn did not seem married the way Uncle Josh and Aunt Nora were, the way my parents were. They had no children and they called each other "dear" all the time, not just on special occasions, and I had heard Aunt Nora tell Mama that "Lottie and Penn have separate rooms, you know, Livvie Lee. Not just twin beds, which are stylish now, but adjoining rooms! Don't you think that's peculiar, Livvie Lee?"

To which Mama replied, "I guess the poor things are just all wrapped up in the good work they're doing for the heathen—"

Uncle Penn Buchanan was a Quaker, a distant maverick relative of Aunt Nora's father, who had come south to visit from his native state of Pennsylvania and had stayed in Churchill to marry Lottie and share her home and mission-founding trips to other countries. He was tall and slightly stooped, which gave him an elderly appearance even before he was past middle age, and he was unfailingly courteous and ineffectual. "Thank you, I might have just a taste more of the boiled custard, that is, if—"

His clothes, like Aunt Lottie's, were cheap and neat and never quite an exact fit. Both Aunt Lottie and Uncle Penn seemed to select clothes with the belief that they would be changing size in the very near future and would grow into the extra folds of dresses or trousers. We felt that this revealed their dedication to spiritual pursuits.

On the other hand, whenever Aunt Nettie Sue wore a dress that was an inch or so too long or a jacket with ill-fitting shoulders, we all laughed to ourselves and treated it as a penalty for her false pride in bright expensive clothes.

Aunt Josie Montgomery was neither married, like Aunt Lottie, nor maiden like Aunt Nettie Sue. She had been married once, briefly, and lived in St. Louis, but somewhere along the way on her return from St. Louis to Churchill she had mislaid her husband. By the time I was old enough to be interested, no one even remembered his name exactly. Mama made a heroic effort one day but the result wasn't very satisfactory. "Now, was he Charles Allen Douglas? Or Douglas Charles Allen? Or maybe just Allen Charles?"

Whenever Aunt Josie spoke of him, which was perhaps on two or three occasions in a decade, it was to say that Mr. Douglas—or Allen—or Charles, whatever his name, had been a perfect gentleman. Whether or not that was a fulltime vocation, I never knew. He wore white in the summer and black in the winter—shoes, suits, hats,—and he was an expert on croquet. He was supposed to have had an impressive fortune when Aunt Josie met him at one of the old summer watering places and married him. I imagine he had considerably less when they parted, not because Aunt Josie was so overly concerned about money but because she was not concerned with it at all. Her needs and wants were her sole consideration and she assumed there should always be sufficient funds available from some source to satisfy them.

There were those who said that Aunt Josie had married just to get away from her brother Pettigrew. He was the eldest of the children and cherished the old English traditions of primogeniture. His father tolerated Pettigrew's notions, which seemed to be aristocratic holdovers from the family's Charleston and London roots, and he failed to notice when Pett's aristocracy deteriorated into arrogance.

Aunt Josie married and fled to St. Louis for a sojourn and when she returned to Churchill she bought her own home, for taxes. It was an ugly old mansion on which her father had held a long mortgage at the bank after the owner went west, seeking oil. Uncle Pett even objected to my country-bred father becoming a member of the Montgomery family. As it turned out, the Montgomerys became Clayburns and that was the only circumstance, finally, that saved the Montgomerys from oblivion. When my grandfather Alex Montgomery had been making those substantial loans to my father during the lean, doubtful years of the Old Mill Field packing shed, he could not have realized that actually he was ensuring the future for his youngest, his favorite, Olivia Lee, and yes, for the others, too.

But those circles making their full turn were still in momentum when I was in Aunt Josie's attic thinking about Stull and his shattering disappointment. It was odd but I realized that I had never been quite so deeply disappointed myself, that I had never mustered for my own defeats anywhere near the pity I now felt for my cousin. His high grades in school, his wizardry with figures—as Aunt Nora said one of Stull's teachers had described his ability in arithmetic—would not compensate for this setback, because it was part of Stull's character to prize most highly the goal he hadn't reached. I knew that Stull wanted to be an athlete—and that he was not. Although football had not yet mushroomed into the passion and obsession that it would soon become in Churchill, in Jackson City, and throughout the South and nation, I knew that the nice aunts playing cards downstairs, even his mother, would never understand what the failure to make the Jackson team meant to Stull. Because Stull and the millions like him, whose hungers and ideas were multiplied into a national credo, eventually removed football, and gamesmanship, from the playing field to the arena of mortal combat. They were the vicarious sportsmen who destroyed sports.

On that afternoon in the attic, I prowled through a pile of sheet music left over from Aunt Josie's St. Louis days, but I didn't really care about the music or anything else in the attic except its solitude because I was busy caring about Stull.

It was several weeks before I saw him again. He had come home from the university for the weekend.

"Nora says Stull wanted to come home to help you out at the cannery," Mama laughed to my father at breakfast.

"Stull is a help," he answered thoughtfully, depositing a prune pit on the edge of his fruit dish. "He likes business. He's quick to catch on."

"Takes after Nora in that," Mama said. She sipped her coffee. "Poor old Josh, he's just as sweet and conscientious—" Many of Mama's sentences died in limbo.

My father nodded. "It's hard on Stull." He pushed away the fruit dish. "You always give me too many prunes, Livvie Lee. Just save those till tomorrow. Don't waste them."

"I'll tell Serena." Mama tossed her head slightly. "Your mother told me when I was first married: a wife can throw more out the back door in a teaspoon than a husband can bring in the front door in a shovel."

"Did Mama say that?" my father smiled slightly.

"I guess she thought the Montgomerys were all wastrels—"

"That football business has been bad for Stull." He brought the conversation back on course again. "I wish Josh and Nora hadn't gone down to Jackson City and interfered."

"But that new coach made Stull the team manager—"

"And now Stull will think he can get by pull what he can't by push. It's not good. I don't like using the company for anyone's personal problems."

"Jonathan, sometimes I just don't understand you at all. If you're so crazy about Stull, seems as though you'd like for him to be happy."

"I'd like for him to be happy," my father spoke mildly, eating steadily between sentences, "but that doesn't mean getting everything he wants. I'm not so 'crazy about Stull,' Livvie Lee, that I can't see his faults."

"Well, I've wondered—"

I could have swatted Monty who chose that moment to come to breakfast with the news that he had a stomach ache. Nothing aroused my mother to action as quickly as announcement of an ache or pain, no matter how vague, and now there was a flurry of baking soda in water, and offers of warm milk, and interrogation. "Did it just start or did it hurt during the night?" "Where was the pain—here? Or here?"

I suspected that Monty's chief pain arose from the prospect of a long day picking beans, but I didn't mind Monty outwitting me when my father told me he would let me ride with him down to the fields on his way to the office. I knew he would be taking Stull to the office, too. Uncle Josh and Aunt Nora had just that spring finished building their big brick house next to ours on a hill at the edge of Churchill. After they moved there, my father spent even more time during the summer explaining and discussing each day's work with Stull.

In my father's high, bouncing Ford we started down to the bean field. "How are you, Jon?" Stull had said as he climbed in the car, but he didn't listen for my answer. Did I just imagine there was a new tightness around his mouth and jaw?

"How's the apple pack coming, Uncle Jonathan?"

"Pretty fair. Shad gave me the totals yesterday. We're a thousand cases ahead of last year at this time."

A pause. "Uncle Jonathan, I've been thinking about Shad Kendrick—"

"Yes, Stull?"

"Isn't he a little slow to be your right-hand man in the company now?"

There was a silence. "He is slow sometimes. You're right about that, Stull. But there are other factors you don't know." We turned from the street onto the farm road. "Shad is one of our company family. He means something in Churchill, in our plant. That counts, Stull."

My cousin didn't reply.

"Stull—"

He turned to look at my father, his face plump and serious. But his eyes were so narrow that from the back seat where I sat they appeared to be almost closed.

"A company like Clayburn Brothers is strange, Stull. It belongs to all of us—and none of us. It's kind of a trust. It's built on trust of many kinds. I don't think any of us ought to use it for ourselves."

"I've never used a penny, Uncle Jonathan," Stull answered quickly.

And my father frowned. "I didn't mean money, Stull. I meant something else. Power, I guess."

Stull looked away.

"That's the real trap."

"I wouldn't know," Stull said. "First I'll have to get hold of a little before I can try it out." Stull tried to grin but the result was a grimace.

"You will," my father said kindly. But there was concern behind the kindliness, too.

All the other bean pickers were in the field, halfway down one of the long simmering rows, when I got out of the car. I watched the dust foam as my father and Stull disappeared down the narrow county road. I could feel the hot rich loam between the toes of my bare feet and the sun's heat on my tattered wide straw hat as I stood, remembering another morning.

It was a Saturday and Monty and I were in Mama's kitchen for a drink of water after riding our ponies. Stull was just coming in the door when we heard Serena's husband call to her from out in the yard.

"Miss Nora called over, asked if we know where's Mister Josh got to, Serena."

And Serena, down in the basement where she was washing one of Mama's linen tablecloths in the laundry tub, called back, "He's around somewhere." Then, lowering her voice: "Likely gone to ask Mr. Jonathan can he take the calf from sucking the cow."

And they laughed loudly, knowledgeably, tauntingly, unaware that anyone heard.

Stull's face had grown gray as putty. The embarrassment, the shame, was almost unbearable to see. We all knew—even kids such as Monty and me—what Serena meant, and we knew that if the Negroes were talking that way in the kitchens all the men on the farms and at the plant had their jokes and winks, too. And the laughter was about Stull's father.

His shame was swallowed by anger. "Why does your mother let niggers go hollering around your house?" he said fiercely to Monty and me. "My mother wouldn't stand for such goings-on."

"Mama's not here," Monty began, but I pinched his arm so he wouldn't say any more.

"My father's the oldest one of this family. My grandmother depended on him most. He—" But Stull's voice broke. His fists clenched. He stumbled down the back porch steps and fled across the lawn.

"I'm glad it's not Uncle Josh who's our father," Monty whispered softly; "I'm glad it's Jonathan who's our father."

I wondered how it would be to know that your father moved in someone else's shadow, that he was not the strongest, the wisest, the best. . . .

Then I went down the row toward the bean pickers. Perlina Smelcer straightened up and wiped the sweat from her face with one big freckled forearm and grinned at me.

"Lord-a-mercy, here's the least 'un now. Come on, Jon honey, grab a basket and pick along here in my row."

I had decided I was sorry for my cousin Stull. And that gave me a pleasant glow of power.

10

The family grew. Clayburn Brothers Company added new plants. The town changed. Mary Clayburn bought the former home of an English timber baron who had come from Pennsylvania to strip the hills and had returned to "civilization and roast beef" as soon as his mission was accomplished. The chief distinction of the house lay in the paneling of its ten rooms. Each room contained a different native wood, ranging from the rich darkness of black walnut in the parlor to the hard, golden grain of oak in the halls and Nettie Sue's bedroom. The Clayburns had bought the Victorian mansion not for this unique feature, however, but because of its convenient location.

The house stood across the street from the offices and expanding warehouse and factory. Jonathan and Cal and Dan and the two girls made their home there, too. Churchill now had two "leading" families. The Montgomerys had been joined by the Clayburns.

Josh and Nora and their children, Stull and a plump infant named Susannah, were left at the Riverbend farm. Delia came to Churchill, too, where she still lived with the family. But Nora had no difficulty with "help."

"It's sister Nora's Virginia superiority that impresses her hired girls and keeps them loyal," Cal once observed.

Cal seemed to overlook the fact that at that time the "girls" had nowhere else to work. And Cal did not tease so often about the Old

Dominion after he married Nora Stull Buchanan's cousin, Miss Isabel Buchanan, also of Richmond.

When the new bride Isabel first glimpsed the two main streets of Churchill, its cluster of frame buildings, brick bank, unimposing courthouse, livery stable, and assorted saloons, she burst into tears. But the novelty of moving into a cottage "all her own"—like a playhouse—next door to the new family which she had met only at her own and her cousin's wedding in the fashionable Richmond church replaced her initial dismay. Besides, as she told Nora during one of their long, comfortable visits together at the farm, she had brought trunks of clothes and linens sufficient to do until she and Cal went back to Richmond for a visit.

Nettie Sue studied voice at a music school in Jackson City, and lived away from home for two terms. Once, in the spring, she brought a young man home for a weekend visit. As could be expected, her brothers, especially Cal and Josh, teased her unmercifully and she never invited him again. And once, when she was practicing her vocal exercises, Dan called in a loud voice for someone to step out in the yard and see what had "gotten into" the howling pups. Occasionally Nettie Sue cried or protested to her mother, but this only changed her face to a mottled red and did not change the boys at all, and so, usually, she tried to laugh and overlook their tomfoolery.

She adored her brothers and acknowledged that their values matched her own, which meant that the music she longed for gradually became only an irrelevance to the important work of the family, a luxury open only to moguls of the Metropolitan's Golden Horseshoe or to penniless immigrant Italians and Russians.

Lottie had better luck with her plans. Her experience with the impromptu nursery at the company, followed by four years at a woman's religious college in Kentucky, convinced her of her call to be a missionary. Her brothers hesitated to approve jaunts to faraway places (indigestible foods, odd diseases, unfamiliar currency), but their mother reminded them of the Bible's admonition to preach to all the world, and they could not oppose both their mother and the Lord.

Lottie did not depart immediately, however. She traveled first to Chicago to work in a settlement house. The thought of the wicked city of Chicago upset Josh and Whitley almost as much as the prospects of the South Seas or of heathen India. But they sent her money regularly, and when the National Canner's Convention met in Chicago, Jonathan and Cal thoroughly examined her situation. The work looked depressing to them but Lottie seemed more mature and practical than they had expected. They encouraged her.

In addition to supervision of production, Dan handled a variety of jobs for the company. He visited machine manufacturers and long-established canneries and learned all he could from their experience.

"We need a wider variety of foods," he said over and over, and his brothers agreed. But it was not easy to find farmers who would grow crops unfamiliar to them, and every new product required a new process.

In Maine Dan observed ways to pack blueberries (called huckleberries back home in Churchill) which he promptly adapted to Clayburn canning. In the Midwest he watched the processing of sugar corn. The greatest triumph of his trip came with the conviction that the fertile acres of the Riverbend and Ransom farms could grow such corn and add a new product to the Clayburn Quality line. His knowledge and enthusiastic innovations gratified the machine and tool companies with which he traded.

"That talk about Southern sleepiness," one Bridgeton, Maine, manufacturer said, "it must be a myth, at least to judge by Daniel Clayburn." And Dan shouted with laughter.

At home he made weekly rounds of the scattered plants. He tried to meet each foreman's complaints and problems. At night and during many weekends Dan worked on new machinery. His main effort still lay in achieving more uniform quality.

"We fill thousands of cans," Jonathan said at supper one night, "and our jobbers and buyers move thousands of cans, but when a woman like Mama here opens one can of our beans or tomatoes for her family to eat, that's the only can we ever made as far as she's concerned. And it had better be good."

Dan's automatic capping machine had solved much of the problem of spoilage, but the size and color and flavor of vegetables or fruits put up at one of the packing sheds, and those put up at another, still varied greatly.

To the tomatoes, string beans, blackberries, beets, sauerkraut, and quartered apples of their first years, they added peaches, huckleberries, sweet potatoes, sugar corn, lye hominy, and pumpkin. But still, as Dan reminded them, Heinz had its "57 Varieties" and some other companies produced even more. So he returned to his machines.

After more than a year of experimenting and another year of improving, Dan put an automatic pumpkin-cutter into operation. The November night that he and Lonas Rankin finished installing the heavy machine in the Churchill factory, and watched it peel and clean and chop a three-bushel crate of pumpkins, Dan exulted.

"Look at her go," he clapped Lonas on the shoulder. "No stopping us now. We'll flood this country with pumpkin till pies are coming out of everybody's ears."

Lonas grinned. "Mighty funny picture," he said.

"We did it," Dan was not to be subdued. "That'll make a difference in the old profit and loss next year." He patted an edge of the motor.

"That's right." Lonas suddenly shivered in the drafty, deserted room. "Turning colder fast, ain't it?"

"I guess so," Dan answered.

"Know so," Lonas said. "Below freezing now. What you going to do with the parts of that machine carrying water? They freeze, they'll bust for sure."

Dan nodded, walking back and forth, muttering. "Why'd our first cold spell have to come tonight?" Then, brightening, he turned to Lonas: "Wait here. Wait right here. It won't take me five minutes to go across the street to Mama's—"

When he returned he carried a pair of thick blue blankets in his arms. "We'll wrap the works in wool," he said triumphantly.

"You going to use those?" Lonas asked.

"The warmest I could find," Dan told him. "Nobody was using them. Mama had them in her downstairs cedar chest where they were handy."

Lonas only shook his head—and helped Dan swaddle the oily, greasy machinery in finely textured blue wool.

As Dan learned the next day, his mother kept the cedar chest in the guest room in order to store special bed linens.

"Now look here," he tried to reason with his brothers, incredulous that they would be more worried about some blankets than their successful new machine, "we couldn't let it freeze, could we?"

"You could have found a little rougher kind of protection," Cal said. "Mama's blankets—"

"I'll have the blankets cleaned. I'll take them to Jackson City," Dan shouted. "I'll buy Mama new ones."

Jonathan interrupted them. "Let's not get too wrought up over a few pilfered blankets. We'd better turn our minds to a bigger problem, now that we know this machine works."

"What's that?" Dan asked.

"Deciding which men we're going to lay off work on the pumpkin line."

Dan looked taken aback. "Do we have to lay off anybody?"

"Well, that's usually the idea of building a machine," Cal exploded.

The curious mixture of shrewdness and naiveté that provided Dan with the skill and originality to experiment also made him, among those who worked for the company, the most accessible and popular of the Clayburns. Just now he gave the impression that he had never grasped the reality that his invention would take the job of some person.

"It will mean a big saving on our payroll," Jonathan tried to tell him.

"But I hadn't intended—" Dan hesitated. "How many will we let go?"

Jonathan considered. "I believe we could do without a half-dozen right now. You've made a good machine, Dan." He received no reply and went on. "Why don't we dismiss only four right now—and we'll see about others later."

"Alex Montgomery and his bank will be glad to see our payroll cut," Cal said.

"Those high interest rates they charge," Dan said, "they ought to be glad for us to borrow all the short-term money we need. I don't care a hoot about Montgomery's bank. It's these men I've got on my mind."

"I'll make you a proposition," Jonathan looked at the pile of work waiting on his desk. "We won't decide today. You go down to the pumpkin line sometime tomorrow, Dan, and you and Shad Kendrick settle on which four men we can spare."

When Dan had left, Jonathan said to himself as much as to Cal,

"When it's perfected and in full swing, that peeler and cutter will save us at least a dozen men—plus as many women."

"That adds up to real money," Cal nodded.

"Dan's inventions could just help make the difference," Jonathan said.

"What difference?" Cal asked.

"Between us and the hundreds of one-horse canners all over this country."

Cal agreed. "But it's like pulling a fingernail for Dan to let anybody go. Even when the season's over he hates to fire them."

This time, Dan did not fire anyone. "I just couldn't," he announced at supper two nights later.

When he looked around the table even his mother did not answer.

"All right, let me put it to you," Dan leaned forward earnestly. "There's Homer Ewbank. He's not the best in the world. But one of the men told me Homer's wife is sick and needs medicine. And there's Orvil Gosnell, sort of lame and slowed-up. I remembered he's been with us since we started. And then—"

"All right," Jonathan sighed. "What did you do?"

"Oh, I laid them off the pumpkin," Dan said triumphantly.

"Then what—"

"I put them to work on a new machine I've got in mind for our ensilage!"

They looked at one another. Jonathan laid down his knife.

"Well, haven't we been talking about using all those wasted shucks and cobs from the three hundred acres of sugar corn we'll can next season?" Dan demanded.

"We have," Jonathan answered.

"Then this is my answer." And Dan pushed back his plate and began to draw with a tine of his fork on the white tablecloth. (When Cal would have stopped him, their mother motioned not to interrupt, and she sat proudly watching—not Dan's drawings but his eager, open countenance, his tousled hair, his dextrous work-worn hands.) "We build one machine to crush cobs, like this, and another to cut the shucks and stalks, and then we blow it all into silos for ensilage. Cattle would thrive on that."

"We blow it in?" Cal asked.

"That's just an idea," Dan said. "We can build the cutter and crusher easily—but it's conveying all that material into the silos that I need to solve. I wrote today to a man in Syracuse, New York, who packs corn and saves his ensilage. I asked him how he handled this problem."

"Those Yankees save everything," Cal said.

"That's why they prosper," Dan answered. "Like we will. Meantime, the four men off the pumpkin line are working on making a cob crusher now." He winked. "We can't stand still. And we'll take the Churchill folks along with us."

They left Dan to his machines. There arose other problems for Jonathan's daily fare. He approached each one with grave attentiveness.

"That typhoid fever slowed Mr. Jonathan some," Shad Kendrick said to Mary Clayburn one day, "makes it easy for anybody who doesn't know better to misread him. Mr. Jonathan's smart like a steel trap, knows just when to shut up."

An order of beans shipped downriver to Jackson City was damaged on route, either in unloading on the crowded dock or at the wholesaler's warehouse. Neither party would admit responsibility for the loss, and Jonathan finally left the matter with lawyer Littlepage Ransom after replying to a militant letter from the wholesale grocer.

"We appreciate the high regard in which you say you have held Clayburn Brothers," Jonathan wrote. "We are going to make certain we do nothing to lose that high regard. On the other hand, we want to make certain that we do not lose our self-respect as a company."

When an autumn drought shrank the river to an over-sized creek, two of the boats hung up on sand spits for a full day, and cases of Clayburn food arrived late in Chattanooga, Atlanta, Birmingham, New Orleans. With natural obstacles augmenting human error, the company finally abandoned all shipment by water. Now they depended entirely on the railroads, and they felt even more sharply the disadvantage of their freight rates.

When Whitley received his law degree from Yale and went to Atlanta as a very junior member of the established law firm of Tarleton, Tarleton, and Dalton, he also found a wife. She was Cornelia Tarleton, granddaughter of the senior partner, daughter of the second

Tarleton, and collateral relative of Dalton, the patriarch of a large Southern clan with "connections" in several state houses.

Cornelia Tarleton fell in love with the idea of a wedding. She shared her mother's dread of the possibility of waiting too long to say "yes" to some beau, and when she understood that both her father and mother approved the character and manner of this new young lawyer (even though he came from the mountains and from a commercial rather than a "professional" family) she encouraged his interest, which needed little stimulation.

As Whit's brothers journeyed one by one to Atlanta to visit him and meet Cornelia, they could not resist remarking on the new circles in which he moved.

"It's all right with us if you want to turn Episcopal, Whit. But we don't know how it is with the Lord. The Bible doesn't mention Episcopalians and we won't either."

"You marry her, Whit, there's going to have to be some rise in the crime rate in Atlanta to bring you enough law fees to keep her in that high style."

And Dan added, "Why, she'll even be wanting you to buy an automobile." Dan himself had secretly studied the machines on display in Jackson City and Atlanta.

"Now I do say Miss Tarleton's as pretty a high-stepping filly as I've ever seen, brother. But I doubt those dainty hands ever put together a meal in their life."

To which Whit replied, "If I'd wanted a cook, I'd have gone courting at a restaurant."

But Jonathan stopped teasing Whit when he learned that Mr. Cornelius Tarleton, Jr., served as special counsel to the Southeastern Railway Company. In fact, Jonathan only marveled once more at how often things worked out to the advantage of Clayburn Brothers, even apparently by accident. For all the setbacks and hardships they had faced, including blight and drought, their progress had remained steady. Crops increased; markets widened; land accumulated.

With each passing season the memory of Laura Rathbone grew less acute; her face became more shadowy, her voice more indistinct; only her body's grace and strength and yielding wildness persisted. And the Rathbone farm, cleared of woods and cultivated, stayed rich and productive. No one mentioned the farm to him, but one day he told Josh that the Rathbone land had been a good buy. Jonathan had pondered the words for days and intended them as a generous compliment, communicating more than the casual remark—but Josh had scarcely acknowledged the comment. And Jonathan understood then that none of the family had had any true idea of that brightness Laura had brought to him, or of the long dark fever which had taken away the quickness, or of what she had meant to him in the buried reaches of his being.

Cornelia and Whitley sailed to Europe on their honeymoon and then settled in the home Cornelia's grandfather had presented them as a wedding gift. "The house is situated in a good section of Atlanta," Whit wrote his family, "and includes three guest bedrooms. Cornelia has a stout woman in the kitchen. So you see we're all prepared for long visits from each of you. Mama, we'd like you to spend a large part of the winter here."

"All those spare rooms will make them trouble," Cal commented.

During the following years, Southeastern Railway granted to Clayburn Company an increasing number of more equitable freight rates. When Jonathan took his mother to Atlanta, Mr. Tarleton arranged for him to eat lunch with a vice-president of Southeastern. Jonathan learned that the man fancied big game hunting. The following winter the vice-president came to Churchill for a wild boar hunt in the nearby Unaka Mountains. When he returned to Atlanta he told his friend Tarleton of the impressive little company that the Clayburns were building. "Unusual family, Tarleton. Unusual. Mother's a woman of character, strength. Sons all have some special function in the business—all except your son-in-law Whitley. And I wouldn't be surprised if he has his own contribution to make."

Mr. Tarleton agreed. "Every company needs legal advice."

"It's a sound company, Cornelius," his friend said. Which constituted the ultimate praise these men could pay any business venture.

By the first of the year, Southeastern Railway had answered Clayburn Brothers' request to meet their midwestern competition in

Arkansas, Texas, and Oklahoma by shipping at the same rate—fifty-seven cents per hundred pounds—to common points within those states. While Illinois and Indiana canners had enjoyed that rate for several years, Clayburn had been paying ten cents more a hundred.

"Damn it, it's not fair!" Nate Lusk had raged.

More quietly, Jonathan agreed. "We also pay high freight costs —six cents a hundred, counting the solder—on cans from Baltimore. That's more than the competition pays. And several of those Indiana and Illinois packers have their own can companies, or at least ones located so near that they meet almost no expense in shipping cans."

"Then how in goddamn hell—I'm sorry, Jonathan, but this gets under my skin and I have to cuss a little to work off the itch—how can we stay in the market against odds like that?"

The following winter Jonathan made a trip to the headquarters of the industry's largest can manufacturer. The official with whom he bargained had never heard of Clayburn Brothers or its quiet-spoken president and quoted a high initial price. Jonathan stood up to leave the office. "We're not buying in job lots," he said evenly. "We're talking about a hundred thousand cases of cans."

The man straightened. "And partial payments?"

"No partial payments. Cash. At least this year."

"Then—" with a gesture urging Jonathan to be seated again " —let's re-examine the situation."

Before he left the office, Jonathan had promised a check for total payment the day the shipment arrived. He had saved more than two thousand dollars for the company. "It takes squeezing all the corners to survive," he told Shad Kendrick afterward, as he dictated confirmation of the transaction.

Nate Lusk welcomed the news that the company could adopt a policy of quoting delivered prices to its customers. "Brokers, wholesalers, retailers, all of them like to know that delivered price when they give me an order."

"Even though the freight schedules are published?" Jonathan asked.

"Most of those boys are too lazy to take the time or make the effort to look up the schedules and figure out our margin. They'd rather have the certainty of all the cost in one package."

"This could be a decisive factor in opening new markets," Jonathan agreed. "As long as we can get Southeastern to give us a fair deal, we'll let you quote delivered prices, Nate."

"So we'll make our pennies," Cal said.

"And our millions," Dan added with a flourish.

But even the pennies seemed threatened when a food broker in Nashville wrote Jonathan that the Durant Company in Illinois had sent a carload of tomatoes, priced at eighty-eight cents delivered, into his city.

The morning the letter arrived, the family, at Dan's urging, was busy considering investment in an automobile. "I guess this explodes any plans for a car," Dan sighed.

"Durant foods are popular," Jonathan said, and reread a paragraph from the letter: " 'This Nashville market thinks no other packer gets tomatoes as ripe or as many to the can as Durant. Send me samples, however, of your apples and pumpkin, also, and I'll do my best for Clayburn.' "

"Eighty-eight cents!" Cal fumed. "Delivered from Illinois! I can't believe Durant makes money on that."

"They're not after money, they're after the market," Jonathan said. He grew quieter than ever during the rest of the day and that evening at home. "With so many canners pushed out of the industry by the Panic of 1907, I wonder what makes Durant so successful it can afford to lose money, or break even?"

Nate Lusk, quick and dapper, who had stopped by the office for final instructions before leaving on a sales trip east into the Carolinas, ventured one answer. "Durant has built up their name. You boys have sold too many cans to private labels—wholesalers and these chain stores, as they call themselves."

"Our private label trade cleared our warehouse during the Panic," Jonathan reminded Nate. "We didn't pile up any surplus inventory."

"Just the same, nobody knows it's Clayburn foods they're eating when they open half your cans," Lusk insisted.

"We need the profit. We don't want to sink any more in advertising," Jonathan said. "I still contend that a good product is its own best salesman."

"Not if you don't have somebody to tell you the name of the producer," Nat Lusk countered.

"Clayburns believe what's inside the can is more important than what's outside on the label."

"Well, I have to sell both." And Nate Lusk brushed a stray thread from his well-pressed coat. "It's a damn rat race."

The next night Dan strode into Jonathan's office on his way home to supper, his overalls and work shirt soiled and wet. He was drying his hands on a hard-worn bandana. "Been helping the boys wash buckets," he explained.

"That part of a manager's job?" Jonathan asked.

"I'll tell you what I told the boys: I'm no better than they are and as able to do anything in this plant."

Jonathan smiled briefly. "No wonder your name's bandied about for Churchill's mayor. You're a natural-born vote-getter."

"Mayoring isn't in my line," Dan stuffed the damp bandana in his pocket and sat on a corner of Jonathan's desk. "But I'll tell you what is."

"Go ahead," Jonathan said, looking up from the letter he was signing.

"I'd like to pay a little visit to Durant."

Jonathan considered. "I don't know how cordial they would be—"

"Not an official visit," Dan said. He started to speak, hesitated, spread his hands and blurted, "As a hired hand."

Jonathan only looked at him.

"I won't tell them anything false. I want to go and apply for a job, take anything they'll give me at their main plant. Whatever questions they ask, I'll answer. Their personnel manager probably never heard of the name Clayburn."

"Well, maybe—" Jonathan began.

"I'll do whatever they put me to do. But I'll keep my eyes and ears open along the way."

"I know that," Jonathan said.

"After all, they did come down here in our territory cutting their prices—"

"Yes."

"And we need to know how they can do it."

On the first of September Dan arrived in a large flat city in Illinois, home of the established Durant Canning Company. In every direction the surrounding countryside stretched out along fertile miles of farmland. No green mountains piled up on the horizon, only dark earth merging with the shimmer of late-summer heat, russeting corn, reddening tomatoes.

" 'Monday morning I walked down to the Durant factory and put in my application for a few days' work,' " Jonathan read aloud to the family from Dan's first letter. " 'I told them I'd had experience at a capping and filling machine for a small company down South.' "

Cal laughed and slapped his knee, looked around at the faces.

" 'Since they needed hands I was set right to work unloading corn and tomatoes.' "

"I hope he didn't strain his back," Mary Clayburn said.

"I guess not." Jonathan turned the sheet of hotel stationery. "He says the third day they posted his name on the regular crew. 'Now I'll be circulating all through the plant. Everything is worked close here. The chemists and processors spend their time and experiments on making everything at Durant rate A number one.' "

"That's what you've been preaching for us, Jonathan," their mother added.

Dan's few days stretched into a few weeks. He packed his letters with information and enthusiasm. His wages rose to one dollar and a half a day.

"Whatever Dan does, he puts his whole strength and heart into it," his mother beamed.

Certain sentences from Dan's letters lodged like cockleburs in Jonathan's mind: "Durant's makes a silver quarter cover all the green on any tomato they put in a can. They don't take them too ripe, either. This could be the weakest thing about our own canning."

"Durant's works the balance of their whole tomatoes into ketchup."

"Durant's pays one and a half times as much wages and works a fourth more men than we do in proportion to output. I'll bring the comparisons home with me."

"I see now that we should make Churchill a central operation and perhaps close out some of the smaller packing sheds. Crops from the farms could be brought in on railroad cars, where they're close enough, or on wagons if we can get our county roads improved. (Maybe I'd better get myself elected to the road commission.)"

"Durant's don't lose a thing. They work all the tomato peelings up for ketchup and tomato sauce for the pork and beans. If we had a central operation we could use our pulp for ketchup."

When Cal wrote Dan in late September that they needed him for the pumpkin pack, he wrote out full instructions for Lonas Rankin to set up and service the machines, and he told his brothers: "I'm pretty well geared up with Durant's now and doing different types of work all over the factory, which is where you learn things. I hate to leave now. Besides, the superintendent has been so nice to me that I want to do the right thing by him. Today was the biggest day we've had so far this year. Everything combined we put up better than three hundred thousand cans. We worked eleven hours. Some days I've worked fifteen hours. But if you need me there I'll come."

Josh, who had come into town that afternoon and was eating supper with his mother and brothers, concluded glumly, "Dan goes into some things a little too wholeheartedly—"

The next letters blazed with optimism.

"I'm confident now that with a little time and work we can get our quality of goods up to or passing Durant's. I want it to pass them."

"We must add three new varieties to our line right away: turnip greens, pork and beans—and sugar peas. Why not peas, Jonathan? Think about it."

"Yesterday was the first Sunday I haven't been to church up here. But the ox was in the ditch, or the tomatoes in the crates, and we had to put in a fifteen-hour day on the tomato line. If you're ordering another carload of cans, be sure and get a few of the five-gallon square size. We'll try them for our tomato pulp, although Durant's still uses barrels here."

"I may buy a car when I get home. It could save us a lot of time and trouble."

With the new ideas for production that Dan brought home in late October, and with Nate Lusk's growing sales force on the distribution side, Jonathan began to hope for an upswing from the lean years of 1907 and '08 and '09. An actual loss in 1908—five thousand dollars —had made them all even more sober than usual.

There were no elaborate gifts that Christmas of 1908 except the box that Whitley and Cornelia sent from Atlanta—especially the new records for Dan's Victrola—and presents from the Buchanans to Josh and Nora and their children and to Cal and Isabel. Nettie Sue and Lottie were shamed by their own small crocheted and knitted remembrances to the family.

When they learned a few months later, therefore, that their brothers were buying the Ransom farm, they asked incredulously, "Why did we pinch pennies if you can spend thousands?"

"Uncle Whit's moving to Florida," Cal explained. "We can't let his land go out of the family. The company needs it."

"Land!" Nettie Sue sniffed. "And the company takes back all the money that is made. I'd like to be able, just once, to go to the Grand Opera and hear Tetrazzini and Mary Garden and Caruso, like Olivia Lee Montgomery does."

"Do the Montgomerys take in the opera?" Jonathan asked.

"Olivia Lee and her mother do—in Atlanta, and maybe in New York—"

"Then you should visit your brother in Atlanta and hear the opera, too," Jonathan said.

In 1911 Clayburn Brothers cleared a net profit of thirty-two thousand dollars. Jonathan analyzed the success and determined the company should not fall below that level again, depressions or no. For the next years his personal life merged with that of the company and the family. Sometimes his family or friends aroused concern among themselves over his unattached state. Sisters-in-law Nora and Isabel arranged numerous acquaintances and opportunities for Jonathan to launch a romance—but for all the pleasant appreciation he expressed, their efforts failed. Mary Clayburn mentioned her concern that Jonathan might never marry. "He can give so much—he needs so much—" But Jonathan seemed to have already undertaken more than it was possible to accomplish. And none of his concerned family or friends lessened their dependence on him.

He kept close touch with the men who tended the farms under Josh's and Cal's supervision and with those farmers who raised crops for Clayburn cans. At the peak of the season in summer and fall, wagons heaped with beans, cabbage, and pumpkins backed up through the main street of Churchill as farmers waited their turn to unload at the factory. Sometimes Jonathan, on his way to or from his office or the train station, would stop for an exchange with one of the farmers.

"Your section of the county making out pretty fair?"

"How are crops?"

"How's the family?"

Always about themselves.

He kept in contact with Nate Lusk and his salesmen on the road. Cal had become the chief sales executive, but his severe shifts in mood —exuberant when all was going well, morose when setbacks occurred —increased Jonathan's burden. Patiently, Jonathan cultivated men who covered the territory from the Atlantic Coast to the Mississippi River and west to the Rio Grande, carrying their sample trunks, cutting their specimen cans, taking orders for spot and future deliveries, introducing new products. They worked to make the Clayburn name known, familiar, sought after. Yet they continued to take many orders for goods to be packed under someone else's private label: Blue Ridge Best, Dixie Sunshine, Waverly's Choice, Southern Pride. Jonathan sometimes wondered if they received a disproportionate number of these orders.

Jonathan studied Dan's machines—and Josh's new beef cattle fattening on ensilage from the crops.

He carried on financial arrangements with the Montgomery bank in Churchill, even when larger banks in Jackson City and Atlanta tried to woo him away, and he negotiated ever larger capitalizations for the company. Alexander Montgomery's wife, Jane, and Mary Clayburn had become close friends—in the church, in the Temperance Union, at ladies' sociables.

Jonathan made and remade agreements with the railroads for shipping rates, and spur sidings, and more careful handling. He was elected a director of the American Canning Association. And, when one of the women who worked on the sweet potato line lost her home in a fire, Jonathan sent a load of lumber from the company warehouse so that her husband and neighbors could start rebuilding the following week.

Or, when Josh and Nora's infant, Susannah, died before her second birthday, it was Jonathan who suggested that Nora should visit her family in Richmond. He bought her the train ticket and brought it to Nora and Josh following the funeral. Nora, pale and quiet with grief, brightened at the prospect of being "home" for an interval.

When Josh asked if Stull would be left at home, Nora clutched the child. "No! I wouldn't go. I couldn't leave Stull."

"All right, Nora. It's all right," Josh soothed her awkwardly, avoiding Jonathan's glance. "It would be better for him to go with you."

"He's all I have left," Nora whispered fiercely.

Josh looked away and his face slowly altered. "I'm sorry, Nora."

And Jonathan, embarrassed by the revelation between them, left the room.

When Josh's and Nora's second girl was born the next year, Jonathan gave little Nancy Ellen a twenty-dollar gold piece. Nora kissed him for his generosity and his thoughtfulness.

Jonathan sent Whitley and Cornelia a supply of Clayburn foods at the close of each year's packing season. At Thanksgiving they remembered him and the rest of the family with Georgia peanuts and pecans.

Future plans and daily details alike composed Jonathan's duty. Only occasionally did his mother or Dan find him standing quite solitary in the yard looking out toward the dark jagged mountains on a moon-washed night. At those times he was private and unapproachable, as though annealed by a pain that came from sources beyond the long fever he had endured. Then his mother would grow silent and Dan would not attempt his usual banter. As for the others in the family, they remained unaware of those private moments.

"Peas? But no one in the South has ever been able to grow sugar peas, at least on a commercial scale," Cal protested after Dan arrived home from Illinois and raised the subject again.

"Gets hot too fast here," Josh said. "Vines get lousy and peas grow tough."

"Hold on, boys," Jonathan interrupted. "No one else in the South has our combination of hot sun and cool nights and river-bottom land."

"We could beat the boys in the East and Midwest by three weeks on all the markets." Dan grew excited.

"You mean we might take a fool gamble like that?" Josh asked. "Why, we have killing frosts in April sometimes." He and Cal looked at each other and shook their heads.

But gradually, through the winter and following year, as they discussed the matter over and over again, each of the four brothers became hopeful about adding peas to their list of foods. A longer growing and canning season emerged as the decisive argument.

"Sugar peas in May and June, beans and greens in September and October," Jonathan said. "Our land would be working double time for us."

"Machinery and people won't be idle," Dan approved. "We'll eat the overhead instead of it eating us."

When the four of them went to the February canners' convention in Louisville, Kentucky, however, they received little encouragement from the agricultural experts or the Wisconsin growers. "No packer south of the Ohio is in sugar peas," one of the older men advised. "Vines would burn up, to begin with—"

"But we have the mountains," Dan interrupted him. "That gives us cool nights for those early peas."

"And our bottomland is rich." Cal winked at the pessimistic Wisconsin gentleman. "Why, children making mudpies from it get indigestion."

The other man scarcely smiled.

"Why don't you pay us a visit?" Jonathan invited. "Look over our situation. Then you give us your best advice on growing peas or not. We'll pay your fare round-trip and whatever fee seems right."

The white-haired man hesitated. The next day they asked him again. He looked at the four earnest faces and said he would like to send his son, a plant expert who had long wanted to visit the Southern Appalachians.

Thus Haley Morrison came to Churchill, a quiet, pipe-smoking, observant man who had studied plant science for his family's Wisconsin canneries but whose interests had broadened to a larger botany. No sooner had he arrived in Churchill than he laid aside the tailormade suit of the city and put on farm clothes, heavy boots, and a loose comfortable jacket. His eyes were dark, observant, and attentive to every person he addressed. Jonathan was pleased by Morrison's tan, weathered face which suggested as much time spent in the fields as in the laboratory. To the Clayburns, advice seemed more reassuring if it came from experience rather than theory.

Quickly, efficiently, Haley Morrison visited the farms and the factory and offered numerous practical suggestions on their experiment with peas. He even directed the planting of a five-acre test field. Then he went into the mountains, drawn back a second day and a third by the variety and luxuriance of the plants growing in the shaded valleys and on the rugged slopes. After the second week, although Mary Clayburn assured him that his visit was no imposition, Haley Morrison arranged to move out into the mountains.

"If I could shake free of Wisconsin," he told Jonathan and Dan, "I'd like to stay in those woods a month."

"You have some place to stay?" Dan asked.

"Oh, yes. Yes, indeed." Morrison tamped fresh tobacco in his pipe. "A man named Rathbone has offered to keep me." In the silence Morrison looked up. "You know him?"

"He's a good man," Jonathan said.

"Yes, indeed. I like him. He and his daughter have rented me a room and will give me meals."

"They know the woods," Jonathan said.

Morrison nodded. "I've already discovered that. The girl has stored up a fund of native knowledge, the kind you never discover in books."

Dan glanced at Jonathan.

When Morrison shook hands with them he said, "I hope you have great luck with the peas."

"And luck to you," Dan said.

Jonathan shook hands slowly, gazing hard at the visitor's face, searching it. "The Rathbones are fine people," he said again.

A few days later Jonathan announced that he needed to go out in the county and that he would initiate the new family Ford to some county roads—if he heard no objection. No one voiced outright disapproval, but Dan came up with numerous instructions. Despite broad hints Dan aimed at him, Jonathan did not ask for any company.

The Grindstone Mountain road, deeply gashed and studded with rocks, stopped short of the Rathbone's house. Jonathan parked at the trail that formed an entrance to Janus Rathbone's woods. When he turned off the motor, silence surged in around him. In the distance a cowbell tolled at regular, lonely intervals.

The trail narrowed but remained easy to follow. A mulch of pine needles and rotting leaves padded it underfoot, and green clumps of Christmas fern and glossy galax leaves lined each side. Eventually the path crossed a rushing stream over a bridge made of long smooth poplars, then followed a low dry-stone wall only recently laid—perhaps during the past two years, Jonathan judged. On the other side of the wall a small, stump-pocked pasture struggled to support the thin stand of grass where a lonely horse grazed.

Jonathan paused and shook his head unconsciously at the rocky pasture, remembering the productive fields on the Janus Rathbone farm now in Clayburn possession.

"It's no river bottom, is it?"

Jonathan started, then saw her just ahead of him, beside the trunk of an immense wide-limbed beech tree in an angle of the stone wall. At first she appeared just as he remembered her—hair long and free, face mobile with each inner shift of thought and mood. He had never seen her barefooted before. She read his thoughts.

"I've been down by the creek. The moss on the rocks felt too soft to trample on with heavy shoes." She held up the shoes and gave a shiver. The water would be icy, even though the sun out here warmed their faces and arms. "I heard the motor of that car of yours and I waited over here to see who was coming up the path."

He looked back at the stream behind him, at its overhanging rhododendron bushes and tall trees, and at the deep woods beyond with their shifting balance of light and shade. "That almost makes up for the poor pasture, doesn't it?" she laughed, gently mocking.

"It's a good place," he said.

"For those who're satisfied with earth keeping more than ploughing." She turned and walked along the opposite side of the wall, taking careful steps in her bare feet, while Jonathan continued along the cleared trail. "There was a rabbit nest here," she paused and parted a clump of grass, then walked on.

"How are you, Laura?" Jonathan asked.

"I'm fine, thank you." The prompt ritual politeness showed a rejection as real as a closed door.

"Laura—" But he could not go on and she did not look around. The dark force and suggestions of the dreams, visions, hallucinations he had had during those long-ago nights of the fever recurred now. Through work and persistent effort to forget he had pushed the Laura of those fleshless orgies out of his consciousness. The fever that had exhausted his body had also cauterized nerve and emotion. Now he knew, finally, that the rare indefinable feeling which had bonded him to Laura Rathbone was burned away. The sickness which had drained his body and the business which demanded his mind and spirit had combined to leave him anaesthetized to the Laura he had known. He felt sadness and regret—and relief, too—in the knowledge.

"We talked like this once before, across a fence," he said suddenly.

She looked at him. Her gray eyes told him nothing; her face seemed guarded. "That was in moonlight. Now it's daytime."

They had come upon the house. It sat in the midst of a grove of beech trees interspersed here and there with tall dark-green spruce and balsam. Many of the lower limbs of the evergreens, though brown and dead, clung tenaciously to the trunks. The logs and planks and shingles and stones of the house had obviously been put together for situation, not for size. Four rooms nestled behind a long wide porch and on either side of a dog-trot, and by the sturdy stone chimney at one end of the building.

The stone wall ended and they came to the shallow open space in front of the building. The spray of the swift stream had moistened Laura's hair. Jonathan could see the wet and bedraggled hem of her gray and white cotton dress. Sunlight dappled through the beech limbs onto her hair and silky golden arms, creating an irrepressible glow. From the perspective of his new sense of release, he knew that he would never encounter anyone who was more awake, more alive, than Laura Rathbone.

"Why did you come, Jonathan?"

As usual her directness took him aback. "I needed to see Haley Morrison."

She did not answer immediately, and he suspected that she had seen right through his lie. Or his partial lie.

"Morrison helped us set up an experiment in growing sugar peas."

"I know."

For the first time he could remember, Jonathan felt awkward talking with her. "He told us he'd always wanted to see the Southern mountains and botanize here."

"He's helping Papa go into the herb business." Laura turned toward the porch before Jonathan noticed the little mounds of roots and stems and leaves piled at neat intervals.

"That's fine," he said. "With all that you and Janus know about the woods and plants you ought to be able to make real money."

Again she didn't answer.

"They say there's a ready market—"

"Everything has its market," she said. She tossed her shoes fiercely toward the porch, where they landed with a clatter and slid apart. "Papa and Haley aren't here just now. Papa took him up to Wolf Pen Gap today."

Jonathan nodded at the reminder. How long ago did it seem to him—how removed from the world of Clayburn Brothers Company —since he had ridden with Janus Rathbone through the fog and to the cave under that gap? (And where were his father's molding ledgers now? Josh and Nora had made a bedroom for young Stull out of the old office-study. Where had they put the big leather-bound account books?)

"Haley Morrison knows more about wild things than anybody since my grandmother." Admiration tinged her voice. "At first, when he told Papa he was a scientist and sometimes teaches, I was scared off—"

"But you're not scared now?"

"Of Haley?" She laughed lightly, clearly. "Why, he's as easy as an old shoe. He doesn't fret a-tall about making things over. He says he wants to know them as they are."

"And you want to enjoy them as they are," Jonathan said.

The cowbell sounded like a faint echo, far away, but it filled the silence between them.

"I have to get back to the factory," he said, wishing for words not stiff as cardboard and not only imitations of what he needed to say. He would like to touch her but he did not know how. Any gesture seemed too little—or too much. "You have a good place here, Laura." He looked around.

"Goodbye, Jonathan," she said, answering what he had not spoken.

Jonathan was not in Churchill when Haley Morrison returned from the mountains on his way home. And six months later he and Nate Lusk were on a sales trip to Texas when Haley Morrison came to Churchill and took Laura Rathbone to startled Justice of the Peace Littlepage Ransom's office, where they were married before leaving for Wisconsin.

"He never even stopped by the office to find out how we made out with our peas," Josh said.

"He'd already seen our letters to his father, telling him about a good harvest on the five Riverbend acres," Jonathan answered. "We'll be putting out a full crop next spring."

"I'm ordering the best hulling and grading machines the manufacturers offer," Dan told him eagerly, relieved that the news of Laura's marriage had not seemed to upset Jonathan. "Then I'll have all winter to adapt them to our needs."

"Pea vines ought to make extra-good cattle feed," Josh added.

Only Cal remained reserved. "We can make a lot, lose a lot, trying something like this."

Since his marriage to Isabel and their constant enlarging and refurnishing of what had once been a cottage near the factory, much of Cal's daring had fallen away. He laughed at his wife's concern for genealogy and social prominence, but he gradually came to share her values and attitudes. Above all, he became fearful of failure.

When he and Isabel had visited in Richmond, and on the one occasion when the Buchanans had come to Churchill, Isabel's parents had made very clear their approval of Clayburn Company's success. They paid lip service to the strong family ties Mary Clayburn had forged and to the reports they heard of Elisha Clayburn's character, but the finances of the cannery received the Buchanans' real attention. Cal, living more than any member of his family in the reflection of others' attitudes rather than in a reality of his own, became easily encouraged, quickly discouraged. He secretly suspected that the strength of his marriage to Isabel depended in large part on the strength of the cannery. And this knowledge had sapped much of his confidence and high humor. When Isabel and Nora, cousins by birth, sisters-in-law by marriage, began to jostle for leadership in the Churchill church, Cal grew uneasy. He made special overtures to Josh so that there would be no tension between them.

Isabel, for her part, did not enjoy the family's Sunday gatherings. "All you Clayburns know how to do is talk about business or that dreadful war in Europe," she stormed one Saturday afternoon, asking Cal to take her to Jackson City for an overnight holiday. "As soon as church is over you're discussing how many acres you'll plant to peas or how many submarines the Germans have, and as soon as you've finished your mother's and Delia's dinner you're figuring how to improve some part of that factory."

"I guess we've made it our lives," Cal tried to explain.

"That's all right for Jonathan," Isabel went on, "or for Dan; that's all they have. But I'm a part of your life now, and Josh has Nora and Stull and Nancy Ellen, and we ought to be considered once in a while, too."

"I try to consider you all the time, Isabel," Cal said. And he took her to Jackson City and fretted about whether or not peas would make a profit, and laughed less and less. And so it went throughout the winter and spring until the May morning when Cal saw in the Jackson City paper the bold black headlines screaming the sinking of the *Lusitania* off the Irish coast.

"More than eleven hundred people killed," he told Isabel at breakfast. "One hundred and two Americans. This may put us in the war."

Isabel appeared fresh and relaxed and happy in a new dark red dress. She knew it complemented her pale skin and accentuated the blush she pinched into her cheeks. "Those heathen Germans!" she tried to sound personally angry. "I hope we kill them all, and that mean kaiser first of all."

But if battles and victors or losers dominated the news, the weather still dominated the Clayburns. The spring nights of 1915 stayed cool, the days warm and sunny. The Clayburns dreamed of raising and canning a first-quality crop here where peas could be put on the market weeks earlier than in the North. They succeeded.

The sample cans they sent up to Wisconsin and to their advisor-friend Morrison drew prompt approval. "As good as the best I ever ate," the older man wrote them. In a postscript he added that his son, Haley, wished to be remembered to the brothers, too.

"Next year we'll put out five hundred acres," Dan said. And they began preparing the land for its second crop.

Cal went with Nate Lusk to offer their first peas to the big city markets. Nate was becoming a first-rate salesman for the company: handsome, shrewd, a man's man, easy to like and enjoy. "You know the knack for success in this job?" he asked Cal. "Getting along with the right folks and getting ahead of the others."

"And knowing which is which?" Cal added.

Nate looked at him sharply from under his jaunty hat brim. "That's right."

Cal turned down Nate's invitation in Birmingham to spend an evening with some girls who were "all right," prettier and smarter than anyone Memphis Gibson had ever introduced in Churchill. In Chattanooga Cal worried about Nate's drinking which left him cross and sick the following morning.

Among the jobbers and grocers they visited they found uncertainty about Southern peas, even after samples were cut and tasted and approved. Once again Hugh Waverly and Son completed the sales trip for the Clayburns: "We'll take the rest of your pack. But we want them under our own Waverly's Choice label." Mr. Waverly tendered a rare smile. "You men would be surprised how big a market our Waverly's Choice is building up for us."

Jonathan had hoped all of the peas might be sold as Clayburn Quality. But he knew the pressures of a first sales trip for a new product, and when Cal and Nate returned with their report he congratulated them.

At the moment Cal remained equally indifferent to praise or blame. His body seemed to ache in every joint and muscle; he felt alternately hot and shivering. He longed only for the luxury of his bed. Alarmed, Jonathan took him home. Isabel sent word to Dr. Maclin to come at once.

Mary Clayburn was visiting Whit and Cornelia in Atlanta. Nettie Sue's letter arrived at midday Saturday. By late evening Whit and his mother sat nervously on the train. Early Sunday morning they walked into Cal's and Isabel's living room. Mary Clayburn was panting slightly from her climb up the porch steps, and she hardly noticed the cluster of whispering friends who sat or stood in a corner of the living room. Nettie Sue, just coming out of the corner bedroom down the narrow hall, ran to her mother. "Mama, it's terrible. Dr. Maclin says he has double pneumonia!"

Mary Clayburn closed her eyes for a moment and her lips moved silently. Then she disengaged her daughter's arms. "We must hold up, Nettie Sue. Go and make us a fresh pot of coffee." She walked heavily, steadily, down the hall.

Only the sound of Cal's breathing, like wind sucked through dry leaves, came from inside the hushed bedroom. Isabel, frightened and disheveled, stood at one side of the bed near the doctor. His sleeves were rolled above his elbows and held by two black rubber bands. He had removed his tie, had opened his collar. His shoulders sagged with weariness. "Come in, Mary," he said. "I thought for a minute you were Dan."

Jonathan crossed the room and took his mother's arm, nodded to Whit who had followed her. "Dan has gone to Jackson City to get some medicine," he spoke softly.

"How is Cal?" Mary Clayburn looked at her son's closed face and heaving chest, at his closed eyes and moist, doughlike flesh; and with one motion, as if in answer to her own question, she went down on her knees beside the bed. "Cal . . . Cal . . ."

Dr. Maclin looked at Jonathan and Whit and shook his head. Then he put an arm around Isabel Clayburn's shoulders and said, "Why don't you take her out, where you can talk, you can tell her how it started—"

"I can't leave my husband now, Dr. Maclin," Isabel spoke in a high, terrified voice. "He might want something."

Slowly Mary Clayburn looked from her son to his wife, pulled herself up to stand again. The anguish in her face could have come only from knowledge. Dr. Maclin sighed a lingering breath of relief. Someone else knew what he knew.

"Yes, take me back to the kitchen, Isabel," her mother-in-law said. "We'll—" She could not go on. But she took the younger woman's arm and moved toward the door. "Cal won't be wanting anything for a while."

When they had left, the effort of Cal's breathing rasped louder than ever through the room. "What do you think, Dr. Mac?" Whitley tried to ask calmly.

Dr. Maclin shook his head again.

A short while later Dan arrived with the medicine, but Cal could not swallow it. Late that afternoon, fighting for each breath, Cal gasped one shuddering gulp of air and was quiet.

When she realized that he had died, Isabel gave a long scream of disbelief and hurt. She could not stop crying. Until Dr. Maclin's sedatives could take effect on Isabel, Mary Clayburn sat by her bed and suspended her own grief until the younger woman could control hers.

"I had prayed," Mary Clayburn told Lottie, who arrived from Chicago the next night, "I had prayed that the Lord would not let me outlive my family. He made me survive Elisha. And now Calvin." Her strong square chin trembled.

"We'll have to have faith, Mama," Lottie said. "But oh, I do wish I could have been here, talked with him just once more, before he died."

"He didn't know us," her mother said. "After I came from Whitley's and Cornelia's, he never saw me—or smiled."

"What will we do without Cal's teasing?" Nettie Sue asked. They all sat around the dining room table, stretched to its full length, drinking cups of scalding coffee, avoiding the crush of friends and relatives in other parts of the house. Nettie Sue's question struck each of them. All at once the two girls were sobbing.

When Josh tried to stop them their mother took him aside. "Let them pour out their grief," she said, "as Isabel, poor child, must do when her parents arrive." She looked at her oldest son's open, hurt, puzzled countenance and reached for his hand. "You have so much more than any of the others, Joshua. Not only your work and home and wife, but a son, too. Cal never had that. You must be very thankful."

"I am, Mama."

But the manner of her speaking and gesture had suggested pity as well as pride.

With Cal's death, Jonathan's work increased. He carried on long sessions with farmers about crops, seeds, fertilizers, prices for the coming year. Nate Lusk and the other salesmen came directly to Jonathan now with problems and plans for breakthroughs on the tightening markets. In addition, the deepening war in Europe was prompting the United States Government to make contact with canners across the country—in case of massive mobilization—and officials came to visit the Clayburns.

Jonathan, with the family's agreement and Whitley's counsel, transferred the stock that Cal had held in Clayburn Brothers to Isabel's name. It seemed odd to think of the young woman who emptied her house and boarded the train for Richmond—surrounded by packages and suitcases and trunks, the barrels and crates in the freight cars—as a widow. She had been in Churchill so short a time, yet she was now a partial owner of Clayburn Company.

And the following spring, Cal's forebodings about the uncertainties of sugar peas as a profitable crop proved to be well-founded. On the twenty-fifth of April Jonathan worked late in his office, but during the afternoon he sensed a change in the wind assaulting his west-side windows. Instead of the balmy warmth of recent weeks that had brought cherries and plums and apples into bloom, he now felt a knifelike chill.

"Long as the wind keeps stirring there's no need to worry, Mr. Jonathan," Shad Kendrick said.

But the wind quieted. At midnight Jonathan and Dan went outside and tested the weather. "It'll be a hard freeze," Dan said.

"We've invested a lot in this early crop. Winter labor, spring labor, seed, fertilizer, new machinery—" Jonathan stopped.

"Maybe the later peas, not in bloom, on the other farms, will pull through."

They looked up at the still, clear sky and walked slowly back into the house.

By noon the next day they knew that all the peas, even the late bloomers, were killed.

"What will we do now, Mr. Jonathan?" Shad Kendrick asked.

For a moment Jonathan paused. Then he turned back to his desk. "We'll tighten our belts, Shad. We'll plug up the leaks that creep into any enterprise. We'll find ways to be more efficient with what we already have."

Shad Kendrick cleared his throat and spoke hesitantly. "I just wanted you to know, Mr. Jonathan: if there's a bad squeeze on, where you can't raise cash real soon, well, I live simple and you can always let my wages go till your squeeze eases up. That is, if it would be any help—"

Jonathan was looking straight at Shad. "That might be a real help," he said. "But the most important thing is knowing that you want to make such an offer. I appreciate it, Shad. I know the rest of the family will, too."

He felt glad to be able to take Shad's offer home with him at dinnertime. It cheered his mother and brothers. "Never know where you're going to find 'unknown assets,'" he tried to smile.

Their mother, who had not smiled often since Cal's death, responded now. "The Kendricks are good people."

Dan joined in, supporting the flickers of optimism. "Feller on the farms asked me today if we would keep on planting peas, and I asked him if he'd stop having babies just because one of them died. This is the latest freeze we've had in fifty years, the old-timers say, and we're not about to be scared off by some freak accident like that."

Their determination waned slightly when Jonathan told Dan after dinner that he would have to stop at the bank and arrange with Alex Montgomery for a new short-term loan to cover the cost of replanting the lost crop. Dan sighed, flung his cap back from his thick brown hair (half the time his mother had to remind him to get a haircut), and returned to the plant.

At the bank, Jonathan had expected to see Pettigrew Montgomery, now a bank teller behind his own latticed window, or perhaps even Randall Montgomery, who was spending less and less time at the store that was supposed to be his family responsibility. But it was Olivia Lee who sat in her father's office.

"You know Livvie Lee," Alexander Montgomery said, not looking up as he laid aside the pen with which he had been signing a stack of letters.

By the nature of Churchill and the institutions, holidays, newspapers, mores, myths they shared, Jonathan and Livvie Lee had "known" each other for a long time. Yet Jonathan realized (at that moment) the falseness of the word. He'd heard the girl's name all his life, had been informed of her presence at various places, but he had never actually "seen" this slender, brown-haired, scarlet-clad creature until now. And judging by the brilliant enigmatic smile she was bestowing, heaven alone knew when he would ever know her.

"Oh, Jonathan and I are at all the same sociables," she said, "but we're never together." Her eyes shone a clear light blue, unlike any others he had encountered before. When she smiled right at him, as now, they disquieted him. In a small high voice with a hint of laughter she said to him. "Do you still parch your own peanuts?"

Surprised, he turned to her father. But the older man only shrugged. Then she added, "Patience and a steady hand and judgment."

Mr. Montgomery glanced at his daughter. Jonathan smiled then. He'd said something like that years ago—to her sister Josie and her brother Jack. But she had been just a child then. Mr. Montgomery looked at Jonathan.

Olivia Lee seemed satisfied by the surprise she had stirred. When she stood up Jonathan noticed her tiny waist, her height, and her pride. She lifted her skirt, as if she were already on the street, and Jonathan saw her ankles, neat and small-boned. Her dress made a soft crackle, like the rubbing together of cricket's wings, as she left the room, and although Jonathan knew nothing about the dress except that it flashed the color of a tanager, he was aware that it appeared more stylish than anything Nettie Sue or Lottie ever wore. And he found Livvie Lee friendlier, more natural, than her older sister Josie.

At home that night he thought further about Miss Olivia Lee Montgomery. That made him happier than thinking about pea vines thawing limp and yellow in the April sun, or hearing reports of Nate Lusk's drinking on the road, or reading of the bloody deaths not long ago at a place called Verdun. In fact, the feeling which stirred in him when he remembered what Olivia Lee had said and how Olivia Lee looked marked the first time he had known precisely that feeling since Laura Rathbone and the fever left him years before. During the interval between, he had experienced both idealistic daydreams and physical arousals, but not the two together, in harmony.

He would ask Olivia Lee Montgomery to ride out to the springs with him next Sunday afternoon. (Would that be his day for the car? The brothers took turns using the high, square, bouncy Ford that Dan tended in the same way that Josh tended his white-faced Herefords.

Josh and Nora drove it for a week, then Jonathan had its use, and Dan, and finally the girls and their mother together took their turn. Each user furnished his own gas and paid three cents a mile into a common purse for upkeep. Perhaps he could make a trade with Josh to use the car this Sunday—) He stared out of his window at the graceful limbs of willow and elm and maple greening with spring. For years he had inhabited the same place as the Montgomerys, yet he had never actually seen Olivia Lee until today, and she had intended for him to understand that no matter how sharp the setbacks, it was really spring.

The following April, of 1917, Churchill abounded with excitement and satisfaction when Jonathan Clayburn and Olivia Lee Montgomery married each other. Shad Kendrick voiced a common approval when he told Dan, "I'd almost given up on Mr. Jonathan ever going to the altar. And here he didn't have to go outside Churchill to find himself a lady."

And Dan wrote to Whit in Atlanta: "Our brother hasn't acted small with Livvie Lee Montgomery. He's given her a diamond as big as a green pea."

The only person who appeared to have reservations about the romance was Olivia Lee's oldest brother, Pettigrew. "He had some Washington and Lee classmate all picked out for me," she explained to Jonathan one night when Pett had excused himself from the room when Jonathan arrived. "Silly old boy who lived on some lonesome old plantation on Virginia's eastern shore."

"I'm a farmer," Jonathan said.

"You're different," she flashed back. "All he cared about was planting and plowing and picking and canning."

"I'm a canner," he said.

"That's you," she smiled. "As long as you can, I won't have to. Oh, I'm just a spoiled town mouse, Jonathan."

"I like you just as you are, Livvie Lee. Just so long as my being a country mouse doesn't worry you and your brother Pett too much."

She laughed and flung both arms around him.

Whit and his Southeastern Railway friends arranged a private car for the honeymoon. On April second, Jonathan and Olivia Lee left for Niagara Falls.

The honeymoon returned Jonathan to the fullness of life. During the years since his typhoid fever, he had been an astute and able businessman, a wise and generous leader of his family. But he had known little emotional richness or variety.

Now he had a wife who was complex and in many ways quite uninhibited—with that unconscious complexity and lack of inhibition born of generations of authority. When she stood before him in her white silk nightgown with its elaborate smocking and hand-embroidered rosebuds, long brown hair around her shoulders, blue eyes wide with uncertainty and timidity yet never flinching in their eagerness, Jonathan realized how dead he had been for so long.

"It's all right, Livvie Lee," he said, sitting on the edge of the starched white sheets in their square box of a bedroom as the train clicked steadily along the rails. He patted the bed.

When she sat beside him he traced one finger over her eyebrows and plump pink cheeks and around her full lips. He did as he had often done during their courtship—in the Montgomery parlor, on Sunday afternoon drives—he kissed her. Then he did as he would never have done while she was still Miss Olivia Lee Montgomery: he slowly unbuttoned the tiny pearl buttons at the throat of her nightgown and he laid a large gentle hand on her bare left breast. He felt its softness and the hardness of the small pink nipple.

"I don't know what I'm supposed to do," she said. Her face was flushed with embarrassment, with excitement, but she spoke clearly. "I guess I don't know much of anything."

The thrill of her innocence and virginity, of his possession of her, of his reawakened, surging body, left Jonathan without need of words. He slipped the gown from her shoulders until it fell around her waist. Then he buried his mouth over hers again and stroked the firm full breasts until he felt her body—not her mind or self-conscious affection, but the nerves and pulse and muscles of her body—responding to his.

The pounding wheels of the train carrying Livvie Lee and Jonathan seemed to mount in the power and rhythm of their thrust. They moved through the night as surely, as inevitably as they had in all the countless nights gone before, yet for this moment, in this place, the couple they transported was unique and solitary.

When Jonathan and Livvie Lee arrived at the hotel on the brink of Niagara Falls, they felt enraptured in a scenic luxurious dreamland, removed from every reality except each other and a world of rushing, spraying water immersing them in mist.

One afternoon they took a ride on the sightseeing boat under the falls. As they returned, still wearing the big raincoats and hats that had protected them from the water, they stood alone beside one corner of the rail.

"That day at the table when I was ten and I stared at you so—" Livvie began, then waited.

"I remember," Jonathan nodded.

"Aunt Vashti had told me of signs that I would meet my Intended that very day."

"Aunt Vashti?" Jonathan said.

"Mama's cook, you know!" she frowned impatiently. Jonathan had already discovered the deep, restless impatience behind this girl's manners and kindness.

"Oh, yes."

"Well, that's why I kept looking at you. I wondered if you were really the one the chicken entrails had foretold."

"Chicken entrails?" Livvie Lee's combination of the romantic and the earthy, the shrewd and the innocent, continued to astonish him. He knew that Josh's Nora, for instance, would never have uttered such a word.

Her eyes gleamed. "Aunt Vashti had lots of ways of reading omens. And when she dressed the chicken for dinner that morning she spread all those innards over the ground and I went out in the yard and asked her what she was doing. 'Telling tomorrow,' she said. 'I don't care about tomorrow,' I told her, 'tell me about today.' And she gave the whole mess a stir and pointed up to me and said, 'Why, little gal-child, you're on your way to meet your Intended today.' 'What's that?' I asked. And Aunt Vashti just cackled, 'Why, that's your True Love. Don't you know nothing, gal-child?' No wonder I was so intent on you, with all those preliminaries."

Jonathan laughed. "I am your true love," he said.

"You're happy with me?" she asked, slipping one long slim hand under his arm.

"Yes, Livvie Lee. Do you need to ask?"

She shook her head with satisfaction. "That's the way I want it to be always."

He bent to kiss her but water ran from the brim of his hat into her face and they laughed and watched their boat negotiate its mooring to the dock.

The next day, on the sixth, they heard that President Wilson had declared that the United States was at war with Germany.

"Let's go home, Jonathan," Livvie Lee said that night, her big blue eyes glistening with tears. "I know Jack will be enlisting. He's already worried everyone half to death talking about going to Canada and getting into the action—"

Before they left, however, Dan telephoned Jonathan to come home via Washington. The agriculture and army departments wanted to enlist Clayburn Brothers' help in providing food for the new war effort.

From Niagara to Washington, from Washington to Churchill—everywhere swelled a great tide of feeling: them versus us, Hun against hero, the catharsis and energy of hate. In one immense bustle of activity, men volunteered for the war to end all wars. In Churchill, Orvil Gosnell's son protested at his rejection by the army because of illiteracy. "What's reading got to do with fighting?" he demanded.

Jack Montgomery left with a jaunty wave. "I'll bring you back a lock of the kaiser's hair," he called to the group of girls and young men who had come to see him off. Then he winked at his brother-in-law and called to Jonathan, "Or one of those French girls' garters."

But Mary Clayburn went to comfort Jane Montgomery after her son had gone. The two older women were not excited or jaunty. They remembered too many one-legged men and armless men and eyeless men and dazed men who had been in the old wars: the War Between the States, the Indian skirmishes, and the Spanish-American affair. Experience had dimmed their enthusiasm for wars.

During the rest of that spring and throughout the summer, an increasing number of strangers visited the Clayburn Brothers cannery. They came to make arrangements for foods to be sent to the camps throughout the South, and to the army overseas. They arrived with requests and regulations and left behind them more work to be done by fewer men. Dan avowed that during two weeks in late August he never pulled off his work clothes. Olivia Lee complained that she never saw Jonathan, that she was already a widow while yet a bride. But she took pride, too, in the fact that nationally he was known and needed.

"It's not me, Livvie Lee," he would protest gently when she boasted of him to her family or friends. "It's the company."

But to her, Jonathan and the company were one.

I I

There came a season one year, just before Christmas, when I learned that there was no Santa Claus. Monty and I found in Aunt Josie's attic the red suit with white cotton trim that my uncle Jack wore when he distributed presents on Christmas morning.

I had believed in that red suit, in the deep chuckle behind it, in the gifts he brought. I had believed totally, unquestioningly, and when I saw the bright limp cloth folded in a box like a discarded chrysalis all that belief dissolved.

I shocked my mother not long afterward when she insisted that I throw away a delectable bite of trout because it had slipped onto the tablecloth and had "all sorts of old germs on it."

I suddenly flared out, "Germs, Santa Claus, and Jesus Christ. That's all I ever hear around here and I haven't seen one of them yet!"

"Jon!" My mother's eyes flooded with tears.

But even then, in my troubled, angry adolescence, I knew that some sickness haunted us, some truth eluded us.

How do we gather so much misinformation during a lifetime? Our minds are turned not so much to learning enough that is true and awesome and useful but in unlearning so much that is stupid and ultimately deadly.

Deep within myself, long after I had shed my last baby molars and erupted wisdom teeth, after I had abandoned two-tone shoes and college pennants, after I had married Teena and established my own family, an astonishing assortment of myths, rumors, hearsay, and hints unconsciously guided my actions. When I was a child—seeing what was supposed to be hidden, hearing all that remained unsaid—the errors and the lore soaked into my mind and my memory like a sponge.

We laughed at the blacks' stories of spells and omens and demons. We smiled at the mountain folks' belief in signs and spirits. Yet the God I knew through my family and the succession of ministers who padded across Churchill pulpits existed only as a glorified scorekeeper made in the image of Churchill's best white citizens. He sat on a throne somewhere a few miles above earth tabulating the "bad" words, the "ugly" thoughts, the "wrong" deeds of those of us who would some day be called up for review—for final reward or demotion. It was a denatured vision of God which nagged rather than compelled—and it led to as many daily rituals and placations as any of the "primitive" beliefs of other less enlightened, or less organized, groups.

We "knew" so much, some of it well-nigh fatal.

We knew the unreality of music and poetry, the practicality of bank accounts and vegetables and machinery. I remember the first time I ever heard that imperative opening of Beethoven's mighty Fifth —not at home, certainly not at the university in Jackson City, but in Atlanta when Aunt Cornelia took me to hear a symphony orchestra. The flesh on my neck tingled. I felt excitement build in me like a fever. Here throbbed the answer to something I was too ignorant to ask. My brother Monty's popular records, Cebo's work songs, Mama's hymns, the lonesome mountain ballads of some of the workmen—none of these had prepared me for another dimension of music, of art, or of words.

We knew:

About Cebo and Serena and by extension all other black people, the ones I met through various associations—each relationship gradually and progressively more formal. At one pole waited Cebo's smoke-saturated cubbyhole adjoining our garage, where I absorbed enough superstition and wisdom and courtesy and anger to last a lifetime; at the other pole existed those racially antiseptic committee rooms in YMCA or church annex or enlightened bank, where I now struggle to recognize the marrowbone errors and fears that prompt each response, each affiliation.

"Oh, Jonathan, son, you don't know. . . ." My mother would look at me with her great blue eyes which could be filled simultaneously with love and rejection as I struggled with the all-inclusive, unspoken wound of race. "You don't know. You just don't know. . . ."

This was her initial warning on most of the questions that mattered—sex or God or race or the work at which I would spend my life. "You just don't know—" And her voice and eyes and gestures suggested experiences of her own so profound or traumatic as to be indescribable, and if only I would benefit from them and from her hard-won knowledge I would be saved a harvest of mistakes.

"Once, when I was eleven or twelve—not a bit more—I went with Mama down to Uncle Randall's store. I loved to go there to play around the counters and look especially at the bright bolts of cloth. A nigra man came in one day."

She turned away from me, stared out of the window at the bare, dark-limbed trees frozen in January ice.

"I can't describe him for you to this day because of what happened afterward, but he wasn't like any of them I'd ever seen before. I know he seemed tall. And different. I remember he bought five pounds of blacksmith nails. 'How's Old Sledge?' Uncle Randall asked, and the nigra didn't smile like all the rest of them I'd seen, but said, 'Able to hit the anvil,' and there was something complicated and independent about the way he spoke, too, and Uncle Randall handed him the nails and he left. It was quiet in the store then. I said, 'Wasn't he a pretty man?' "

My mother's eyes widened at the memory of that moment. "Mama and Uncle Randall looked at each other. I could never forget my mother's face at that moment. If I had spoken blasphemy or walked through Churchill stark naked, she couldn't have been more overwhelmed. 'Olivia Lee,' she whispered, and took my hand and we left the store and started toward home very fast without even buying whatever it was we had come to buy at Uncle Randall's store.

" 'Olivia Lee, we don't ever ever remark on a nigra's looks—' her voice lowered and I knew something of special importance was taking place between us, '—especially we don't ever remark on a nigra man's!' "

Just the memory of that moment held my mother spellbound. Finally she looked at me again and said, "You can't imagine how many generations of trouble and experience lay behind Mama's warning, Jon. I know. I think I sensed it even then because I had heard my great-grandfather Montgomery tell how it was in South Carolina after that hateful war. Something called the Red Shirts—I guess they stayed sort of secret—had to protect the womenfolks as best they could. Oh, I don't know all that old history, Jon, but it was an awful time. . . ." And her vagueness, her hints, etched a more troubled, violent picture in my mind than accumulations of precise, detailed historical or sociological accounts could have done.

All this contributed to put Mama's "nigras" in their place, us in our place, convenient arrangements for security and comfort and prosperity—*our* security, *our* comfort, *our* prosperity. But it also played the part of blindness, ever since my mother was warned as a little girl not to see "them." And partial, voluntary blindness for a lifetime became our condemnation, our imprisonment.

I also "knew:"

That black skin smelled special (I did not refute this with the simple evidence of my own senses in relation to whites and blacks with whom I worked and played and ate and talked); that Cebo and Serena and the others somehow acted childlike when compared with my busy father and uncles and well-dressed mother and aunts.

There was my knowledge of Churchill:

The outer noonday crust of toil, uprightness, a code of honor and civilization; and the underlayers of seething survival of the fittest, the savagery of which erupted in items in the Churchill weekly newspaper, items of bootleggers ambushing and ambushed on the highways, of a farmer's barn and livestock burned by unknown parties, of a mountain woman "stomped to death" by her husband, of thievery and threat. All I "knew" amounted only to a half-known half-truth, which equalled a whole lie.

There was my knowledge of my family:

A dichotomy intensified by the town and county where the Montgomerys—earliest leaders, urban, never free of awareness of their "aristocracy"—and the Clayburns—solid pioneers' descendants, relatively unimpressed by their own prestige or power—accepted complementary roles in the community.

In my growing up I "knew," for instance, that the Montgomerys descended from a line of plantation owners who inherited their natural right to be served by others; that they, being "artistic" and refined with inclinations toward occasional china painting or fox hunting, relegated work to a secondary status. But I actually knew that the Montgomerys measured their tasks to themselves, gauging their work to their own strength or fatigue or pleasure; the Clayburns measured themselves to the job to be done, summoning all their resources to meet demands on muscle or imagination or determination.

Thus, the Clayburns could not take prosperity or its privileges for granted, while the Montgomerys always did, even when their money and privileges no longer existed.

My mother had a deep instinct for noblesse oblige, for giving freely and beautifully to all who pleased her or touched her sympathy or affection; my father paid the bills. Uncle Pett gave a grand, useless statue of the county's first judge (a Montgomery, of course) to Churchill's courthouse square; his father paid the bill. Aunt Josie kept the big white-columned house when she could not even pay the taxes, much less pay for paint and roofing and guttering and repairs to steps and verandah. I took it as natural, however, that the Montgomerys should live as if they had money and the Clayburns as if they had little.

The Montgomerys remained attractive and shed an aura of pleasure. They played cards and danced—and the Clayburns did neither, although they permitted rook and an occasional pat of the foot when music at a party grew especially rhythmic. The Montgomerys went on long, glamorous journeys and the Clayburns traveled only on honeymoons or conventions—or, like Aunt Lottie and Uncle Penn, when they went to do good in foreign fields.

While the Clayburns considered tomorrow and its needs, the Montgomerys concentrated on today and its possibilities. Small immediacies consumed the Montgomerys' attention: what they would eat at the next meal, which suit or dress they would wear, with whom they would spend the evening, where they would go on an approaching holiday. And once they decided what they wanted from these limited fulfillments, they would press to any extreme to have their desire. Their primary weapon was flattery; their ultimate weapon lay in the tantrum.

The Montgomerys were known for their fearsome tempers. With the exception of Alex, whose contacts with impersonal vaults and deposit boxes and printed paper seemed to have damped down the blaze of his temperament, the others would be likely to fly into a fury at a moment's most unexpected notice.

If casual assumption or cajolery or pouting did not win them their way they resorted to a pale-faced screaming tantrum in which they hurled, plunged, buried any weapon of words into the unsuspecting flesh and spirit of their victim. The size of their threatened disappointment or defeat bore no relation to the size of this weapon they used. They ended by destroying—as if a child, desiring a butterfly and unable to capture it, had turned a shotgun on it, determined to have the impulsive wish fulfilled by any means available.

The saddest, inevitable fact: they won their immediate goals—the food, the place, the event, the way they wanted—but they lost the larger rewards of life, respect of those whose respect they valued, friendship of those they most admired, and finally the love of those whose love they wanted, needed, desired above all. For a poached egg (when they had asked for scrambled) they would forfeit the peace of a marriage. For an evening's diversion (if duty threatened to interfere) they would sacrifice the authority of friendship.

Their rages grew of long heritage. They told of great-uncles who had lain on the floor and kicked until servants came and pacified them with whatever they demanded: a special food (creamed chicken livers for breakfast, apple turnovers at bedtime), or some other outlandish favor. They told of a grandmother, youngest of her family, who, as little more than an infant, had screamed and cried and broken fine Minton china when she did not get the bonnet or dress or trip to the circus she wanted.

Along with heirlooms of silver and rosewood and mahogany, along with legends of lavish sociability and leadership, the family legacy included the flaring nostrils, white and tight; the blazing eyes; the hard mouth blasting forth blasphemy and destruction; the raging body and unreasonable mind that won its moment's victory—and lost everything. This remained as part of the legacy of black slavery, this white self-slavery whose adherents believed in the paramount importance of its own whims and wishes, believed that each should be fulfilled.

Thus my Uncle Pett Montgomery had mastered his home—until his wife, the gentle, sheltered daughter of one of Jackson City's best families, ran away in desperation with a sewing-machine salesman from Chicago and left Pett to nurse all his victorious little tyrannies and his wounded pride.

Thus my uncle Jack Montgomery had volunteered for the army and left jauntily, confidently, to joust with an enemy who would crumble in a few days before his high humor and good-natured jokes or his alternating pouts and angers. When he found that by some incredible misunderstanding he had become part of something not only unyielding to any of his persuasions but totally indifferent to them, Jack Montgomery underwent a shock, a shock far more severe than that from the shell which exploded one morning in the tin bowl where he had washed his face only seconds before, which sent him to the hospital for twenty-one unconscious days and many weeks of recovery. From then on, Uncle Jack lived as though he had discovered that the best a man could do in this accident of a world was to reap all the enjoyment possible from it.

Error and fable and partial fact compounded into all that I learned or "knew" about these people and situations. I am now trying, in my adult life, to sift the one from the other.

Just such a compound formed my knowledge of my cousin Stull. Though it made me envy and dislike him in those earlier years, I now realize something else. Another feeling. Another dimension beyond my own skin.

I consider how Uncle Jack used to tell of Stull's visit to Memphis Gibson's. I wonder how that relates to Stull's relationships with Clara and Eugenie and Mrs. Schroeder.

Uncle Jack's eyes flashed with droll wickedness. "Stull Clayburn had been mooning over that high-stepping girl in Jackson City, the old senator's granddaughter, but she wouldn't give him a tumble." My uncle's voice lowered and I couldn't hear the tidbit that made the other men laugh maliciously, derisively.

"Well-sir, that young man may be a genius in his university mathematics courses and he may be the Clayburn that wears the big britches some day, but I tell you that it was old Jack Montgomery who let him in on the well-known scientific and social theorem that—" and his tones became baritone "—in the dark, all cats are gray."

Again the laughter, subdued this time, but laced with fierce personal knowledge and agreement.

"Do you fellers realize," Uncle Jack went on, "Stull Clayburn might have gone all the way through that university and come out yon side and never laid any woman a-tall—if I hadn't come to his rescue?"

They chuckled in anticipation.

"He was growing up plumb ignorant! That Jackson City society girl had him so razzle-dazzled he never tried to see if she would put out for him. Fact is, I doubt if she ever let him take her out more than a couple times; he's such a stick. But I told him one day, what you can't have by asking, you can always buy." Uncle Jack slapped his wallet pocket. "Good hard cash."

"Yes sir-ee." The other men's words rattled and gurgled in their throats.

"With poor bumbling Josh for a pappy and all that Clayburn Sunday piety cluttering up the rest of the week, too—well-sir, how's a young feller like Stull to grow up?"

Uncle Jack paused. I could feel the sweat on the palms of my hands, and I wiped them softly against my trousers. I heard him say, "On our way out to Memphis Gibson's I could tell he was nervous as a nigger at election, but you know all he asked me? The only thing he said the whole ride out was: 'When do I pay them?' I tell you what, it sort of took me back. 'Them?' I said, 'How many of Memphis' girls are you planning to take on tonight, boy? You'll be doing well to take care of one—' 'All right, then,' he said, stand-offish like his pappy, and scared and mad at me, too, 'When do I pay her?' I let go the teasing. 'You needn't worry about that a minute, son. You pay old Memphis whenever you leave, and in case your mind's somewhere else and you start to forget, she'll be right there to remind you.'"

Again, his voice lowered in order to emphasize the privacy and drama of what he had to tell. But it left me out. Strain as I would I could not hear anything until another explosion of laughter broke the silence: ugly, knowledgeable—infinitely knowledgeable—laughter.

"That young feller came downstairs walking like a man. He handed Memphis a bill, and she stuffed it in that peg leg of hers fast as a trout snapping up a fly. You should have seen Stull's face then. He didn't know under that long skirt of hers old Memphis had one wooden leg where she socks it all away. 'You're right much a man,'

Memphis said, knowing a likely customer when she sees one, after all the drunks and deadbeats she has to contend with. 'You come back to see us just any time, sweetheart.' And that Stull never said a word, just walked out the door, climbed into the car, and waited for me to get in and start the motor."

After a silence, Uncle Jack said, "You know the only words that young buck said all the way home?"

"No, Jack. What?"

"What'd he say, Jack?"

"About the time we came across the railroad tracks he spoke up: 'I figured there would be more to it.' Like he was considering a case of tomatoes or kraut, or some new machine for one of their runs—"

Eruptions of laughter. Strange laughter mixing guilt and suspicion and an undercurrent of nervous agreement.

"Oh, he's a greedy one, that feller is," Uncle Jack Montgomery whistled softly. " 'More to it . . .' And him killing his first sheep."

I heard the factory whistle, its long hoarse call echoing across the town, and I knew I had to go home. But I couldn't leave Uncle Jack's story, especially when he was getting ready to add a postscript.

"I've done my part toward the education of Mr. Stull Clayburn. I reckon he'd had enough Shadrach, Meshach, and Abednego; he was ready for hatrack, cognac, and in-the-bed-we-go!"

Snickers, nudges, thigh-slapping cackles.

"Well, that's history now. Happened last winter. And you know what I learned from the golf pro down at Jackson City Country Club last week? Stull, if he'd had the nerve, could have had free from that senator's granddaughter what he paid one of Memphis' sorriest girls for!"

That brought the final male uproar.

Never before had I heard anyone say my cousin Stull lacked nerve. I wondered about his mysterious experience. For different as we were, I came to learn that Stull and I had something in common. Call it lack of flair, as my Uncle Jack did; call it shyness, as my mother did; call it coldness, as Clara did of Stull, or superior self-confidence, as Teena once did of me; whatever it was, it set us apart from that swaggering, insatiable carnal contest indulged in by the Nat Lusks of the world.

I wondered that day how I would pass my first test, even though I was incredibly ignorant (stuffed on hearsay and folklore and anatomical misinformation) and held only the dimmest realization of what went on at "Memphis Gibson's house." I can scarcely believe, remembering, how troubled—almost frantic—I became then and through years to come at that uncertainty, that wonder.

Did it trouble Stull, too?

When Stull met my distant cousin Clara Montgomery from Charleston and married her a few years after I had overheard Uncle Jack's account of the visit to Memphis Gibson's, I stood awe-struck. (Aunt Nora had suggested to my mother that she ask Clara up to Churchill for a summer visit. "Stull is spending all his time at the company," Aunt Nora confided. "He'll never meet a girl that way.")

Clara resembled a Dresden doll—but she didn't break. Pink and white and blond, she rode and swam and danced—rumors circulated that she even smoked cigarettes—and lived up to every legend of the Montgomerys. By what power did Stull seem always to win the best of everything?

12

When the summer season reached its peak, Jonathan sometimes returned to his office at Clayburn Brothers in the evening after he had finished supper and had helped Olivia Lee put rambunctious Monty and Jon to bed. He saved some of his paper work and many decisions until those evenings alone. A few years before, he would never have returned to his office any night unless an emergency arose. But since the end of the war the tempo of pleasure, of conversation, and of competition, was changing character. Men like Jack Montgomery came home from France with a craving to live swiftly, actively. The war had destroyed more than soldiers' bodies and battlefield terrain, villages with strange names and the specter of the kaiser; it had demolished a way of life, an attitude of innocence, an anticipation for tomorrow. In his brother-in-law who had spent five months in a hospital in France and another six months in various other unnamed dwellings in Paris, Jonathan saw the experience of war and its aftermath: cynicism and bitterness at the slaughter, confidence and brashness in the unconditional victory.

In recent years there had been an increasing number of decisions for Jonathan to face at his square oak desk. They reflected the widening role of Clayburn Company in the world and the multiplication of Jonathan's responsibilities, both in Churchill and in larger regional and national circles.

Jonathan concentrated on no single level. If he had to form a

270 /

committee with other canners across the country to seek effective ways to petition the government not to sell surplus wartime canned goods from coast to coast at cheaper rates than the manufacturers could ship them, he also had to decide whether a new screen should be put on the back door of the Riverbend packing shed. While he determined whether or not cherries might be grown commercially in some of the lower mountain valleys, he also tried to heed Olivia Lee's hints about her brother and find some job Jack Montgomery could fill.

In Olivia Lee's understanding, "the factory" was a vast private preserve. It existed to keep her husband occupied, to generate funds for whatever her children might want, to provide repairmen when a furnace went out of order, and to supply fresh vegetables whenever Cebo's kitchen garden ran short.

"Call the factory," she would say when any difficulty arose around the extensive brick house and encircling lawn and trees Jonathan had provided for her. At the factory Shad Kendrick would try to meet her problem and would send any necessary workmen or mechanic, as Dan Clayburn had instructed.

"That will lighten Jonathan's load a fraction." Dan slapped Shad on the back.

In the matter of hiring Jack Montgomery, however, only Jonathan would finally decide.

The first Wednesday night in August 1923, Jonathan returned to his office. At home the boys had been catching fireflies in the early dusk and showing their father the trophies. They protested his departure, but when he took them on each knee and let them hold his gold watch (Jon could already tell time, an achievement his aunts and uncles considered awesome at his age) they grew quiet. "The hands will be here and here," he pointed, "when I see you next, at breakfast."

"Will you go to sleep before then?" Jon asked.

His father laughed. "Of course. I'm only human. You and Monty set me a good example and I'll be home and asleep before you know it."

"That would be good for you, Jonathan," Olivia Lee said. "You need more rest from that old factory. You've looked sort of pale lately. I was mentioning it to Nettie Sue just the other day. Serena," she called into the house, "Mr. Jonathan and I are leaving now."

Jonathan drove Olivia Lee by the church. Summer was the only season when he skipped any church service, but everyone in Churchill understood. People walking along the sidewalk and standing on the church steps nodded or spoke.

"Dan will pick you up after prayer meeting when he gets Mama and Nettie Sue," Jonathan said. "That is, if I'm not finished with my work. Dan's anxious to show off his new car."

"All right, Jonathan." Olivia Lee gathered her beaded drawstring purse and New Testament and palm leaf fan from the seat. "I'm so glad our prayer meeting services this month are taken from the New Testament. It's so much more cheerful than that Old Testament." She closed the door behind her.

Jonathan had to smile. Livvie Lee made the world around her her own private property. She stood at the exact center of an intensely personal universe—and most people and events in it were rated on her own special chart for their degree of pleasantness, for their lack of demands on her. Apparently Job and Jeremiah had not scored very high on that scale.

As he drove toward the cannery he could hear the voice of the church choir (Nettie Sue's tremolo mingled in there somewhere) raised in its first hymn. A sound simple and familiar, it flowed like golden honey through the early evening stillness. He knew not only the middle names and the faces of those who sang, but he knew their histories and rumors as well: grandfathers tough as sole-leather, cousins gone West for various secret and obvious escapes whose names had become dim memories, painful losses by death and disease, good fortunes, loves, and hates.

And yet—secure and intimate as this world seemed, there lay something else . . . out there. . . .

Jonathan glanced toward the mountains in the distance, toward Wolf Pen Gap far away, dark masses against the night sky. This country he knew, though deep within itself a mystery, a violence, lay coiled, alive, waiting. He was aware of what prompted this turn in his thoughts.

That afternoon his uncle Whitley Ransom had come by the office. Since failure of the Florida venture and Uncle Whitley's return to Churchill, Jonathan had given him a job as keeper of the company's time-clock. ("That Mr. Ransom, he tried everything," old Cebo grumbled, "nothing but a turn-from and a turn-to." But Mary Clayburn had been happy to have her brother in a regular job.) Today, excitement animated his florid face. He told the tale as he had heard it that morning from the sheriff, a tale of bizarre superstition and cruelty that had taken place in isolated Metcalf Cove only yesterday.

Eighty-year-old Esau Metcalf, father to Edom who had worked for Elisha and Mary Clayburn when they first began farming at the Riverbend Farm, had grown increasingly frantic in his religious zeal during the spring and summer. When Esau said he heard witches, no one paid any attention, except to laugh. When he said he saw witches, a few of the more lonely listened and shuddered. But then Esau vowed that his three fine cattle were bewitched.

All night long two nights before he prowled the stony, winding road up and down the cove, moaning that witches were riding his good, sleek cows and turning them into wild brutes. Not more than a half-dozen families still lived in the steep, neglected moonshine-whiskey corner of Metcalf Cove, but two or three of these had shouted to Esau to go home, and one man had set dogs on him.

Esau waited until the first light of dawn and then took his lantern and dragged heavy chains from his barn down to a deep ravine behind the barren pasture lot. In the middle of the ravine there grew an immense yellow poplar. Surrounded by gullied hillsides and scrubby second-growth saplings, the poplar stood like a sentinel preserved from an ancient era. No one could guess how it had escaped the woodsman's ax or lumberman's saw in years past. But it did not escape Esau Metcalf.

He fastened a chain around its trunk. Then he went back to the pasture and led the two thoroughbred Guernseys which had been his only pride during recent years, and the aging brindle cow which was half-blind, down into the ravine, talking to the animals so that they moved with docile patience, until he hooked chains around their necks and cinched them close to the rough tree-trunk, where they began to pull and balk. A pair of neighbor boys crossing the head of the ravine heard Esau muttering to the three tethered, uneasy cattle as he paced back and forth around them for an hour, two hours, heaping dead brush and wood into a huge pile around the poplar and among the restless cows. The boys waited and watched, had no need to hide since Esau stood oblivious to everything except his task.

At long last, he unscrewed the small cap from the lantern's base and emptied a stream of kerosene onto the piled brush. From his threadbare shirt pocket he drew a long match. Cupping his calloused hands as a shield against any stirring of air, he struck fire and dropped it onto the kerosene and debris. The blaze leaped, spread, soared. The cattle plunged against the chains, wild with fear.

Before the boys fled they saw old Esau circling the tree, tears streaming down his white-whiskered face, crying, "Witches burn. Taste your own torment. Come out of the fire if you can, devil witches."

The blaze from the dead brush licked at the poplar trunk, seared the maddened cattle, intensified as a breeze fanned it to fresh heat. The crackling sticks and Essau's chants were drowned by the bawling of the cows, a sound of hoarse animal pain and terror. The smell of burning limbs and leaves was submerged under the sickening smell of hair and hide and flesh singeing and roasting alive.

When others from Metcalf Cove, guided by the breathless boys and the columns of smoke and the macabre sound and stench, finally arrived at the ravine, the fire was too well established, the animals too near death, for any help.

"The old man let them bring him in to the courthouse meek as Mary's lamb," Whitley Ransom concluded. "But all he would say to them was, 'Fire's the only brew for witches.' Over and over."

Jonathan now shook his head, remembering his uncle's sudden startled uncertainty as he had finally stated, "Foolishness to believe in witches and spirits and ha'nts and such. Isn't that right, Jonathan?" And Jonathan wondered if a deep memory from the peat-smoked bogs of old Ireland, from the wild Cornish coast of England, stirred in this ferocious blood. Hadn't Whitley Ransom himself, years before, in a drunken rage, tried to shoot the evil spirits out of forty hogs in the middle of summer? Jonathan's wondering faded as the cannery came into sight.

The sauerkraut line was running late this evening. The office echoed emptily, however, as Jonathan took the key from his pocket and unlocked the door. He glanced at his watch—happy as he recalled the faces of his two small sons only a few minutes before concentrating on the numbers and hands and telling time. He would have at least three good hours to work here, as soon as he reminded Dan to take

Livvie Lee home after he retrieved their mother and Nettie Sue at the prayer meeting. Jonathan unbuttoned his collar and hung his coat carefully over the back of his chair.

The first matter he must attend to was the Churchill Can Company. After years of planning, the Clayburns had built this factory in the midst of the business slump of 1920–21 when canneries and other businesses were failing on every hand and food prices had collapsed. But ever since the first wagonload of cans from Baltimore had been hauled down the dusty road to that crude tomato shed on the Riverbend Farm, the Clayburns had found themselves at a disadvantage in buying one of their costliest production items. And Clayburns did not like to be at a disadvantage.

Two giant monopolies controlled the supply of cans to hundreds of canners, most of them small, unorganized, and unable to effectively protest any price hikes. Clayburn Company, being in the South, had the additional squeeze of the old freight inequities to fight. Whit helped out but each new shift in prices brought a new crisis.

Carefully, persistently, the Clayburns developed plans for establishing their own manufacturing works, and two years before the Churchill Can Company had been incorporated. Its two hundred thousand dollars authorized capitalization was equally divided between common and preferred stock. Under Dan's direction, Clayburn Brothers installed machinery in a new building constructed next door to the central Churchill cannery, placed orders for sheet steel, and hired—upon recommendation by Haley Morrison—a plant superintendent from Wisconsin. (The letter from Haley Morrison telling of the new superintendent's qualifications also mentioned in a personal postscript that he and Laura were parents of a son. "Laura wishes he could grow up in her mountains," Morrison wrote. "And I agree. I only wish it were practical.")

The distinctive feature of the can company, however, lay in its ownership. For several years Jonathan had given thought to ways in which his family's company could become a closer part of the community's life. "I wouldn't want to see us become a self-sufficient empire at the edge of town," he sometimes said to his brothers. "We ought to be part of Churchill in every possible way."

And Dan had suggested, "Why don't we give anyone who works with the company a real stake in its future?"

"You mean open the company's ownership to the public?" Whitley, who had taken Calvin's place on the board, protested.

"No," Dan shook his head. "But this new business would suit to a T. Why not let anyone who works for Clayburn Brothers buy stock in the can company? The fortunes of the two are interlaced."

Jonathan agreed. "We'll call it the Churchill Can Company. This county needs some industry if it's ever going to prosper and grow. A can factory ought to create good will."

"And profits, too," Josh said. "If we sell cans to Southern canners—and I think they'll rush to give us orders with our f.o.b. Churchill instead of Baltimore or Ohio or some other Northern point—then someone stands to make a pretty good haul."

"We hope so," Dan said.

"Well, then, why give it away? It's one thing for you to be free with profits and money," Josh said, and the others felt that they heard echoes of Nora in his words, "you don't have anybody but yourself to look after. I'm responsible to a wife and children."

"So are others, Josh," Jonathan interrupted mildly. "We seem to be pretty fortunate so far." And behind his words lodged the reminder that he, even though president, received no more salary or dividends than any of the others.

Dan and Jonathan—and Churchill—had gotten the can manufacturing plant.

Shad Kendrick, investing every penny he possessed in Churchill Can Company, became its first general manager and owner of a large block of stock. Nate Lusk invested all he had and then borrowed from his brother-in-law, Colonel Gideon Wakely, to buy more stock. And Colonel Wakely, afflicted with a harsh, twisting rheumatism in his later years, emerged once again as part of a new Clayburn venture.

"They're shrewd boys, Nate," he said. "You throw the bottle away and stick with them and you'll be on easy street someday."

Prospects of the Churchill Can Company aroused enthusiasm throughout the town and county. And even some of the most improbable employees became stockholders in the new plant.

The first months of production confirmed their enthusiasm. Clayburn Brothers Company alone had used almost ten million cans, and an additional one million had been sold to various small canners in Jackson City and adjoining states. Except for some delays of shipment in tin plate scrap and some fights over freight cost (the crucial difference between eleven dollars and fourteen dollars a ton), the can company had had smooth sailing.

But recently Lonas Rankin had brought Dan his savings from years of work with the Clayburns and had asked if the money could go into the Churchill Can Company. And Dan was backing him in his request.

"It wouldn't be wise," Jonathan's father-in-law, Alexander Montgomery, said when Jonathan mentioned Lonas Rankin's wish to invest. "Not wise at all. This can business is one of the best undertakings Clayburn's could have started in this region. And it has cemented friendship everywhere. But to let Lonas Rankin in on an equal basis—" He shook his head.

"Craziest fool thing I ever heard of," Josh said. "Why, half the other investors would pull right out if he came in."

"Since you didn't favor letting any outsider in to begin with, that ought to suit you fine," Dan answered.

"From all that I've heard since I was a child," Livvie Lee had said that night at supper, "that Lonas came in a gnat's heel of being lynched once over some stolen money. I should think he'd be perfectly satisfied now just to lay low and not stir things up."

Her words turned Jonathan's memory back to the wet, dark morning he and his mother had stood between Lonas and the surly men on horseback. He could see, as clearly as the desk before him, the way the cold sweat had gleamed on Lonas' skin while his gaze never flinched and his shoulders never sagged for an instant.

But he remembered, too, the red summer of 1919 not long past, one of the war's bequests, when there had been a race riot in nearby Jackson City with six Negroes shot and one lynched from a railroad bridge and two blocks of homes burned to ashes, and across the country hundreds of black people flogged and branded, tarred and feathered, burned at the stake. A man could not let his thoughts dwell on such upheavals for long at a time. There had also been unease and suspicion and rumors in Churchill.

Jonathan returned the incorporation papers of Churchill Can

Company to their place. He would go along with Dan on this—at least until the intensity of reaction to Lonas Rankin's boldness could be determined. But he was troubled.

He picked up a letter on his desk where Shad Kendrick had left it for first attention. Nate Lusk, asking for a shave in price on several canned items, had sent it from New York City. Nate was reporting on a contract with the Great Atlantic and Pacific Tea Company and the tough competition he faced.

"It's a tremendous market, but I believe we can make a big cut of it ours. They shave everything close. I was mistaken in my idea of the kind of buyer I would run up against here in New York. It's not a yes-or-no proposition, even worse than the jockeying line of our Southern jobbers. I've cut a good many cans working the trade here, and I've not been ashamed of a single Clayton product. If we can get hooked up with one of these expanding chain outfits, we'll be in fine shape. It looks as if they'll be the coming thing."

The letter suggested two portents. One related to future marketing, of course. Were these "chain stores" catching on, with their quick turnover, lower prices, standardized procedures, reduced personal services? If so, could Clayburn Brothers work with them and still make a profit? He figured the fraction of a cent difference that Nate had proposed for Atlantic and Pacific Tea. It looked permissable— not good, but permissable. He jotted down an answer for Shad to type the next day. Shad's business course had included the secretarial rudiments of typing and Clayburn Brothers made use of this skill to hold overhead down, keep the budget lean.

The other problem was Nate himself. During the war he had married, had gotten a son, Nate, Jr. whom they called Nat, and the Clayburns had hoped this would settle him into more sober habits. With the government using the largest part of their pack each year, there had been no need for aggressive salesmanship during the war years and Nate had taken over some of the growing burden of paperwork, much of it created by government procedures. He had also helped make many arrangements for the Churchill Can Company. After the armistice, however, when peace arrived sooner than business or government foresaw, Clayburn's had sent Nate and some of his old sales force back on the road—first to create good will and renew contacts, then to sell whatever surplus stood in the warehouses or whatever crops could be canned that season.

Nate's old habits returned—enlarged and intensified. As business increased, as Clayburn's market expanded to include the Midwest and parts of the Northeast, Nate remained away for longer and longer periods of time. He supervised the other salesmen and cultivated brokers, jobbers, wholesalers in all of the large cities. And Nate liked cities. His clothes became a topic of conversation in Churchill—as did his drinking escapades.

One night three months ago in Memphis he had been arrested for public drunkenness and disorderly conduct. Before Jonathan could get money to him he had spent a night in jail.

"Clayburn Brothers represented by such a man!" Mary Clayburn protested to Josh and Dan. "What would your father think?"

"But Nate does a good job for us," Dan said. "Except for his drinking."

"That's a mighty big exception," his mother said. "All some folks ever see or know of this company is Nate Lusk's face and antics. If you want the Clayburn name to be associated with such habits—"

"We'll do whatever you think right about it, Mama," Josh said.

"I'm sorry for Nate. And his sister Drusilla is one of my dearest friends and has her cross to bear with the colonel for a husband. But I don't see how you boys can have the good name of Clayburn dragged through bars and taverns by a drunkard!"

They had promised to fire Nate.

When he came into the office, however, Jonathan reversed their decision. Nate was not wearing his natty clothes, his face was drawn and contrite, and he was subdued as a wayward child discovered in its mischief.

"One more chance. That's all I ask you boys. One more chance. And if I let you down then you can call me every name but the right one and fire me without notice."

No one answered.

"I swear I'll go straight this time. And even the Lord said we should go an extra mile—" He held up his hand to forestall Josh's answer. "I'm not asking for a mile. Or even a yard. Just give me a few inches to keep my foot in the door and I'll prove old Nate Lusk to you." It was the finest sales job he had ever put across.

"All right, Nate," Jonathan said at last. "One more chance. But Clayburn Brothers wants an upright reputation. You represent this company right—or not at all."

"Shake on it!" And Nate held out his hand. It trembled only slightly.

Reading his report from New York, Jonathan wondered how Nate was getting along. Dozens of new clubs and entertainments opened in New York every night. . . . But the orders continued strong. He hoped Nate would make it. The company needed his salesmanship. He would try to help Nate.

He heard a car speed into the company parking lot and skid to a halt just under his window. This was odd. Even the last workers in sauerkraut had long since left for home.

He pushed his chair back from the desk and stood up, pulling his coat on as he went to the window. He leaned over the sill and looked out to the parking lot. In the dim light he could see a man—hurrying —"Hello, who is it?" he called.

"Mr. Jonathan." It was Shad Kendrick's voice. But it was not Shad Kendrick's normal voice.

"Shad? Is that you, Shad?"

"Yes, Mr. Jonathan." But he was running now. Around the building. Up the three outer steps and down the hall to Jonathan's office. He appeared in Jonathan's doorway, his face white and his eyes wide with alarm. Tears rolled unnoticed down his rugged cheeks.

"Shad! What's happened?"

"You've got to come, Mr. Jonathan. Down to the railroad crossing in town—"

"What's happened?"

"It's your mother—and Mr. Dan—"

Jonathan did not wait to hear more.

They both ran now. Out of the building. To Shad's car. And then they were rushing along the street, past warehouses and the mill, past homes and a church and the Montgomery store, past the bank.

"Mr. Dan was driving across," Shad explained, grasping the steering wheel as if it were a lifeline, "and a switch engine was backing up from the siding at the lumber yard."

"Didn't he see it?" Jonathan leaned forward, not looking at Shad, urging the car on with his body.

"Not till too late. There weren't any lights on the engine. And the car stalled—"

"Good God!" It was a prayer and a curse and a horror.

"Miss Nettie Sue was in the back seat. She jumped out."

"And Livvie Lee?" The words came out as little more than a whisper.

"Miss Livvie Lee?" Shad puzzled. "She wasn't there."

"Then Dan had already taken her home."

"But Mrs. Clayburn, your mother—" Shad seemed as slow as the car.

"Yes?"

"She couldn't get out so nimble. And Mr. Dan he kept trying to start the car."

"Are they hurt much?" Jonathan asked.

Shad Kendrick could not answer. He looked at Jonathan quickly, furtively, then back to the road, and he pressed the accelerator.

They came to the railroad crossing between Churchill's two main streets. The switch engine sat on the rail, the huge Cyclops eye of its front light flooding the scene. The rear of the engine loomed dark and blank.

From the edges of the night, people were approaching, looking, whispering, huddling in confusion and dismay. A hush lay over the scene of wreckage, as if the roar of the engine, now silenced, and the crash of Dan's car, now twisted and tumbled on its side in the street, and the initial screams, now subdued to sounds of crying, had given way to an awed disbelief of what had happened here.

Jonathan was not aware of leaving the car, of running up the gravel crossing. He was aware only of two bodies, crumpled in distorted, motionless heaps a short distance from each other.

Dan wore overalls. He had been working on a new lid conveyor and dispenser for the can-making plant. ("If my idea proves right and we can get a patent on it," he had said to Jonathan at noon in one of his bursts of enthusiasm, "every canner in the country will want this machine.") Blood and dirt now stained the torn overalls. One arm, the shirt sleeve ripped away, lay flung over his head, partly covering his face. This defensive, even childish, gesture made him appear frail and vulnerable against the iron machine just beyond.

Jonathan's throat and chest seemed squeezed by steel bands. He turned to his mother.

"Jonathan! Jonathan!" Nettie Sue cried his name and flew into his arms, her dress tattered, her hair loose and wild. "Mother . . . and

Dan . . ." She repeated the names over and over. "What could I have done, Jonathan. What should I—"

He held her close and by will power broke the invisible bands around his throat. "Nettie Sue, you did all right. It wasn't your fault. Sh-h, Nettie Sue—"

But as he looked at his mother's body he could not go on. Gently he gave Nettie Sue to someone standing nearby—was it Alexander Montgomery? he never knew—and walked the few steps to where Mary Clayburn lay. Although her body had been battered and broken, her face was open and only slightly smudged, fully staring up into the starry summer night sky.

Jonathan slowly, carefully, pulled off his coat. He knelt beside her and spread it over his mother's face and shoulders as reverently as if it were an altar cloth. He smoothed her skirt over her legs—the lame left leg that had always hindered her, that must have dragged her back in that frantic final effort to escape from the trap of the stalled car as Dan tried the motor over and over and the locomotive engine bore down upon them, hugely, relentlessly. . . .

He buried his face in his hands and wept.

Nearby Shad Kendrick, wearing no coat, pulled off his shirt and laid it over Dan Clayburn.

Gradually Jonathan became aware of the growing crowd, of individuals in the crowd. He stood up.

"We'll take them now, Mr. Clayburn, if it's all right." Jonathan recognized the hesitant voice of the undertaker whose establishment stood nearby, just down the street.

"Yes." He nodded, unsure whether or not his throat had uttered a sound.

Then there were Josh and Nora and young Stull arriving—Nora taking Nettie Sue away with her to their car; Josh stricken and wordless as he tried to grasp his mother in one last hug of affection and grief; Stull awkward and stunned and inarticulate, withdrawn to one side, watching.

He saw Pett and Jack Montgomery, and deacons from the church who had not yet gone home after prayer meeting when the accident occurred, and Whitley Ransom who stared at his sister's body and for once was silent. Lonas Rankin finally picked up Dan Clayburn and carried him as gently as if he were a sleeping baby up the street, into the darkness, toward the Churchill funeral parlor. The undertaker's assistant ran beside him, protesting, unheeded as a buzzing gnat by the strong, crying black man.

There were familiar faces and strangers. And their voices made a chorus, its individual words undecipherable but its overall message one of shock and grief and inadequate comfort.

Someone pushed an object into Jonathan's hand. He looked at it and recognized the Bible he had seen his mother carry to church for half a lifetime. Its cover was askew now, and some of the pages hung torn and wrinkled. "It was laying inside the rails, near her—" the man's voice trailed off.

"Thank you," Jonathan said.

He looked at Shad Kendrick who stood nearby, bare-chested, waiting. "Bring Nettie Sue and Josh and the others up to my house Shad," he said. "I'd better go up now and see about Livvie Lee and the boys."

Dan had taken Livvie Lee home first. That was why he was on the opposite side of the railroad tracks from the church and the cannery and their mother's home. If Dan and his mother and Nettie Sue had not had to take Livvie Lee home. . . .

He looked once more at the wreckage of Dan's new car—the hood, running board, and door demolished on one side—and at the milling crowd, at the stains—surprisingly small and dull of color—already disappearing in the dirt and gravel. It all seemed as senseless as the burning of innocent cows, the wanton slaughter of quail. He asked Stull to drive him home.

Later he would have to come back down to the undertaker's and make necessary arrangements. He would have to decide the formalities of death. But first he hoped he could see their faces just once more, before the blood was gone, the flesh altered: his mother's broad, grave, strong countenance, and her youngest son's, so much resembling her own except for the added dash of humor which had crinkled the lines edging his eyes and mouth.

For the first time since he was a youth and had come to Wolf Pen Gap with Janus Rathbone and had seen where his father was ambushed and killed, Jonathan cried out, silently: Why?

13

My father was a voice: calm, firm, edged with steel and kindness. And a hand: warm, secure, leading and loosening. And a glance: tolerant but perceptive beyond comfort.

I remember the voice.

It is an afternoon in October. Sunlight falls around me and over the porch where I am whittling a block of pine wood to a nub, to nothing. Motes of dust whirl and shimmer in each shaft of light. The afternoon stretches out from me like a golden sea, limitless in time and goodness.

In the house behind me voices rise and fall. I hear them without listening, listen without knowing. My father and mother, Aunt Nora and Uncle Joshua, Aunt Nettie Sue, Aunt Lottie and Uncle Penn, and Uncle Whitley and Aunt Cornelia, are sitting in my grandmother Clayburn's tall living room. She is not there. And my Uncle Dan is not there.

Aunt Nora, plump and alert as a partridge on its nest, is sitting in my grandmother's chair but the chair is too large for her. She clings to it tenaciously.

"Did you have to bring the boy, Jonathan?" Uncle Josh asks when we arrive.

"Little old Jon won't bother anybody, Joshua," Mama answers. "He couldn't go to Monty's Sunday School picnic and Serena has the day off. I didn't intend to leave him there alone."

"That's all right, Olivia Lee," Uncle Josh says hastily as if he were fleeing from angry bees. "I just thought he might find it tiresome."

"He can play Dan's Victrola," Aunt Nettie Sue offers, then quickly covers her mouth with her hands. Tears flood her eyes.

I look at the machine with the picture of the listening white dog in front of a speaker shaped like a giant morning glory. I can't believe that Uncle Dan would never again be cranking the handle energetically around and around before he carefully laid the needle into the grooves for "Roses of Picardy" or a Harry Lauder song or "Semper Fidelis."

I am embarrassed by their talk of me. "I'll sit outside and whittle with the knife Uncle Dan gave me," I offer.

My mother stiffens. "I thought we hid that knife," she says to my father.

"Jon found it," he replies.

"But he might hurt himself—"

"I'll be careful," I promised, clutching the neat, bright pocket-knife.

"Jon must learn to respect tools," my father says. I hurry outside, happy over the reprieve from security.

I can smell the rich pine of the slim block of wood as I sit cross-legged in the October sunshine on the porch and draw the thin blade of my knife down in smooth long slashes. I hear the voices inside the house.

"The railroad is making a handsome settlement." Uncle Whitley's voice has a deep professional tone.

"You've handled it well, Whit," my father says.

"Of course, it's nothing more than they should do," Aunt Nora speaks decisively. "Killing two perfectly innocent people—"

"But we still appreciate what Whit has done," Uncle Josh interrupts her.

"Yes," Aunt Nora says. "Oh, yes, of course we appreciate that."

Aunt Nettie Sue is crying softly, as she did at the funeral 'way back in August. But everyone cried then, even my father. When the ancient character they called Brother Pryor, in a long black coat and a voice that rasped like a crow's call, spoke of the sturdy, unselfish, industrious hands of Mary Clayburn and her son Daniel, hands which had built for their family, for Churchill, for the nation, I saw tears run down my father's pale cheeks and I looked away quickly, ashamed to intrude on the terrible privacy of that moment. Then I saw that everywhere in the crowded church there were people crying unashamedly.

"—That's the question we must decide now," my father is speaking to his family gently, urgently. "You've heard Whit's summary of a partnership and a corporation. Do any of us have questions?"

"If we wanted to, could we go on as the partnership we are?" Aunt Lottie asks.

Uncle Whitly answers patiently. "No, Lottie. Anytime a partner dies—in this case two—the partnership must be reorganized."

"That's why this seems a proper time to incorporate," my father continues. "Our idea is to issue only common stock in return for whatever interest each member now owns in Clayburn Brothers. That way everyone will have voting rights."

I can hear my mother drumming lightly with her fingertips on the arm of the red velvet sofa. She is bored by talk of business arrangements and money.

"If brothers Jonathan and Whit think it's the right move for Clayburns to become a corporation, I think we should agree," Aunt Lottie says. "Don't you, Penn?"

"Emphatically, dear," Uncle Penn answers.

There is a pause. I watch a layer of pine curl behind the cut of my knife.

"One other thing—" Uncle Whitley's voice breaks the stillness. "As all of you know, neither Mother nor Daniel left a will. We must make some decision about the disposition of their shares in the company."

"Oh!" Aunt Nettie Sue gives a quick sob. I hear the subdued murmurs of my mother comforting her.

There is a long silence.

My father speaks slowly and distinctly. He has given much thought to his words. "I have a proposition," he says. "We divide Mama's and Dan's interest in Clayburn Brothers between Nettie Sue and Lottie."

Someone in the room sucks in a quick gasp of air.

"Our business has been blessed with success and prosperity. It seems to me that Josh and I have nice enough homes and about as much money as is necessary for anyone's comfort; that's true of Whit, too, and sister Isabel up in Richmond. I think it would make Mama and Dan happy to know that the girls own their share of Clayburns."

A brief buzz of reaction hums through the room. Surprise and appreciation from Aunt Nettie Sue and Aunt Lottie. Surprise and suspicion from Aunt Nora. Ready agreement from Uncle Whit. Reluctant agreement from Uncle Josh.

I do not hear all the words. Aunt Nora mentions Stull. Then Uncle Josh says, "But we'll go along with whatever the rest of you decide."

After a while my father says, "I mentioned my idea to Livvie Lee last night and called up Isabel on the phone. They both agreed that it would honor Dan and Mama best."

"Oh Jonathan's so smart when it comes to anything financial," my mother repeats her usual vow of fiscal ignorance and personal dependence. "And for his family," she adds, "he'd give the shirt off his back."

"That's right, Livvie Lee," Uncle Josh says. "And Jonathan's plan has our approval. Doesn't it, Nora?"

"If you say so, Josh." Her voice is barely audible. "What with the railroad settlement and all that stock, Nettie Sue and Lottie will certainly be well fixed."

"We know they'll be good stewards," my father says. "Nettie Sue for the family and Lottie and Penn for needy people in distant places. But none of us ahead of the others in wealth, or in means for service."

"Thank you, brother Jonathan," Aunt Lottie says. She and Uncle Penn have been making arrangements to begin mission work in Argentina. They will leave in November.

"We'll employ our new providential resources to serve to their ultimate," Uncle Penn adds. (I can almost hear Uncle Dan, in some distant corner, laughing at Uncle Penn's big words.)

"If it's settled then, I'll draw up papers for these transactions when I get back to Atlanta," Uncle Whit says.

A few minutes later as they come out on the porch I hear my father reassuring Aunt Nettie Sue. "Mother would be happy with the arrangement, Nettie Sue. She wanted you and Lottie to have security."

"I still can't believe they're gone, Jonathan."

"I know, Nettie Sue." He pats her shoulder. "Down at the cannery I still set things aside to show Dan, to talk over with him—" I have never heard my father's voice break. Is he sad, or tired? Or both?

I look down at my bit of pine block and see that I have whittled it away to the heart, no larger than a kernel, a seed.

I remember his hand.

The midwinter day is cold and we are in the mountains beyond Churchill walking along a stream. Monty, wearing a red stocking cap, walks on one side of my father holding his hand and I walk on the other side. My cap is green.

"There's a rabbit," my brother cries as we come to an open field and he sees the brown bundle of fur huddled by a stone wall. He snatches his hand into the grip of an imaginary gun as he sights along a barrel and fires. "Bang, bang, bang! That rabbit's dead."

But our father does not nod approval. "He was sitting, Monty. A man doesn't fire at any animal till it has a running chance—or till a bird is on the wing. There's no satisfaction in unfair advantage."

Monty is crestfallen. He has little to say for the next few minutes.

"I wish I had more time to be out in the woods with you boys," my father says. "I'm going to work toward that." When he speaks his breath forms small white clouds that dissolve in the cold air.

The stream beside us is noisy under a rim of ice as clear as shards of glass. Beards of ice drip from overhanging rocks. Except for the rushing of the water and alarms of a distant crow who has spotted us, there is no sound. The cold holds all living creatures in its fierce grip. I am happy, thinking over the promise that our father will be taking us to the woods more often.

"Why are we going to see Mr. Rathbone, Father?" I want to know. Vaguely I recall that name from the Clayburn legends and recollections I have absorbed.

"I need to ask him something." The tone my father uses is unusual and I look up at him. He looks down at me and smiles. Then he smiles at Monty, too. The pressure of his large hand is reassuring. "Janus Rathbone is a good man."

"Why does he live so far back here away from everything?" Monty asks, confident once more.

Our father smiles again. "He has a daughter who used to wonder why other people wanted to live in town, so far away from everything here." When Monty and I do not respond, my father adds, "And Mr. Rathbone's business is here. You've seen his big herb warehouse in Churchill, down near the railroad water tank." We nod. "Well, those herbs are gathered by folks up in these mountains and brought to Janus for him to ship to medicine companies in New Jersey and New York."

Monty and I are impressed. We look more closely at the woods and field and stream-bank around us.

"Is he rich?" Monty asks suddenly.

Our father's eyebrows lift. "In a good many ways, yes," he answers slowly.

"What happened to his little girl?" Monty persists.

"She grew up," our father replies, "and she married, and she went to Wisconsin to live with her husband."

"So we were right after all, and she did leave here!" Monty says triumphantly.

"I don't know who was right. But she did leave." My father releases our hands and shivers, tightening the collar around his throat.

We come to Janus Rathbone's cabin and soon grow warm. He is a white-haired man, old as Santa Claus to me, but his face is lean and ruddy. It lights up with surprise and pleasure at the sight of my father.

An orange fire, feeding on green hickory logs, fills his big room with heat and light. From rows of sacks along the walls there rises the sweet and spicy and astringent smell of dried roots and leaves, plants and stalks and blossoms. While Monty and I explore the house, the men talk. Then I hear my father ask, "Do you know where Lonas Rankin is—or what's become of him?"

Mr. Rathbone shakes his head.

"I had word that he stayed here with you for a while."

"So he did. After your nephew let him go at the factory."

"What?" Father's voice is sharp. Monty and I sit down very carefully and quietly.

"Stull. Mister Josh's boy. He told Lonas a bad situation was building up—ever since Mister Dan got killed and Lonas didn't have him to work with any more. White men needed Lonas' job. The Klan was stirring. Trouble brewing."

My father's face is stern. "I didn't know Stull had spoken to him. Where did Lonas go from here?"

"Now I couldn't say. He named something about a stranger from Ohio had come in with big odds on the dice games."

My father watches the fire. "Could it have been a trap for Lonas?"

"Could have," Mr. Rathbone says. "Likely he suspected that."

"How long ago did he leave?"

"More than a week."

A forestick on the fire breaks in two and sparks dance up the chimney.

"You had any threats or trouble, taking him in like that?"

Mr. Rathbone looks at my father. "Not many folks threaten me," he says. And they laugh as if they share a special secret knowledge.

"Any black pepper handy, Janus?" my father asks, and they laugh again.

As we leave the warm, aromatic room my father says, "You hear anything from him, let me know."

"You can count on it," Mr. Rathbone replies.

My father pulls on his coat. "What do you hear from Laura?" There is a pause, an interval. I hold my mittens to the fire to warm them.

"She may be coming back here to live in the next year or so. She and Haley and the boy." Mr. Rathbone hands Monty and me a dried bit of sassafras root to chew on. "Haley will take over my little herb business—"

"Little?" my father says. "Not to judge by that warehouse you've built."

"Well," the older man shrugs, "in comparison to Clayburn Brothers . . ."

We walk down the mountain faster than we came up. Monty and I cannot slip on patches of ice because our father's hand holds us up. I am wondering about the man named Lonas Rankin and why my father or Stull should be so concerned over him.

We come to the place where our car is parked and drive into town quickly, steadily. Our father does not smile or point out special sights or give us bits of advice. He is quiet except for an answer to one of Monty's rambling questions. We pass a county school—one room for seven grades with a black metal coal-stove flue reaching out of the wall—and Monty sighs. "Father, do I have to go all the way through the books? I may not be very smart in books. It takes so long. There's kindergarten and grammar school and high school and then college—" His serious face is troubled.

Father slows the two seater, Model T Ford from twenty-five miles an hour until we are hardly bouncing at all. He speaks to Monty. "You don't have to go to school at all, son. But remember, when the Lord wants to make an oak He takes a hundred years; when He makes a squash He takes two months. It calls for time and hard work to make a man."

"Yes sir," Monty says meekly, gazing at some of the oak trees we are passing.

We come to the plant and Father parks his car near the office door. "You boys wait here. I'll be back in a minute."

When Father returns to the car Uncle Josh is with him. Father walks now as if all need to hurry has vanished. Monty and I tumble onto the back seat so that Uncle Josh can sit up front with Father.

"Stull was only doing what he thought best, Jonathan," Uncle Josh says. "That's all I wanted—to do the right thing. You know that, don't you Jonathan?"

Father nods. Monty and I are completely quiet. We have never seen him in just this mood before.

"We wanted to do right by everybody—"

As our car crosses the railroad track my father says, "Lonas Rankin helped Dan make every piece of machinery he invented here."

"But this place was going to blow apart, Jonathan," Uncle Josh says. "Without Dan around, the other workers wouldn't stand for Lonas. Especially after they heard he wanted stock in the Churchill Can Company."

"I know a handful of people were worked up even before I went to that meeting in Indiana trying to get some stability in lye hominy prices. But I never thought of Lonas leaving."

As we climb the hill toward home we can see the distant mountains where we talked with Mr. Rathbone. The air is clear and cold. Perhaps that is why my father's words ring so sharply. I liked Janus

Rathbone and his house and I pledge to myself that I'll go back there again.

"I've fought the moonshiners and liquor interests in this county," Uncle Josh sighs, "and I've withstood their threats. A man can take on only so much—"

"I don't expect more of you, Josh." My father speaks slowly. "But Clayburn Brothers must stand for something, too. Not just cans of food."

As we turn in the driveway between the two houses my father says, "When did they find him?" I look at Monty. I realize that my hands and feet are chilled.

"Word came just after you left with the boys. I guess the sheriff came across the body early this morning. A pack of dogs called his attention to that cave above the river. Lonas had been shot in the heart and stomach. Playing cards were scattered everywhere."

Father stops the car in the driveway but no one moves.

"Doctor thinks he's been dead more than a week."

Father nods.

"The sheriff says it was a gambling fracas."

"There won't be an investigation?"

"No." Uncle Josh's voice is so low I can't really hear his answer but I see him shake his head.

Father nods again. "You remember when Lonas used to help Old Sledge, the blacksmith? He was a fine specimen of a man."

"He was that. But there was always something about him, some insolence." Uncle Josh frowns and lays his hand on the car door. "If he'd just known his place, he could have done anything. If only he'd admitted his place—"

I remember my father's look.

It is another year. Five years. The heat of mid-summer seals the early evening in a breathless quiet. No breeze stirs and supper's smells linger in the air; fireflies seem to glow over and over in the same spot suspended in the twilight; no leaf moves.

The ice cream freezer stands abandoned on our back lawn, the ice around its now empty cylinder melted to a slush of salt and water. I am sulking under a boxwood on the line between our place and Uncle Josh's, for I believe that I turned the freezer crank longer than

Monty did and yet my mother let Monty have the wooden spoon with its leftover nuggets of fresh peaches and rich ice cream. Mother and Aunt Josie are lying now in hammocks, settled like pale moths on the evening lawn, laughing and talking softly, swinging ever so gently in the motionless air. Inside the house I can hear Serena rinsing the last dishes, slamming cabinet doors, and talking with Monty. I suspect my brother has cajoled an extra piece of angel food cake out of her and I retreat farther into the boxwood.

The side door, the one to my father's study, closes and he comes out onto the side lawn. "Oh, Jonathan," my mother says happily, "sit down here with us—"

He bends over the long net hammock where she is lying and kisses her lightly on the forehead. I am embarrassed and look down at a firefly between my feet where I am crouching but I hear him. "I wish I could, Livvie Lee. You understand. This month is the very peak of the season."

Mama says, "Next summer I want it to be different."

"It will be," he promises. "I'm going to delegate more of the work to the young ones. In fact, Josie, during the fall and winter next year I just might take your sister and her boys on a trip out West and then around the world."

Aunt Josie nearly falls out of her hammock. "You hadn't mentioned a word to me about it, Livvie Lee."

"We haven't left yet," my mother answers.

My father smiles briefly. "But I've been laying aside the *National Geographic*s. We'll have a year to plan—"

Around the world! My mind boggles at the thought. And I am included.

"But right now I'd better get across the river," my father explains to Aunt Josie. "I thought I'd go and speak to some of the farmers. They've hauled their crops a long way and will spend half the night waiting to unload."

"Come home soon," my mother says. She reaches up and catches my father's hand and they look at each other.

"Well now," he glances around, "I thought maybe I had two helpers around here who'd like to go along—"

I break from the boxwood like a deer flushed by the hounds. "Yes! I'm here. I want to go—"

"Whoa there." He winks at my mother. "I thought maybe you were already in bed, asleep—"

"No sir." I try to sound matter-of-fact.

"What about your brother? Where's he?"

I go reluctantly to the kitchen door and open the screen and stick my head into the warm room. "Father's walking all the way to the plant and coming right back. I'm going with him. You want to come, Monty?"

"Serena was telling me a tale—" Monty hesitates.

"Sure." I let the door slam and race back to the side lawn. "Monty's talking to Serena. He doesn't want to go."

My father and I walk down the hill and across the river and through the town. Only once does he take my hand: at the railroad crossing. His grip is strong. "Step lively," he says, looking up and down. Although the accident was a long time ago—five years—the pain in his face hurts me, too.

When we approach the cannery, the wide field to the east and the street in front of the weigh-in shed are filled with a line of trucks and wagons. There aren't many trucks, but the men who drive them are mostly younger, prouder than the others. The wagonmen are rough, patient, independent. They have fed and watered their teams and now they gather, a few in each cluster, and talk quietly, occasionally erupting in deep slow laughter. One or two are dozing on their wagon seats.

The ripe smell of tomatoes permeates the motionless summer air. A faint reminder of the day's run of ketchup lingers in the night. Tomorrow it will saturate Churchill again, when all of these tomatoes are processed, cooked to pulp, strained and seasoned, bottled. Monty and I are working inside the cannery this summer for the first time, helping off-bear from the canning machines to the iron retorts where everything is cooked. Our mother thinks the work is too hard, too hot, for us. But each morning we go with our father back to the "upper shed," to the first of the Churchill plant's three packing units.

As my father and I walk among the farmers, the men straighten and peer at my father like drowsing birds aroused on their roost. My father knows many of them and calls their names.

"Hello, Jackson Foster. . . . Sneed . . . Howdy, there, Tracy Morrell. Things going all right up on Kilbuck Creek? . . . And Grover Harris: I didn't know you were tending a crop this year. . . ."

When he does not know their names he nods, or sometimes he stops and shakes hands and learns who they are.

After we have passed by I can glance back and see the men looking after my father. Pride swells up inside me like a balloon stretched to bursting whenever my father lays his hand on my shoulder and says, "This is my boy, Jon." The men shake hands with me.

As we come to the edge of the empty lot and turn around I see the factory looming in front of us. It blots out the town, the mountains, even the full moon coming up on the horizon. It fills the world.

My father says: "Is it big enough for you?"

I nod.

"For me, too." We walk toward the river which runs behind the plant. "There's no need to be the biggest or the richest—or the only cannery in the world." His tone indicates that he is talking to himself more than to me and that what I overhear has passed through his thoughts more than once. But he says no more.

At the bank of the river an open ditch leads from the factory, a ditch of waste and slime, and empties into the running water. "We'll have to see about that—one of these days," my father says, as if jotting down a note.

We walk along the river a little way. Then we turn back toward the street on the west side of the factory, a street deserted and dark.

"It wasn't very long ago," he meditates, "when there was nothing here at all, Jon. Now there is a warehouse full of good canned food and more coming every day. All waiting to feed people. . . ." We go slowly and he looks at the brick building and attendant sheds as if he is searching both sides of the present: yesterday and tomorrow.

Twilight has faded and we walk home by the full moon and the occasional electric lights Churchill has installed along a few streets. My father has grown even quieter than usual but I feel that there is some intangible web of communication between us and I walk lightly, hardly breathing, because I do not want to shatter it.

We make our way up the hill slowly. The light of the full moon casts dark shadows of trees, shrubs, telephone poles. My father's shadow goes before us, ten feet tall. As I watch it I become aware of his breathing, hard and fast. I move closer to him. In the darkness no one can see that I am holding my father's hand. He smiles at me.

When we reach home everything seems the same, although Aunt Josie has gone home and Serena has gone to bed. The lamp in Cebo's garage room has been out since suppertime. ("Man and beast meant to sleep with first dark, wake up with first light," Cebo says.)

Mama is still in the hammock and Monty is playing records—Gene Austin crooning out some lonesome love song of the sort Monty likes, sentimental and narcotic.

"I must have dozed off," Mama says, hurrying to go in the house with us. "Josie does wear me out sometimes with all her parties for Clara and Stull and every new bridge game—" She interrupts herself to ask my father, "Would you like a glass of milk . . . some angel food cake . . . anything, Jonathan?"

"No," he shakes his head. "I'm sort of tired tonight. I think I'll turn in early."

That night I dream of a river of tomatoes. Tomatoes rolling, tumbling, flooding through the cannery, the town. Gradually the red juice changes, however, and turns into a torrent of dark, muddy, foul water full of debris and waste. It rushes over me and I gasp, struggle for air—and awake.

I am eager to describe my dream at breakfast but there is no opportunity. My mother is worried, fluttering like a winged bird between Serena's stove and Father's place at the table. To her, it is both calamity and challenge when someone in her orbit does not wish to eat.

"But Livvie Lee, I've already thrown up once this morning," my father says as Monty and I begin to eat our oatmeal. "The hot tea is all I dare try now."

My mother squeezes a heavy stream of lemon into the teacup as she sets it before him. "Stop by the doctor's office," she says. "Promise me, if you don't feel much better by mid-morning that you'll stop by."

"All right, Livvie Lee. But it's only a little upset stomach."

When Monty and I pass through the line of trucks and wagons into the main canning shed, one or two of the farmers nod to me. I nod back, trying to seem laconic although I am elated at their acceptance, their greeting. The whistle atop the warehouse blasts out its hoarse call. Another day has begun.

The bottles rattle by in a steady stream throughout the morning. The aroma of cooking ketchup spreads like a heavy blanket over the plant. When I stop for a long drink of water one of the men tending a cooker grins. "Takes water to make steam," he says.

I have not heard the noon whistle when Shad Kendrick is suddenly standing by the machine where Monty and I are waiting to lift off the next metal basket of bottles. "You boys ready for a breather?" His voice croaks in an odd strain.

"It's not dinnertime yet, is it?" I ask.

He shakes his head. "Not quite. But it's all right—" He turns sharply, motioning to us.

As Monty and I wipe our arms across our sweaty faces and follow Shad Kendrick we notice that although the rattle of machinery and the hiss of steam is still noisy, no person in that big shed seems to be moving. Everyone is looking at Monty and me. I walk faster.

Shad is already in his car by the time we overtake him. I notice that the car is sitting right in the street. Several people are standing near the door to the main offices under the long sign which proclaims "Clayburn Brothers Company, Quality Canned Foods."

"Why are you taking us home?" Monty asks. "Where's—"

"Your father? He's—well, he's pretty sick—" Shad Kendrick says. "He asked me to drive him home a couple of hours ago—" Everything he says seems to remain unfinished.

Monty and I sit stiffly, feeling the black leather seats of the Ford against our sticky skin and damp clothes, taking in the full spicy richness of the ketchup smell with every strained breath of air.

When we turn into our driveway I see a strange assortment of cars there, as if Mama were entertaining her Missionary Society or Thursday Club. But I recognize the doctor's car—and Uncle Jack's shiny sports roadster—and Aunt Nettie Sue's—

Before we are in the house I hear a sound of crying. I run toward the front door. "Don't let the children come this way, Shad," someone calls—but I am already through the door. I have seen him.

My father is lying on the blue velvet couch in the living room. His face is the color and texture of the paraffin Serena sometimes lets me chew: gray, waxy, cold. His lips seem to have sunk away and disappeared. His eyes are closed. The blue threads of vein in their lids offer the only color anywhere in his face.

Before anyone can hold me back I have flung myself across his chest. My face touches the familiar white smoothness of his shirt, and the clammy coldness of his cheek. I pull away. I do not know this stranger. Where is my father?

I feel Aunt Nora's arm around me, guiding me away. I hear her say, as if from a distance, "Poor child. Poor, poor, children. When *will* that undertaker be here? Come with me, Jon—Monty—your mother wants you upstairs with her."

Monty breaks away and runs out the back door to the garden. I hear him sobbing under the pear tree.

The following days are a blur of people and sound. Bits of words, glimpses of faces, tableaus and tones of voice build into a mosaic. It threatens to overwhelm me, but it will not substitute for him, for the voice and hand and eye that fortified my world with an equal measure of love, wisdom, steadfastness.

They take my father away—and bring him back. Now he is totally unreal to me, this wax figure, this shell.

"Clayburns die young," my great-uncle Whitley Ransom says with inbred Irish superstition born generations ago under smoke-filled thatch and salt mist. "There was Elisha." He shakes his head and the men on the porch shake their heads, too. "And Cal. Then Dan. Now—" He nods toward the window of the room where my father lies.

My mother's eyes are wide with shock and the pain of an unexpected blow. "What did I do wrong that the Lord should punish me so?" she asks. No one answers her.

"Whatever will Olivia Lee do without him?" The friends' headshaking and doubts.

"Poor little Miss Livvie Lee, never acquainted with care or burden when she was coming up; now the big load laid on her tender shoulders all at once." Tears from Vashti and the old black friends who have gathered in the kitchen to help Serena.

Uncle Joshua next door looks incredulous, confused. When my Uncle Whitley arrives from Atlanta they come next door to talk with my mother and Monty and me several times before the funeral.

"Jonathan always did right by everybody," Uncle Josh repeats over and over. "He didn't have an enemy in the world."

" 'Most anybody has a few enemies," Uncle Whit says. "That's the way you judge a man. But Josh is right, Olivia Lee. Jonathan must have had the respect of even his enemies, what few he may have had, and of more friends than we even suspected."

My mother nods, tearing at the bit of wet linen handkerchief in her hands.

"Brother Jonathan . . . he can't be dead. . . . What will we ever do without him?" Aunt Nettie Sue, distraught and stricken in her grief, asks precisely the question that lies at the heart of all our thoughts.

Nate Lusk comes in a haze of alcohol. "He was the fairest man I ever dealt with. Jonathan Clayburn would give a fellow a second chance. He was a man. Livvie Lee, I want you to know, and I want these sons of his here to know, that if there is ever anything—"

Uncle Jack Montgomery takes him away. Uncle Jack and Uncle Pett welcome the people who come to our house, and their manners, bred from an old Charleston tradition, please everyone who basks in the courtesy of Olivia Lee Clayburn's brothers.

Sometimes Uncle Jack talks with one or another of the businessmen who have come from Jackson City or even farther away. Their language is like a code: call money, Anaconda, bears and bulls, investment trusts, and margin. Margin is mentioned often, like a password. Their voices are animated and confident as they talk, and I know this has something to do with stocks and bonds, with all the rumors of people becoming fabulously rich this year. ("Jack is playing a pretty fast game," I heard my father say only last month.) But Uncle Jack and the men with whom he talks exude an air of prosperity.

There are so many—the preachers and farmers, the cousins and salesmen, the bereaved and the curious—that I escape sometimes to Cebo's little room. The door which has always stood open except in the bitterest of winter weather is closed since my father's death.

The old man is nursing his grief, but his bloodshot eyes and shrunken skin are dry as parchment. His wrinkled face appears too dehydrated to permit easy weeping. I tell him about my dream: of tomatoes like a river and the river becoming a relentless murky torrent drowning me. When I finish he reaches a thin skeleton of a hand out toward my arm. "It was a warning sent," he mumbles. His knuckled fingers pat my arm. "You your father's son, boy."

Those five words spoken by Cebo comfort me more than all the platitudes and sympathies of the days and weeks that follow.

I catch sight of Janus Rathbone when he walks from the entrance toward our sitting room made strange by pulled shades and tall stands of lighted candles and flowers banked to the ceiling and overflowing into hallways and other rooms. Janus wears a blue serge suit with white shirt and dark necktie; he looks like a different person. But his face is still striking in its bony strength. His large rough hands dangle awkwardly from the white shirt sleeves. When I speak to him outside the room he seems glad to see me.

"I've known your father for a long time," he says. "Ever since *his* father died. I always hoped—" His Adam's apple bobs up and down above the old-fashioned celluloid collar and I never hear what Janus Rathbone had always hoped.

Finally he says, "I'm not much of a hand with words. But if you ever need anything, boy—" He shakes my hand.

Telegrams come like a yellow snowfall to my mother's room. One covers two pages and is from Aunt Lottie and Uncle Penn in Argentina. Another is from Aunt Isabel in Richmond. The room smells of ammonia and lilac toilet water and the doctor's medicine bag. He gives Mama sedatives.

The morning before the funeral I see Stull. During all the accumulations of feeling and episode and condolence he has been around, of course—he and pretty Clara doing errands, carrying messages, meeting trains, talking to newspapermen or representatives of various national associations on the telephone. But this is the only time we have really spoken.

"I'm sorry about your daddy, Jon," he says. He holds a cap in his hands, shifting it from one hand to the other. He is uneasy—with me! We are dealing in a currency he does not know—words; we are delving in a medium he does not trust—emotions.

"Yes, Stull," I say, swallowing, looking just above his head, "It's pretty bad."

He nods. "I've been up at the plant making arrangements about this afternoon's shut-down—" he begins.

"Did they run yesterday—and the day before—and this morning?" I had not thought of the wheels turning and the food cooking, of Clayburn Brothers going on with my father no longer there.

"Uncle Jonathan would have wanted it to keep running," Stull says.

Now I notice that the odor of hot ketchup is, indeed, in the morning air drifting up from the factory. The heavy sweetness of carnations and tuberoses, roses and gardenias, has overwhelmed the familiar ketchup of previous days.

Uncle Whit stands beside me—my mother on one side, he on the other—during the service. Mid-summer heat wilts the mountain of flowers and intensifies their stifling fragrance. Under her long black lace veil my mother sobs. A friend of Aunt Nettie Sue's from Jackson City sings "In the Sweet Bye and Bye."

At the cemetery we sit under a canvas and look at the casket and vault, which is supposed to contain my father, and listen to the final prayer. Uncle Whitley leads me away. I like it because he lays his arm on my shoulder and does not take my hand. Monty is on the other side of my mother. As I leave beside Uncle Whit, her brother Pett comes and helps her toward the undertaker's square black limousine.

"Don't ever forget your father, Jon," Uncle Whitley says. He is very handsome in his tailored city clothes.

"No sir," I answer.

"I only wish you could have known him longer," he says, ignoring people who start to approach him and then hesitate when they see us talking. "He was an example, a plain everyday sermon to anyone who knew him."

"Yes sir." Something in my voice makes him look up sharply.

"Oh, he wasn't perfect. His feet had their share of clay—" Uncle Whit pauses "—but his head and heart had more than their share of goodness, generosity—"

I do not answer this time. I nod.

"Well, no need for another sermon today, eh?" He would like to smile at me, I think. I fix my gaze on the horizon.

From the cemetery there is a sweeping view of the mountains. In the late afternoon sunlight they stand out bold and clear. They seem far off, awesome, unattainable—yet I have already been among them and eventually will know them all. Janus Rathbone will help me know them. He is old but he is tough, like Cebo. They last.

When we come home, Mama doesn't seem to notice any of the people eddying around us: strangers, friends, relatives, well-spoken, uncouth. In the living room she stares at the blue sofa, back in place now that the casket has been removed. Serena brings her a cold drink of water with ice, but she takes only a sip. The black veil is draped over her arm and her gloves have fallen on the floor behind her.

"I'll never forget the way he looked," she whispers. "He came in from the car, and smiled at me, and lay down—right there. Then all at once—" a flick of her hand "—he was gone!" Her words are almost inaudible. "He's gone now."

I walk slowly down the hall, unbuttoning my hot coat and shirt. As I pass my father's study I pause and look in the door. The first object I see, squared neatly on the window sill behind his desk: a pile of *National Geographic* magazines.

"That's the way I'll think of him," I decide. "Away on a trip. Not a Clayburn Brothers sales trip or convention or company visit, but an exploration. My father is on a journey, exploring. It may take quite a long while."

This moment sticks in my mind: just before the noiseless professionals place my father's heavy casket on well-oiled rollers and slide it from our home into the ready hearse, I try to disappear behind a bank of flowers—and come face to face with my cousin Stull.

He is gazing at the box holding my father. Tears trickle down his round cheeks and chin. "He was good to me." Stull speaks more to himself than to me, but I know it costs him effort. "He taught me everything I know. Everything that amounts to more than a belch and bamboozle."

Then I see that his hands are clenched into two fists, one pressing against the other. The fists tighten and harden until their knuckles stand up like sharp stones straining under the skin—straining to strike out.

14

Early in his planning, Stull Clayburn dismissed all consideration of age. He would let others concern themselves—or become side-tracked, as he put it—by that inconsequential factor. He would forget age, except, of course, where he could turn it to his advantage, perhaps to deceive people into believing he was naive or inexperienced. There were many areas in which he was lacking sophistication, but that would not affect relationships he considered essential. At least at the beginning of his career. He would remember that he was young only when he could capitalize on the fact. Otherwise, he would depend on what he knew or intended to learn about the intricacies of finance and the business of canning. He could do nothing to improve his birth date by one minute. He could do a great deal to improve his participation in the world of industry and fortune.

This concentration had the effect of making him appear older than he was and thereby confirming his decision. His heavy, slightly awkward body and his deliberate manner of looking at people—as if appraising them by some special and authoritative standards—added to the impression of his solid maturity.

Actually, Stull Clayburn suffered from a mild case of myopia and since he refused to succumb to the use of glasses, which he considered professorial or unmanly, he had to peer intensely at things or persons around him in order to gain a necessary view of their presence. People often were simply not visible to him unless they spoke or had over-riding purpose.

When his uncle Jonathan died, Stull surveyed the situation care-fully. Clara, whom he had married six months before, found him preoccupied at meals in their apartment above the garage at the Mary Clayburn family home. Stull had wanted to live here because it was across from the cannery and because the expense would be only token. Aunt Nettie Sue, the only one left in the old house since the death of her mother and brother, had said, "Why, Stull, I'd like to *give* you and that sweet Clara use of the apartment as a wedding gift—for just as long as you can use it!"

Stull's mother sent for some pieces of her family furniture from Richmond ("After all, he is a Stull Buchanan namesake") and hired a professional decorator from Jackson City to come and put proper touches on the apartment's interior. Nora Clayburn wanted her son to enjoy comfort and tradition, if not luxury—and she had no inten-tion of giving Clara's Montgomery relatives any reason for pity or disdain when they came up from Charleston to visit.

But Stull's awareness of the apartment was slight. Mahogany highboys and cottage curtains could not clutter his view of the future. After his uncle Jonathan's death, Stull's attention to his vivacious wife diminished, too.

"How do you like my new dress?" she would ask after a shopping expedition to Jackson City.

"Yes."

"Yes what?"

"Yes, it's all right."

"Is it too short?"

"I said it's all right."

"But I don't want it to be just 'all right,' " she pouted. "I want it to be a lollapalooza—"

But he was as uncommunicative as he had been on their wedding night. There was no play, no subtlety, no sharing in him. Clara had wept secretly and bitterly that night but the next morning she had decided that he was only shy and self-protective; her impulsiveness and gaiety must help bring him into an awareness of all that romance, love, and sex might be.

Her resolve came to nothing. At night his body asked for only one thing, and when it found that release he rolled back to his side of the four-poster mahogany bed and lay impassively, thinking, planning, until he fell into a heavy sleep. Often there was no word spoken between them during the whole ritual. Sometimes Clara enjoyed it; usually she did not. At first she pretended ecstasy each time they were together, but when she discovered that Stull didn't really care—so long as she wasn't sulky or uncooperative—she abandoned all pretense.

She tried to understand that this was a "turning point" in the company, as Stull told her it was, and that their lifelong future (hers as well as his) might be determined during these immediate months and years. And since Clara was almost as self-centered as Stull (a lifetime of family pampering and St. Cecelia society nurturing had produced an instinct for survival that was both shrewd and elemental), she quickly decided to leave her practically new husband to his own pursuits while she found her pleasures where she could. There were all kinds of time-consuming clubs and parties and entertainments in Churchill—and now that the new highway to Jackson City had been opened, she was discovering a whole fresh field of diversion there.

It did not matter to Clara at all that Stull frequently discussed his plans with his mother. Clara had taken the advice of her older relative Olivia Lee Montgomery Clayburn: "I've found out that a woman saves herself a lot of boring talk and silly work if she doesn't know one thing about money: where it comes from, where it goes, or how much there is lying around." A shrug of her soft white shoulders. "I just assume there's enough."

Nora Clayburn was the only person with whom Stull could talk easily or carelessly. He knew instinctively (he was neither self-analytical nor even interested enough to state it to himself) that she cared for him beyond all others and that she needed for him to succeed as her husband Josh had not succeeded. In addition, she was astute and strong. She had been a good Clayburn for a long time. She knew that the company could be far more than any of the brothers who founded it had ever planned.

His father had been president for only a month when Stull turned to his mother in impatient frustration. "He's a housekeeper. A good housekeeper, Mother. But so is Shad Kendrick. A company has to have a leader."

"I know, Stull," she said. She was beginning her knitting for Christmas charities; her needles clicked rhythmically.

"You don't know what he was ready to do today—"

"No—" She waited.

"I got to the office a little late this morning. I'd gone by the machine shop to see if they ever got that pumpkin-cutter fixed. And he was dictating a letter to his secretary telling the lye hominy committee of the national association that Clayburn Brothers wouldn't be attending any more meetings."

The needles stopped. "Wasn't that the committee your Uncle Jonathan suggested to fight price cutting on hominy?"

"Of course it was." Stull was pacing up and down the room. "It was that committee he'd gone to organize when all that hell broke loose over Lonas Rankin, when I learned my lesson about a lot of things. But the point is, Papa would have just let that committee go —along with profit on the one product where we can outstrip any other packer. Nobody can grow hard-shelled Hickory King corn like ours."

"Did he say why he'd made that decision?"

"He mumbled something about keeping Clayburn a family business, that he couldn't deal in the bigtime, all the things he said when the stockholders elected him president."

Nora Clayburn looked up, alarmed at the sarcasm in her son's voice. It was stronger than she had suspected. "There wasn't much choice at that election, Stull. Your Uncle Whit is a lawyer in Atlanta, he and your father already had a big responsibility as legal guardians for Jonathan's boys. Certainly your uncle couldn't take over the company and leave his life's work. And the family thought you were too young. So that left only your father—"

"I guess I'll always seem 'too young' to old fossils—"

"Stull!"

"I'm sorry, Mother." He stopped walking and stood in front of her. "After he went in as president he told me he wanted me to help him. But he won't take any of my suggestions. He won't listen. He won't risk!"

Nora Clayburn shook her head. "No," she smiled slightly, "that was Dan's—and Jonathan's—department."

"Well, I've grown up in Clayburn Brothers. I know more about this company now than Papa does." Stull paused. "You know I do."

"Yes," and she resumed knitting.

"And I'm going to use what I know."

"Naturally."

He sat down and folded his hands behind his head. "I'm going up to Chicago day after tomorrow. I wired one of the hominy packers that I'll be up to see what we can do about that jack-leg firm in Indiana that undercuts us all on hominy every blasted year. Last season we didn't show a dime profit on lye hominy."

His mother looked up in surprise.

"Not a penny. Our other vegetables and fruits carried it. By all rights it should have been one of our big money-makers—" He broke off. "Well, we'll try to improve that. And while I'm in Chicago I'm going to look around—"

"I want you to do whatever is best for your future."

"It'll be best for all of us," he said. "But Papa is going to kill Clayburn Brothers."

"It's a pretty healthy concern," Nora Clayburn said.

"At the stockholder's meeting after Uncle Jonathan's death, I pointed out that the company could take one of three directions."

"I remember."

"It can go backward and be a little family business, whittling down its production and its market to a limited area here in the hills; or it can inch forward and 'feed the South'; or it can leap ahead and become a national enterprise, find new capital, build more plants, earn bigger profits."

"I guess I know which you favor," she said.

He stood up. "Well, Papa's way isn't my way. And I'm going to find out all I can in Chicago."

She smiled at him as he left. "Tell Clara to come and stay with us—"

He looked puzzled.

"While you're away. She might get lonesome."

"Oh. Yes, I'll tell her."

Clara visited in the big brick house on the hill while Stull was in Chicago. She rather liked being out of the cramped apartment and having servants again ("like at home") and being waited on. Then she stayed again later in the fall when Stull went to Richmond (for family reasons, he said). He returned from that trip unusually pleased and even brought Clara and his mother a small bottle of perfume each.

Everywhere Stull went throughout the country that autumn of 1928 he found feverish optimism and excitement. Industry, real estate, businesses large and small, everyone—except a more or less silent stratum of farmers—was burning with speculation on the future. The ugly war's excess profits' tax and other hurdles to expansion had been cut away. The pace of growth and change was set by the automobile manufacturers. Americans had invented a vehicle to release their restlessness, their rootlessness, their insatiable quest and exploration. Iron and steel—and coal mining and dozens of other allied industries —boomed as the hunger for cars intensified. Sand in the balmy states of Florida and California was synonymous with the gold of El Dorado. Cities were flourishing. For the first time, more Americans lived in towns than in the country.

But at Clayburn Brothers everything sat on dead center. Nothing at Clayburn Brothers was feverish—except perhaps for a single day's rush to finish the turnip greens or late beans.

Stull heard of a fellow in Jackson City whom he had known casually at the university who had made a killing in the stock market in recent months. And the fellow was a dolt! Yet now he was rich— and independent. Stull brooded about this.

Jack Montgomery was the only man in Churchill who seemed to Stull to have caught the spirit of '28. He drove a Stutz Bearcat and belonged to the new Sequoyah Country Club in Jackson City. He played golf over the converted cow pasture and on Saturday nights in the pebbledash stucco Tudor clubhouse danced and drank just enough to stay merrily tipsy.

Once Jack Montgomery sneaked every bottle of bootleg liquor out of the members' lockers and poured it all into one of the guest-room bathtubs and invited everyone to a "Jackson City champagne" party. It ended as a wild success, and from that night on the local moonshine whiskey was known as "Jackson City champagne."

Another night Jack Montgomery and the daughter of one of Jackson City's prominent surgeons ran away to Florida and were married. By the time they returned, Jack had made token down payment on a thousand acres of Florida real estate and the surgeon had threatened to horsewhip Jack—or at least have him barred from the country club. Jack promptly threatened to inform the public about the number of abortions the surgeon performed for his friends each year, and hostilities stood at an even draw. Before the year was out, the justice-of-the-peace marriage was annulled. Jack received a handsome settlement, and everyone—including the surgeon—celebrated with Jackson City champagne. Jack's friends congratulated him on being the sparkling hero of an otherwise dreary season.

Through all of this, Jack Montgomery made money on the stock exchange. He had bought into the Radio Corporation of America and the profit this move reaped for him, at least on his broker's reports, had fired his confidence. A dread yellowish dawn on the battlefield; "that scrap between the krauts and the frogs," as he now called the war; those foul-smelling trenches which had devoured his buddies and changed America and the Western world: all of these had become bygones, drowned in a flood of paper prosperity.

Stull looked at the Stutz Bearcat and heard the envious laughter over aging Jack Montgomery's escapades and investments. The only thing that won Stull such admiration these days was his appearance at a party—with Clara on his arm. Not that she stayed on his arm long.

"Honey," her Charleston charm was at its thickest in the early hours, "would you get me something to drink? I'm fairly pa-a-arched!"

Or, "Honey, don't those little bitty sweet things look good—"

And as Stull went to fetch, he might hear Jack Montgomery or some younger blade saying, "Yes siree, those little sweet things *do* look good!"

Stull had no gift for small talk. And made no effort to remedy his lack. When others admired Clara he looked at her and agreed. But the parties seemed more and more familiar to him. The people were the same ones they had seen the night before, or weeks before, and many of them Stull had known since childhood. Until he married Clara he had never suspected that there was such a rich social life in Churchill and Jackson City. He began to go out less and less often.

"I've heard their jokes and gossip," he answered Clara's protests, "not once but a dozen times. This is second-string social life, anyway. . . ."

"But what will we do?" she cried. She did not want to forego next

Saturday night's fun for the nebulous possibility of next year's big-time entertainment. "I just can't read those reports and financial pages you bury your nose in. What can I do for—"

But he only shrugged and set down his coffee cup and left for the company across the street—where his father was puzzling over a decision on labels for the next season's pack. Nate Lusk was standing near the window.

"The chain stores are taking us over," Nate said. He wore a jaunty new hat and looked very prosperous. "By God, half the trade doesn't even know the name Clayburn Brothers Quality. It's all A & P, Piggly Wiggly, Kroger. I'm right back where I was at the beginning of this game. We've got to turn this private-brand business around, Josh."

"Well, I don't know—" Josh Clayburn could walk over a river-bottom farm and judge what the land would grow, he could look at a Jersey heifer and tell what her worth would be in two years' time —but these realms of marketing and competition and a public's fickle tastes made him uneasy. "What do you think about it, Stull?"

"You know what I think," his son said. "We talked it over during Christmas holidays. Last week I gave you an analysis to take home."

"I haven't had time yet—" Josh Clayburn turned through some papers on his desk. "Well, we'll see about it, Nate—"

In his frustration Stull went down to the warehouse to make sure that the skeleton crew there had thoroughly mopped up after a blowing winter rain two days before. A supply of shipping cartons had been soaked under a leak in one corner of the warehouse roof. The men seemed surprised to see him checking on such a detail. Did they think his Uncle Jonathan was the only one who would do that?

On their first anniversary, Clara told him that she was pregnant. Stull reacted with mixed emotions. He was surprised and pleased with himself and uncertain of what this might mean in his plans. "Of course, I'm proud, Clara. I just didn't think it would come so soon."

She was satisfied with herself, too, but scared of the pain she was to undergo. "Well, what did you think might happen with all that tumbling around in bed?" she asked, and Stull was surprised to discover a streak of coarseness in his fluffy-haired little belle.

One day in late spring, however, when he came home from the cannery, Clara was in bed and his mother and the doctor were with her. "She called me this morning, not long after you'd left for work," Nora Clayburn told him. "She's had a miscarriage, son."

"But she's seemed fine. Just a little upset stomach sometimes at breakfast. That's what I thought was wrong this morning—"

"It's no one's fault," his mother said.

The doctor told them later that the child would have been a boy.

Two weeks after Clara's miscarriage, while she was in Charleston recuperating at her parents' home on the Battery, smelling salt air and enjoying fresh bowls of symmetrical, odorless pink camellias in her room each morning, Stull wrote for his Uncle Whitley to come to Churchill, if possible, to advise on an important company decision.

Whitley Clayburn arrived on Friday afternoon. Nora invited her sister-in-law Nettie Sue, Stull, and Jonathan's widow and two boys, to dinner Friday night. "Whit will want to see Livvie Lee and Monty and Jon sometime while he's here," Nora said to Josh. "After all, you two are the boys' court-appointed guardians, even if Livvie Lee isn't going to let anybody else 'guard' them. It will be a good way to get that obligation out of the way before Stull wins Whit's attention."

"Well, I can't understand why the boy's gone to all this trouble," Josh fretted. "We can reach a decision about this label business without so much stirring up—"

"He isn't a boy," Nora Clayburn said, "and I'm sure he intends for a decision to be reached." If Josh had listened more attentively to the tone of finality in his wife's voice he might have been better prepared for the meeting in his office on Saturday morning.

It was a meeting in which Josh Clayburn saw his son for the first time as a businessman, in which Josh Clayburn won the decision and lost the fight, in which he secured a present moment of comfortable familiarity by opening a strange and possibly treacherous future.

The immediate problem to be solved was basic and thorny, but it might have been any one of a dozen important decisions awaiting direction. The fact that it involved the scope, the growth, the very identity of the company, gave it an emotional dimension besides.

Whitley listened to his brother and nephew as they discussed the chaotic situation of private labels.

"I've not kept up-to-date in the canning world," he said at last. "I just hadn't realized that these private brands had multiplied so fast during the last decade."

"Like damned rabbits—" Stull began, then caught his father's troubled frown and murmur.

"No need for cuss-words, son."

"They've expanded all right," Stull went on impatiently, "right in proportion to the growth of the chain stores. When the chains began using more and more of their own brands to build regular customers, squeeze out a little more profit, then the wholesalers did likewise. Even more than likewise, some of them went whole hog for their own brand names—"

Whitley looked at Josh. "Couldn't you still put the Clayburn name on the label?"

Stull answered. "We do. 'Packed by Clayburn Brothers.' But who reads the fine print on a tin can? Most people do well to read the name of the product, know whether they're buying corn or applesauce."

"How much of Clayburn's pack this season will be under private labels?"

Stull did not look at his uncle but at his father. "Eighty-four and a half percent," he said.

Whitley Clayburn raised his dark prominent eyebrows. "That much?" he said.

"That much," Stull said and pulled a paper from the file on the table before them, "and it will be more when this order goes through."

Whit looked at the paper. "Waverly wants all their order packed under the Waverly Choice label?"

Stull nodded. "And since they went chain they're our biggest customer."

"That's why we ought to think twice before we do anything to go against them," Josh Clayburn said.

"No." Stull leaned forward. "We've got to reverse the trend and we've got to start right here."

"But if we can food just for the Clayburn Quality line we'll have to put on a lot of promotion. We'll have to spend more money on advertising, increase Nate Lusk's sales force by a hundred percent or so."

"Right," Stull said. "And when we get the Clayburn name better known, we'll go nation-wide—not just South and Midwest—and we'll build our own customers so we can sell to any wholesaler or chain or anybody else."

Whit nodded. "That may be fine for the long range," Josh said. His face was lined and troubled. "But we should slip into it by degrees. Just yesterday, Stull, you heard from Mr. Hugh Waverly about that letter you wrote hinting we might cut down our private label sales. And he asked us not to move hastily, to help them out with Waverly's Choice a while longer—"

"And help them keep their cash register ringing," Stull said bitterly. "Don't you see? They want our food, our quality—and a slice of our rightful profits, too."

No one spoke.

"They'll come to us," Stull said finally. "Waverly, Nate's customers, all the others. We put up a good product and we stand behind it; we sell at competitive prices. We've got to take the initiative—for ourselves."

Josh nodded. "But gradually. With Waverly's last. They've been friends for a mighty long time."

"Now," Stull said. "With Waverly's first."

The pause was longer, quieter than before. A switch engine on the siding behind the factory came to a noisy standstill. Finally Whit Clayburn looked at his watch. "Well, we've really used up the hours," he said. "I'm glad to have some solid information about the label situation. Of course, I'm not here in any official capacity."

Whitley Clayburn saw the force and reason of his nephew's arguments. But he also understood the lack of confidence his brother felt in his position as president. Whitley judged it more important at this moment to buttress the strength of Josh and keep the company on an even keel than to agree with Stull and change the course of Clayburn Brothers' merchandising.

"Why don't we follow your father's advice," he said to Stull genially. "Here and there cut out the private brands, move increasingly back to the Clayburn label, give the Waverly Company a few years—"

Josh was nodding happily, almost forcefully. A loose forelock of hair bobbed up and down on his forehead.

But Stull was pushing back from the table. "If that's the way the company wants it," he said. "But it will have to go ahead without me."

The two older men looked at him.

Stull stood up and started toward the door.

"What are you talking about?" his uncle asked.

"Leaving," Stull said.

"Now hold on—" his father was taken aback.

"My judgment doesn't count for anything here. Anybody can run the errands."

His uncle seemed less perturbed than his father. "Well," he said. "Well, well. You leave Clayburn Brothers. You have any idea what you'll do next?"

"Yes, a good idea."

"And—?" his uncle pursued.

"There's a canning outfit in Illinois, just south of Chicago, that's run into some hard times. I've asked the creditors if I can try my hand at running it for a year. If I fail, no salary. Expenses only. If I put it back in order, or at least enough so that it's possible to expect some profit the following year, they'll repay me with stock."

His father and uncle listened.

"I know the canning business," Stull said. His round jaw was set and hard.

"You've already had talks with them?" Josh asked.

Stull nodded.

"But your Uncle Jonathan never thought you'd be going outside this company," Josh said. "Why, you'll be working for the competition—"

"Don't you see, we can't both run Clayburn Brothers?" Stull asked. "Right now, I've got all that's sensible on my side and Uncle Whit knows it, but he's giving in to you. That's no way to run a company."

"But we've always thought of our family, too. Your uncle Jonathan thought of his family—and even you will admit there wasn't any better businessman—"

Stull looked away. "Uncle Jonathan just never thought of himself," he said. "Maybe he didn't have to. But he and I, we're different—"

The word seemed to reverberate throughout the room.

Josh Clayburn looked down at his hands. His chin trembled for a moment as if he might cry. Whitley Clayburn walked to the window and stood facing it, hands clasped behind his back. He remembered that it was Stull who had compiled the financial report to give to the stockholders after Jonathan's death. It was Stull who had written this year's annual report. It was Stull who had kept dozens of questions from burdening Josh's desk these past months as they had burdened Jonathan's for more than a quarter-century.

"This isn't any sudden decision for you, is it?" Whitley said. "You've been looking into this Illinois cannery situation for quite a while."

"Long enough," Stull said. It was almost as if he were already with the other company and not a part of Clayburn Brothers at all.

"You might do well to think it over a bit longer—"

"I've thought," Stull said. "If they're willing to take a risk on me, I'll give them a try—"

"They don't appear to have a great deal to 'risk,' " his uncle said drily.

When Josh and Stull told Nora Clayburn that night about Stull's move to another place and another company she did not seem totally surprised. But for a moment there were tears in her eyes.

Later that night when his mother found Stull in his old room, with the university pennant pinned to the wall and the picture of the Jackson U. football team below it, writing to Clara about the move they would be making, she paused at the door and waited.

As if he knew what she was asking, Stull suddenly laid down the pen and leaned back, clasping his hands behind his head. "I had everything on my side today—words, logic, even sense—but I didn't have one thing. I lacked muscle."

She waited.

"When I come back to Clayburn Brothers, I'll have muscle," he said. "That is, if I come."

"You'll come back," she said, and closed the door softly. She had wanted to hear him state the conditions. Next time she would be on his side. For she knew, had known all along, that he was going to be the leader of the pack someday. Jonathan was a rare breed—but he was just the forerunner for her Stull. After all, Stull wasn't just a Clayburn, he was a Virginia Buchanan, too. His strength wasn't only of earth-rooted mountain stock; it was also the fruit of the Tidewater. She could hardly wait to tell Livvie Lee next door that Stull would soon be leaving Clayburn's, that other companies were seeking his talents, his genius. And it would be a long time before anyone could tell whether Monty or Jon would amount to anything.

Stull and Clara took leave of their apartment over Mary and Dan Clayburn's old garage, left the Clayburn Brothers Company, left Churchill, and Jackson City, the people who were friends and the people who pretended they were friends, left the family.

The small town of the Wabash Canning Company huddled in the flatland of Illinois, hot in summer and chilled in winter. There were no nearby mountains to break the winter gales or generate summer breezes. Two main streets, one north-south and the other east-west, bisected to form a perfect square. On one corner sat a bank, on another a Methodist church, the third corner boasted the bright red machinery of the International Harvester dealer, and on the fourth corner a drugstore offered a variety of satisfactions ranging from vanilla sodas in August to chilblain salve in January.

Stull's and Clara's small white house was on the street running north and south. (All of their solid midwestern neighbors, as they met each in turn, made up some special joke about the appropriateness of their location on the *south* street. Stull quickly tired of their stale humor. But Clara capitalized on it and spoke with a broader South Carolina drawl, which her new friends loved.) The neighbors they met were more prosperous and less interesting than the people they had known in Churchill.

Stull spent most of his time at the Wabash cannery on the eastern edge of town. Clara discovered Chicago, only an hour's train ride away, with its Loop and its rattling elevated, its lake and museums and stockyards, its ugliness and energy. She went to concerts and plays and dozens of movies and took up art lessons. The wife of one of the Wabash Company vice-presidents joined her in the class, and that made a useful relationship for Stull at the factory.

For his part, Stull was encouraged by the way things developed. Before he came to Illinois he had thoroughly investigated the background of Wabash's desperate situation. He saw that the company had small, potentially efficient plants located in three Wisconsin towns and one other Illinois crossroads, that they held at least two valuable brand names—Wabash and Golden Harvest—whose acceptance throughout the Midwest had been built up over a couple of decades. But the company's recent management had followed an erratic pattern. Because of too many high salaries at the top, forced plant sales, and inattentive owners, it was little wonder that bankruptcy threatened.

Stull had been introduced, at his first lye hominy committee conference, to Sherman Wright, a short bespectacled Eastern investment banker whose words crackled as crisply as new money. He was in Chicago "checking out" some questionable holdings. Stull asked Sherman Wright to show him the Wabash enterprise.

As they drove down to the little town, Wright told Stull that the major creditor of the shaky company was National Metals, which had provided, on credit, the cans for the unprofitable operations of the last two seasons.

When Stull met with Mr. Wright again, this time in the banker's spacious suite at the Drake Hotel rather than in the dreary Wabash Company town, an official of National Metals was also present.

"I've brought along a friend you should know," Sherman Wright said, taking Stull by the arm and steering him toward the bay window where a tall, broad-shouldered man in a London-tailored pin-stripe suit stood with his back to the room. "Worth, this is the young fellow I was telling you about: Stull Clayburn."

The stranger turned. His clothes, cut to a perfection of fit such as Stull never attained, wrapped him in an air of urbane ease and gentility. But his face—swarthy, blemished, slashed by a barely discernible scar across one cheek, with dark eyes direct and sharp as an arrow—was neither urbane nor gentle. The sleek dome of his balding head contrasted with the deep network of wrinkles furrowed around his narrow mouth and nose and eyes. In that countenance there was the leashed appetite and cunning of a lion, the raw force lurking beneath the surface of his well-massaged body, ready for antagonism, expecting it, relishing it. He shook hands with Stull, looking at him, speaking not a single word.

"Stull, this is Mr. Worth Franklin," Sherman Wright went on, "president of National Metals. I think you two have something in common." A slight, sardonic smile creased the banker's face briefly, then disappeared.

Neither Stull Clayburn nor Worth Franklin noticed. They were watching each other too closely—the older man with a mixture of unconcealed skepticism and reluctant interest, the younger one with deceptive earnestness and attentiveness. They were each probing to discover how the other might be useful to him.

At last the president of National Metals said, "Met you three years ago. American Canners in New York. You were with Jonathan Clayburn. He your father?"

"No," Stull said.

"A pity," Worth Franklin said.

"He was my uncle," Stull explained.

"Unusual man." Worth Franklin drew a flat silver case from his pocket and offered thin cigarettes. Sherman Wright chose one, lit carefully, held the lighter for his friend. The dull rich glow of sterling blended with the muted harmony of deep-pile rugs and draperies and polished furniture in the impersonal hotel suite. Stull did not want a cigarette. What he did want was Worth Franklin's confidence and authority and the money that made possible that total conceit.

"More than five hundred canners in your part of the country lost their shirts," Worth Franklin was continuing almost casually, "while Jonathan Clayburn kept his company alive and growing—"

"There were five brothers," Stull said.

The brown eyes turned to him quickly in amusement. "So. That's the way it is: you don't want to let Uncle Jonathan have all the credit." He considered. "Anyway, the company succeeded—"

"While the Wabash Company failed," Stull added.

The banker glanced quickly at Worth Franklin and frowned. Franklin's face had darkened. "Yes-s, more or less," he demurred. The two older men were seated now on a deep sofa, its back to the bay window.

"I can make Wabash Company earn a profit," Stull said. Sherman Wright and Worth Franklin looked at each other.

"He plows a straight row." Franklin's face crumpled into a dozen crevasses as he suddenly, mirthlessly, laughed aloud. "No looking back, eh? On your own—and hungry?" His words seemed as much reminiscence as comment on Stull. "Well, it's the angry, hungry young bastards I like. Sherman, did you bring the Wabash file with you?"

And the banker reached for the pigskin bag which had been waiting on the desk all the while.

Sherman Wright and Worth Franklin did not like to be associated with failure. When it involved only an ailing midwestern canning venture they saw nothing but favorable odds for them in accepting Stull Clayburn's proposition. Besides, the National Metals lawyers had drawn up their bear-trap contract which protected that company as thoroughly as any mortal document might—and Stull acquiesced readily to all provisos but one. He would not even discuss arrangements beyond one year.

"Leave your options open?" Worth Franklin said. "Everything in the turmoil it is now, that suits us, too."

Stull arrived at the Wabash Company at the beginning of the canning season. He found no contracts with farmers for their crops, machinery and equipment in haphazard condition, labor scarce and demoralized. Stull inquired, persisted, and discovered some of the old workers who were eager to have jobs again, if there was any hope of pay. He worked with a mechanic who would come on Sundays, a full day before the production line started each Monday. And luck was with him on the crops that season; the broad fertile Illinois acres broke all records for bumper yields of tomatoes and corn. Canners who had made contracts were forced to pay prices higher than the market, while Stull and the Wabash cannery bought all the vegetables they needed on a cheap open market.

Former customers of the Wabash Company were induced to place orders for the more popular brand names, and Stull found new outlets in Chicago. The company had become something of a symbol to Midwesterners and they were glad to see it revitalized, happy to help save something from failure in a time when the fear and expectation of failure gripped most undertakings.

For Stull's initial success was just ripening to certainty when the bottom fell out of the financial world. The stock market plunged. Banks failed. Margins and mortgages were called. Businesses closed. Men leaped out of windows and hoped their wives and children would receive some fraction of worth on the over-borrowed insurance policies they left behind. Well, Stull wondered, how was Jack Montgomery now—and the rest of Churchill? How were the newly rich of Jackson City? His mother wrote that everyone was very depressed. It was a word that would find common use in the following years.

People still ate, however. The Wabash Canning Company withstood the initial shocks of the national situation and accumulated a small profit for the first season of Stull's management. That profit took its toll, however. A new element had entered Stull's work, infiltrated stealthily, gradually, relentlessly, like slow poison seeping into a familiar water supply with invisible power: the element of fear.

Dozens of impressions, facts, situations fed that fear: the hard countenance of Worth Franklin which never relaxed its guard and its ramming insistence; the crumbling foundations of companies he had always thought of as Gibraltars; the crazy, careening course of markets, of investments, of all the solid and hallowed world of "the economy." The only antidote he knew to such uncertainty and fear was work.

He immersed himself in the Wabash Company the way an Indian devotee would immerse himself in the Ganges or a cripple would immerse himself in mineral baths. There were no "hours" for him, no fulltime or overtime, but all the time. There were no separate or complementary interests in his life—only the Wabash Company.

And even as such single-minded labor exhausted him, sapping his mind and body and even the urgency of sex, it exhilarated him. He felt slightly perplexed the first time he tried to reach a climax with Clara and failed. But the grueling day he had spent with the overseer and a new crew of migrant pickers in the fields, and the anxiety of receiving cancellations from two brokers in the Northeast, had left him preoccupied and tense. He was not even sure he found Clara alluring any longer. She cared about none of his work or problems, only the money and the social and cultural prestige it could maintain. With scant time for introspection, Stull Clayburn poured all of himself into the Wabash cannery—and shared whatever was left over with his wife and such few friends as they had.

Just before the end of that hectic summer of 1930, Clara announced she was pregnant again; it came as a special surprise. This time Stull was happy and he told Clara so and assured her that although the world seemed upside-down he wanted and needed a son now. She was happy, too. Having a baby would give her something to do besides read all the doleful headlines and listen to everybody's crazy, frightened talk on the radio. What did they think? Money couldn't just disappear. People didn't just starve.

And later in the fall Nora Clayburn wrote Stull that his father had suffered a heart attack.

"Some union sent an outside organizer in here to snoop around and see what the labor situation is at Clayburn Brothers. Your father called in the sheriff and police chief and they all told him exactly what the labor situation is. That terrible old troublemaker, I can't tell you who he was but he had one of those long foreign names no one can pronounce, left town right away. About an hour after he'd gone your father began having chest pains. The doctor calls it a minor attack but it frightens us. I think the family might like to have you reconsider returning to Clayburn's."

Stull did not sleep that night. The next day he was on the train from Chicago to New York.

They sat around the room like an isolated herd of spring range cattle—or pictures he had seen of western buffalo just before the big herds disappeared—slightly shaggy, wary and uneasy, suspicious of some shapeless threat they sensed but could not define, awkward and innocent in their dormant strength. He could hear the shuffling of their ample, well-shod Clayburn feet even though the restiveness was muffled by his mother's richly patterned old Sarouk. He could discern the alarm in their naive faces and unnatural nervous gestures and he knew that they were ripening toward a stampede. The trick would be to time their rush to his advantage and to steer it in the direction he wished.

But Stull Clayburn knew he must not make the mistake with his family that Sherman Wright and Worth Franklin had made with him. For under the family's disarming ingenuousness lay a shrewed self-confidence, an impulse to survival, which made it knowledgeable in unsuspected ways and formidable in its resoluteness. He had discovered that where candor was an unaccustomed weapon, it was also a powerful one.

For instance, there was the day in Worth Franklin's executive offices of National Metals when Stull had asked: "Why should I be interested in staying with a run-down canning outfit in the Midwest, building it up for the profit of a New York investment banker and a metals monopoly—all right, near monopoly—when I can return home and help run a successful cannery and get a proportionate share of the profits for myself and my family?"

"All right—why?" the older man returned skeptically.

Stull had looked at him unblinkingly. "Because I mean to make the two into one company."

The eyebrows lifted, wrinkling the forehead back to the beginning of the smooth, shiny scalp.

"And I'll run that company."

Worth Franklin moved his hand slowly across his bald head. "No more proportionate shares?" His eyes almost gleamed.

"No," Stull said.

"Rocky time for business—"

"For some business. Clayburns is in good shape. It'll pull through. Combined with Wabash it'll come out on top." Then he had presented Worth Franklin with the hand-written projection of what he had accomplished with the Wabash Company and what he would achieve by the plan he had designed.

Worth Franklin had only glanced at it before he pointed out: "But Clayburn stockholders have to agree to this. That's the key."

"Of course." Stull was unperturbed.

"Why should they?" A faint flush made the scar on his cheek stand out whitely from the other deep lines. "They're no fools. They hold all the aces."

"They'll come along," Stull said.

"And I want to know why."

Stull put the answer plainly: "Because they're in a crisis. They need me. They believe in a Clayburn. And I'm the only one available."

The wary and experienced head of the company whose tin supply had helped Wabash canneries survive and fail looked at the round-faced, fresh-skinned, indifferently dressed young fellow whose head was as packed with figures and plans as the crowded sheets of paper he had presented. "I believe you," Worth Franklin said. "Yes, I believe you. Now—" he picked up Stull's prospectus again—"let's see how we can squeeze the best deal possible out of this opportunity."

"We'll need a first-rate lawyer," Stull said.

The older man read carefully. "A chance like this doesn't come but once in a lifetime. I see you plan to make the most of it—"

Stull nodded. Frowning, he remembered the long evenings he had spent on those papers with Clara behind him, fretful, demanding.

"Talk to me, Stull. Tell me what's going on out there in the big world. Can't you understand what it's doing to me to stay shut up in this suffocating mousetrap of a house—"

"It was the doctor's orders, not mine," he said.

"That's not the point. I'm the one who has to suffer. I just can't stand this confinement another minute—"

"You wanted a baby."

"Well, kiddo, it wasn't just my idea. It takes two to make a baby, or hadn't you noticed? Oh, sweetie, don't you even want it?" The big eyes brimmed with tears.

"You're acting silly, Clara—"

"Now you've turned against the baby—and against me—because I'm misshapen and ugly!" Tears coursed down her cheeks.

"I'm doing my job, Clara. Your job is to have our son. Mine is to provide a living for both of you. But you make it pretty damned hard—"

"I'm so lonesome—and bored—"

"—All your whining and nagging—"

"—And I'm scared."

"Whose fault is it if you're a coward? My mother had her children down at the old Riverbend Farm, never even near a hospital—"

"And look what she produced—a heartless monster! Oh, if your precious mother were here I bet you'd talk to her, tell her about all those documents you fondle over—" She seized a sheaf of papers from the table under the fringe-shaded reading lamp and let them fall down her loose kimono around her slippered feet.

Stull struck her flat across the mouth.

"You dumb little bitch."

He picked up the papers and took them with him when he closed the door on her screaming and left the house. He spent the rest of the night and the following day in his office at the Wabash plant, setting forth details for the merger he anticipated. As if the anger released against Clara had focused all of his thinking and skill, he worked more steadily and clearly than at any previous time. Even after he went home and found Clara pale and exhausted by the tantrum she had indulged in when he left, even after she awakened him the following night and made him drive her to the town clinic where she miscarried again ("Yes it is—was—a boy, Mr. Clayburn"), Stull could not feel the total involvement that was expected of him. The whole episode seemed unreal and remote from his inner self. Clara would have other children. He would see to that. Meanwhile, it was up to him to make sure that his own creations incubated full term, that they did not miscarry.

Thus he had been candid with Worth Franklin, and at the Wabash Company—with other canneries tottering and failing as rapidly as banks around the country—his performance had won Sherman Wright. With money scarce, thousands of businesses in shambles, and the future murky, Stull Clayburn had received the support of a powerful segment of the eastern financial and industrial community. Of course, that support had not come without a price—the price of participation in Clayburn Company's continuance—but that was a condition Stull had been willing to meet in his move to blot out the raw wounds from a lifetime of disastrous athletic encounters, from decades of pride embittered by his father's secondary role in the company hierarchy.

Now at last he was back in Churchill. His father, as president, had called a meeting of Clayburn stockholders. His mother, asserting her anxiety over Josh's health, had invited the stockholders to meet at her home.

"Joshua is in no condition to go up to that company office," Nora Clayburn told her sister-in-law Lottie. And Lottie agreed.

"Poor Josh," Nettie Sue exclaimed when she arrived at the meeting, her expensive navy blue felt hat slightly askew above her tinted hair. "He doesn't look well at all, does he?" Her question, her words were addressed to no one in particular. "Three weeks ago he seemed so much better, when Livvie Lee had us all to Sunday dinner with the new preacher. I thought then how well brother Josh was looking since that heart flurry six months ago. But oh, he has lost ground—"

Stull Clayburn and his mother did not look at each other.

"Well, don't let Josh hear you say so, Nettie Sue," Nora Clayburn whispered emphatically. "We want to build up his optimism as much as possible."

"Of course, Nora," Nettie Sue cried. "I'm not that stupid."

Then Whitley arrived, driven from the train station by Shad Kendrick. He greeted his sisters and brother and nephew, handed a tissue-wrapped package to Nora. "Just a little house-gift Cornelia picked out at Rich's. She was sorry not to come this time, Nora, but one of the children isn't so well. I see the prodigal's back from the West, Stull."

"Yes sir," Stull shook hands with him.

Stull watched them gather and greet and sit. His father sat on the blue velvet love seat, pale and quiet, having called their informal family meeting to order. When the light buzz of conversation had quieted, Josh said, "Stull has a proposition he wants to bring to you. You can hear him out and then make up your minds what you want to do."

Stull wondered if anyone at the threshhold of a great enterprise had ever had a less auspicious introduction. But that was all right. It confirmed his decision, his proposal.

They sat around the room, heads lowered, listening to him—their son and nephew—as he wore an old familiar suit they remembered from his wedding, as he spoke in brisk unfamiliar accents. They listened and shifted, and again he thought of the huddled cattle or buffalo sniffing strangeness, suddenly alert to danger. Slowly . . . slowly . . .

Forget Worth Franklin and Sherman Wright now, their merciless eyes, their trip-hammer calculations as cold and predictable and welcome as steel compared to these veering, memory-ridden, religion-haunted minds that might choose the most unexpected caprice or allegiance. The dangerous bolting from his plans, the cranky old mavericks to bring to herd, were not in those mighty oak-paneled offices in New York but right here in his mother's living room in Churchill. God, he would be glad to be free of this family!

Slowly . . .

At last he finished. They looked at each other. Only Josh did not look at anyone. He was looking at his hands resting on the cane he had used to walk from the bedroom. The veins in his hands stood up like meandering blue ropes, so hard was his grasp on the carved ebony head of the cane.

"Well, I don't know—" Aunt Nettie Sue spoke first aloud, her voice sharp and high and trembling as if she were reaching for a top note in "O Jerusalem."

"Nor I." Lottie was trying to present her reasonable affirmative self but she was obviously shaken. "I'm sure Penn might comprehend the details of this, the financial arrangements and all, better than I do—" They all knew that Penn would understand less than she did, but Lottie insisted on creating for him a businesslike mask of efficiency.

"Well, it sounds to me, if I understand the English language a-tall," Nettie Sue pursued her own line of thought, disregarding her sister's low, even voice, "it sounds to me as if Clayburn Brothers is going—" They looked at her, waiting while she searched for the word. She glanced at her brother Whitley, but he gave her no prompting whatsoever as he sat with his arms folded over his vest and coat and looked straight ahead. She began again. "The way it seems to me, Clayburn's and this Wabash Company will be like the gingham dog and the calico cat: they et each other up."

There was a startled silence.

"Oh, Nettie Sue, don't be silly!" Nora's voice was sharp. "Do try to be practical, just once!"

The others grew even more agitated. When had they ever heard pink and blue Nora, pleasant, accommodating, sweet Nora, speak so harshly? Her emotion underscored the gravity of this decision.

To Stull, his mother's voice was reassurance of the astuteness and constancy of her support. He knew why she had maneuvered for this meeting to be in this place—not because of Josh's heart but because of Stull's need: the need to win, which would meet a muted opposition in Josh's and Nora's home. To the older Clayburns, home meant a sanctuary. They would not easily betray its hospitality and its forms.

His mother was pressing this advantage for all its worth. "Don't you see, Nettie Sue—" always choose Nettie Sue for the attack, the one the boys had teased out of professional singing, out of marriage, out of everything but querulous devotion to her mother and sister and brothers—"don't you see that Stull wants to come back to Clayburn Brothers? He wants to relieve his father of a burden, he wants to keep the company going—"

"Going right out of the family, I'd say!" Nettie Sue cried. Stull could not help but respect her naive shrewdness. She had struck straight to the heart of the matter, at least to that central issue he felt would trouble them most.

"Then you don't consider Stull one of the Clayburns?" Nora asked.

"Why of course I do, Nora—"

"Then how can you say the company will be out of the family? Stull will be leading it—"

"Brother Joshua's son as president. Of course that would make us all happy; that's what we've all wanted," Lottie intervened.

"Then how can Nettie Sue suggest that Stull is just—just letting it all go?" Nora's eyes were as angry as her voice.

"Well it is true, isn't it, Nora," Nettie Sue replied, "that Clayburn's won't belong to us anymore? Won't Clayburn Brothers be bought by that Wabash Company, with the big New York banker—Sherman somebody—and that tin-can man—"

"And Stull."

"Yes, and Stull, Nora." Nettie Sue's voice was growing subdued as the others sat silent.

"Technically, that's right, Aunt Nettie Sue," Stull answered her himself, patiently, pleasantly. "But it's only a formality till we can reorganize as a Delaware Corporation—"

"Why Delaware? Why not reorganize right here in our state?"

"There are tax advantages in Delaware, Aunt Nettie Sue." He had slipped that time, telling more than was necessary, saying too much. Stull's voice became gradually more firm and authoritative. He glanced toward his uncle but Whit Clayburn was still silent, preoccupied. "With business conditions as they are in this country today, we need every advantage we can scrape together. I think Uncle Whit will verify that." Still his uncle did not respond.

When Nettie Sue's blue hat bobbed in a nod of agreement, Stull did not wait for her to speak. "And you've noted, of course, that Clayburn Brothers stock is all exchanged for preferred stock in the new company. That means no dividends can be paid to anyone else before the preferred holders have been paid."

"Yes indeed," Lottie said.

"You'll always be safe, protected."

"That's nice," Nettie Sue nodded rapidly, eager to be agreeable when she could.

There was a pause. The ticking of the tall grandfather clock in the hall just beyond the sitting room was all at once clear and loud.

"Brother Josh, you haven't told us yet how you feel about these
—these rearrangements," Lottie said.

Josh did not look at them. He was gazing again at the cane and
at his farmer's hands—large, rough, sure—forming a knob on its
handle. "If you want Stull's plan, that's all right," he said slowly. "If
you want me to stay on and do the best I can, that's all right, too.
Either way, I'm willing to do whatever seems best for the family."

They glanced at each other, their uncertainty returning.

Stull did not look straight at his mother but he saw her clearly
at the periphery of his vision. Her small plump body was tense and
strained. Her shock was obvious. He remembered when he had left
this house last month and she had whispered, "Go on and make your
plans, Stull. I'll see to your father."

He had been happy enough to leave the adjustment in her hands.
Especially after his father's initial reaction. Stull had come down on
a quick, secret sortie—no one but his parents knew he was in Churchill except Bessie, their cook. Even his sister, Nancy Ellen, across the
street, and Clara (who thought he was on a trip to Chicago), did not
know that he had come home to test Joshua Clayburn's reaction to
the new company Stull was forming.

Only Stull and Nora Clayburn were present when that explosion
came. At first Joshua had shown stunned disbelief. Then, when he
comprehended that his son was in earnest, he responded: "No! You
cannot do this!"

The color rushing to his cheeks heightened the air of outrage and
command Joshua had assumed. His health had improved steadily
since his heart attack and he seemed in full presence again. But his
hands shook as he turned through the papers Stull had given him.
They shook so fiercely that the onionskin sheets trembled like dry
leaves on a dying limb. "You'll not carry out any such scheme! I
forbid it!"

Stull found it difficult to believe such vehemence in his father.
"What's wrong with my proposition, Papa?"

"It turns our company over to strangers—"

"I'm no stranger, Papa."

His father had peered at him for a long, troubled moment. "No
member of the family has ever used his position with Clayburn Brothers to get ahead of the others—"

"Maybe that's why the company is in a predicament today—"

"No! That's why it's in such a strong position. All our earnings, except for salaries—and they were always small enough—went back into the company. We had cash reserves when the panic came."

"That won't keep the business running forever—"

"It'll keep it out of the hands of National Metals and the New York banks—where Wabash Company is!"

Stull understood then that he could not wage his campaign through appeals to tradition or profit. In fact, he must avoid these at all costs. He would win the family's support only by exposing their fatal weakness. And that was essentially the weakness of the man before him, who happened to be his father.

"Papa," he said slowly and deliberately, "how long do you really want to be the president of Clayburn Brothers?"

The older man was rocked off balance by his son's shift of emphasis. And he answered the only way he knew—openly, honestly, tritely. "Only until you'll come back and take over the reins."

Stull leaned toward his father then and said, "This is the way I'll come back. The only way."

Each of them heard the sharp quick suck of Nora's breath. The needlepoint on which she had been pretending to work crumpled to the floor. She did not even notice. "If that's the way you want it, Stull, the way you think best, then we'll welcome it—"

"Wait!" her husband said. The high color had drained from his face, replaced by pallor and an expression of bewilderment. "Wait—"

"Not another minute," Nora Clayburn said. "I've waited all my life."

Josh turned toward her slowly. "I don't understand—"

"You never did. All those years when everyone was making the decisions, when we were stuck down on that muddy, isolated Riverbend Farm while the others were up here in town—important, respected, comfortable, close to everything—all that time I was just waiting for my husband or my son to become *the* Clayburn."

Neither her husband nor her son spoke. Each of them looked at her as they had not seen her for a long time.

"Well, you never wanted that, Josh. You were satisfied—yes, that's the very word, satisfied," she repeated it scornfully, "satisfied as long as you were warm and well-fed to be one of the family, a hewer of wood and drawer of water. And I never said anything. I went along. I waited for Stull."

They listened, astounded that anyone could summon such self-revelation, even to her closest blood.

Tears had welled in her eyes. "When that business professor at the university told us about Stull's quickness in economics, in math, well I knew then that all the disappointment over football would fade soon enough. I knew that my waiting would be rewarded." She shook her head impatiently, as if to dry her tears without acknowledging they existed. "And now Stull has found a way to make Clayburn's bigger and better than ever—"

They still did not speak and she went on, easing slightly, "What was it the Frenchman said, 'Every day in every way I'm getting better and better.' All right, Stull, go ahead and make it bigger—and better."

"Nora—" His father spoke so quietly that Stull could not catch all the cross-currents of emotion in the one word. "Nora, I don't know what to say."

"There's no need to say anything, Josh. Just give your son your support in this wonderful plan he's worked out."

He looked away from them. "I can't—"

"You can't do anything else," she said. "If New York bankers and one of the country's big industrialists can believe in your son's ability, can't you?"

"It's not his ability that worries me," Josh said. "And they don't have anything to lose."

"And what have you got to lose?" she asked sharply. "Stull is your son."

Stull had left shortly afterward. Just before he went down the hill to catch the Chicago Limited which would stop in the Illinois town where Clara would be waiting in their troubled doll's house, he had his mother's reassurance. "Go on with your plans, Stull."

Behind them, on the stiff Victorian chair in the hall, Josh Clayburn rested. He was breathing in hard, rasping gulps as if some invisible wound were making impossible demands on him. But for the first time he had refused his wife's and son's sympathy and attention.

"Go on to your train," he had said to Stull. Then, with a new breath, "Give pretty Clara our love. Tell her—tell her we were mighty sorry about losing the little boy."

Stull was momentarily startled. He had never thought of it as "a little boy" at all, but only as a fetus at some indeterminate stage of development. "Yes, Papa, I'll tell her."

His mother had stood under the Corinthian columns and waved him good-bye.

No one knew he had been in Churchill last month. And yesterday he had returned for the stockholders' meeting. His father's worn face and dependence on the cane—the difference wrought in only a few weeks—had shocked Stull. He knew why Aunt Nettie Sue had whispered in alarm about her brother. But still, it seemed that Josh was unconvinced, despite all of Nora's efforts, about the proposed merger.

"Stay on—do the best I can—I'm willing—" he had just told them.

"Josh, you can't!" Nora Clayburn cried. Her voice cracked. Whitley turned to look at her slowly. Nettie Sue and Lottie were taken aback by her vehemence. "You've given the best years of your life to the company—now you're sick and you deserve a rest." She turned on the others: "You have no right to ask it of him, especially now that there's someone else to take the responsibility. I don't want to be another Clayburn widow!"

Lottie nodded, glad to understand the devotion of her sister-in-law. She leaned forward in her chair and reached out timidly to pat Nora's hand. Nora did not seem to notice.

Stull wanted his mother to be quiet now. His uncle Whitley's stern face and continuing silence disturbed him. Ultimately the acceptance or rejection of his plans would depend on his father and on Uncle Whit—and he wished the women would give over now.

"Uncle Whit," he said, "I'd like to have your reactions to our discussion."

The older man's bright eyes, under their thick dark brows, looked at him directly. "Two questions occur to me. First, where's Isabel, or a spokesman for Calvin's stock?"

There was a pause.

"I own Aunt Isabel's shares," Stull said.

Astonishment stood out on their faces like a fresh blistering brand.

"Well!" Nettie Sue gasped. "This is the first I'd heard—"

Josh looked up at his son for the first time that morning. "Cal's stock?"

"It was Aunt Isabel's when I purchased it," Stull said.

"May I ask when this transaction took place?" Whit asked.

"Last spring," Stull replied. "Aunt Isabel was nervous about the future of the company. I didn't want to see her stock go outside the family—"

"So you set her mind at rest," Whit spoke drily.

"I bought her shares," Stull said.

His father was speaking, to no one in particular, as if to himself. "Such a transaction must have taken a sizable chunk of money."

Stull nodded, cool, alert, in command.

"I think this just demonstrates Stull's faith in Clayburn Brothers," Nora said. "A faith Isabel obviously couldn't muster."

Now that the family had lost their last grasp at assurance and serenity, Stull wished to conclude the whole business. "And your second question, Uncle Whit?"

"Was Olivia Lee asked to join us at this meeting?"

The stillness came again suddenly, chillingly.

"No." The word rose hoarsely from Stull's throat and he had to repeat it. "No. You and Papa vote Uncle Jonathan's stock."

Jonathan. The name became a presence in the room. A disconcerting presence, invisible but potent.

"As legal guardians for Monty and Jon—"

"I am well aware of the official rights your father and I exercise," Whit interrupted.

For the first time that morning a flush mounted from Stull's throat to his forehead; his eyes gained a glitter of emotion. "Then Aunt Livvie Lee had no reason to be here."

"Along with these rights," Whit continued, "we have certain responsibilities, legal and personal. I think Josh would agree."

Josh looked at his brother and nodded.

"We must each determine our personal responsibilities to Jonathan's wife and children. But I think we all know what Jonathan would do for ours if the situation were reversed—"

"Oh, Jonathan always thought of his family first," Nettie Sue said. "I think Livvie Lee should be here!"

"Well, I can tell you all, Livvie Lee would avoid like the plague any discussion of finances," Nora asserted firmly. "She's told me often enough how she hates business." There was no response. She added, "Besides, we all know how emotional Livvie Lee is."

They knew. They knew the near-hysteria with which Livvie Lee had rejected Josh's proposal, the year after Jonathan's death, that the boys should be sent to one of the private Southern military academies. They knew the fierceness of Livvie Lee's loyalty to her Montgomery kin—especially those two brothers, Pett and Jack, who had run through their father's estate in the final year of the Big Boom and were early victims of the Big Crash. They also knew Livvie Lee's generosity and impulsiveness and innate sense of beauty, for they had often benefited from her bounty.

Whit would not argue with one sister-in-law about another. He would have to drop the subject of Livvie Lee's absence. "What is germane to our decision on Stull's proposal," he said, "is how it will affect the stock Jonathan's sons will inherit."

"Exactly," Stull said quickly.

"And I think it will reduce the value and power of that stock," Whit said. "Indeed, of all the Clayburn stock."

"How is that?" Lottie asked.

"We'll be trading our interest in a perfectly sound company on an equal-share basis with a company that is on the rocks—"

"Hold on!" Stull interrupted. "That's not accurate."

"Since it's founding thirty years ago, how many years has Clayburn Brothers failed to show a profit?" Whit demanded.

"One year," Stull replied.

"And how many years has this Wabash Company failed to show a profit?"

"The past six years—till this year," Stull said. "But the facts are not quite that simple. Wabash is a larger operation than Clayburn's. Acquiring it would bring Clayburn's at least a half-dozen items not offered now, a wider diversity. It would bring two labels which have good acceptance in the Midwest. That would extend our market in areas where rail costs have been a disadvantage. And Wabash Company would bring the financial backing of one of the major New York banking firms and the country's biggest tin-can manufacturer. The company's profit this year was small—but it indicates the company's possibilities." He paused. "And while Clayburn's did make a profit, it was less than for any year in a decade. It's the direction that's as important as the figures sometimes. And Wabash is on the way up."

"And you made the difference," Whit said.

Stull nodded. "I believe I did."

"And you would be the difference in the new company?"

"I would be president," Stull said.

This was the moment. Which way would they break? But it appeared they were still undecided.

"And you wouldn't consider—" Aunt Lottie cleared her throat and began again "—you wouldn't consider coming back to Clayburn's without this—this—"

"Merger?" Stull offered.

"This merger," she finished.

"No," he said.

When no one spoke, Stull knew he would resort to his last weapon. He had planned it, honed it, carefully—hoping he would never use it, knowing he would if the need arose.

Slowly, deliberately, he turned to his father. "Papa," he said, with condescension and coaxing in his voice as if he were dealing with a recalcitrant, slightly retarded child, "Papa—"

"Yes?" Josh's eyes fixed on Stull, still trusting but hiding none of the hurt or bafflement he was experiencing.

"What was Clayburn Brothers adjusted gross income last year?"

"Right offhand, I couldn't say—to the dollar—"

Stull did not move his eyes from his father's as he went on, "Could you tell us the net difference in profit between the cans you let Waverly and Son have under their private label and the cans you sell under your own Clayburn Quality brand?"

"I'm not sure there is much difference."

"Oh, there's a difference," Stull said.

"I'd have to check. Shad Kendrick will have it all down—"

"And what," Stull's voice lowered a fraction; he spoke more slowly; "as president of Clayburn Brothers, what plans do you have for meeting next season's demands for short-term capital?"

Josh looked at his son and at the other faces all around him. "We'll see about that, like we always have, when the time comes."

"Alexander Montgomery is gone and so is his bank. Short-term capital isn't as easy as it always has been. Most canneries are cutting costs and inventories to the bone."

Josh's shoulders slumped perceptibly.

"Of course, there's the matter of standard cost-accounting procedures, too. That's long overdue. And bringing expense of new equipment and repair into proper entry—"

The aunts and uncles looked at Josh, and away, at each other.

"And I had thought," Stull's words were regular and precise as hammer blows, "that Clayburn Brothers might take the lead in the industry by being first to use enamel-lined cans. What's your standing on enamel-lined cans, Papa?"

"I—don't know."

"How about new items—baby food, frozen food, dog food?"

His father did not look up.

Stull gathered his papers in one big clutch and slipped them into his commodious cowhide briefcase and snapped the lock. He stood up.

"I'd like to come back to Clayburn Company and work for you," he said, looking at each one in turn. "I've given you my terms." And he walked out of the room, down the hall, and upstairs to his bedroom.

By the end of the week the family had agreed to sell their shares of Clayburn Brothers stock to the Wabash Company of Illinois.

"I don't like it," Whit summed up his own attitude. Pacing the floor at Nettie Sue's where he and Lottie had nibbled at lunch in an effort to reach some decision, he said, "But I have a law practice in Atlanta. I can't uproot my family and try to run a canning company."

"Poor brother Josh," Lottie said. "I never understood before how anxious Nora is to have him relieved of some of the burden."

Whit looked at her but made no answer.

"If only Jonathan were here," Nettie Sue said.

It was fortunate that Nora had not heard Nettie Sue's wish, for she would never have forgiven her.

To Stull such a remark would have made no difference. Jonathan was dead. He, Stull, was alive. Now it was his turn. Those were realities.

When the new Clayburn stock was issued, a large portion of the preferred went to various members of the Clayburn family. Stull Clayburn acquired twenty-three percent—or the controlling single block—of the common stock, the voting stock. And he was the sole

Clayburn on the new board of directors. For the first time, strangers, outsiders, others shaped the destiny of the company that was now Clayburn's in name only.

Joshua and Whitley went to see Jonathan's widow. They explained to Olivia Lee that she and her sons would be receiving regular dividends from the new preferred stock and that this should provide amply for their needs. Eventually, when Monty and Jon became old enough to receive their inheritance, it might be worth even more than now. That is, if Stull made a success of the new and larger company.

Olivia Lee did not make any serious attempt to follow explanations or understand the organization of this new Clayburn Company. She lived in a daily world of specifics and details by which she understood larger events and trends: wondering why Stull, who had been so constantly at her house when Jonathan was alive, had not come next door to see her or bring her news of Clara while he was home from Illinois; peeved by the gradually growing indifference of a factory plumber or electrician who, at one time, had responded with alacrity to her crises; grateful to Shad Kendrick for his unfailing solicitude and respect.

But when Olivia Lee heard, soon after the reorganization and establishment of the new company, that Shad Kendrick had been fired, she was incredulous. She went next door immediately and found Nora finishing a needlepoint chair cover.

"Nora," she appealed to her sister-in-law, "we must do something about Shad Kendrick."

"Shad was always a favorite of yours," Nora murmured, placing her needle carefully.

Livvie Lee was startled. But she would deal with Nora's quips tomorrow. Now she must do something for this man who had been so faithful to her Jonathan. "Why, Shad is the one who's been with the Clayburns the very longest."

"A new broom sweeps clean," Nora said.

"Well, it's a shame. Poor old Shad, they have this new baby, you know—imagine being married fifteen years and having your first child and these awful hard times and no job! When he came by to see me I wrote him a check for two hundred dollars, he looked so hurt and pitiful, and I thought the company ought to pay him some kind of bonus, or whatever they call it."

"That was a foolish thing for you to do, Livvie Lee," Nora said. She drew her thread carefully with a gentle tug. "The company's not a family affair anymore, you know."

"But Stull is president!"

"And he's answerable to a board of tough bankers and business-men who want what we all want, I guess, profits."

"Well, if they can't afford a measly little two hundred dollars, I'll just give it to Shad Kendrick myself. Out of my tithing money." As she turned to leave, Olivia Lee asked, "They're not letting Nate Lusk go, are they?"

"No," Nora said, examining the design of her handiwork, hold-ing it at arm's length. "But I understand he is upset—"

"Oh?" Olivia Lee waited.

"The Churchill Can Company is to be closed."

"Closed?" This was really important news. "But it makes good profits." Olivia Lee came back into the room. "I can tell you, people all over this county will be upset about that." She was excited and her blue eyes widened. "I remember Jonathan saying, that very last sum-mer, that one of the best things he and the family had ever done was organize the Churchill Can Company and let all the people in the cannery and around this area become stockholders along with the family. It gave them a responsibility, he said, a stake in the losses or profits—"

"Of course I remember all that," Nora was nodding impatiently. She did not mention that one of the conditions under which the new Clayburn Company had come into being was its ten-year contract with National Metals Company for purchase of tin cans—and the closing of the Churchill Can Company.

"I'll bet Nate Lusk *is* mad. He owned a lot of that—"

"He'll quiet down. There's nothing he can do about it now," Nora said. She tied her thread in a final knot and snipped it close. "Times change, we have to look ahead."

Suddenly Olivia Lee paused and looked at her sister-in-law. And she said, very quietly, "Most of us look ahead, Nora. But some of us don't want to forget to look back once in a while."

She left Nora sitting by her sewing table and went back along the path through the boxwood hedge to her own house.

Since Livvie Lee had watched the undertaker lower Jonathan's body into the red clay of Churchill Memorial Cemetery—could it be years ago?—she had not felt the reality of his death as completely as she did now. Now he was dying in another, different way. She felt as though her head and chest might explode in one huge burst of bafflement and rage and loneliness and lament. Only God could forgive her roiling emotions. She would ask forgiveness, tonight, on her knees.

Within a year after Clayburn Company succeeded Clayburn Brothers and established central offices in the Illinois home of Wabash Company, the Churchill Can Company was dissolved. Shad Kendrick's share of the payment to can company stockholders went to his widow and infant son. Two weeks following his final day at Clayburn's Shad had been found in a remote field of the old Riverbend Farm crumpled beside a rifle which had been fired once. What he had been hunting at that season, no one knew. Himself? That was all he had brought down.

Nate Lusk invested his can company money in the new Clayburn Company common stock. He was put in charge of the Southeastern division with headquarters in Churchill.

And two years later, to the surprise of the national financial community, Clayburn Company purchased giant Durant Foods and became Clayburn-Durant Incorporated. Durant was one of the oldest, best-known names in the canning industry.

"Why, do you remember when Clayburns was just beginning and brother Dan went up there and worked for the Durant people the whole month of September?" Nettie Sue asked.

"And nearly all October, too," Nora nodded. "I remember Josh and Jonathan and Cal thought he never would come home—"

"He was just a common laborer," Nettie Sue went on. "He learned a whole lot at that huge plant—doing hard manual work and keeping his eyes open."

"That was what he wanted—"

"And now the little fish has swallowed the big one," Nettie Sue said triumphantly. "To think!"

In the midst of the depression, when failure seemed to many

people more likely than success, Stull Clayburn found the Durant Company in deep trouble and took a chance. He investigated the large, respected company and discovered that he could take that chance because the original Clayburn Company had avoided precisely those pitfalls which had undermined Durant: high salaries and dividends depleting reserves, large year-end inventories, expensive national advertising programs, and use by food stores of the popular Durant brand goods as "loss leaders" in sales promotions.

The executive offices of Clayburn-Durant, Inc. were consolidated in the imposing, downtown midwestern metropolitan building that had been the home of Durant. In the spacious corner office on the top floor, with its view over the city toward the farmland beyond, surrounded by heavy polished paneling, Stull felt at home. More at home than in any of Clara's picturebook rooms and disheveled houses. He was glad to be free of them. For between the Wabash Company merger and the Durant purchase, Stull and Clara had indulged in an angry, lengthy divorce.

"She wants to take me to the cleaners," Stull told Sherman Wright during a business trip to New York. "And I don't intend to work my tail off for some lazy bitch to live like the Queen of England."

"Get a good lawyer," Wright said, speaking from the experience of three bankrupt marriages and three successful divorces.

"I intend to," Stull said. "You have a recommendation?"

He did. Madison Davis, a legal surgeon for Hollywood and New York marriages who was almost as famous a celebrity as many of his clients, handled all of Sherman Wright's business of this sort. He agreed to take Stull's case. When Madison Davis was through, Clara had only the little home they had lived in when Stull was with the Wabash Company (and had been unable to sell), their big Packard car, a modest sum of cash, and five hundred dollars' monthly alimony. To many of their old friends in Churchill, caught in the hardships of the Depression, Clara's settlement seemed like a great windfall; to those in New York who knew where Stull Clayburn was going, the settlement was token. And Stull had achieved his main purpose, which was to keep all financial arrangements in cash, so that he would surrender no stock in Clayburn-Durant.

"She cost me that much a month in silk stockings and long distance phone calls," Stull said.

"At least she's got the legs for the stockings," Madison Davis said.

Stull couldn't have cared less. He had discovered that there were hundreds of girls with good legs who were available on a nightly or weekly basis—without permanent demands—who would not drain all his time and thought from important matters.

The family had scarcely recovered from the confusion over Stull's financial transactions, and his emergence as the central controlling power in what previously had been their common family enterprise of pride and profit, when this new revelation sent them reeling.

"Divorce!" Aunt Nettie Sue cried, as she and Nora and Olivia Lee sat in her living room on an early spring afternoon.

Nora only nodded, her eyes red with crying. "If only they could have had some children—" she murmured.

"Oh, yes!" Nettie Sue seized the thought. Each of the women knew their common premise: it was Clara's Montgomery willfulness and waywardness that had wrecked the solid Clayburn character which held marriages together. If only Clara had been more patient, if only she had carried her babies full term.

"This is the first divorce in the Clayburn family," Nettie Sue said.

And Olivia Lee, remembering not only her brother Jack's escapades but lively anecdotes of Ransom family history as well, retorted, "Well, it may not be the last."

"Oh I hope so!" Nettie Sue plunged on openly, sincerely. "Everything is so topsy-turvy. With this New Deal government threatening to run business, and banks clamped tight as turtleshells, and all these hard times—" She looked at her sisters-in-law, "I do hope our young ones will hold on to some of the spirit, the principles, the—the way it was."

Nora answered. "Whatever Stull does, Nettie Sue, I can promise you it will serve to make Clayburn-Durant bigger and better."

It was a proper answer, but Nettie Sue found it in some way deficient, less than she expected or needed. She looked at Olivia Lee. "As far as Jonathan's Monty and Jon are concerned, I guess we'll just have to wait and see," she said.

15

Funerals bound us together. Not weddings, although there were enough of those, nor births, which were plentiful and well celebrated —but the ritual of death and burial, constant, certain, yet each time unexpected and in some special way shocking.

During the years after I finished Jackson U. and went to Clayburn-Durant, during those years when I lived successfully disguised to myself as businessman, and husband, and father, and citizen, and sometimes leader—whatever that meant—during that long, self-satisfied and deeply unsatisfying time, my chief relationships with Churchill, beyond the work of the cannery itself and its contact with the home office, were continued or begun or completed at funerals. And like the crumbling edges of a mountain slipping away in puny fragments, leaving the great whole minutely, forever altered, each burial ceremony—brief or interminable, completed in rain or chill or sun—marked the breaking off of some small but unique segment of family. For each one carried his own special talents, deficiencies, mysteries, and above all, idiosyncrasies.

I had been at Clayburn-Durant only nine months when Stull said one noontime, "Uncle Whit Ransom died this morning. My father just called."

I hardly knew how to reply. Great-Uncle Whit Ransom was barely more to me than family legend as a boy and more recently as a long, yellow-stained white mustache drooping from a hollowed face. "Was he still at the sanitorium?"

"I suppose," Stull nodded impatiently. Uncle Whit had been at the state tuberculosis sanitorium during all the recent years we could recall, coughing and bellowing away his ninth decade. "You want to go down for the funeral?"

I looked at Stull in surprise.

"He was Grandma Clayburn's brother. She was one of our company's founders. We can't afford to let him be buried without some notice." Stull spelled it out as if for a slow learner.

"I guess I could go—"

"Even Papa was upset telling me. Down there they still set store by someone's dying. But I can't get away." I knew why he couldn't get away. He was flying to Hollywood to spend the weekend with that little French singer.

Thus I represented the company at our half-forgotten great-uncle Whitley Ransom's burial. The day blew gusty with erratic winds and clouds, but the preacher beside Uncle Whitley's open grave remained calmly certain: "The Lord giveth, the Lord taketh away. . . ."

The wind had been blowing that long-ago Sabbath morning in family legend when Whit Ransom, in nightshirt and bare feet, had fired the boiler and blown the whistle on the Ransom farm cannery just to tumble his starchy Clayburn nephews out of their comfortable pews. Then he had preached them his own sermon. "You boys need to raise less corn and more hell."

Now the last of an older, wilder strain in that generation was gone.

When Aunt Josie died I went back to Churchill on my own. She was a Montgomery, not a Clayburn, so I went for my mother's sake and not for any company reason. With my mother at the funeral home were Uncle Jack and Uncle Pett (who did not die for several more years), gracious, exuding largesse and appreciation for every comforting friend or distant relative or curious stranger.

"Josie did love nice things and a good time," Mama said, tears welling over the expression of hurt and loss in her eyes—as if this taste for pleasure which her sister had indulged was exceptional.

I thought Stull would go to Churchill when Nate Lusk's cirrhosis of the liver finally proved fatal. But Nate made the mistake of dying the day Stull flew to Vegas to marry Eugenie. Eugenie sang on the Clayburn-Durant radio Homemaker's Food Show for six months before the sales department discovered that her husky voice appealed more to midnight than to midday audiences. By that time she didn't need to sing any longer. She and Stull had met in Hollywood and he had been intrigued by her piquant Gallic features, petite figure, lilting accent, and breathless attentiveness whenever he spoke. Her compact body, round and firm, always lightly perfumed, expressed unshakable —indeed, absolute—self-confidence, and this, too, enchanted Stull. With eyes set too far apart in her round face, and one eye suffering a slight cast so that it never seemed to be focused in precise harmony with the other, Eugenie was not pretty; but that cool assurance and chic figure she maintained created assets more memorable than any skin-deep prettiness.

Stull was triumphant when Eugenie agreed to marry him. As the marriage turned out, Stull might just as well have gone to Nate's funeral.

"Old Nate was one of the best we had." Stull shook his head as he asked me to go to Churchill, while checking the plane ticket West which his secretary had just brought in. "Nate could have sold corsets on Fiji if he'd set his mind to it. You tell Nat how we feel about his father—about him taking his father's place."

"How do we feel, Stull?" I asked.

"Dammit, we want him at the top if he can cut the mustard."

"Then we're talking about Nat, not Nate."

Stull glared and did not answer.

But the son was too much like the father for me to have worried. I could almost watch Nat stepping into those brown and white shoes, those white flannel summer trousers and dark winter pin-stripes of his father's; echoing the ribald stories; consuming the good meat and drink and bright-eyed girls. But he was ambitious beyond Churchill, too.

After the funeral, as we rode from the cemetery in the long anonymous limousine, Nat asked, "What's the chance of my going up there to the head office one of these days, Jon? Hell, my father lived his life for Clayburn-Durant."

"That was his life. Now we're talking about yours," I echoed Stull.

He glanced at me across the white carnation on his black lapel. "My father pulled together a damned good chunk of C-D stock. And I know a lot about sales for this company. Hell, that's what I was weaned on!"

That and Kentucky bourbon, I thought. But he'd made a sound assessment; within the year he was up at our Midwest headquarters.

At old Nate's burial some of the glad-hand, the zest to sell and convince and fail and resell, the loneliness of the road, the insatiable appetite, the piston drive toward success in all its crude innocence, also disappeared.

The only family funeral I missed was Uncle Whit's, and I was sorry for that. Between my uncle Whitley Clayburn and his brother —my father—Jonathan, there had been a curious unspoken bond of rare respect and understanding. The heart attack which had brought my father down so suddenly was repeated now in Uncle Whit, who without warning slumped and died on his judge's bench. When Aunt Cornelia called me, talking with me the first of all the family, I was in bed with a bout of pneumonia (reacting to a new drug called penicillin), and I told her why I could not come to Atlanta for the formal services or to Churchill for the burial. Later, after I wrote her, she replied: "Your uncle Whitley often doubted that he and Joshua had been the stewards to you and Monty that Jonathan would have wished. It was, I think, the only real regret of Whitley's good and distinguished life. I know you will understand."

With Uncle Whit's going, there went a part of the Clayburn conscience.

Twice Stull returned to Churchill funerals: first to his father's, three years later to Aunt Lottie's.

Uncle Josh's casket was the most expensive ever seen in Churchill. Stull himself ordered it. Three entire rows of church seats were occupied by Clayburn-Durant board members, business associates of Stull's, industrial and political leaders of the state. Their conservative grays and blacks and navy blues established a formidable wall against which the awed and nervous young minister's Christian sentiments of green pastures and treasure in heaven thudded softly and disintegrated.

In the midst of the rhetoric and the mellow music ("A Land That Is Fairer Than Day"), the banked flowers and elaborate white silk and silvered metallic box, Uncle Josh's agreeable, weathered, farmer's countenance and hands seemed a discordant, irrefutable reality.

Stull and his mother and sister, Nancy Ellen, stood together for a long minute before the lid was closed and gazed at the strange familiar person no longer a person. I looked at Aunt Nora, heavy now, still upright, with a tilt to her black velvet hat, and I wondered if anyone remembered that day in family legend when Nora Stull Buchanan arrived from Richmond, Virginia, and awkward, shy, determined Joshua Clayburn warned his brothers that she was bespoken. Then Stull, dry-eyed, led Aunt Nora to her seat. And with Uncle Josh, the Clayburn brothers were gone, the eldest going last, as the youngest had been one of the first.

For Aunt Lottie, arrangements were simpler. Uncle Penn, as she had stipulated, requested that in lieu of flowers donations be sent to an orphan children's home and the Churchill cancer fund. Odd visitors, unknown to any of the family except Uncle Penn, filled random corners of the small church chapel: two elderly women wearing good cloth coats and expressions of esoteric good will; a well-dressed Negro couple staring straight ahead; a tearful girl of college age; a stooped old man with murky glasses and a kindly, genteel face; a tall black woman I recognized as a teacher in the Jaybird Grammar School.

But it was not so much Aunt Lottie's funeral which consolidated her family as it was her will. The only surviving partner of Littlepage Ransom's law firm read it in Grandma Clayburn's parlor, now Aunt Nettie Sue's. All of the Clayburn-Durant stock (and that was all the worldly wealth she owned) was to be put in trust. Its income and its votes would go first to her husband, Penn, and then to her sister, Nettie Sue. When both Penn and Nettie Sue were gone, the trust fund would be used to establish a home for "needy girls."

"That's just like Aunt Lottie," Monty pronounced in the silence, "always thinking of others." Aunt Nora and my mother did not respond.

Aunt Lottie took with her an impulse toward a world larger, poorer, more terrible than the Midwest and the South that was our circumference.

Later that year Uncle Penn entered a "retirement home" where he held the vesper services each Sunday, reading from Paul Tillich and C. S. Lewis, and where his skin grew more like parchment—until he simply did not wake up one morning.

These were only undercurrents in the reality of my Clayburn-Durant life, running deep and unexamined beneath the rapid rush of everyday decisions, struggles, pressures. Yet now I know that those moments, suspended in carnation-smell and dutiful handshakes and lowered voices, flowed beginnings into consequences and, more than all the brisk hours at the expanding cannery with the regional executives and the sales force and the production men, carried at least part of Clayburn-Durant along the mainstream of yesterday into today. . . .

16

"**N**at?"

"Spea-king." The word proceeds as precisely as the footwork of high-wire acrobats.

"Stull there?" I ask. Dampness following last night's rain drips from the oak leaves outside my motel window.

A pause. "Yes—and no."

"Well, which is it?"

"Let's say he's here in body but not in spirit."

I wonder how the old charade is going. Does Aunt Nora still pretend she is unaware of Stull's drinking, that she cannot smell the reeking breath, see the wavering eyes and trembling hands? Do the others, Nancy Ellen and the cook and Nat Lusk and Stull himself still make believe there is a secret about the drinking? (Someone had told my mother, during the long months in the mid-fifties when Stull and Eugenie were negotiating their divorce, that Eugenie had said Stull was a boor when he was sober and a lout when he was drunk. And Mama had told Aunt Nettie Sue, "I guess it will come as a shock to some folks that Jack Montgomery, who at least had the war as an excuse—he would jump every time one of the boys lit a firecracker —isn't the only person in this family connection who has bottle problems." But she never mentioned it to Aunt Nora.)

I say to Nat: "Just wanted to tell Stull I won't be flying back with you this afternoon."

"Trouble?" Nat is abruptly alert, the thickness on his tongue dissipated by alarm.

"Not especially." Let him sweat a little.

"Something new about that farm woman's sickness?"

"Perlina's death, you mean? No. Nothing new that I know of."

"Then what the hell—"

"Let's say it's personal."

"Oh." Mingled suspicion, relief, curiosity.

I know that if Stull had been on the phone he would have said, at this point, "Forget 'personal.' What about that raider who's prowling around Clayburn-Durant? I know the son of a bitch is there. I can feel it in my bones. You don't think, do you, that I shoved this company into the big three of canning without developing a nose for scavengers? And you'd better get the scent, too." But Stull is not on the phone. He is in a half-stupor upstairs in his mother's house.

Nat is speaking again. "Jon, I almost forgot. Your secretary called here last night. She didn't know where you were staying when Monty said you weren't at his house."

"I decided not to impose on my brother and sister-in-law this visit, such short notice and all."

"Well, Stull was mad as hell about it. He thought you'd be here next door."

"I'm not exactly on the moon. Just here at your friendly Vacation Lodge—"

"Okay, okay. Anyway, your secretary said that plant science fellow, Lex Morrison—the spray man—tried to reach you all day yesterday."

"What was on his mind?"

"He's coming to Churchill. Wants to see the land, vegetables, cans—everything connected with the use of his spray on our experimental pack."

"Sounds like a good idea," I say.

"If he can keep his mouth shut. Seemed to me he worked up too big a sweat in Stull's office Friday when he heard we'd run into a little rough weather."

"I'll be here when he comes, Nat. I'll show him everything. And this afternoon I'll be going out to Burl Smelcer's myself."

His breathing is heavy on the phone. I can imagine his puffy eyes examining the ceiling, the walls of Aunt Nora's house. Nat married a wealthy niece of Aunt Nora's, a giggling naive girl from Richmond who assured Nat of a lifelong berth with Clayburn-Durant, three children who are now in distant boarding schools, and her own lonely, secret, heavy drinking—and whenever Nat comes to Churchill he stays at Aunt Nora's house.

"Is that smart?" Nat asks. "To go out there—with those people —maybe set them to wondering?"

"I've known Burl and Perlina since I was a boy."

"But folks like that, they're pretty shrewd."

"Why not let me handle it, Nat?" I interrupt sharply.

"Sure, Jon. No offense. What the hell. . . . Only don't offer any money."

My anger will spill over if I answer him, so I simply say, "See you next week, Nat."

"Sure. Stull and I will be down for the Jackson U. homecoming next Saturday. Ought to be a humdinger."

"How was yesterday?"

"Lousy. Damned quarterback couldn't call the plays; the pass receiver slid on the turf, broke his arm; we won by one point."

"That wasn't a defeat."

"It's not the kind of win a fellow likes." He sounds just like Stull. Have I been at Clayburn-Durant long enough, I wonder, to have the sound, the spirit, too?

"Maybe next week will be better."

"It damned well better be. Stull will see to that." A hint of mystery and promise shades the way he speaks.

"May the right team win," I offer. Neither he nor Stull will sense the irony in such a statement. The right team is their team. Always.

"I'll tell Stull you phoned," Nat says.

"And I'll see you next weekend. Meanwhile, I'll call my office Monday. And Nat—tell Stull I may be asking a friend, a friend from New York, down to visit."

"Sure, Jon." Nat hesitates. "Anybody I know?"

"No. No, I'm sure you don't know her."

We hang up. The silence inside my sealed room is total, except for the whirr of an alternate heating-cooling unit and purr of a small refrigerator near the television set. I see brown autumn leaves stirring outside but I can hear no wind. I see a bluejay dip across the driveway but I can hear no scream. Under the fluorescent light of the mirrored bathroom I shave hastily. I want to get away before Stull can return my call.

First, however, I must talk to Monty. I dial his number.

"Kate and I were just leaving for church—"

"I don't want to hold you up."

"No, you're not. No sir. Where are you anyway? Why don't you come to church with us?" Good old Monty, saying all the right things. We arrange to meet for Sunday dinner—at another motel, near the one where I am staying. "I think they give better servings than that Vacation Lodge," Monty says. "But if you'd rather—"

"No. Wherever you suggest will be fine."

Then I try to call Deborah. (In the beginning was the number and the number was with Deborah and the number was Deborah.) There is no answer. It hasn't occurred to me that she might be away from her high, sunlit, austerely furnished apartment at this hour on Sunday morning. I ask the operator to try again. The rings are insistent—and fruitless.

Oddly, with little apparent reason or connection, I remember the night Eugenie called me. "Jon, I'm divorcing Stull. Tomorrow morning I leave. For good. But right now he's down in the hall shooting at invisible labor organizers. God, I think he's gone mad! He says they're out to get him. He's already ruined the chandelier. I've locked myself upstairs. Jon, if you don't want me to call the police to come and tame your cousin, you'd better come out and quiet him yourself."

I went to the sprawling, pretentious house and found Stull standing rumpled and wild-eyed and barefoot at the front door. His gun was empty. The hall was a shambles. Shattered glass and splintered furniture made it hard for him to walk.

"They're after me." He clutched my shoulder. "They'd like to get me. But I've fixed them. This time. I'm warning them though; they'll never take over Clayburn-Durant as long as I'm alive."

"Where's Eugenie?" I asked.

He took his hand away. His eyes narrowed. "Upstairs. Says she's leaving. Can't take it." He sank into a sofa which creaked beneath his weight. "Let her go. Goddamit, let them all go. They all want your money, your time, your brain—"

"What about your child?" I asked.

He looked at me. "She's a girl," he said. As if I hadn't learned that the day she was born, a half-dozen years before. "Let them all go—" He waved a pudgy hand.

When I left him in a fitful sleep on the sofa that night in that desolate mausoleum of a house to which even Eugenie's delicate French imports had brought no real change, Stull seemed to me the loneliest man I had ever seen. Selfish, impossible (how many times would I have to desert Teena at night or over a weekend to nursemaid Stull?)—but lonely beyond even his own recognition. "A girl." The way he had spoken of his daughter, dismissed a segment of his life— its potential, its emotion, its meaning—as decisively as if he had cut out a useless, troublesome appendix.

The rings at Deborah's number continue until I hang up. The day is not starting well. I remember long lonely Sundays of my childhood in this town and I yearn for Deborah's voice.

I slip my wallet into my pocket, after I glance at a snapshot of my children. Lee and Ellie are at one of Ellie's horse shows and my small daughter, cool, poised, confident, is holding an immense silver trophy half as tall as she. My slim awkward son appears embarrassed. Yet his eyes seem to look straight to me, and I wonder now how much he might like to know something about this world of Clayburns and Churchill. Yes, Lee might really care.

I flee the motel room.

During the hour before I meet Monty and Kate I drive around Churchill: past the house where Aunt Josie once lived (now a rundown duplex apartment with peeling paint and shutters awry); past the Clayburn-Durant factory and Grandma Mary Clayburn's town home where she and Dan and my father and the two sisters lived and Aunt Nettie Sue lives now (I will need to see her presently, while I am in Churchill); past the renovated air- conditioned church (no such luxury at my mother's funeral); past old landmarks in a personal landscape and new outcroppings of industry, business, prosperity. Fast foods. Easy loans. Trade-in motors. I have not really looked at the town for a long time. I drive out along the new highway leading to the mountains in the distance, through the river-bottom farms where new textile and furniture industries have devoured wide swatches of land. All changing—and yet, as the French proverb holds, the more it changes the more it remains the same.

I discovered that last Friday morning when I was caught between George Hodges' computers and the smell of ketchup.

"Computers," Nancy Ellen's son, George, said to me proudly, "expand the memory of man a trillionfold."

But I want to know if they can respond to the warm richness of tomato ketchup cooking, if they can recapture the desolation and loss of a day when the town was permeated with that aroma and life was altered beyond recall? My father, Jonathan Clayburn, wrenched by sudden pain and ancient weariness, had left me, left us all, before we could speak—or ask—

And we searched for answers, for certainty and meaning in the labyrinths of machines, laboratories, charts more sophisticated than the pattern of the heavens on a starry night. We reached for meaning in power, the small, fragmented but nevertheless tangible power of a company's products and payroll and financial mystique. Yet the meaning eluded us.

In my car, along a back-country road bordered with both the gorgeous profusion of heather-colored Joe Pye weed and a glut of random garbage—rotting paper, plastic, metal, cloth, rubber refuse— I am finally at the heart of the cross between the programmed computer and the prodigal fluid evocativeness of ketchup.

When I arrive at the commercial dining room, Monty and Kate are already there. "Rushed right over after church to get us a good table," Monty pumps my hand self-consciously, good-naturedly. His hair has begun to gray during the past year. His smile comes and goes hesitantly. "This is a popular place on Sundays. Yes, sir." The heartiness of his voice is belied by the confused expression in his eyes.

"I can see this is a favorite spot," I reassure him. The ritual of Sunday noon which I remember so well has been transferred from the family tables to the motel restaurants. "Hello, Kate."

"Hello, Jon." She is already looking at the menu. Her brown hat matches her brown hair and brown mood. "How long are you in for?" She makes it sound as if I am a sailor home on leave.

Her directness embarrasses Monty but I have known Kate since she was a little girl and defiantly delivered eggs from her father's poultry farm—"the big brown ones" my mother liked best—and always asserted, in grammar school, that she "was just as good as anybody," although I never heard anyone question that she was.

"Most of the week, I guess."

"Well, then, Jon," Monty glances around the room as we sit down, waves at a couple of friends, "you'll have to come on up to the house—won't he, Kate? It would look funny, you staying at a motel for a whole week instead of coming up to your old home."

I'm shaking my head. "It's all right, Monty. I'm settled in now. Besides, I'm expecting someone else."

They both look at me. "Well, then—" Monty begins.

"It's tentative. I'll know for sure tomorrow—I hope."

I can almost hear Kate's sigh of relief.

"Well, you know you're always welcome," Monty says.

A waitress brings us two more menus and water. "You all right today?" Monty asks her.

The waitress nods, pleased by Monty's personal notice and I realize again that there are qualities my brother preserves which I have long since abandoned.

"You can take that slop away," Kate pushes back her glass. "Since Churchill began drinking from the river instead of our old mountain springs reservoir, our water tastes like something manufactured by DuPont."

We laugh but when I take a sip I remember how sweet the water tasted from the gourd Cebo had at Grandmother Clayburn's Riverbend Farm when I was a shirt-tail boy and Uncle Josh and Aunt Nora lived there. I agree with Kate.

The waitress brings our salads (tossed hunks of whitish lettuce under a blanket of mayonnaise mixed with lumps of blue cheese) and cellophane-wrapped crackers and Monty asks me, in his best confidential tone, "Anything wrong at Clayburn-Durant?"

I try to laugh again. "Just like old Monty. Not, Is everything okay at the Clayburn-Durant canneries? But, What's wrong?"

He grins sheepishly. "Well, you're back so suddenly—for a whole week—" His eyes can be wide and hurt as Mama's once were.

"Sure. I was teasing. But it's all right, Monty. Clayburn-Durant is in good shape."

"Nothing troublesome to affect the stock?"

"Not at the moment—"

("Monty worries so," Mama always said. "He's a Montgomery that way. Don't tell him about problems unless he just has to know, Jon. He's like his Uncle Pett and Aunt Josie. They couldn't bear unpleasant things. Some people brood—" Thus I always felt that I must strain my conversation with Monty through a filter so that there would be no harsh lumps of dispute or challenge but only a smooth tasteless pablum.)

"Of course, most of my stake is in insurance anyway," he is saying, "all for Kate and the children. A man can't have too much insurance." Monty has taken to heart the slogans of his own business. His agency is the largest in Churchill. It was Uncle Whit who first suggested that Monty might like to go into the insurance business, and then brought him clients even from Atlanta and his own prestigious law firm there.

"Whatever you have, somebody's waiting out there to grab it." Kate has finished her salad.

"But of course, I do try to keep some Clayburn-Durant stock. Sometimes I wish I'd gone with the company like you did, even if Stull has been a wheeler-dealer."

"And a drunk," Kate says.

"After all, it's our family name, too, and our father's—"

"Sure," I interrupt. Monty's aimless dissatisfactions reduce my own current questions to a petulance I cannot accept. I see in my brother tension between what he has been taught is "right" by the church he accepts and what he observes is "necessary" by the company he also accepts—and it is a tension resulting in paralysis, a limbo avoiding responsibility. He risks neither mistakes nor evil himself; he is free to observe others' failures—perhaps my own this very week.

I am simultaneously sad and angry at this judgment of my brother. I want to reach out my hand to him. ("Do you remember how we went hunting in the woods with old Janus Rathbone after our father died, and how he taught us the names of trees and plants and animals as if they were friends of his?") I want to look at him openly, directly, long enough to see. ("Do you remember the night before I married Teena and we sat up together talking after the rehearsal dinner, two country boys in the big city, slightly awed by the confidence and importance of Teena's father—president of a big midwestern milling company, director on a half-dozen major boards, member of innumerable clubs—and slightly intoxicated, too, by both the champagne and a rare sense of togetherness? And you said, 'Mama liked Teena, Jon. Mama liked pretty, happy people.' A pause. 'I'll never forgive him for her death, Jon. I'll never forgive Stull. After he put through that big Wabash Company deal and gave away the Churchill Can Company stock, in which Mama owned most, to Worth Franklin's big can monopoly; after that Mama always believed she was penniless. And everybody else thought she was rich. Of course she was somewhere in between, but it was what she *thought* and *feared* that mattered. That was why she didn't go to the doctor and the hospital in time on a simple appendectomy—' And you couldn't finish, Monty. Because we had talked this over a dozen times, and neither of us had yet accepted the suddenness, the uselessness, of her death only six short months before my wedding to Teena.) I want to speak to him about some of the thoughts and memories that flooded over me in the old machine-trampled field on the Riverbend Farm last night. But I do not know the way. There has always been a wall between my brother and me. We have, in crises and emergencies, reached over it, around it—yet never through it, straight and penetrating.

"How are the children?" I try to look at both Monty and Kate when I ask this. (Is it strange that we have spoken of so much else before we speak of our children?)

"Fine," Monty says.

"Able to throw away money like dishwater," Kate looks at me. "What's Lee doing in Europe?"

"Finding himself." I cannot resist the impulse to say the very thing I know will infuriate her.

"What did he lose over there?" she asks. Kate was such a scrubbed, open-faced, good-hearted girl, speaking her mind in wit and anger and candor. How did she become this sharp woman, impatient of all need to think and weigh and yield and understand, adamant in her need for black and white solutions, sheep and goat separations? With the rude innocence of an earthquake she shatters what she presumably wishes to settle and hurls asunder all that she presumably wants to cherish. Her own five children (they are Monty's, too, of course, yet somehow I think of "Kate's children"—do I even include Monty in that category?) are no longer in Churchill.

I do not try to answer her but smile and shrug and accept the plate of Sunday dinner which the waitress is setting before me. It is rich, drowned in grease, heavy with starches and sugar. (I remember Deborah and delicate Dover sole and ambrosia—with a dash of sherry?)

When we have finished dessert—thick wedges of nutmeg-laden chess pie—I ask Monty if he would like to ride out to Burl Smelcer's with me.

"Burl Smelcer's?" Kate repeats.

I nod. "Heard his wife died. I used to work with them down on the farm. You remember Perlina, don't you, Monty?"

"Of course I do. I carry her burial insurance policy."

This news surprises me. "Did she have life insurance, too?" I ask.

He shakes his head. I feel relieved by his answer and am shamed by my relief.

"It's that spray, isn't it?" Monty leans toward me. "Clayburn-Durant is afraid that new spray might have had something to do with Perlina Smelcer's sickness—" Monty will not use the word "death" unless there is no alternative.

"How'd you hear about the spray, Monty?"

"Price Sims. He was telling me about it up at the country club right after they'd put up the first run of vegetables from those fields. Talked like it was the greatest discovery since the wheel; really held back the aging in any plant they used it on."

"We hope so."

"But you're worried?"

"We want to be sure—" How can I try to capture the whole simple-complex crucial situation in words without sounding official (and officious), like a company spokesman, an apologist?

"I'll bet so." Kate lays her napkin on the table. "With all the consumer and environment nuts running around loose, I'll bet even fish-eyed cousin Stull is worried about his spray invention."

"We'll *all* be worried if a poor woman has died because of something we've done—or not done," I assure her. "But this seems most unlikely. As far as we know not one of the Smelcers has even considered such a possibility."

"Of course not," Monty says. "We didn't mean any criticism of you, Jon. And we won't discuss this with a soul, will we, Kate?"

"Not likely anyone would be all that interested."

"Don't kid yourself, Kate. This could be red-hot. With all the public worry about pesticides and additives—and much of it perfectly legitimate—" I break off, then continue, trying to confide in them. "And that's where Stull is back in the Middle Ages. He thinks he can handle Washington—because he handled the company's big income tax settlement twenty-five years ago. He thinks he can ignore people —because he's accumulated factories and produced canned goods and profits. But the weather-vanes are veering even in Washington—and Stull will find out that people matter."

"Why yes," Monty says. I can foresee a cliché struggling to surface.

"It's not as easy as it sounds," I rush on. "We all say we care, but that's cheap. What if it cost us a couple of hundred thousand dollars—and that's what it may cost Stull—just to care about Perlina? The cost may go higher if we have to give up the new spray and lose that competitive advantage."

"That's a lot of money," Kate says respectfully.

"Love of money is the root of all evil," Monty asserts.

"And lack of it spurs a lot of evil," I answer.

We push back from the table and I leave a tip for our eager young waitress.

"Sure, I'll drive out to Burl's with you," Monty says. "When are you going?"

"Right now. I want to get it over with."

"Then I'll take our car home," Kate says, as we make our way to the cashier and the door.

As Monty and I drive out of town he looks through the windshield as if viewing the town through my eyes. "Guess Churchill seems pretty one-horse when you come back now from the big city." His tone is teasing and indifferent but I know that the question arises from the sensitivity of self-consciousness.

I shake my head. "No. It still seems like a pretty good place—"

Monty relaxes. His moods can change as quickly as our mother's once did. "I'll tell you one thing, Jon: that can-manufacturing outfit you re-established here—folks say it's making more money for Clayburn-Durant than any part of the Churchill operation."

"Yes." Profit-and-loss breakdowns on each segment of our operation are filed in my memory. "Making our own cans cuts down on our chief cost. And we're selling cans to other food processors in this region. It was a good move."

This idea was one of the two primary suggestions that won me Stull's special confidence during my years at Clayburn-Durant. The first time he admitted that I might be an asset to the company was in the early period, when I began pushing his policy of developing Clayburn-Durant's own label, cutting down the private label business to its logical limits. That is, I fought for national distribution of our products and heavier advertising as our chief protection against price competition. Stull and the other decision-makers were slow to commit real money to advertising. I prodded. And I aroused our sales representatives to the trap in which our "exclusive" distributors were catching us: too many were using Clayburn-Durant as "assorted-car" suppliers, while giving more profitable "straight-car" orders to the competition.

I can remember my very words at that sales pep-talk. "It's up to you men to remember—and don't ever forget—it's not only prices that count but *relative* prices. Don't you forget that a thousand cases of lima beans bring us a profit equal to five thousand cases of other items. Pork and beans yields your company three times the profit of other items. Same with our fancy peas and asparagus. Clayburn-Durant can't just sit back content with full-line orders. We have to get in there and scramble for those profitable volume items."

Stull understood that language—and its results.

He also understood, several years later, when I proposed that Clayburn-Durant set up its own can manufacturing in Churchill, at one of our midwestern plants, perhaps in the Far West, too.

"When we buy cans we have really only two major sources to choose from. When we fill those cans with food and are ready to sell, we have about thirty-five hundred separate canners to compete with. We're buying at the seller's price and selling at the buyer's price—and that's a hell of a way to try to make a profit. Now we can cut down the bleeding a little if we make our own cans."

I didn't remind anyone that Jonathan Clayburn had once put up the initial investment for the Churchill Can Company, a highly profitable concern that made cans for Clayburn Brothers and which was widely owned by the people who worked at the cannery.

I didn't remind anyone that the Churchill Can Company, in which Stull Clayburn owned no stock, had been sold for a fraction of its real value to Worth Franklin's National Can at the time of the Clayburn-Wabash Company merger, and that National Can then made a ten-year discount to Clayburn Company for cans, saving the company perhaps a million dollars or more, the company in which Stull Clayburn now owned the controlling block of stock, in which Worth Franklin, too, held a substantial interest. The National Can Company discount had long since expired, Worth Franklin had drowned while swimming off his yacht in the Caribbean on a cruise with Stull and Mrs. Schroeder and a half-dozen other guests, and now Clayburn-Durant needed to make some fresh move to reduce the cost of its cans.

Stull understood the necessity of my proposition. He understood the profit that resulted almost immediately from the installation of the can-making plant adjacent to the Churchill cannery, and later at the can plant near our largest Illinois cannery.

These, with the computer decision, were the special achievements Stull granted me, although it was administrative housekeeping at a half-dozen levels, company and community and government diplomacy in various forms, and liaison between Stull and almost everyone else which had been my grab-bag of vice-presidential tricks during recent years.

("You do the work and Stull draws the salary," Teena had said one day, trying to be light, desperately earnest, after we knew she was hopelessly ill. "Don't you let that scheming Nat Lusk or that ambitious veep in charge of production bounce into the president's chair when Stull steps into chairmanship of the board, Jon." I squeezed her hand and tried to smile. "You deserve it, Jon. And the company needs you. The only trouble is—I wanted to be here to help you—" It was the nearest we came to breaking down in each other's presence.)

I say to Monty, as we leave Churchill behind and head toward the Riverbend Farm, "Did I ever tell you about the time Teena and I were engaged and I needed a raise from Stull?"

"No," Monty answers, not urging me to tell now, uninterested in such an ancient history. He wants the current picture.

But I am on an orgy of remembering. "Teena and I went to see Stull and Eugenie. That day the stucco fortress was as pleasant as I ever saw it, perhaps because everyone was outside at the swimming pool, including the new baby girl and the English nanny Eugenie had employed. When I told them Teena and I were engaged Eugenie pulled the dark glasses from her eyes a moment and looked at Teena, all fresh and Junior League in her round Peter Pan collar and little string of pearls, and said, 'Poor dears.' Stull only grinned, like the Cheshire Cat in *Alice in Wonderland,* and finally said he hoped we'd be happy."

"That's more than he ever wished Kate and me," Monty says.

"Next morning I tried to see him at the office. I needed a raise if I married Teena. Stull was all tied up. Same story the following day. It was ten days before I finally got in to talk with him. And when I walked in the office, before I could clear my throat and present my case (I'd rehearsed it a dozen times), Stull was telling me about the rough slump the canning business was going through, and the necessity for maximum effort from everyone.

"Then he put it to me: he realized my time and attention would be divided now that I was getting married and I wouldn't be worth as much to the company. However, he had decided to keep me on and at the same salary, even though I wouldn't be as valuable to Clayburn-Durant. I forgot all about my raise and ended up thanking him for what I was already getting."

"That sounds like old Stull," Monty says. "Yessiree."

"Later I got the raise. But not till Stull made sure I was putting Clayburn-Durant beside Teena in my loyalties, in my attention."

"You were good to Teena," Monty says. "You were just a struggling junior executive then."

"I was a flunky for Stull. And I gave Teena everything I could —but time."

Far down the highway I can see where the road to the farm cuts off. I begin to slow down. The upland fields and second-growth trees appear peaceful and familiar. "Then fate, or God, or whatever name you choose, left her without any time at all."

"I sure did hate it, Jon—"

"Well." I slow to make the turn, drive down the long oak-lined corridor to the farm, veer off before we come to the house so that we will find the field where I stood last night. "Well, we didn't come to resurrect Teena."

"Before we change the subject, Jon," Monty leans toward me confidentially, "is there anything—you know, anything serious with this—this New York woman who may come to visit?"

"Deborah?"

He hesitates. "Is that her name?"

"Deborah Einemann."

The hesitation is even longer. "Oh."

"Yes," I say. "It's serious. It's the most serious relationship I've ever known."

Monty has a lot to think about as we come to Burl Smelcer's house. Automobiles surround the square unpainted dwelling on the rise that is no more than a bunion on the surface of the land. There are two tall sheltering trees—a black walnut in front, a sweet-gum in back. At one end of the weather-beaten house is a clay-chinked stone chimney, at the other end, a flue. Blue wood smoke billows from each this afternoon.

Monty knows many of the people who are arriving or leaving or standing and waiting—for what, God knows. They like Monty. "He may be a Clayburn, but he's common as an old shoe," they praise him. They like him, too, I know, because he seems to have chosen to stay in Churchill, thus affirming their own lives, over which they have little control.

Inside the house Perlina's casket and her massive presence, though finally motionless and silent, dominate the small room. Her blue dress is of a synthetic material which is smooth and shiny as a mirror. The skin of her face is also drawn unnaturally smooth so that only traces of hard work, wind, and sun remain beneath the rouged cheeks and powdered forehead. Her hands, however, folded across her mounds of bosom, are not so easily camouflaged: larger, rougher, more veined than any man's. I recall how those hands clutched a water-dipper—not by the handle but cradling the bowl between them in one full encircling, thirsty grasp—or a hoe or a crate of vegetables. And I am shocked to see that Perlina's hair, drawn back from her face and coiled in a high crown atop her head, is gray. Her neck and arms are old. I have not seen her in a long time.

Clutched in her hands are three sprays of artificial flowers—lily of the valley. "She was always partial to them little lilies," Burl Smelcer, standing beside me, says. "Had a patch out there in the chimney corner. Ever' spring that come around she'd tend and feed them. And whenever they blossomed she'd say they smelled sweet enough to be angels' breath. Now wasn't that something? The florist woman down in Churchill let one of my girls have them make-believe lilies.''

Who would have thought that Perlina's coarse hands nurtured such fragility, that the light fragrance of those white bell-blossoms filled some need in rough-shod days? Suddenly, irrelevantly, I think of Bonita Fredericks—golden, pampered flesh in soft white shirt and well-made jodphurs, as I had seen her Friday, and in long, low-cut silk for a long silken evening, perfumed with a scent that cost dearly, by the quarter-ounce, as I had seen her many times this summer— and I know that underneath her sheen Bonita Fredericks is harsher, harder, more invulnerable than old Perlina Smelcer with a skin like bark and a laugh like a sonic boom. We wear our callouses under many guises.

"She was a mighty clever woman," Burl Smelcer says. I understand that he is using the word in its old meaning: generous, obliging, open-hearted.

I try to say the right words to him. Monty reassures him about the burial insurance. Burl says simply, "It'll come in handy. Seems like me and Perlina stay caught between the hard place and the rock these days."

As he motions us to sit down, some of the women—daughters, daughters-in-law, cousins, neighbors—who have been crowding the room retreat into the kitchen. Most of the men are in the yard or on the porch, and through the open door we can hear the murmur of their talk and occasional muffled laughter. Heat from the hickory logs on the fireplace feels good in the damp chill of the gray afternoon. The cloud of white puffed satin that lines the lid of Perlina's casket reflects brightly through the room.

"I'm proud to see you boys again," Burl Smelcer says. His black suit of ancient vintage and limp white shirt with its narrow frayed necktie hangs loosely on his wizened body. His seamed face has lost the ruddiness I remember and has gathered instead a pallor of age, exhaustion, illness. "Just the other day, down in one of the river-bottoms, I picked up a well-nigh perfect arrowhead and I said to Perlina when I came in home, I said, 'Wouldn't Jonathan Clayburn's chaps like to have found this one, way back yonder when they were in the fields?' And she said, 'Lord yes, them little fellers were sharp-eyed as chicken hawks—when they set their minds to it.' I'm proud you boys come to see us."

The fact that strikes me now, however, is not that I am here but that Burl Smelcer is here, just as he was when I was a boy, as he has always been, owning neither land nor home nor even his own strength —which he owes on a dozen due bills. On the company's accounts he is one of "them": tenant, labor, abstract item. Face to face, here, now, he has become Burl Smelcer, unique, individual to me. That reality fills the room. It embraces Perlina (sixty baskets of tomatoes in one day, a thousand heads of cabbage—a dozen children, several dead) who still seems alive.

"It's hard to give up somebody," Burl Smelcer says. "Somehow Perlina didn't seem like the dying kind."

(I think of Deborah. Tenacious of life with a vigor that is fed from well-springs which are the source of creation itself.)

Tears are running down Burl's cheeks. He does not even bother to hide them or wipe them away. When drops of water form on his nose he rubs them away with the back of his cracked, chapped hand. I smell a vague whiskey breath as he speaks—not strong and over-powering but enough for comfort, an interlude of ease in the midst of his aches.

"You boys come out here to see me and Perlina like this and that means a lot." (His appreciation shames me; we are here through fear and self-protection, not the neighborliness he craves and grants us.) "You take Josh's boy, Stull, and some of the others that have put on them rambling shoes and left Churchill. They come back in too big a hurry to live. You hear? That Stull, he used to come riding up in a big car through the farms once in a while, hasn't even done that for years, I reckon, and he'd never set foot on the ground, never speak our names to a one of us old-timers. He don't seem to understand we live this side the grave just once—and we got to be friends. You hear?"

Monty is nodding, easily, agreeably. But I wonder if he can really answer yes to the nervous, habitual question Burl asks. "You hear?"

"Now your daddy, he liked to make money all right, and he was Scotch-thrifty, but he enjoyed it, too. He took time out to look at folks and speak. He was a family man. You hear? And when a pinch was on, your daddy and your uncle Dan was the first to roll up their sleeves and pitch right in—"

In the kitchen there is a clatter of pans and the smell of strong coffee brewing. Music blares softly from a radio—the nasal, melancholy country music of a young man giving his all to the Nashville sound. Burl Smelcer wipes his nose.

"These upstart experts, they come down here now from the company's head offices, way off up North someplace, telling me how to plant peas in this ground. And I been growing peas here for more years than they've lived."

"Burl," I have to ask him now, I cannot wait or hide any longer, "what killed Perlina?"

He looks at me quickly. I sense that he knows what I am asking, but I cannot be sure. "She had high blood," he says, "and sick headaches from away back, only more often lately, and the doctor says she being fleshy like she is—or was—didn't help any—"

"You can't say one specific cause then?"

"A young fellow at the undertaker's and some lawyer in town asked me about—what is it called, autopsy?" He shakes his head slowly, fingering the frayed necktie nervously, looking into the fire. "I didn't want them doing all that to Perlina. Seems like a body don't have any right to himself, to his loneness anymore. You hear? I wanted Perlina to have—" he fumbles for a word that will encompass all he wishes, then gives up the effort—"to have herself to herself."

"Sure, Burl, sure," Monty shifts in his straight-back chair, disliking this familiarity with death.

"We've always lived close to the bone, Perlina and me," Burl says, "but no man ever saw one of us come on hands and knees for anything. And I wouldn't want to use Perlina now—"

We look at each other.

"Clayburn-Durant has always been fair with us," Burl Smelcer continues presently. "It's big now, and we don't know none of you very close, but I reckon in a way we're still neighbors."

"Sure we are," Monty is relieved to be able to turn to agreeable conversation. "Churchill, this county, we're all still mostly homefolks."

I can tell by the shrewd expression which flickers on Burl Smelcer's face that he does not buy Monty's excessive claims, but he only says, "Along the way we've got to put some trust in one another. You hear?"

And I nod yes. I hear. But this time, finally, I do begin—just begin—to hear.

"Burl," I stand up. "I'll be at her funeral."

He grips my hand. "It's set for tomorrow at two o'clock. Our boys from the army will be in by then. At the Open Door Holiness Church. Perlina will be glory-proud to know you come—"

When Monty and I are back in the car, I drive away as quickly as possible. The rutted farm road jolts us.

"Hey, take it easy," Monty protests. "What's wrong with you, anyway? You left old Burl back there like you'd been stung by a horse-fly."

"I'm ashamed. Can you understand that, Monty? A middle-aged, 'successful,' practical businessman—and ashamed of his practicality, of business as usual?"

Monty begins to nod half-heartedly, then cocks his head and sniffs. "What's that smell?"

There is a putrid foulness spreading through the car. We examine our shoes. On my right one, spread over the heel and into the edges along part of the sole, is slippery yellowish dung. In my rush from the house to the edge of the yard I have unwittingly stepped in it—human or animal, I do not know. Or care. The stench is nauseating. We stop. I find a rag in the glove compartment and as thoroughly as possible I clean my well-made British shoe.

"Isn't there even an outdoor privy on that place?" I demand as I rub—wondering for some strange reason what Teena's father would do if one of his golf shoes were dirtied thus, or Sherman Wright, the haughty elderly banker who only recently retired from the Clayburn-Durant board because he could not bear to leave the balmy pleasantness of Palm Beach for meetings in the more mundane parts of the country.

"I didn't notice," Monty says. He grins. "Well, you've been trying to get back to earth."

Back in the car the odor still clings. I roll down two windows but the air does not help. When we come to another wide place in the road —where one of Clayburn-Durant's mechanical cultivators is parked awaiting its next assignment—I pull aside. While the engine idles I pull off my costly imported shoes and open the car door. I drop them into the bramble-covered ditch.

In my stocking feet, I drive Monty home and go back to my room at the motel.

"Deborah?"

"Yes, Jon. I'm here."

She explains that she had gone to a friend's this morning and only returned late this afternoon. I would like to admit to her the dismay, the sense of solitary isolation that clutched me in those moments this morning when the phone rang and there was no answer. But I cannot make such confession—even to Deborah. "My friend and I," she is explaining, and her voice is strained and tired, "we were asked to make depositions, record memories, for a trial next month in Munich. A former guard, surely one of the last—"

"I'm sorry, Deborah." I want to hold her, to feel the gaunt, bony aliveness of her body next to mine, warmer than mine but needing me.

She tries to laugh, comforting me, dismissing herself. "It's all right."

"Deborah: marry me! Come to Churchill."

A half-beat of silence. "In that order, Jon?"

"No. Come to Churchill tomorrow, next day, sometime this week. Can you, will you, Deborah? And after you've seen what it is, what I am, if you'll marry me—"

"I know what you are." Her voice is quiet, certain.

"Today, Deborah—" It is a relief to try to tell someone—"today I went with such condescension, such selfishness, to see an old farmer on the Clayburn home-place here. I went looking down on him—and now I'm going to just try to live up to him. He knows some of the secrets, the way you know them, Deborah. And I need you to help me."

"I need you, too, Jon." Always, always, she knows the right answer, the word that will heal and not wound, the invitation that will liberate without division.

"You'll come?"

"On Wednesday. Arrangements have been made for one more session with the Munich lawyer—"

I tell her plane schedules to Jackson City and we arrange her flight. Then I ask, holding the phone very close, "And the other? The marriage?"

"Yes," Deborah says, "whenever you wish, Jon."

It is as simple as that, as all great triumphs, as the few watershed moments which divide our lives into distinct entities. As simple and incredible as Mozart's Jupiter and Shelley's *West Wind* and Brueghel's *Winter Hunters.*

"I'm acting like a sophomoric kid, Deborah," I laugh and shout, confessing, "but I don't care. I won't settle down with my middle-aged anxieties before I've taken a chance on some of my younger creativity. I want to recapture it, Deborah."

"Yes, Jon, yes." She is urgent, approving.

"I hope Lee will understand the double vision I'm groping for: Stull's know-how and Lee's know-why."

"He'll understand."

"I love you, Deborah."

"And I love you," she says.

"I wish it were already Wednesday."

When Lex Morrison calls on Monday morning to say he will be arriving in Churchill that afternoon, I make arrangements for Price Sims to meet him, show him the fields, laboratories, warehouses, give him details on our use of his spray.

After Perlina Smelcer's funeral in the afternoon I go to the cannery and find Price Sims and Lex Morrison in the laboratory. Morrison is wearing a tweed car coat and he has the frank, outdoor look I remember. We shake hands.

"How about it, did they get Perlina preached into heaven?" Price Sims asks.

I know he is expecting some droll anecdote. When I do not reply at once, Price explains to Lex Morrison. "Those people really put on a good show at a funeral. They holler and cry, sometimes they even throw themselves across the casket or in the aisle. They work off all their grief and troubles, that's a fact."

"We never mind a little emotion down here in the mountains."
I look at Morrison but mean Price Sims.

They seem surprised that I identify with this place and people all
at once. I am surprised, too. It is as if the years in the city, in the
central offices of the company, the years which gradually filled around
the edges with golf and riding, symphony and Little League and PTA
and Human Relations committees, winter vacations in Florida or
summer holidays in Vermont, the years when any of these could be
dropped to rescue Stull at a party or on a jaunt where his drinking
created a problem, when I finally became an executive vice-president
and received the key to the private rest room and went with Stull on
pineapple trips to Hawaii and tomato paste ventures in Spain or
Portugal—the years after Eugenie until he met Mrs. Schroeder of St.
Louis and she became his mother-mistress—it is as if those years
rolled away and I am only Clayburn and Churchill again.

"I'm sorry about the woman," Lex Morrison says. "If I thought
the spray had anything to do with her death—"

"No one thinks so," I tell him.

"Actually, it won't be any further problem, at least for the immediate future," Morrison says. "No one will be using that spray for
a while."

I look from one to the other and notice that in spite of Price Sims'
effort at banter they appear discouraged.

"That's right," Price picks up a can from the lab shelf and holds
it under the electric opener. "We've just had our ass kicked in."

"What's wrong?"

"Morrison and I brought can samples up from the warehouse."
He lifts the lid and tosses it in a wastebasket. "There."

I look at the tomatoes he holds close to my face. They have
disintegrated into a dull red pulp. "That's what's wrong."

"Here, look at the other cans." Along the sink there is an array
of tomatoes, greens, beans—all marked by that muddy color and soft
pulpy consistency. "They held up fine the first weeks. We've been
testing cans at regular intervals here in the lab. But these were some
of our first pack—and they seem to have gone to pieces after six
weeks."

I look at Morrison and he nods, soberly.

"What do you think about it?" I ask.

"Only one thing to think: we don't know enough. Some combination of chemicals, some way the natural ingredients and the man-made factors influence and alter each other, some action of the cooking or storage—any or all of these will have to be explored."

"Meanwhile?"

"Meanwhile, no spray."

I pick up one of the cans, jab my finger into the beans that are supposed to be green but now are pale and grayish. They dissolve like pudding. "Price," I dry my finger on a handkerchief, "empty the warehouse of every case of this stuff and bulldoze it underground."

"Nat Lusk said Stull was really high on this spray. He might want to try to salvage—"

"I've taken the responsibility, Price. Get rid of it."

"That will take a little while—"

"Damn it all, I didn't say do it tonight. I said begin. And lock the warehouse up till the cases can be hauled away."

"I'll see about it right now."

After Price Sims has left, Lex Morrison and I stand awkwardly for a moment. "We usually have better-controlled test situations before we use any product," I explain. "Good Lord, we've had a perfect record up till now, we must have been doing something right. But regulating growth, halting the aging process, it's become one of Stull's obsessions—and you happened along just when the tomato strike last year was still a sore spot."

"For my part, I'm relieved to have the spray out of circulation." Morrison shakes his head as if he has just come out of a deep dive. "I think I can perfect it, make it work safely, one of these days. But I'll have to go at my own pace, in my own way."

"And Clayburn-Durant can stay in touch."

Morrison nods. After a moment he says, "There's something else—"

"What's that?"

"While I'm here, I was wondering if I could find the whereabouts of the house where my grandmother and her father used to live."

"Laura Rathbone? Janus?"

He nods, apparently half-embarrassed at mention of such personal, long-past subjects.

"More than a chance," I tell him. "I know exactly where it was and still is, I suppose."

"You do?"

"Not long before my father died, he took me with him when he went to see Janus Rathbone."

"My grandmother was already away by then?"

"Oh yes. She'd left years before." I sit down in a chair and prop my feet on the lab desk, happy to forget for a little while those wasted cans of food and lost advantages of super sprays and company infighting.

"Is there a chance? I haven't reserved tickets for my return flight yet."

"That we could go out to the place? Why not?" He is young and eager and he deserves something affirmative from this trip.

For the first time he becomes actually excited. Excited and pleased. "She meant so much to me, you see. She would let me help her in her garden. She took me on trips out into our woodlands. And she told me—did she ever stop telling me?—about these Southern Appalachian hills and valleys. From the time I was a toddler till I went away to college, she filled my mind with knowledge of plants and trees and growing things. I think she must have loved my grandfather very much to leave this place."

"It's surprising you haven't been down here before, considering all your grandmother's stories."

"Oddly enough," Morrison hesitates, looks out of the window, "I've wanted, and not wanted, to come. She made the country seem so special, so extraordinary."

"I understand."

"Just as she remembered the Clayburns, at least some of them, in such high praise."

"My father especially, perhaps. Everyone seems to remember him."

"Yes." His reticence and embarrassment are evident. How much does he know, I wonder, about a girl named Laura and a young man named Jonathan, who are now only dust and memory? I wonder at how little I know of them.

I promise to take him, the next morning, to the log house in the mountains.

Both of us are staying at the Vacation Lodge Motel and we meet at breakfast. After Morrison has been introduced to grits, and made an unsuccessful attempt to eat his portion with bacon and scrambled egg, we go out to my car. The weather has begun to clear although there is a heavy morning fog. As soon as we are in the country we begin to pass fields of brown cornstalks wound with morning glories. Their pink and blue and purple trumpets splash bits of color across the subdued landscape. The country road to Janus Rathbone's has been paved.

"Used to be a muddy cow path when I came out here in my father's Model T," I tell Lex Morrison. "But after World War II the sheriff bought some land on top of the mountain and the county paved the road."

"Politics—the same everywhere," he answers, but his attention is focused on the landscape around us.

I think about Laura Rathbone and my father. I remember the distant pivotal day when old Cebo shattered my illusion of perfection and said, "There was one a long time before your mama."

"One what, Cebo?"

"Somebody."

"What kind of somebody?"

"A girl."

The enormity of this, that there could have been anyone, ever, besides my mother, took a little while to grasp. "What kind of a girl?"

Cebo rubbed his knuckles, his gaze far away. "Hair always flying, feet always running. Full of laughing, of questions. Never bearing to see anything hurt. That was the girl."

"Would the girl, and my father, have married?"

Cebo looked back at me then but gave no answer.

"Did they like each other so much?" I persisted.

"They liked each other."

"Then why didn't they marry? Why wasn't that girl my mother?" The thought stunned and intrigued me.

"Clayburn folks follow ordered ways, make use of this world. That girl dance to another tune, don't listen to 'use.' When her pappy sells trees to the Clayburns for making crates, she dusts that farm behind her, won't live where the green is gone, goes way back in the big woods. And your daddy don't see her any more."

"You're talking about Janus Rathbone's daughter!"

"That girl named Laura," he nods.

"My father took me to their cabin once, after the girl had moved away—" I have to have time to consider all this, to sort my feelings and memories and disillusionment.

I pried among the older ones of the family, asking everyone separately, secretly, about the girl named Laura Rathbone.

"I remember her," Aunt Lottie nodded. "She made trouble in the packing shed when we were putting up tomatoes that first summer. Colonel Wakely was very upset."

Aunt Nora had not forgotten her. "A little hussy: no breeding, no decorum. The others of the family were always so careful and generous with her. But I knew, right from the first, that she was a fortune-hunter. She knew the Clayburns were on the way up. Why, right when your father had been near death with typhoid fever she came to see him. I gave her her walking papers."

My mother was last. "Oh, there was some little mountain girl your daddy liked. Everybody knows some little girl like that before he's married, I expect. What mattered to me was that he didn't know one after we were married. And your daddy didn't." My mother was supremely confident in her awareness and dismissal of Laura Rathbone. Her assurance reassembled my own trust and faith.

As we near the end of our journey, I discover that I cannot drive Morrison all the way to Janus' place. There is still a short distance, from the dirt road branching up the hollow to the house itself, which is marked only by an overgrown trail. Morrison is even more prepared for the country than I am, for as we walk along the path his poplin slacks turn off the blackberry briars and Spanish needles better than my flannel material. When I notice that there are a few bent bushes along the way I wonder if someone may still be living on Janus' place, although Monty assured me at dinner last night that it has been deserted for years. There are many such deserted places in the mountains since the last two decades of migration to cities, jobs, opportunities.

At the edge of the yard we pause. The cabin looks empty and sturdy and very much smaller than I remembered it. The stream rushing past also seems smaller.

But what really strikes me is the absence of trees. Where Laura's and Janus' house once sat in a tiny clearing surrounded by a canopy of forest—evergreens and hardwoods mingled in a rare variety and compatibility—with a rich ground cover of ferns and galax and mosses, there now remains only a graveyard of rotting tree laps and jagged stumps. Here and there, sourwood, sassafras, dogwood, and laurel are thrusting up stubborn shoots, but these are poor reminders of the spacious forest that was here.

"Looks like the sawmill beat us to it," I say.

Morrison only nods.

"I wish you could have seen it the way it was when she was here."

"I wish so, too," he says. "I can tell by the size of these stumps what giants they were."

We walk toward the cabin. Morning sun slants across the porch, the broken steps, the steep wood-shingled roof. New-fallen leaves create a soft cushion underfoot. There is no sound but that of water over the boulders in the stream.

We stoop to enter the low doorway and stand in the dark living room. I remember the light of the fire from my boyhood visit and I describe it to Morrison. I tell him the details I remember of knowledgeable Janus, of the aromatic herbs, of the house.

"It's just as I pictured it," he says. "And in another way it's totally different. But I can imagine her here—"

We go across the dog-trot, the wide breezeway, and push open the door to the room that was once a kitchen. I glimpse a row of gleaming glass jars ranged along the wall.

"All right." The voice rasps suddenly and harshly from the shadows. "What are you sons of bitches up to?"

Morrison is as startled as I am. We stumble into the room, propelled by a shove from behind. There are two men inside, crouched in a corner putting the capped Mason jars into pasteboard boxes. The third man follows us from behind the door, a squirrel-rifle in his hands. In another corner a yellow cur dog lies in mangy lassitude. He growls with an ugly show of teeth at Morrison and me and then subsides.

"Moonshiners?" Morrison exclaims.

"Give the feller a little silver star," Squirrel-Rifle says. "He knows the answer right off. Only that wasn't the question I asked you, Mister."

"We came to see where his grandmother used to live," I speak up quickly, believing mountain men may just understand and accept this improbable truth. But these are three ugly characters—not for the filthy overalls and army fatigues they wear, nor for their tobacco-stained teeth and greasy felt hats, but because of the utterly blank, unresponding stare of their dark eyes and the half-moronic, meaningless smirks on their stubbled faces.

"What grandma?" one of the men in the corner asks.

"Laura Rathbone," Lex Morrison says. When there is no reaction, he begins an explanation. "She left, a long time ago—"

"Old Janus was a mean bastard," the man with the gun says flatly. "Sent me to the pen once." No one speaks. "Five years." The only sound is of the creek rushing outside. "Said I set his woods on fire. He helped the state agents find a can of lamp oil somebody had left in my barn."

One of the other men titters.

"You don't think I set any woods afire, do you?"

"No, Lonzo, I don't. I sure don't."

"Then stop your damned peeking and lickspittling."

"What you aim to do about them?" The other man on the floor stands up, jerks his head toward Morrison and me.

They survey us sullenly.

"What's your name?" the one called Lonzo asks.

"Morrison, Lex Morrison. From Michigan."

"And I'm Jon Clayburn."

The men look surprised. "Clayburn?"

"I don't live in Churchill. I'm at the main offices—"

"I don't care if you're the President from Washington, D.C. You come snooping into others' business—"

"And that ain't healthy." The second man grins.

Lex Morrison turns to each one. "Look here—"

"Yeah?" The insolence of Lonzo's tone is chilling.

Suddenly, without plan or warning or purpose, innocent Lex Morrison and I have stumbled into a nightmare. I need to be numerous other places, especially at Aunt Nettie Sue's, and I'm in this ridiculous situation. In the middle of weekday morning sunshine we are threatened and I am frightened. I know of too many encounters others have had with the dark subterranenan violence that moves just below the veneer of Churchill and this county: the ubiquitous guns and the wanton shooting, the stompings, knifings, pistol-whippings, the grinding auto wrecks, and slaughter. Yes, there is no need to deceive myself; I am scared. And the chief reason is the realization that I have no means of reaching these men, no hope of arousing any jot of reason or sympathy, no bargaining assets I can think of.

The man who is still crouched on the floor draws a long, gleaming knife from the side of one boot. With a single quick stroke he separates the pasteboard lid from a carton and kicks it aside.

The pasteboard strikes the dog against the wall. With a startled yelp the mongrel leaps out, tail between his legs, hair on neck and shoulders bristling in fear and anger. Before he can bite, one of the moonshiners catches him in the ribs with a blunt, brutal kick. His howl is high and anguished. The animal slides across the empty floor, snarls, prepares to find his adversary and attack.

Then swiftly, before any of us is aware of his intention, the man with the knife is across the room. With a single movement he gathers both of the long brown ears into his grasp and lifts the kicking plunging dog off the floor. With his right hand he brings the gleaming blade of the knife down across the taut stretched neck in a savage powerful slash. Blood gushes in one warm red spurt. A moan drowns in the dog's throat and becomes a strangled gurgle. Only a remnant of skin and bone seems to hold the gaping hole together. Blood splashes on the floor, scattering small stains over a wide reach. Lex Morrison and I stand frozen in shock and revulsion.

The man hurls the dog aside, then methodically draws the bloody knife-blade across his sleeve, wiping it clean and shiny once more. But he does not return it to his boot. He holds it loosely in his hand, muttering, "That ought to take care of the damned cur."

"You dumbbell," Lonzo says. "Messing everything up like a butcher's shed. What's that prove? Huh? Tell me."

In the momentary pause I rush to speak. "Look, you fellows got no trouble with Mr. Morrison and me. We got no trouble with you. This is all a crazy mixed-up accident."

"What are we supposed to do then?"

"If you've got any smarts worth the mention you'll let this stranger and me walk out of here and go on about our business."

"While we go about ours?"

I look at Morrison and nod.

"I'm a chemist, a plant scientist, not a revenuer," he says.

A slow, unpleasant, victorious grin begins across Lonzo's face. "You know that feller there is just itching to dull his blade against one of your rib bones."

The other two men shuffle closer.

"Then git!" Lonzo shouts suddenly. He lifts his squirrel-rifle in a sweeping arc toward the door, motioning Morrison and me ahead of him. "Out!"

And we get out. Across the breezeway and the porch, down the steps, through the overgrown yard.

Behind us we hear the men come onto the porch, their heavy shoes clumping against the boards. Their laughter is harsh, derisive, triumphant. A shot crashes through the stillness, aimed just above our heads.

When we come to the car Morrison and I are out of breath. I start the motor, turn around, head toward town. As we turn from the dirt road onto pavement, the man beside me begins to laugh. "Wouldn't you say we presented a comic sight—in full flight through the brambles while those outlaws took pot shots at us?"

"Troops retreat, regroup, reconnoiter," I laugh, too. We both laugh excessively, relieving our tension. "What a hell of a friendly episode that was."

"Would they really have harmed us?" Morrison asks. "If we'd resisted?"

I nod. "Don't kid yourself. You saw that dog, didn't you?"

"I think maybe that was one of the most savage things I ever saw."

"Well, that poor old mongrel wasn't causing half the trouble we could cause them if we don't keep our mouths shut."

Morrison nods. We come down the highway into the outskirts of Churchill. People pass us going about their daily business. At a new shopping center women are coming out of the laundromat, chain grocery, and sprawling discount store. Several cars are parked at a hamburger stand. Is it possible that we had our lawless encounter only a few minutes and a few miles from this normal bustle?

I know Morrison is experiencing the same incredulous sense of disorientation when he says, "Maybe we just dreamed it, all that back there."

"I wish so. But they're real, all right." Morrison brushes at a spot of blood on his poplin slacks. He is still rubbing when we come to the motel.

The desk clerk hands me a fistful of messages. All but one are phone calls from Stull: return the call immediately, phone operator 20; reply as soon as possible. The other message is from Aunt Nettie Sue. She is inviting me for dinner—supper in her vernacular.

I have lost all appetite for lunch. My impulse to call the sheriff is chastened by the thought of Monty who lives here and might be made my scapegoat. How do I know who is financing that illegal whiskey operation, behind the menacing trio we met? My mother's and father's old brick home where Monty and Kate now live is as vulnerable to fire as his insurance agency is vulnerable to unseen pressure.

"It makes me mad to think we'll let those men go unchallenged right here in what used to be my home-place," I told Morrison as we parted.

He understood. "It's hard to know what to do."

While I pretend to be deciding, I readjust to my usual work-day tempo, slip into the schedule I have established even here. And it takes only a glimpse below the surface to tell myself I do not want to bother; why risk fighting those ruffians at their brutish level? Especially when I am already engaged in one contest that can make or break me. Why is is that every crisis seems to peak at the same time? Why, for God's sake, does everything have to come at once?

I shower, put on a fresh shirt, and return Stull's call.

His greeting is direct. "What the hell is going on down there in Churchill?"

(I wonder what he would say if I really told him, described the encounter I had just survived.) I explain about the experimental vegetable pack and its disintegration in the cans. "Apparently the tomatoes, beans, greens held up well for an initial period after they were sprayed, even after they were canned. Then they had a complete breakdown, just fell apart. The color, consistency, flavor, everything."

"There must be a few good ones."

"I've never seen anything like it, Stull. Neither has Lex Morrison. He came down—"

"What's he got to do with it?"

"It's his spray we used," I remind Stull. "He feels pretty responsible."

"Everybody's feeling too damned responsible." Stull pauses. I can imagine him looking at the paper jungle on his desk, pushing it all aside as he leans forward. "The business about that woman's sickness all settled?"

"Nothing to settle," I answer. "Burl Smelcer thinks he and Clayburn-Durant and all of us are just one big neighborhood. No suspicions."

"Why should there be? We've always looked out for him."

"Well, now he's looking out for us. Stull—"

"Yes?" Impatiently.

"Isn't there some way Clayburn-Durant could give Burl Smelcer that house and garden patch where he lives? Not as any pay-off," I hasten to explain, "but dammit all, Stull, a man and woman put their whole life into a farm, work like mules, they ought to have a piece of ground they can stand on and call their own before they're ready to be put under it."

"Would that be on the Riverbend Farm?" Stull asks.

"Sure. You know, where those northernmost fields are. Burl's house is up at one end; the company wouldn't miss it."

"Well, Clayburn-Durant doesn't own the Riverbend Farm."

"What?" I glimpse my startled face in the motel mirror. "Hasn't Riverbend Farm belonged to the company ever since Grandma Clayburn and Uncle Dan were killed and the company bought the farm to settle the estate?"

"It did. But then I bought the farm myself. Last year."

That news hits me like the cold shower I have just been under. "You did? From the company?"

"Sure. I thought you'd heard about it."

"I would have heard if it hadn't been a pretty well-kept secret. Why dammit, Stull, Monty wanted that place for years. To remodel the house. To live there. Are you planning to live there, Stull?"

He is indifferent to my anger. "I guess not," he says. "I may give it to charity."

"Then why gobble it all up, Stull? Why grab the Riverbend just to give it away?"

"Because it improves my tax situation," Stull explains, open in his indifference to my knowledge of his maneuvers—indeed, proud of such maneuvers that prove him a hard-headed businessman. "When you're giving land to a school or church or hospital, I've found appraisers tend to be generous in their evaluation of your gift." He almost chuckles. "For the hundred thousand I paid for that farm I expect to get a quarter-million tax deduction. You'll have to admit that's worth scrambling for."

"So you're not even keeping the farm. But Stull, when you bought it you were trading with the company. There's something called conflict of interest, you know."

After a moment he answers hoarsely, "Don't lose sleep about it, Jon. I've set up a foundation to give the Riverbend Farm to Jackson University. My lawyer says there won't be any conflict of interest suit since all the money's going as philanthropy anyway. The prestige will be good for everybody with the Clayburn name."

"Then it's all settled."

"That's right." His tone alters slightly. "Look here, you'd better come on home, Jon. Nothing more to do down there. We'll have to re-examine this whole damned spray deal. But Churchill doesn't seem to agree with you. Come on back and take that sexy Bonita Fredericks out on the town."

"I already have a date here, Stull." I hold my voice slow and steady. "She's coming down from New York tomorrow. Deborah Einemann."

"Who?"

I repeat the name, as if his question is sincere and not an implicit insult.

"What kind of a name is that?"

"It's her kind of a name," I answer.

"Looks like you've kept some little secrets of your own."

"Maybe it's catching," I answer.

There is an interval.

"A Jew," he murmurs.

I wait and then very deliberately I tell my cousin, "You keep your goddamned dirty prejudices to yourself, Stull."

"Hold on, Jon—"

"*You* hold on. Hold tight. I'm staying here in Churchill this week. I have things to do here. And I have a lead on that other business. You know, who it is that's trading heavy in Clayburn-Durant stock."

His voice changes. "Well?"

I do not answer promptly.

"If it's that lousy Stu Siegel prowling around—"

"It will all be here when you are, this weekend, for the big game."

"You just be sure it is, Jon boy." Stull's voice has turned cold and mean as an auger boring in. "Because if it isn't all there, and with some sort of solution at hand, Jon Clayburn may be just another bright executive on the beach peddling a profile résumé."

I hang up the phone. My hands are clammy. The threat Lex Morrison and I faced this morning was a primitive child's game compared to the menace here. This is for keeps. We have called the numbers for a showdown play.

Aunt Nettie Sue is old. It has been a long day, and by the time I arrive at her house for dinner perhaps I am ready to notice any sign of age.

The veins in her hands stand up in blue ridges, coursing between the knobs of her knuckles and joints. The creased flesh of her neck folds like contours of an eroded upland farm. Her hair, which may be a wig, is the color of straw and chaff, dry and wispy. She kisses me, draws me into the familiar house where Mary Clayburn's photograph dominates the hall, feeds me and questions me, stirs admiration and sympathy.

"Jon," her fingers on my arm are chilled, as icy as the variety of stones in the rings she wears. "I can just see you sitting on your father's lap—oh, long, long before brother Jonathan died—and you would hold his big gold watch and tell everyone what time it was."

"I remember," I nod.

"Sit here, Jon." Her voice, which once rang with tremolo throbs throughout the church has grown high-pitched and cracked. "My girl just comes in by the day now. I hope you'll like what she's fixed and left for our supper."

"I will, Aunt Nettie Sue."

"Jon," the blue eyes with their milky pupils are searching, fearful, "I hope nothing is wrong at Clayburn-Durant. The stock seems a little unstable right now."

And thus we eat, remember, probe.

"Whatever happens, I know you and Stull will do the right thing, Jon," she says. I want to ask her, How do you know, Aunt Nettie Sue? Because our name is Clayburn? Because you hope, or trust? How do you know?

Instead, I say, "Aunt Nettie Sue, I've come to ask about Clayburn-Durant."

"Oh Jon, have you? Have you, really? I'm so glad. It's been so long since I've really talked with anyone about the company. Not since Lottie died, I guess. They used to come and talk with Lottie— and me, too, because I was there—but Lottie never did look, well, realistically, you know, at anything involving the family. But for so long we were all involved. Just every breath we drew was part of Clayburn Brothers."

"It was Clayburn Brothers then," I remind her.

She urges the silver platter of fried chicken on me again, and nods. "Of course, it's a big organization now, known across the country and all."

"That's what I want to talk about."

I call Deborah again that night. After we have finished talking I lie awake until the darkest, loneliest depths of the morning, thinking back, thinking ahead.

Snatches of sentences echo like antagonistic motifs in my wandering mind.

From the mid-thirties:

"Chicken and feathers, feathers and stew, get them before they get you." Uncle Jack and Uncle Pett sat at my mother's breakfast table discussing for the two hundredth time the "what-ifs" of the Depression, their "bust" as Jack termed it, their "financial reverses" in Pett's words. "They got us down, then kicked our teeth in," Uncle Jack raged. "Not only lost our money but took most of the property Papa left us, too. Lord God, there was nothing fair about it."

"When I consider a Gosnell owning Uncle Randall Montgomery's store," Uncle Pett shook his head in disbelief, overcome by the impropriety of fate. "Olivia Lee, the waffles aren't quite as crisp as usual this morning."

"I'll speak to Serena, Pett," Mama said. "Meanwhile, I was thinking—if either of you were interested—I heard by the grapevine that there's a night watchman's job at the factory—"

"Night watchman?" Uncle Pett's fork froze in mid-air.

"Well, it wouldn't mean much work," Mama explained defensively, "and the way I heard it, the pay would be good. Those notes I signed for you and Jack—they're being called, and with no Clayburn-Durant dividends to live on during these past five years—well, I'm just in a sort of squeeze, I guess."

"Night watchman at a cannery!" Uncle Pett's face was mottled. "Maybe you can overlook that the Montgomerys have meant something, been somebody in this town since its beginning. But I can't forget so easily, Olivia Lee." He pushed back from the table and a knife clattered to the floor.

"Hold on, Pett," Uncle Jack said. "Livvie Lee didn't mean anything."

"If she means that she begrudges us the food we eat here while we're getting straightened out and finding suitable employment," his voice was rising, "then I, for one—"

"No, Pett," Mama cried. "You know you're always welcome in my home. I love having my family with me."

"Then why do you say we're squeezing you?" Uncle Pett stood, wadding his napkin into a ball, throwing it on the table where it landed in his coffee cup and splashed brown stain on the fresh linen cloth. "You throw those old notes up to us—"

"I don't throw them up to you, Pett. I'm just trying to explain."

But he raged on until at last he was satisfied and my mother was reduced to tears and then he and Uncle Jack returned to breakfast and ate three more waffles and sausages apiece. The only aspect of my return to military school that made me happy that year was the knowledge that I would miss those tyrannical blow-ups, those petty tempests.

When Uncle Pett died years later of a stroke, Monty told me at the funeral, "Pett gave me Grandpa Montgomery's diamond stick-pin. He said you were a Clayburn and didn't honor the Montgomerys. But if you want the stick-pin, Jon—"

My laughter in the hushed funeral parlor offended Monty. "I don't want the stick-pin, Monty. After all, when Jack died I inherited his Stutz museum piece. We each ought to have something to remember them by."

"They loved Mama," Monty said.

"But mostly vice versa," I told him.

And from the mid-forties:

Worth Franklin, shaved, massaged, Italian-suited (shortly after I came into Clayburn-Durant's central offices, during a trip to New York), invited me to his club for lunch. Mellowed leather and deep-pile carpet cushioned the confident male voices settling important decisions and comparing golf scores in the dining room beyond the bar.

"He's a genius, a bastard and a genius, your—" Worth Franklin hesitated.

"Stull's my first cousin," I said, tasting the bullion.

"Then first cousin Stull Clayburn's one hell of a financial operator and if you're bright you'll learn from him." The older man drained his cup at one gulp and pushed it aside. He leaned toward me. "I understand your father and uncles had a lot to do with this company in early times. But you ought to know about Stull."

"I know a good deal about him," I said. But Worth Franklin hadn't brought me to lunch to hear my ideas.

"Stull brought Clayburn's and the Wabash Company together, reorganized, made a modern corporation. He found the Durant Company in trouble and paid a bargain quarter-million for it and made that much back the first year of ownership. He took over New York Machine and Tool and made it into Clayburn Equipment Company and saved Clayburn-Durant three-quarters of a million in annual taxes."

"Till Internal Revenue began an examination—and he had to make a 'settlement' in Washington."

"Well, it wasn't a bad settlement, I can tell you that." Worth Franklin looked at me with the fixed fierceness of a hawk concentrating on a chicken. "And you watch the way he goes about getting Clayburn-Durant out of the baby food business in the next few months. Old Stull will shake loose from that money-loser."

I could agree with him heartily this time.

"Just the way he did back in the thirties, early forties, when he saved nine years of paying cumulative preferred stock dividends—and then settled with the preferred holders for a fourth the amount due! That's horse trading. That put some zip into the common stock."

"Which Stull held. And you. And Sherman Wright's bank. But some of us, some of the family in Churchill, we lost most of that seventy-five cents on every dollar."

Worth Franklin paused, regrouping his forces. "Maybe so. But whatever Stull did for Clayburn-Durant helped you, too, helped every one in the long run."

"It just didn't hurt everyone the same in the short run," I said. "Especially considering the less-than-starvation salary of seventy-five thousand a year that Stull took all those hard-up years while the stockholders had no income."

"Look here," Worth Franklin propped his elbows on the table and spoke very clearly, "I don't know what kind of standards you're judging Stull by, but you'd better begin to remember which side of the executive table you're on now, Jon. Good men are hard to find."

"Yes," I agreed. "They are."

He leaned back in the leather chair slowly, and looked at me. His eyes became unpleasant slits and the expression on his leather-skinned face was both genuinely puzzled and harsh. These were the moments a business course had not discussed. He waited until the waiter had placed our lunch before us, then he said, "I've been on the board of your company for a long time. I'm on eight boards—plus my own National Metals—but I've been interested in Clayburn-Durant especially. I thought it would be good to have someone else named Clayburn on the way up. Stull's done nothing about training any successor. You might be the answer. But frankly, you puzzle me."

"Oh?"

"I get the feeling you're not all with us. There's something less than one hundred percent about your support of the company."

I separated a chunk of avocado and lobster and savored the blend of flavors with the special chef's dressing. Worth Franklin was so eager to tell me something, whip me into shape for Clayburn-Durant. Maybe I could tell him something, by my silence. And although Teena and I needed an improved salary and I knew Franklin's judgment would carry weight with Stull, with the board, I wouldn't go along so easily. After that luncheon I told Teena it would be a while before I got the key to the executive wash room. It was.

Not until years later, after I had worked with research and production to develop Readi-Maid frozen meals—and then nursed them along through the test markets, distributors, advertising programs, and after public acceptance had turned Readi-Maid into one of Clayburn-Durant's chief non-seasonal profit-makers—did Stull make me his executive vice-president and present me with the coveted key.

And the mid-fifties:

"You ever hear of Modigliani?"

The name rolled in Stull's mouth like warm wax, unmanageable, distasteful.

"Yes," I said, "but I'm no expert."

"Well, who the hell is he?"

"A painter who was born in Italy, lived in Paris—"

But Stull didn't really want to know. "To hear all the talk about him last night—Modigliani this, Modigliani that—you'd have thought he was a stand-in for the Second Coming."

I had seen Stull's face last night at the party when Eugenie and Stu Siegel were rapt in their exchange on art.

Stu Siegel was in town to see Stull and to launch an exhibit of the world-famous Siegel Collection at our city's new art museum. No one knew which of the reasons for his visit was paramount. For years Siegel Enterprises had put out feelers toward Clayburn-Durant; ownership of Clayburn-Durant would extend the empire of one of the country's wealthiest men, whose conglomerate eventually included textiles and steel, newspapers and soft drinks, pulpwood and meat packing.

But during recent years Stu Siegel had become a collector of art as well as of companies. His presence was as well known in Bond Street as in Wall Street. His touch for selecting painters and styles who were "comers" was as skillful as when he selected industries and managers. Big, balding, modishly dressed, he was assertive in a manner that seemed carelessly frank and voluble, which in reality was carefully noncommittal and secretive. His conversation during an evening could appear to contain nuggets of experience, advice, significant anecdote; but when assayed, the words added up to fool's gold, revealing nothing more than was already well known about Stu Siegel.

The city's art museum had been a growing point of controversy —only one among many—between Eugenie and Stull. She had become acknowledged queen of the knowledgeable art lovers and art students, as well as of the social-climbing would-be sophisticates who didn't know umber from magenta or Giotto from Orozco but who realized that if their midwestern metropolis were to join the twentieth century it would have to boost at least a nodding acquaintance with the fine arts.

"Den mother to a bunch of deadbeat paint-slingers," Stull said of Eugenie, but he let Clayburn-Durant make good on the fat pledge with which Eugenie had launched the construction campaign.

As Stull used money to control Eugenie, she used art to embarrass him. Her French accent, of which only traces remained when Stull first met her, grew almost impenetrable. Her dress suggested Montmartre more than the Midwest, and for the huge Beaux Arts New Year's Eve Ball of which she was principal patron, she brought back a haute couture creation from Paris and became the sensation of the season.

She spent lengthy sessions with the museum's director, and at any gathering where Clayburn-Durant people were present she quoted the director's witticisms frequently and at length. Nat Lusk voiced the unease of many in the company when he growled, "Eugenie's got herself a pet poodle in that art fellow. If I was Stull I'd cut that fairy's water off." To Nat, any man who preferred a paintbrush to a target-pistol, any man who would immortalize a female with a palette rather than use her on a pallet, would have to be "a fairy, a queer—and damned queer at that."

By the time Stu Siegel came, the museum was finished—and so

was Eugenie's and Stull's marriage. Neither seemed particularly astonished by the disintegration, only determined not to be outwitted by the other in the money settlement. There was never any question about the child—she would be with Eugenie. Stull was pulling out of marriage to free himself from the responsibility of such attachments, not to assume it. But before she left, Eugenie was determined to repay her husband's tyranny—long boring evenings of financial discussion, alcoholic weekends of football fantasies and self-centered soliloquies, humiliations at home and abroad to which his limitations had subjected her—of which she had kept careful and bitter account.

I had watched at the close of dinner that night of the country club art patron's party, as Eugenie leaned toward Stu Siegel, the low round neck of her ruby-colored velvet dress falling forward ever so slightly and sufficiently as she slowly accepted the flame he held for her cigarette.

I had heard her light laughter as they danced briefly after dinner. And I had seen Stull's face as Eugenie and Stu Siegel, on a sofa in one corner of the club's bar, talked on and on, by turns animated and subdued, until the music in the ballroom stopped and there was no more dancing and the guests were either leaving or settling down for the serious hard drinking.

"Well, dear wife," Stull approached Eugenie, and no one except perhaps Eugenie and me could realize the almost total inebriation that teetered behind his overly straight walk, his carefully chosen speech. "Is this high-level negotiation secret or may the rest of us common folks be privy to your enlightened thoughts?"

Stu Siegel stood up. The bald white of his head glistened in the glow of the overhead chandelier. "We were discussing museums, collectors—"

"Yes, Stull dear, do sit down and 'enlighten' us with *your* thoughts on the subject." The hard brightness of Eugenie's mismatched eyes, the flaunting sarcasm of her voice, alerted some of the drifters in the bar. I could see Bonita Fredericks and several of her friends moving in closer, keen-eyed, sharp-eared, ready for the smell of blood.

Teena, in a far corner with Nat Lusk's wife who was by then quietly, desperately drunk, made no move to come closer. Teena sat with her feet curled up under her long flowered skirt, round chin cupped in one hand, elbow propped on the heavy upholstered chair arm, and listened patiently to the pathetic girl's repetitious gibberish. At that moment I loved Teena. I blew her a kiss across that hot, smoky room.

"Your wife's a delightful art authority," Stu Siegel said to Stull. "I had no idea—"

"But you did have ideas," Stull winked slowly, ponderously. "Concerning my wife—"

"We were discussing Modigliani, dear," Eugenie interrupted. She set the long ivory cigarette holder between her lips and inhaled a deep draught of cigarette smoke. "What are your thoughts on Modigliani, Stull dear?"

"I haven't a thought in the world about him—or her—or it."

The smoke wreathed around Eugenie's neat trim head in a pale blue halo. "But you and Mr. Siegel here have so much else in common, Stull. You like business and canneries. And profits. Oh my, Stull, there are just oodles of profits to be made from —'pictures.' "

"Well," Stu Siegel was bored by this cross-fire. He wanted no part of it. "A person is caught up in the art world, really, for more than the profits, Mrs. Clayburn." He glanced at several of the others in the room who seemed to have drawn within earshot.

"Why is a person caught up in this art fad, Siegel—really?" Stull asked.

"Is there any reason why we shouldn't sit down in a civilized way?" Stu Siegel asked. He resumed his seat beside Eugenie, not bluffed by Stull, disingenuous and superbly casual. His face, however, showed the creases of many years of trading—in companies, in canvases, in people—and his weariness at having to cope with such sticky and unprofitable situations as this. "We buy companies, Clayburn, you and I, when they're in trouble, have some flaw we know how to cure. But we buy paintings because they're as nearly perfect as human genius can make them."

Stull looked at Stu Siegel. Whether or not he saw him was debatable.

"The perfection—ah, that's the answer!" Eugenie waved her cigarette holder in a long sweeping gesture of homage. "Which do you prefer, Stull dear: the genius of Picasso in his blue period, perhaps? Or Renoir and his light: light on the Seine and the boating party, on a delicate lady's hair and skin?"

"I prefer," Stull said suddenly, "the genius of that fella that draws the covers for the *Saturday Evening Post*. And I bet he could just about buy and sell those foreigners—"

Eugenie and Stu Siegel looked at each other; one of Eugenie's eyes cast slightly upward as if in mock despair.

"Norman Rockwell does very well, indeed," Stu Siegel said, his evaluation including both art and money.

"The All-American Boy," Eugenie said. "But darling, forgetting the *Post* for a moment—what of those pictures of sunsets and cattle in meadow-streams and all those bewhiskered grandfathers scattered through your mother's house?"

"You leave my mother and our pictures out of this," Stull blazed. He stood up, turned to get his drink, and lost his balance. As he fell across the chair, his hand struck the glass on the end-table. Remnants of Johnny Walker sloshed over the upholstery, ice skidded across the floor, and glass shattered into a dozen sharp fragments.

I left my seat at the bar and went to help Stull regain his balance. He grabbed my arm fiercely, stood up, then shoved me away. He didn't bother to smooth his rumpled dinner jacket or straighten his black tie. Stull looked right into Stu Siegel's horn-rimmed glasses. No one in the room was even pretending to be unconcerned now.

"Siegel," Stull's tongue was only slightly thick and hesitant, "you can take all your smart-ass talk and your arty crap and stuff it."

Stu Siegel was getting to his feet again.

"And as for Siegel Enterprises, you'll have to find some cannery besides Clayburn-Durant to go with that little horsemeat-packing operation you picked up off the bargain counter." Stull held up a hand, blocking interruption from either Siegel or me. "And if you try to get your goddamned greasy hands on my company, I'll go to the anti-trust boys. Clayburn-Durant packs a good amount of government meat and there could be threat of monopoly in Siegel Enterprises, with its meat operation, trying to take us over—"

Stu Siegel resembled the angry, self-controlled banker or merchant prince of the Netherlands, Spain, Italy, as represented on any number of those fabulous canvases he had pursued and finally captured. "You're a drunken boor, Clayburn." His tone was authoritative and final. "I wouldn't trade with you for a paintbrush, much less a canvas. And I don't want even one can of your pork and beans, much less 'your' company." He strode from the room.

Eugenie's eyes glittered. "And there you are in a nutshell, dear."

Stull, flushed, turned to her. "Don't you ever sleep in my house again—you conniving little French slut."

The episode was the talk of the town.

And Stull called me to his office and wanted to know about Modigliani.

For an instant I thought he might actually wish to know. And I remembered the past we shared—paradoxically rich and arid, offering us so much, excluding so much.

"Let's face it, Stull," I said in his office, his cheeks puffy and sallow from the night before, "there's a whole world we missed out on when we were growing up."

He listened, looking out the window.

"And part of it was exposure to art. To the excitement of ideas, to experience of emotion as a conscious fulfillment—or frustration—but something to be sought as human, not shunned as trivia or weakness."

Stull remained standing with his back to me, but I went on. "The sad part, Stull, is that it wasn't due to meanness or plotting that they shut that world away from us. They themselves didn't know it. And it wasn't in them to seek it out. But we missed it, too, Stull."

He turned to me then and for the first time that morning I saw him almost laugh. "What the hell are you talking about? You sound like some green college kid who's just had his first lay."

My anger paralyzed my throat. Stull must have seen my fury for his tone softened slightly.

"This whole art deal is just one big dirty end of the stick, as far as I'm concerned. I've earned my money; I'll spend it wherever the hell I please. Why, when I mentioned the frauds to Eugenie—" He paused, as if the name scorched his tongue "—she said of course there were frauds, but there were experts, too, and you had to take risks. Well, I like to be my own expert. I don't need anybody else's risks."

"But—"

"I know football," he said. "I like football. I'll buy Jackson University a stadium and some players. That ought to be as good public relations as giving a goddamned museum some painting. Maybe better, back home."

"Undoubtedly better."

"Then what's the matter with it?" Stull demanded. "I notice there are a hell of a lot more paying customers for football than for all this art business."

"They're two different things," I answer, suddenly weary at the futility of this absurd conversation. "A man needs several kinds of food—"

"You're talking to a canner." Was he intentionally obtuse, or was he putting me on?

"Okay, Stull. Forget it. I wash my hands of the whole insane evening—and yours and Eugenie's little trade war."

We turned away from each other, convicted of the chasm between us. As I left the room he muttered, "Modigliani," and laughed sourly.

And in the mid-sixties:

The week after Teena's funeral, when Lee and Ellie were still with Teena's mother on the family island off the Maine coast, Teena's father came to my office at Clayburn-Durant.

"She was our only child, our life. You made her happy, Jon. We can't repay you, wouldn't try, but we want you to have, now, half of the estate that would have been Christine's. The other half eventually will be Lee's and Ellie's, of course. But we would like for you to have some independence from your cousin—if you want it. Christine told us, you see, about the squeezing years, at first—and the demands, the embarrassments, recently. We wish we had done more while she was living—"

I was abashed by his admissions, for I knew how hard they came. "We didn't want, or expect you to do more," I said. "And I think you're too generous now. You should reconsider. And I want to think about it."

"There are no strings attached," he said shrewdly. "You're pretty young—to me, at least, enviably young. And you'll go ahead in your work, marry again—" his voice broke. "Do whatever seems best to you, Jon. And for Lee and Ellie. They're all that we have left of Teena."

His voice, his arrangements about the stocks and bonds and money, fade—in my mind—into Aunt Nettie Sue's voice and arrangements today, at supper tonight. . . .

As I fall asleep, I remember waking up early this morning, meeting Lex Morrison, encountering the men on the mountain in Janus Rathbone's old cabin. And I wonder if all our lives did not take a different turn because the Clayburns never accepted or even faintly understood Laura Rathbone.

Deborah, too, is a stranger. But I will never let her go.

17

When I drive to meet Deborah at the Jackson City airport my throat is dry, my stomach knotted, with excitement and anticipation. The plane settles like a noisy, glossy gull—and Deborah is coming down the steps, across the landing field, through the gate. Her five-feet-three inches seem taller because she is thin, thin with the modish angularity of fashion models or the emaciated boniness of past disease. But I know it was a disease in others and not herself which left her so.

She wears a black and white wool coat and soft white leather boots and a white scarf at her throat. Her hair, drawn back from her face in smooth severity, and her large eyes, seem dark and shiny enough to match her black kid gloves or handbag.

"Jon!" She stands on tip-toe and I wrap her in a hug which smashes us together in a long, warm reparation.

We claim her luggage, a single medium-sized bag—like Deborah, spare and simple. Everywhere else there is a bloated too-muchness, organizations for every purpose, all choking in fat, sinking under the weight of their own self-perpetuation. But Deborah can control appetite, not satiate it; savor life and not devour it, or be devoured.

"Deborah," when we are in the car I take her hands, now free of gloves, and I hold the knotted, twisted joints between my own warm palms, "you meant what you promised on the phone?"

"Of course, Jon. I'll marry you." No artifice, no ruse to make me reassert my need of her, no bargaining with our mutual need.

I lay her hands, fresh and cool with scent of soap and lilac cologne, against my cheek.

"Has it been difficult, Jon?" Her voice is warm with concern.

"No. That's not the word. Tough, because I'm facing the whole reality with a toughness I've avoided before. But exciting, too."

We kiss.

I back the car from its parking place and drive toward the highway. "Are you tired, Deborah, or could I show you some of the landmarks? There's so much to share—"

"I've never been less tired in my life," she says.

We swing by Jackson University where I try to give her the essence of four undergraduate years of arid business courses, bridge and basketball and fraternity high jinks, the syrupy refrains of "Stardust" and "We Could Make Believe" and Guy Lombardo's sweetest music this side of heaven. We pass the football stadium and I ask her about Saturday.

"Stull and Nat Lusk will be flying down for the big homecoming game. Stull will want us to join them. He always has a box on the fifty-yard line. His mother used to come to every big game of the season, till she was unable, at ninety-one, to stand the ride down from Churchill and back. Stull can't comprehend that anyone would choose to miss a ball game. You see, down here it isn't a game at all but a ritual, an enormous rite of autumn. But you, Deborah, you're free to choose. We'll do whatever you wish."

"I wouldn't think of missing something so—so essential," she smiles at me.

On the way from Jackson City to Churchill lies the Riverbend Farm. In the autumn sunlight the upland woods, the wide empty bottomlands, the winding river in the distance, stretch lonely and timeless around us. I show her the old brick house where Mary Clayburn received word of her husband's death and reared five sons and two daughters, the stump where Cebo's mother's great oak tree once stood, the woodland where Jonathan Clayburn and Janus Rathbone and others built the first tomato packing shed. And on a rise beyond the northernmost field, I point out Burl and Perlina Smelcer's house. All of this now Stull's, only and solely Stull's. And not even that for long.

"I'm glad to see it all with my own eyes," Deborah says as we drive away. "It's not what I expected at all."

"Your provincial New York cliché of magnolias and mint juleps?" I tease.

"Perhaps, a little. And yet it is also what I expected—" She gazes out of the car window at the blue-shadowed mountain range on the horizon, at the golden-brown corn shocks and stalks of tobacco on the small farms, and I know that she is feeling the first tug of this place and season.

In Churchill we drive past the sprawling Clayburn-Durant plant and warehouse. I tell her about Lex Morrison's visit and our experience at the old Rathbone place in the mountains.

She shudders slightly. "They might have killed you. It becomes so easy after the first barrier is breached by blood." She reaches out and touches my hand on the steering wheel. "They could have done it—so carelessly."

I squeeze her hand.

"Where is Lex Morrison now?" she asks.

"He went home this morning. But you know what? He claims he's coming back here to buy his great-grandfather's old house. When he leaves the university laboratories, he'll live here. He even called the lumber company that owns the place and made them give him a price before he left."

"What of the present tenants?" Deborah asks drily.

"Morrison says he won't relinquish all the best corners of the earth to savages—old or new. But the bootleggers will find another hide-out. We just happened to surprise them. And ourselves." I try to smile at my own anti-heroic recollection.

As we pass the gabled, turreted, imposing brick ruins of my grandfather Alexander Montgomery's home, I tell Deborah of my generous, party-loving mother, Olivia Lee, who bore the pride and then the neglect of being Jonathan Clayburn's wife. I look at Deborah, wanting her to share all of the secrets as well as the openness of my life, as I have shared hers during many long weekends in New York.

"My mother wanted to protect anyone she loved. It was her flaw and her virtue. She was compelled to protect—from sneezes or stumbles or stomach aches, and later on from disappointments and heartbreaks—whenever she could. She had to feed, and protect—"

"A perfect Jewish mother," Deborah says.

We look at each other, smiling in surprise. "Maybe we have more in common than we know," I say.

"Of course."

"And Mama was devoutly religious. Orthodox Baptist."

Deborah nods. "Questions, departures from the old ways, alarmed my darling mother."

"And mine. I never deliberately meant to hurt her, and yet I know how mortally I wounded her conviction that there was a real, coal-burning hell toward which I was headed. She shielded me from broken arms, and from a good many knocks I should have experienced, but she couldn't safeguard me from hell."

"And my mother couldn't safeguard her family from the living hell that exploded all around us. And it killed her. I remember when she saw my brother herded down the corridor, toward the furnaces —she collapsed—and she died the following week, cheating all their neat mechanical contrivances for killing." Deborah is trembling. I have begun half-casually a conversation that suddenly verges on the brink of the abyss.

"I've worn you out." I realize it is very late, that I have brought her from the plane to all this newness of place and people, to all this past, abruptly, emotionally. "I'm sorry," I tell her, as we arrive at the motel and find a parking place.

"Don't be sorry for giving me a new life," she says, looking at me. The white scarf around her throat reflects light on her face.

After I have helped her find her room and open her suitcase, we sit for a moment quietly. Then, as if continuing her sentence from the car, she says gently, "All these years, there were friends—friends who wished to marry me, care for me. But you wanted to care for me *and* me to care for you. There was something I could give as well as take. And you had a family, a past, something I had lost, lost so violently and irretrievably that sometimes in the night I used to waken and wonder if there had ever been anyone, if I had imagined it all in a nightmare—"

I close my arms around her.

"And that is part of the reason why I wish to marry you."

"I'm glad," I murmur against her hair.

Her body is tense against mine. "I'm afraid. I've seen it happen. When we cut the tap-root we're free to destroy the earth and each other."

I hold her close. "We needed to find each other. Now I'll tell you why I love you in such a special way."

"There's no urgency—"

"Yes, there is. I want to tell you. I must. Because I loved Teena. She was kind and she loved me and our children, and God knows she did her best during those last months. I could never think of her without love. But you've taken me beyond Teena. You've shown me endurance against hate, against some awful darkness I can't even imagine. You brought life out of death, Deborah. You're the most beautiful person I ever saw."

Tears, the first tears I have ever seen her shed, run down her face. The surge of love between us at that moment is born of sex but also a dozen other hungers and fulfillments and joys which merge to make it an experience rare as birth itself. It is a kind of rebirth.

Friday morning I check with Price Sims about the disposal of the spoiled canned goods.

"We located a ravine back in that knobby upland on one of the farms. Makes a natural land-fill spot. Ten or twelve truckloads of cans already dumped there." As he talks, Price shows me the emptying warehouse.

"Good. And early next week you should get our machines into those fields around the Smelcer place. If it's not too wet, have them turned good and deep."

"Plow the spray residue under," Price Sims says, putting his hands into the pockets of his brown-checked, wash-and-wear, stay-creased slacks as we walk from building to building in the chilly morning air.

"About all we can do now," I tell him sharply. "Even Lex Morrison didn't have any sure answer, but he seemed to think breaking up the ground and leaving it to leach out during the winter would be best."

"Damned scientists," Price Sims says. "Always so ready with their big discoveries and claims, then scatter like pa'tridges whenever we need hard answers."

I think he sounds like Nat Lusk.

We have arrived at the can-making operation. As we push open the heavy outer door the clatter of sheet tin, the rattling of empty tins and whirling lids, is deafening. Overhead, networks of lines of shiny cans bang along mechanical conveyors and disappear into the storage lofts. The ceaseless din, the glaring reflection from the new metal, seem unnoticed by the handful of men running the operation.

"Sounds like money to us," Price answers when I mention the noise. He is shrewd enough to remember that this can factory was my baby, years ago.

I need to reassure myself, too—before Nat's and Stull's arrival. "It's made a difference," I tell Price Sims, "a big difference. Not in sales, where it would stand out in a splashy showing, but in savings."

"And that's the way to meet a budget: add up a profit," Sims agrees. "That's how to make the buckle meet the tongue."

The strong earthy smell of sauerkraut permeates the air as we come back outside. "They're stirring the vats," Sims says, unaware that a long time ago this was one of the jobs I performed in the open sheds at the farthest corner of the plant. "It's our last kraut run of the season."

"It's the ketchup I always remember best," I answer, and he is obviously puzzled by my naive, irrelevant, wandering conversation.

At the motel, Deborah has finished late breakfast and a walk around the empty swimming pool. We leave for our day's pilgrimage.

We go see Aunt Nora and my cousin Nancy Ellen, who has come by her mother's on an errand. As I park in front of the tall, familiar brick house, next door to the home where I grew up, I remember that before my marriage to Teena my mother wrote Aunt Nora the longest, most informative note announcing our engagement. Not to Aunt Nettie Sue or Aunt Lottie or even Aunt Josie, her own sister, but to Aunt Nora. And I know she wrote Aunt Nora first and most not because she liked her best but because she feared her more. My mother, in her own way, knew the uses of power: the power of family acceptance or rejection, the power of diplomacy. Aunt Nora was more or less the family arbiter, and although my mother might defy her in her own lists, Mama was determined that Nora Stull Buchanan Clayburn should accept and assist Monty and me, and whomever we might marry. Aunt Nora had approved of Teena: of her manners, her money, of every outward appearance. That was one of my mother's small triumphs before she died.

But now there is Deborah.

"The air is chilly this morning." Aunt Nora reigns from her small needlepoint-covered settee in front of the fake electric fire in the fireplace, while Nancy Ellen arranges chairs for us. We speak of weather and airplane travel and how Churchill has changed. "Where are you from, Miss Einemann?" (Aunt Nora called Christine "Teena" the moment after their first introduction.)

"New York now," Deborah says. "Before that, Germany."

"Oh." Aunt Nora and Nancy Ellen look at her again.

"During World War II Deborah was in a concentration camp. All of her family were killed. She was considered dead." I want to plunge them into the knowledge. I want these nice comfortable people to realize some small part of her childhood horror. . . .

"How dreadful," Nancy Ellen says. She is short, like her mother, but her face is wide and placid as Uncle Josh's was, not given to fleeting expressions or easy laughter. She has, like her brother Stull, the Clayburn gravity, and her mother's judgment. Aunt Lottie called her the salt of the earth.

"How old were you." Aunt Nora asks, her tiny blue-veined hands clutching the pink shawl around her shoulders, "when you were in that—that place?"

"I was ten years." Deborah's voice is soft but it fills Aunt Nora's Dresden blue and pink rooms.

"Ten!" Aunt Nora exclaims. "It was a wicked nation—"

Her words linger in the brief stillness before Deborah answers. Deborah's hands hold on to the arms of the chair where she is sitting and I realize how hard it is for her to dredge up these memories. "There was a guard over one of our women's barracks, a fair-haired, clear-eyed young man who hadn't the butcher's face and hands of so many guards, and I wondered how he could survive that place, his work of persecution and murder. One day, as he watched me scrub latrines for the camp's headquarters, I asked him quite directly. He answered without a second's hesitation: 'Jews are different.' "

They were shocked—by the latrines, not by what Deborah had told them. In fact, they were not quite sure what she had told them.

Was she trying to say that Germans were not different from themselves?

Deborah's fingers tightened on the chair. "To believe someone is not like us is to protect ourselves from caring. Or from our own humanity. It's such a tiny crutch, but it can support a holocaust."

Aunt Nora's wrinkled face is rigid. She has not renounced her assertion of difference, but she will not be impolite, either, especially to so strange a stranger, the kind she had always expected me to find.

"I hope and pray there will never be another war," Aunt Nora concludes the conversation.

Nancy Ellen passes candy from an over-sized five-pound box on the marble-top coffee table. "Stull always brings Mama chocolates when he visits," she explains.

"Stull will be coming again tomorrow." Aunt Nora's face lights up. "He never misses the homecoming game at the university. Only the time he was visiting that man, that Trujillo about a plant in the Dominican Republic, he missed then. But not often. Jon, you and Miss—Miss—"

"Einemann."

"Yes. You'll be going to the game tomorrow, won't you?"

"I suppose so."

"It should be the best of the year. If they win this one over Alabama, they'll go to the Orange Bowl. Everyone knows that."

"Yes, Aunt Nora."

"Of course," her mouth tightens so that the network of tiny lines puckers around it like a purse-string drawn fast, "Alabama always has taken special delight in defeating Jackson U. They'd like nothing better than to win tomorrow and knock us out of the Bowl bid."

Deborah watches this old woman, full of tenacity and fierceness over a football game.

"Your Uncle Josh," Aunt Nora goes on, "was captain of the first team at Jackson University, you know."

I know.

We go to Monty's and Kate's, next door. They are finishing a quick lunch and invite us into the old breakfast room.

"Debbie, it's good to meet you. We want you to feel right at home here. This was our parents' house; Jon and I grew up here, you know—"

"Yes," Deborah nods at Monty's urgency.

"—He'll probably want to show you all around."

"Just don't notice the dust," Kate intervenes. "I work full time as assistant manager at Churchill's new discount store and I don't get much time at housekeeping. Help's no good."

"Dust won't bother me," Deborah reassures her.

"Then you'll get along fine here," Kate offers us peanut butter sandwiches, a coke, but we decline. I remember some of the lavish meals my mother served here. "You down from New York to see how the country people live?" Kate asks Deborah.

"To see Jon's family," Deborah looks at me.

"We're going to be married," I tell them.

A shadow, a hesitancy, flickers across Monty's face. Then he says, "Now that's fine. That's just dandy. Old Jon here needs a wife. And Lee and Ellie need a mother." He hesitates. "What does Stull say about it."

"He doesn't know yet," I reply.

"What business is it of his, anyway?" Kate demands.

"Well, we want you to come and eat with us, stay with us," Monty says as we leave. "We'll work it out. Friday's such a busy day, in my insurance office, at Kate's store, you know—"

We go to Aunt Nettie Sue's. After I have explained the house to Deborah, I explain Deborah to Aunt Nettie Sue, who says only, "I'm glad. People were meant to be married."

The striking of the hall clock echoes through the crowded, empty rooms and seems to emphasize the loneliness Aunt Nettie Sue has let us glimpse.

"I'm glad you'll be together for Jon's fight—"

Deborah looks at me quickly.

"Oh, Jon didn't call it a fight," Aunt Nettie Sue's laughter is high and shrill, "but I've usually been able to guess what people wouldn't tell me. Even back when brother Cal used to tease me so about my voice, I knew it wasn't the singing that troubled him but the independence of my wanting a concert career."

The ticking of the grandfather clock is loud and regular during each brief silence.

"And I knew, way back at the beginning, that brother Jonathan

and brother Dan would have something big before they finished building—if only the terrible old accidents and the illness—" she fumbles
with the amber beads around her neck. "Anyway, I suspect I know
real well what Jon's talking about. And it's a fight. Even though we've
always been such a close family—"

Deborah nods, knowing that to listen is all that is necessary here.

"That is, we were a close family."

"Jon has told me," Deborah says.

"Jon was always like his father," Aunt Nettie Sue says, and even
at this late age I am extravagantly pleased to have her say so. As I
stand I put my arm around my aunt's proud, weary, unyielding
shoulders.

"Thank you for bringing this dear girl to see me, Jon," Aunt
Nettie Sue smiled wistfully up at me. At the door she stops Deborah.
"You have a beautiful speaking voice. Do you sing?"

"Sometimes. For my own pleasure."

"I'm so glad!" Aunt Nettie Sue nods toward me shyly. "I think
Jon inherits some of his pleasure in music from me."

"I'm sure of it," Deborah says. And gives Aunt Nettie Sue both
of her hands.

Aunt Nettie Sue squeezes them, feels the burls, then looks down
in astonishment at the knotted, twisted joints and fingers.

"They were broken, one by one, when I was a young girl,"
Deborah says. "Before that, I had played the piano, at home, for my
father every evening."

"Poor child, poor, poor child—"

"It's all right now. I learned to live with it."

"Come back," Aunt Nettie Sue says. "I'll play the piano and
you'll sing!" She is triumphant at the neatness, the wholeness of such
an arrangement. So are we.

"And Jon, I'll wait to hear from you."

At dinner that evening Deborah eats even less than usual.

"A few spoons of soup, a forkful of salad, a bite of meat—how
will you survive this pace?"

She smiles at me but it is a tight, forced smile. "I'm nervous about
tomorrow, Jon."

"But Deborah," I lean forward in my captain's chair, "you told me once you were truly free of fear, you'd seen the worst face to face."

"I only said I was nervous."

"But why should you be even nervous?"

"There's Stull to meet—"

My surprise is complete. "Stull?"

I try to think of something, in addition to the many things I have already told her, which might help her know him better.

"Look," I lean across the table, "Stull and I were talking once about a big union fight we'd had at one of our plants. It left scars, and I had the bright idea that he should go out there and get to know some of our workers—their families, where they live, how long they've been with the cannery. Stull listened to that proposition about one-half minute before he said, 'I'm running a company, not a political campaign. You want to know the biggest discovery I ever made, Jon, way back when I was still at our Churchill plant? To produce, people don't have to like you. They just have to fear you, to know you have the clout. That's something you'd better learn. Fast.' "

Deborah listens intently. I explain to her what "clout" means. She nods gravely.

"Then there was another time, a few years ago after Eugenie left, before he found Mrs. Schroeder, when I had to go out and spend the night at his fortress. Even the couple who had lived with him so long were uneasy. The next morning I was in a storage room beside the kitchen. And he had six king-size freezers there, each stuffed to capacity. Two were packed with steaks. One held only beef and pork and lamb roasts. One was crammed with lobster and shrimp. Another had gallon after gallon of rich, pure-cream ice cream."

Deborah takes a sip of water, as if nauseated.

"It was obscene," I conclude. "But when I asked him later why the stockpile, Stull only said, 'You never know when someone might attack.' "

"Attack him? Attack the country? What is he so afraid of?" Deborah asks.

I shrug. "Everything, I guess." Then I add one final piece to the puzzle. "You'll meet Mrs. Schroeder, Deborah. She goes everywhere with Stull, except to Churchill. She's a plump, pleasant, middle-aged widow. Stull met her in St. Louis about five years ago. Her husband had made a fortune as a brewer so she doesn't need Stull's money.

Maybe that reassures him. But more than anyone else I know, Mrs. Schroeder looks like Aunt Nora. The way I remember Aunt Nora thirty-five years ago."

Deborah understands. She nods.

"For the first time Stull has found a woman with whom he's content. Clara, Eugenie—they made demands, wanted time and affection along with sex and an allowance. And Stull couldn't give himself. He already belonged to the company, outright and in fee simple and in every way. But Mrs. Schroeder apparently asks nothing, except to care for him, admire him."

"Will they marry?" Deborah asks.

"Probably not. I guess that's the thrill Stull gets out of the whole arrangement, and it's really quite domestic in the dullest sense: the thrill of feeling that he's a big league sophisticate now, complete with mistress. To those of us who were once Southern Baptist country boys, no matter how long or far we've been away, that's quite a lark, you know."

"So—"

"So—that's Stull. A bird's-eye view. No need for you to be nervous about him, you see."

"Not for himself," she says. "I suppose I have known many like him. But for what he means to you."

"I don't understand."

"I'm a released prisoner of war. You're still a prisoner."

I lean back and take a long drink.

"You're a prisoner of war with Stull, with Clayburn-Durant."

"I'm breaking free. This weekend."

"Then I'm right to be nervous." She waits a minute. "And Jon?"

"Yes?"

"I've never been to a football game."

I begin to laugh. "Well, that is a crime. As the French would say, in Churchill it is worse than *une crime.* It is a mistake. Oh, for God's sake, don't worry about that, Deborah."

She looks away from me.

"The stands are full of dumb broads, as Nat Lusk calls them, who might as well have never watched a football game, either, for all they know. They can't tell a forward pass from a punt return."

"I'm not sure—" she begins and breaks off.

"Well I am," I promise. "Tomorrow you'll be initiated into the great American ritual. You heard Aunt Nora this morning?"

Deborah nods.

"You can see what Stull and I were brought up with."

"Then it's all bound up together—"

"Maybe. But remember, you and I are the ones who are together now. It's a new ball game." She looks puzzled and I explain. "That's just a saying. It means something fresh, different, is beginning."

"Oh, I hope so, Jon." Her vehemence startles me.

"Meanwhile, you just relax about tomorrow, and have a good time."

Deborah was a truer harbinger than I of things to come that Saturday.

By the time we arrive at the massive concrete tiers surrounding the emerald football field, Stull and Nat Lusk and an affable middle-aged couple are already there. So are sixty thousand other people, with a final five thousand of the expected capacity crowd streaming through every gate and artery.

The afternoon is crisp with a high blue sky arching above the jagged horizon of mountains in the far distance, the uneven skyline of the city in the near distance, and the immense bowl of the stadium around us. The atmosphere sparkles with anticipation and excitement, pulses with latent energy straining to be released.

In Stull's box, introductions are made, seats resumed. It is obvious that Stull and Nat began fortifying for the game while they were on the plane this morning.

"Well, hel-lo," Nat Lusk says to Deborah, holding her hand until she pulls away. "Hello and where have you been?"

"I've kept her in a pumpkin shell," I tell him sharply, irritated by the shopworn routine of his notorious womanizing.

"Clayburn-Durant pumpkin, I hope. And you've kept her very well," Stull says. He motions to the seat beside him. "Sit here, Miss Einemann." His effort at pleasantry is a surprise.

Deborah glances at me. "Yes, thank you." She sits and I take the place beside her. Nat winks at me.

The strangers are a Jackson University trustee and his wife whose names I have heard all my life and seen immortalized on at least two campus dormitories. Mr. Trustee is a retired road-builder and state legislator. He has acquired his money from highway contracts and his prestige from state politics. As for education, he has proudly proclaimed in fifty years of public speeches that his own experience of it was confined to a grammar school report card and the college of hard knocks. As a living symbol of how richly a man can succeed without higher education, he would seem an anachronism as trustee of a large university. But he is on the board as a watchdog, a sentinel of common sense and hard-headed practicality among the ivory-tower scholars and do-good reformers who might otherwise corrupt the halls of learning. A Tyrolean-style hat perches jauntily on the back of his head and the flamboyant plaid jacket and overcoat he wears almost cancel notice of the ebony cane he wields. "Pesky stroke, left leg," he slaps the cane and leg together, exclaiming in disgust as we are introduced.

"Dear!" his blond wife, with hair teased into a frothy pyramid above her well-creamed, delicately rouged face, reprimands humorously. "We promised not to mention that, didn't we? Nothing unpleasant today." She flashes a brilliant empty smile at each one of us until she reaches Deborah. "What did you say your name is, dear?" she asks, leaning across me. When Deborah answers, she nods and smiles and sits straight again, patting wisps of hair into place.

People swarm around us, finding seats, calling to each other, many pausing to speak to Stull or to the trustee, making special obeisance, establishing camaraderie.

"Good to see you, fella."

"Sure thing. How's it going?"

"Down the track. Good enough."

"Ole Jackson going to take this big one?"

"We'll mop up that damned Crimson Tide, fade 'em to a pale pink."

"That's the way. Think positive."

"You know it, fella. We gotta have this one."

A practice cheer rises from the student section across the field. "Beat 'Bama."

And Mr. Trustee alerts a friend: "An extra bonus coming up today. Just wait till half-time, you'll hear a big piece of news—" He nods toward Stull who sits impassively looking at the field.

Deborah is watching the women who crowd by in their tweeds and knits and furs and suedes. I glance at Mr. Trustee's wife, swaddled in the mink coat which matches the highlights in her hair, at the heavy jangling memory bracelet weighting her arm. The solid gold charms are so crowded on each link that they overlap each other in a massive jumble. I look at Deborah in the black and white coat, fitted slightly to her lean and supple figure. The essential accessories— shoes, bag, gloves—well-made, well-cared-for. Nothing else. She is an eloquent statement of herself—herself only, fully. These others seem preening parrots of each other.

"You have something to tell me?" Stull asks suddenly, across Deborah to me. It's an old technique he has used for years, the surprise attack, and I have grown inured.

"Yes," I answer.

"You'd better." He adds, reluctantly. "I suppose you and Miss Einemann will be having dinner together?"

I nod.

"Then Nat and I will take you out. We'll all eat together." Before I can agree or disagree he leans toward Deborah and says in an unusually soft, winning voice, "You'd like that, wouldn't you, Miss Einemann? You'd accept dinner from two lonely gentlemen, wouldn't you?"

"Why yes—"

"Then it's all settled." He pauses. "And Jon, come on up to Mama's tomorrow morning. Early. We'll talk."

"No, Stull." I have thought this all out days ago. "You come out to the motel. I have a good roomy suite. We can talk there."

Anger blazes in his eyes, in the look he gives me. He says, "It won't be as pleasant, but if you insist—"

"I insist."

"All right."

"Come any time, I'll be up early." I promise, as the Jackson team erupts onto the field below.

Pandemonium: applause, cheering, whistles, the band. Mr.

Trustee waves his cane in the air. "Look at those boys! They're the stuff men are made of."

"They're all right," Stull agrees smugly. In his camel's hair overcoat his appearance is barrel-like and slightly passé. "But I can remember when we played *football*. The whole game—offense, defense, whatever was needed. Now they've got this 'platoon' system," his tone heaps scorn upon the word, "one defensive, one offensive. Not a single real *football* player in the lot."

I identify the teams for Deborah. "It's the crowd that I watch," she says. "Somehow I hadn't—expected it." She is looking at the sea of colors opposite us, with scattered splashes of blue and red as clear and vivid as the hues in a stained-glass window. But there is a troubled shadow on her face, too.

"Two-to-one odds on Jackson." Nat Lusk, sitting on the other side of Stull, suddenly calls out. No one accepts his offer. "Three to one—and I'll give two touchdowns."

"Don't be a fool, Nat," Stull says. "You're sitting with the Jackson fans. Nobody's going to take you up—publicly. No fun left in the game. That is—" He looks around at Deborah.

She doesn't know what he is saying.

"Unless Miss Einemann here would make a wager with us. Since she doesn't have any special loyalties to either team she wouldn't mind betting against old Jackson, providing a little interest."

"But I don't understand—"

"Just to make things lively." Stull's eyes are focused tightly on her face. "You'd take up a little bet with us, a few dollars—"

"Look here, Stull," I interrupt, not knowing whether to be amused or angry at his childishness.

"No, Jon, it's all right." Deborah's voice has become certain. There is an undertone I do not understand, however. "I'll agree to your bet, Mr. Clayburn."

"Stull. Please, call me Stull."

"All right, Stull. And I'm Deborah. And we will make a little gamble."

"Good girl!" Stull's eyes are glittering now. "A hundred dollars?"

"I don't like this, Stull," I begin.

"Ten to one?" he asks Deborah. "A hundred if I lose. Ten if you lose?"

"I'd rather it should be even," she says.

"But then it wouldn't be as exciting," he answers. "Anyway, you're going to lose. Ten to one it is, on old Jackson." He is stimulated by this new element of risk, of personal stakes. "I'm going to beat you, Deborah," he warns happily.

I can understand Stull's wanting this wager, but I cannot understand why Deborah has allowed herself to be drawn into it. With Stull, everything must be a competition: business, work, play, relaxation. Buying a frozen food plant, presiding at a board meeting, playing gin rummy, watching wrestling on television, football—he is lost, without identity or satisfaction, unless there is a clearly defined enemy.

With a long roll of the band's drums, the kick-off comes. Jackson U. receives the ball and runs halfway down the field before there is a tackle. The crowd goes wild.

The team functions smoothly like a well-oiled machine. There is a Jackson touchdown. And another.

"Watch that steam engine roll," Mr. Trustee cries.

Then the Alabama team begins to challenge. It completes a long pass across the goal line.

"A goddamned bomb," Stull grumbles.

"Even a blind hog finds an acorn now and then," Nat Lusk comforts him.

But Stull does not respond. He cannot just win, or be ahead, or succeed. He must demolish the other side.

In the second quarter a Jackson guard is injured and lies unmoving on the green artificial turf. Men bring a stretcher and carry him away.

"It's that damned make-believe grass," Mr. Trustee mutters. "Why, one of the sports writers said that stuff is so hard and hot on a sunny day that a player's covered with 'rug burns' if he slides at all."

"It doesn't do much for knee-caps and back injuries, either," I agree. "Besides, who wants to look at a field of that synthetic stuff."

"Everybody wants to—when it's raining," Nat Lusk says. "Artificial turf lets the game go on. Hell, a fellow doesn't want to give up his whole Saturday to see a mud-battle. Any player that can't stand a few scratches ought to shape up or ship out."

The game goes on. One minute till half-time Jackson scores again. And kicks the extra point. 21–7. Cheerleaders somersault through the air. There is a long shout from the crowd.

"Well, Deborah, looks like you chose the wrong side," Stull announces triumphantly, standing heavily, laboriously.

I start to say, "She didn't choose at all," but two other men have joined Mr. Trustee, and now they surround Stull and walk toward the nearest exit.

Down on the field the visiting band is playing "Dixie," followed by "The Stars and Stripes Forever," and is executing an elaborate march.

Nat has already left our box, clutching the flask bulging in his coat pocket. Mrs. Trustee stands. "I guess there must be a little girl's room somewhere—" and she disappears.

Deborah and I are left alone, with people shoving around us, the old grad behind us calling a little more loudly and incoherently all the time, the music drifting up through the clear autumn air.

"Why did you let Stull draw you into that stupid betting game?" It is the first time since we met that I have been deeply irritated with Deborah.

"He had to have an adversary," she answers, responding only to my question, ignoring my irritation.

"But why did you have to make it you?"

She looks at me. "I was already the adversary. I always have been. He knows that."

After a moment she points toward the field below us. The Jackson band, blazing green and gold with sunlight showering like twenty-four-karat dust from the magnificent moving horns and the director's baton, has encircled a small grandstand set up on the stiff artificial turf. A cluster of men are ascending the stand. As the band concludes with a flourish, the president of the university speaks into the microphone.

He announces the presence of "a loyal Jackson alumnus, a great and wonderful benefactor of our university." And I see that Stull is beside him. He announces the gift of one of the state's great family farms and homes to the university. And I know that the Riverbend bricks and oaks and bottomlands are now forever the stranger's.

Stull acknowledges the introduction with a brief step toward the microphone and a few sentences mumbled out of the mike's range. Then he makes an old V for Victory sign. The ebullient president rescues him, announces that the generous sum to be realized from the sale of this gift will be invested in enlarging this very stadium—to ninety thousand seats, no less!—and improving its facilities, with an additional athletic dormitory underneath.

"And henceforth, the name of this whole wonderful complex shall be the Stull Clayburn Stadium."

Applause arises from the packed seats and the standing spectators. Three blond, whirling cheerleaders tumble across the synthetic grass. Cameramen from the Jackson City papers snap their shutters; flash bulbs explode.

Then the phalanx of graying, overcoated dignitaries descends from the grandstand and walks back across the field as the bright indefatigable band plays a chorus of "For He's a Jolly Good Fellow."

I laugh aloud. "The Stull Clayburn Stadium. Great God and little junipers!" It was one of Uncle Jack Montgomery's exclamations when absurdity reached new pinnacles.

Deborah watches me closely.

But she cannot see what is actually happening. I am indulging a fantasy, a fleeting estimate of what the scene may be in Stull's mind at this instant. Through a maze of sour mash and buried memory, does the twin monster of regret and triumph stir? Those weekends long ago when his heart and lungs and legs and muscles were still young but he was not an accepted part of it all —balanced against today when he owns it all? He may not be one of the swivel-hipped, broad-shouldered, swaggering athletes who walks as if he carries deed to the earth itself—but now Stull carries deed to them. Soon his name will be emblazoned above this entire arena, although he cannot focus and see any one single person or square foot clearly and in depth. Soon the arrogant young athletes will learn that the shouting ends and the music stops and time happens to everybody. Then they can prove whether they're men or boys. Old Vince knew. Good old Lombardi. Winning isn't the best thing; it's the only thing. Stull's name in concrete on this stadium will show them all.

The band is in its last throes of ecstasy and a medley of waltzes as Stull returns to his seat, accompanied by two young university vice-presidents who shake hands and depart, and by Nat, whose face is now a mottled red.

"Damned newspapermen," Stull says. "Prying into your life."

People from nearby seats come to speak to him, slap his shoulder, extend thanks.

As he settles into his place he looks across Deborah, to me. "Well, Jon?"

"Congratulations."

He waits for me to say more, and there is an awkward pause, broken by Nat. "The Stull Clayburn Stadium. That has a damned good ring to it."

When I still do not respond, Stull says, "Our trustee friend and his wife, they went to watch the last half from the president's box. Said to tell you two it had been—"

"A ball?" I suggest.

The old grad behind us shouts, "Buddy, if I had Alabama and hell, I'd go to hell and rent Alabama out."

Boos arise from scattered followers of the Crimson Tide.

The game resumes.

Jackson captures an Alabama fumble and begins a push down the field.

"Go. . . . Go. . . . Go. . . ." The student section chants and motions in protracted unison. "Go. . . . Go. . . . Go. . . ."

But the march stumbles. And fails. There is a tedium of plays, huddles, tackles, misfires. Two other players limp off the field. Slowly but surely the visiting challengers gather momentum—and score. Excitement mounts in their cheering section this time.

"Get in there and *play,* Jackson," Stull mutters.

There is more time-out, during which those in the stands grow restless.

"Okay now, Jackson," Nat calls, "let's get the hell with it—down the field!"

"Don't think I've lost yet," Stull says to Deborah.

"No," she agrees.

The advantage shifts back and forth between teams. The score is like a fever patient's thermometer climbing slowly, steadily. 28–28.

Alabama tries for a field goal and racks up three more points. For the first time they are actually in the lead.

"Three lousy points," Stull mutters. "We can grab that back in one good play."

As the kick-off comes, five minutes remaining in the last quarter, the entire stadium rises to its feet in unison, watching, yearning. The Jackson deep-back runs—and runs—then, as clearly as if he were on slow-motion camera, one foot slips on the hard turf and he falls. The ball skids from his grasp. And is recovered by the enemy safety.

A deep groan rumbles from several thousand throats. No one sits down.

Another play is begun and ends in a first down for Alabama. There is cheering from its minority group of students and supporters, but the applause is engulfed in the ominous silence of the bulk of spectators.

An unexpected end-run, the goal line is crossed again and Jackson falls farther behind on the giant score-board. A long, low murmur arises from the grandstand—not a word, not a cheering signal, but a deep unconscious response and warning.

The kick for the extra point is good. The murmur gradually expands to a surly visceral roar.

"The sons of bitches are knocking us out of the Bowl!" the old grad screams.

"Get in there and fight!" Stull strikes his right fist into the left palm.

The smacks and grunts on the field have become audible even at a distance. But Jackson cannot regain the initiative. Anger throbs in the air. Jackson loses its last chance as the clock ticks out the final minute. A dark, malevolent growl moves through the multitude which seems welded by a single ravening lust of enmity and revenge.

"Jon!"

Deborah's choked scream is almost drowned in the cresting uproar, but I feel her hands as I look down at her.

"Jon!" She is clutching my coat desperately, turning her face away from the stadium, burying her ears between her arms, trembling violently.

I hold her tightly. Her fear frightens me. I can feel her fragile, sensitive body against mine, shuddering with more than fear, with terror.

"What's wrong with her?" Stull asks, out of the rising and receding swells of sound.

When he asks, I know. My dull-wittedness is redeemed by a glimmer of insight. "She's heard this crowd before—" I begin, then drop the effort. Her panic is mine. "Come on, Deborah." Keeping an arm around her I push her out of place, past Stull and Nat and into the aisle.

"You won our bet," Stull calls after her.

"Shut up," I answer. "Shut up—" And into the walkways which are suddenly choked with people as the game ends and the crowds flood from their seats. "Heil!" I call to them furiously. No one notices. "Sieg heil!" And they think I am drunk as I shield Deborah and force a passage through the mob, down the vast ramps.

Sunday morning is clear and chilly. Last night's frost is harvesting the leaves in heavy windfalls. A few red maple leaves, flung against the expanse of my sliding motel windows, cling there, flattened like hands pressing against the smooth cold glass.

I awaken with the first streaks of daylight and stand for a long time before the window, looking toward the mountains, watching them emerge in their jagged profile and shadowed contours and solidity. After orange juice and coffee, I open my briefcase and check through some of its papers. Relief for the tension between Stull and me is not there, however, and I snap the lock shut.

Stull arrives at eight-thirty—the old office hours when Clayburn Brothers headquarters were in Churchill. He is sober and ready for whatever the action is. Although his face is slightly pouched and his hands are not quite under control, he is all together, ready, poised. He did not indulge in his usual Saturday night anesthesia, even after Jackson U.'s defeat.

"We missed you at dinner," Stull says. "Nat and I ate at the Baron of Beef."

I read the scene as if I were there: Nat, patting the perky miniskirted waitress on her rump, cajoling: "Brenda, Wanda, whatever your sweet name is, how about bringing me a double Scotch from one of those padlocked cupboards back there—and on the double quick?" Then, swilling the drink: "Now sweetheart, you tell that chef to break out a couple of his prime twenty-four-ounce New York sirloin strips. And one of them—let him burn it up. Charcoal outside, raw inside.

And Brenda, baby, a baked Idaho drowned in sour cream. Some green stuff. With oil and vinegar. Okay?"

Then he and Stull eat from the slabs of meat sizzling on hot platters, Stull holding food in his jowls as he talks.

"How's Nat this morning?" I ask.

Stull glances around my room. "Nat better watch it. He's going heavy on the sauce."

"Nat's got too much of his father in him," I answer. "The drummer, peddler, agent, salesman, huckster—you name it. Whatever people want, he gives them; whatever they buy, he sells; what they'll pay, he asks; where they move, he follows. Old Nat, like Nate Lusk before him—they'll survive."

"Glad you think so, Jon." He looks at me suddenly. "Say, what happened to that girl yesterday at the game?"

I look at his plump, self-satisfied face—which reflects at the same time deep, divisive dissatisfactions—and at his soft white hands. "The crowd, the shouting, reminded her of bad times—"

"The Germans," Stull nods.

"The Nazis," I correct.

"But all that happened a long time ago. Say," Stull's voice carries a new tone, "that—that thing on her arm. Did they actually do that in the camps?"

"They actually did. It's a number, in her flesh. At Auschwitz they took away names and gave numbers."

"Did she—was she ever—mistreated?"

The curiosity glinting in his eyes sickens me. (Did I perhaps look like this when old Cebo told me of his mother and her dying? What is it that both repels and fascinates us about human torture? Is it the totality of power—and subjection?) "She was mistreated."

When he understands that I'm not going to say more, he pulls off his coat, hanging it on the back of a chair as he asks, "How'd you ever find, or want, somebody so—well, so different, Jon?"

I have to laugh. I can imagine him discussing this with Aunt Nora and Nancy Ellen and Nat. "It's Deborah's difference I love." I blurt out the word in these alien surroundings, even try to explain. "Deborah's difference enlarges me, makes me another—maybe better—"

Stull turns a chair from the window impatiently and sits down. "I don't know how she'll fit in at C-D," he says.

"I don't know how C-D will fit in with her," I answer slowly and deliberately.

"What does that mean?"

I sit down in the chair on the opposite side of the low coffee table and face Stull. "It means that I've been taking a long hard look at Clayburn-Durant."

"And what do you see?" He fits the tips of his fingers together in a tent and looks across at me.

"I see my son Lee and a whole generation of brains and potential turning away from anything called 'the company.' I see a whole public suspicious and resentful of something called 'business.' I see an industry and a person I don't like very much: Clayburn-Durant—and myself."

"Now that's too bad." Stull's sarcasm is as heavy as his clenched jaw.

"No, it's good—"

"You want out?"

"I want to know what direction we're going—"

"Hell, if you don't know that—"

"I want to know whether we're going for bigger and bigger—or bigger and better." We look at each other fiercely. "I want to know if a corporation, if *this* corporation to which I'm giving my life, is more than a profit-and-loss statement. Is it in the end a machine, or is it a human experiment—of, by, and for human beings?"

Stull gives a long derisive sigh. "That's quite a manifesto. Has all the right words."

"You know damn well it's more than words."

"Not to me, it isn't. It's words and crap. I've already heard all about the 'dehumanizing machines.' You tell me: are people less human now because we don't build our pyramids with slaves pulling the twenty-ton stones into place? Are we less human because we don't wrench open the ground with ox-drawn plows and gouge out meager crops with sticks and stones? I can remember some of the drudgery down on the Riverbend Farm, when we broke our backs all day for a dollar. Some of the people lived like damned hogs and didn't want better. Now you tell me how letting machines take the burden off a man's back, how giving some men food, and others a chance at a profit for the money they risk, is so 'anti-human,' to use one of your big words."

"Don't dodge the issue, Stull." I look away, toward the immense mirror at the opposite end of the room. "Of course machines are necessary. But how far do we go—with our computers, for instance? Our mechanical memories. If all the computerized information that we're storing up about each other makes us so cautious that we hesitate to ask questions, so fearful that we won't try something new or different or even dangerous—then we're not enslaved by machines; we *are* the machines."

"You're the computer advocate," Stull reminds me. "You and George Hodges have pointed out their necessity, their good—"

I nod. "That's the point, Stull. They're not good. They're not evil. They're something more dangerous. And that's what those of us who control the computers are in danger of becoming, Stull, not good or evil—just impersonal."

"Crap, nothing but—"

"And that can breed the greatest evil of all. Like the number on Deborah's arm. Like Burl and Perlina Smelcer."

He is taken aback. "Look here, you've been screwed up ever since we began the experiment with that arrested-growth spray. Now nobody knew how it was going to work, nobody could guarantee whether or not it would pay off, but dammit all we owed it to our company, to our stockholders, to try and take a risk—"

"For profits—"

"Sure, for profits. What else, what better? You think there's something wrong with profits?"

"Not something wrong. Just something else."

"You're full of cute little riddles this morning but—"

"Of course I'm not against C-D profits," I interrupt sharply. "I just want to know how much profit and what it's costing."

"Such as?"

I lean forward, elbows on knees. "Isn't it time to set up a realistic accounting system? One to include damage to air or water or land, to the health of a human being?"

"Look here, I don't know who that 'system' you're talking about belongs to. But I know damn well who C-D belongs to: its stockholders." He jabs a stubby forefinger toward me.

"You don't even believe that, Stull. You repeat it—like a litany, a slogan—but even more than making a profit you believe that C-D is your turf, and more than that it's your image, your genius. Stull, you believe that C-D is you."

"You're damn right. I think this company's part of me. I've given it everything I am. And I've done it the hard way. Nobody ever gave me anything on a silver platter in this business."

I stare at him, disbelieving my ears. I shake my head slightly as I say, "Are you kidding yourself? Do you honestly think you did it all alone?"

"You better believe it—"

"My father himself gave you something priceless. He shared his experience, his knowledge, his time—and God knows he had little enough of that, as things turned out—he gave them all to you. I know; I was there. And what he shared was worth more than any amount of money, if that's what you mean by silver platters."

Stull flushed. "We take what we can wherever we can."

"That's right. And we cut some corners, we count on a lucky break or two, and after a while, when we're on top, when we have that precious key to the private wash room, and the reserved parking space, and the plane in the hangar, the fuzz-on-the-shoes deep carpet and the oil portraits in our paneled office—when we get all that, everybody's so busy telling us how smart and indispensable we are, even while they're sharpening the ax to cut us down, that we lose all touch with practicality, all perspective."

"Are you accusing me—"

"Lord no, Stull. Time's past for all that. None of us is a devil. We're only ignorant and arrogant. That may be worse. We just stay here, ignorant of our past and its consequences, arrogant while the waves wash in and threaten to destroy us."

"What in the hell are you talking about?" Stull asks distinctly. "Are you challenging what I've done for C-D?"

"No, Stull. You just took Jonathan Clayburn's advice and help and training, you took a company the family had created for all the family—and you manipulated it all to your own private fortune."

"I made this company big. I made it pay off big. And don't you forget it. For myself, yes—and for the rest of the family and stock-holders, too." He slaps his fist on the arm of the chair for emphasis. "Oh, I know they didn't appreciate my work. They whispered and fretted and shook their heads about 'brother Jonathan' or 'Uncle Dan' or 'Grandmother Mary'—but, by God, when they looked at the stock market columns each morning and saw old C-D prices rising, they were happy enough. Oh, I understood them. They lurked there in the shadows, secretly deploring the rumors they heard, relieved that they didn't have to face up to those jugular fights, but wanting me—and through me the company, their company—to get ahead. And all the time it took more and more to get ahead: brains, nerve, instinct, sweat, choices between family and company—"

"I know, Stull."

"You don't know a goddamned thing. You don't know just how much the family helped make C-D what it is today: tearing open your little dividend envelopes every quarter, wanting to be sure they kept coming—with a little more from time to time. Even Aunt Lottie—good, unselfish, unworldly Aunt Lottie and Uncle Penn. Oh, I know how the Worth Franklins and the Sherman Wrights felt—piss or get off the pot. Then I discovered that some others felt the same way. Only they fooled themselves that they were apart and different and better. Aunt Lottie would write me about her mission work, and how she 'knew' I would do 'the right thing' at C-D, and then at the close she'd slip in the clincher: 'How are the dividends looking this quarter?' "

If I hadn't laughed at Stull's recital, he might have seen the tears in my eyes. It only goads him. "Not Aunt Lottie, not a one of you was one whit different from me—only uninvolved, except of course to share the profits. No, you didn't go out on any limbs. But you sure enjoyed the sweet dividends and the satisfaction of condemning me. Well, I laid it all on the line. Oh, you're pretty superior, Jon—hinting I lost my soul for filthy lucre. Well, if I did, by God, I lost it by my own decision—and not by default!"

I never heard Stull, sober, speak with such candor or feeling. A delicate blue vein bulges at the edge of his forehead. "There's no cause for me, for anybody, to be self-righteous, Stull. I remember my Uncle Jack used to say that a halo has to drop only a few inches to become a noose. I'm not claiming any halos." I attempt a laugh, to defuse the atmosphere.

"A measley quarter-million," he is speaking to himself as much as to me, "and I got the Durant outfit that's been this company's backbone. But who remembers that? Who—"

"That's just what I'm trying to tell you. I've been remembering. I'm sorting all the pieces that fit together to build C-D: Elisha Clayburn's land and Jonathan Clayburn's vision, Dan Clayburn's and Lonas Rankin's way with machinery and your—"

He looks at me with such hostility that I realize he cannot acknowledge any part, any power but his own.

"Okay, Stull," I finally abandon the effort at explanation, at understanding, "I grant that you've lived and succeeded by your code. My father by his, you by yours. And now I have to live by mine. It isn't my father's; it isn't yours. It's my risk, my stake."

Stull leans back. "What is it you're trying to get, Jon?"

"Not get. Be. I want to be someone, Stull."

He shakes his head, convinced I am playing with words again. Then he stands up, his eyebrows lifted in sarcasm and boredom. "Well, all along I've half-expected you to leave the company."

"Oh?"

"I've seen you weighing and thinking and judging—even when you've put through one or two good sound ideas for me. But this food business is a hard, rough racket. It takes know-how and toughness."

"I'm no wet-eared beginner," I remind him. "I've been in this a long time."

"Long enough to know it's a man's game."

"Long enough to know there are plant managers on the firing line every day. And workers who bring their skills and muscles and put out their best day after day. But there are buffers between them and you, Stull. You don't see the real C-D any more. It's not in some broker's office or at one of those dinners our public relations agency stages."

"Well, wherever the real C-D is, Jon, we're getting the work done." He walks around the room. "So don't fret about it after you've gone. But before you leave and this very educational, philosophical discussion is finished, I wonder if you'd be so kind as to instruct me what, if anything, you learned about the takeover bid on us. You've had enough time to find out."

"Yes, I know something. There *is* someone buying heavy in C-D stock. That I know."

"Well, I knew that a long time ago."

"But he's not after C-D, Stull. He only wants you, your place."

"They're the same thing—"

"Not quite."

"And who is the bastard? If it's Stu Siegel's outfit—"

"It's Jon Clayburn, Stull."

He whirls to face me. Once and for all I have canceled out every past surprise he ever foisted on me. In the pause between us he breathes heavily. "You? What the devil are you talking about?"

"We're talking about C-D."

"But you're getting out—"

"Why should I get out? This isn't some melodrama where your dreamer rides off into the purple sunset to write a book."

"Jesus! Whatever is going on in that addled brain—" He sits down abruptly.

"I'm staying, Stull. I want this business to be exciting again, the way it was for my father and Uncle Dan and Uncle Cal. I want it to have purpose, purpose everyone can share. And that is as worth the risk as what you wanted. I may get clobbered. But I want my turn."

"Turn?" He tries to laugh. "You think this is some kid's game —to take turns?"

"I'll tell you exactly what I think." I stand and put all the harshness and force I can muster into my voice. "A few days ago a toothless old farmer named Burl Smelcer taught me something about trust—mutual trust and community. And I'm not ready to forget it."

"You can skip the goddamned riddles."

"There's no riddle to it. When Clayburn Brothers started, Stull, they didn't have any medical benefits or pension plans or a single bowling team. But they had one thing. And that was a sense of community. I know, because I saw it, heard it, felt it for myself—with my father among the wagon haulers of tomatoes and cabbage, out in the fields pulling beets and picking beans with Perlina and the others. You must have known it—"

"It was different then. Everything was smaller, slower."

"Then all the more reason to value that spirit wherever we find it today. And if Burl Smelcer can still believe in C-D, I intend to give him some reason for that trust."

"Just what do you plan?"

"Well, to start with, no more field experiments with the food people may eat—"

"Then you'll lose the initiative. C-D is a business, Mister, and I promise you, if C-D doesn't take the chances some other canner will."

"That's the cheapest excuse there is, Stull: if not me, someone else; if not my company, some other company. As for chances, nobody has the right to take risks with somebody else's life."

"Oh, to hell with it!" Stull's tense hands grip the chair. "You're not going to do anything with C-D." He watches me as I walk over to the window. "So. You've been buying stock."

"Not quite as much as your 12 percent."

"You just shoveling smoke then?"

"A little more than that."

"You rob a bank?"

"Not quite," I tell him. "Teena's money bought a sizable block—"

"Teena's money?"

"Her family gave me a share of what she would have had."

"Oh? I hadn't heard—" Stull's eyebrows are raised, his mouth pursed.

"I think they thought, too, that I might want to leave C-D—"

He nods, respecting Teena's successful father.

"But I have some other stockholders with me, too."

"With you?"

"Now, if you put my name before the board to be next president and chief executive officer when you become chairman—"

"I'll be damned." It is almost a whisper. "I never figured you had so much ambition."

"Maybe it's something else, Stull. After all, why should I be the one to leave? There's too much to do."

"Go to hell."

I swing away from the window. "You listen. In the next ten years there can be a real revolution in this world—and we'll be at the center of it. We can concentrate on refining more and more luxury items for affluent customers, Stull, or we can help develop foods to feed the world."

"We're a business, not a ladies' missionary circle."

"And what's more businesslike than meeting the biggest market in the world? Hunger. Belly hunger driving some people. Hunger for purpose driving others."

"Do you know what you are? You're an idealist."

I stand in front of him and answer slowly. "You'll have to do better than that. Idealism or not—labels don't matter. But it was Jonathan Clayburn's risk and dream that made the first money in this company. It was your risk and dream that made bigger money. Now maybe it's time for new risks—"

"Whose stock have you got?" Stull blunts my outburst. I wonder if he has heard a word I said.

I sit down. Now we are opposite each other, face to face. "Do you want a proxy fight, Stull?"

"I want to know who's with me."

"For God's sake, Stull, we'll be on the same team. You know you're reaching retirement, you must have thought about it—"

"Don't you tell me what I'm reaching, what I've thought about."

"Here it is then. I have my own stock and what I've bought with Teena's money. I have the votes of two other members of the board who are less than satisfied with your performance. I'm sure I can get the proxies of whatever stock Siegel Enterprises owns. And I have Aunt Nettie Sue's proxies. With her mother's and Uncle Dan's and Aunt Lottie's stock—and she's never sold a share, she's the only really big stockholder left in our family, except you, as you know well enough."

Stull says nothing. He is talking inwardly, figuring quickly, from memory. . . .

"A proxy fight can be sticky." I keep the statement matter-of-fact.

"Brings a lot of slugs out from under the rocks," Stull says. "But I'll handle them. I'll handle—"

"If it became necessary," I tell him slowly, "I'd go to the full board, Stull."

"How far do you think you'd get there—except with the two grumblers you've cornered?"

"I could tell them I'm ready to confront a stockholders meeting and accuse the board of gross dereliction of duty."

"What dereliction?"

"For paying a quarter-million dollars in salary and bonuses and benefits and expense accounts to a president who's on the job a quarter of the time. Because he's a sick alcoholic."

Stull's face is frozen. His hands are balled into fists but there is nowhere for him to strike. He starts to speak but words do not come.

"Did you think it's only the winners who can play rough, Stull? Don't you think there ought to be some of your clout for a few of us idealists who may not want to come in last?"

"You'd do that?" he asks hoarsely. "You'd spread a lie and humliate my mother?"

My hands are clammy. My throat is tight and dry. But I look at him steadily. And I nod. "I promise it."

Hefting himself out of the chair with his hands on the over-stuffed arms, he stands a moment as if regaining his balance. Slowly he crosses to the straight chair and removes the coat he hung there. As he pulls the coat on, his mouth moves wordlessly, then clamps tightly shut. He turns to me. "I could fight you and win. You know that."

"We'd all lose."

"The way it is—" He cannot bring himself to the words. Suddenly he digs into his pocket, brings out his wallet, and counts out five twenty-dollar bills. The new bills rustle like juiceless leaves on winter oaks. With exaggerated ceremony and precision Stull lays the money on the dresser in front of the mirror. Using a stubby forefinger he separates each bit of paper until a crisp green fan is spread before him.

"Give that to your friend," he says.

We look at each other.

Stull goes to the door. "The plane's coming this afternoon." Reluctantly he asks, not looking back, "Will you be ready?"

"I've been ready, Stull. And Deborah will be with me."

"Okay." Stull opens the door. "You tell her. She won."

I am exhilarated—astonished, terrified, above all exhilarated—by the morning's encounter.

When I go to her room Deborah takes only one glance at me and runs laughing across the room. "Jon! Jon, I'm so glad."

"Don't make it too big a deal," I try to play down my own

excitement and eagerness but then I have to laugh with her and add, when she stands so close on tip-toe and looks into my face, "A riddle for you: what is it that's the craziest, most artificial category in the world, Miss Deborah? Give up? It's age. Not nationality or—"

She is already nodding. "Perhaps—"

"Oh yes. Today I'm thirty—just more experienced. I'm twenty-five—only smarter. But who'll believe it?"

"I'll believe."

"Then it's true. By official proclamation." I release her and she goes back to the mirror where she finishes combing her hair. "Now I must call my housekeeper and tell her you will be coming home with me this afternoon."

On the telephone Mrs. Alexander is her usual correct, efficient self. "Oh yes, Mr. Clayburn, you received a cable from Athens this morning." She opens it and reads a request from Lee for money. "He sounds a twinge homesick to me, Mr. Clayburn." I agree and thank her. She seems pleased that we will be home for Sunday night supper.

I stretch into one of the lounge chairs and give Deborah a quick summary of the talk with Stull. But I hesitate to tell her of my final threat to make Stull's drinking a public issue, a matter for stockholders' debate—and in the end I do not mention it at all.

As I finish, she says, "Jon, about yesterday, and the game, I'm sorry for my foolishness. I promise it won't happen again. It's been so many years since I went to pieces like that."

"Don't, Deborah. Don't apologize to me, or anyone, ever, for your feelings."

"I guess it's been so many years since I cared about anything, anyone—so much," she finishes, with a tentative smile at me, in the mirror.

I smile back, via the mirror. "Let's be married this week, without any fanfare."

The telephone rings. Deborah answers, then hands it to me. It is Monty in the lobby with Kate and Aunt Nettie Sue. "Church was out a little early. We came on over. You do remember, Aunt Nettie Sue asked us all to eat together?"

I remember. I have just forgotten the time.

We eat in the motel dining room. Two moments come alive, stick in my mind. One is when Kate turns to Deborah across the cluttered table and says in plain tones, "You've seen hard times, haven't you?

Well, life isn't any rose garden. But any time you need somebody in this family to take your part you let me know. I don't think the Clayburns, or anyone else, are something special."

Monty gives an uneasy chuckle, glancing at Aunt Nettie Sue. "Why no, Kate. None of us—"

Kate ignores him. "I like you," Kate says to Deborah. "Remember."

And Deborah accepts with complete seriousness. "Thank you, Kate. I won't forget."

The other moment comes at the end of our meal, as we are parting. Aunt Nettie Sue looks at me brightly from under the bronze-feathered brim of her Sunday hat. "I'm so glad you came and talked with me about my Clayburn-Durant stock, Jon. It was just like your father used to do—keep us all informed and all—" She breaks off.

I pick up a glove she has dropped. As she clutches it with her purse she looks at me from wide wrinkle-crusted eyes and says, "You do think the company will have a good year, in the dividends and all—"

My stomach knots ever so slightly. And I think: now it begins.

When they have left, Deborah goes to finish packing her suitcase. I walk to the rear of the gaudy, sprawling motel building and stand looking at the blue, saw-toothed ranges out there.

"Raring up there like so much proud flesh, ain't they?" Burl Smelcer's voice jars the silence. I turn in surprise and he grins with friendly toothless pleasure. "Didn't mean to rattle you."

"No, no, that's all right."

"I been waiting up there the longest—" he says.

"I'm sorry. I wasn't expecting anyone."

"No. I reckon not." He is wearing the same wilted shirt and tie and coat he wore at Perlina's funeral.

"I didn't want you to get back North till I'd seen you again."

"Sure." I look at him but he keeps gazing off toward the mountains. "Anything special?"

"Sort of special." His hesitation baffles me. It's not like the Burl I know. "You see, there was this young lawyer feller came out to see me day before yesterday."

Another pause. I wait.

Burl spits onto the concrete. "That young feller seemed to think

I wouldn't be doing right by myself if I didn't make the canning company—"

"Yes?"

"Well, if I didn't make Clayburn-Durant admit whether or not they'd harmed Perlina."

"I see. And maybe pay you—and the young lawyer—something?"

"Well, maybe." He faces the mountains. "It was talked of."

I look off for a moment, too. Then I take a deep breath.

"We can't, Burl. As far as we know, there wasn't anything harmful in that spray. But combined with other chemicals, under varied conditions, well, Clayburn-Durant couldn't guarantee one way or the other."

He faces me. There is deep suspicion in his look. The familiar work-worn countenance is half a stranger's.

"And you can't prove one way or the other, either," I add.

"But I don't reckon you'd like to have all that brought out." He watches me closely.

"No," I say, "we wouldn't. Especially since we won't be using that spray again."

He considers. "Maybe that young lawyer was just wanting himself a soft job."

"I wouldn't know," I answer. "But I can tell you one thing: he didn't mourn Perlina like I did, Burl. And it wasn't all because of any spray."

He nods. "Well—" But then he adds, "You might be able to think of something you could do—"

We stand a moment awkwardly.

"Poor folks have poor ways," Burl Smelcer says. He winks. There is nothing personal or humorous in that wink. He turns to leave. "Perlina would've been proud you came to see her buried— what with such a big business and all you have on your mind." He spits again. "You think about that lawyer's proposition."

"Nothing to think, Burl," I tell him as he walks away.

Believing in Burl Smelcer's neighborly trust I charged Stull's defenses. Now all that is left is to laugh or howl. I'm not twenty-five, or even thirty, and so I laugh. Well, if the Burl I imagined doesn't exist, I must invent him, at least make him possible.

A chill trickles down my spine like ice water. Two realities present themselves. First, I have won: in the contest with Stull I am victor. And second, Burl Smelcer is still waiting.

Knowing, remembering how the kernel of our victories is defeat, that the winner may become a reincarnation of the enemy he thought to vanquish, I pause—and feel my hand clutched inside my jacket pocket. I consider Burl Smelcer and the revelation he has flashed into my insulated life, calling into account both the realism I serve and the idealism I cherish.

Now the real contest begins. Within myself. What do I want? Want above all? And what am I willing to pay?

Before I go to join Deborah I look again toward the mountains. I think of Jonathan Clayburn and of Lee. Have I invented them? Tonight I will send Lee money and a message: Come home. To make the Clayburn-Durant I want I'll need computers, research, image, luck. But most of all I need my father and my son.